Also by Brandon Mull

Beyonders

A World Without Heroes

Seeds of Rebellion

Chasing the Prophecy

Fablehaven

Fablehaven

Rise of the Evening Star

Grip of the Shadow Plague

Secrets of the Dragon Sanctuary

Keys to the Demon Prison

Candy Shop War

The Candy Shop War

Arcade Catastrophe

FIVE KINGDOMS

SKY RAIDERS

BOOK 1

Brandon Mull

ALADDIN
NEW YORK   LONDON   TORONTO   SYDNEY   NEW DELHI

ALADDIN
An imprint of Simon & Schuster Children's Publishing Division
1230 Avenue of the Americas, New York, NY 10020
First Aladdin paperback edition January 2015
Text copyright © 2014 by Brandon Mull
Cover illustration copyright © 2014 by Owen Richardson
Also available in an Aladdin hardcover edition.
All rights reserved, including the right of reproduction in whole or in part in any form.
ALADDIN is a trademark of Simon & Schuster, Inc., and related logo is a registered
trademark of Simon & Schuster, Inc.
For information about special discounts for bulk purchases, please contact Simon &
Schuster Special Sales at 1-866-506-1949 or business@simonandschuster.com.
The Simon & Schuster Speakers Bureau can bring authors to your live event. For more
information or to book an event contact the Simon & Schuster Speakers Bureau at
1-866-248-3049 or visit our website at www.simonspeakers.com.
Cover designed by Jessica Handelman
Interior designed by Ellis M. Lee
The text of this book was set in Perpetua.
Manufactured in the United States of America 1114 OFF
2 4 6 8 10 9 7 5 3 1
The Library of Congress has cataloged the hardcover edition as follows:
Mull, Brandon, 1974–
Sky Raiders / by BMull, Brandon, 1974–
Sky Raiders / by Brandon Mull. — First Aladdin hardcover edition.
pages cm. — (Five kingdoms ; book 1)
Summary: Whisked through a portal to The Outskirts,
an in-between world, sixth-grader Cole must rescue his friends and find
his way back home—before his existence is forgotten.
ISBN 978-1-4424-9700-9 (hc)
ISBN 978-1-4424-9702-3 (eBook)
ISBN 978-1-4424-9701-6 (pbk)
[1. Fantasy. 2. Adventure and adventurers—Fiction.] I. Title. PZ7.M9112Sk 2014
[Fic]—dc23   2013032734

For Liz,
WHO WANTED SKY CASTLES

Castles in the sky sit stranded, vandalized.

—"A Dustland Fairytale,"
by the Killers (written by Brandon Flowers)

CHAPTER

1

HALLOWEEN

Weaving down the hall, Cole avoided a ninja, a witch, a pirate, and a zombie bride. He paused when a sad clown in a trench coat and fedora waved at him. "Dalton?"

His friend nodded and smiled, which looked weird since his mouth was painted into a frown. "I wondered if you'd recognize me."

"It wasn't easy," Cole replied, relieved to see that his best friend had worn an elaborate costume. He had worried that his own outfit was too much.

They met up in the middle of the hall. Kids streamed by on either side; some dressed for Halloween, some not.

"Ready to score some candy tonight?" Dalton asked.

Cole hesitated. Now that they were sixth graders, he was a little nervous that people would think they were too old to go door to door. He didn't want to look like a kindergartener. "Have you heard about the haunted house on Wilson?"

"The spook alley house?" Dalton clarified. "I heard it has live rats and snakes."

Cole nodded. "The guy who moved in there is supposed to be a special-effects expert. I guess he worked on some big movies. It might just be hype, but I keep hearing amazing things. We should check it out."

"Yeah, sure, I'm curious," Dalton said. "But I don't want to skip the candy."

Cole thought for a minute. He *had* noticed some sixth graders trick-or-treating in his neighborhood last year. A few kids had looked even older. Besides, did it matter what anyone else thought? If people were handing out free candy, why not take advantage? They already had the costumes. "Okay. We can start early."

"That'll work."

The first bell rang. Class would start soon. "See you," Cole said.

"Later."

Cole walked into his classroom, noticing that Jenna Hunt was already at her desk. Cole tried not to care. He liked her, but not in *that* way. Sure, in the past he might have felt excited and scared whenever she was around, but now she was just a friend.

At least that was what he kept telling himself as he tried to take his seat behind her. He was dressed up as a scarecrow that had been used for archery practice. The feathered shafts protruding from his chest and side made it tricky to sit down.

Had he ever had a crush on Jenna? Maybe, when he was younger. During second grade, the girls went through a phase when they ran around trying to kiss the boys at recess. It had been disgusting. Like tag, except with cooties involved. The teachers had been against it. Cole had been against it too—except when it was with Jenna. When she was chasing him, a secret part of him wanted to get caught.

It wasn't his fault he kept noticing Jenna during third, fourth, and fifth grades. She was too pretty. He wasn't the only one who thought so. She had modeled in some catalogs. Her dark hair had just the right amount of curl, and her thick eyelashes made her eyes look made-up, even when she wasn't wearing makeup.

He sometimes used to daydream about older jerks picking on Jenna. In his imagination, he would come along and save the day with a burst of bravery and action-movie karate skills. Afterward, he would be forced to suffer through her tearful thanks.

But everything had changed at the start of sixth grade. Jenna had not only ended up in his class, but by pure chance the seating chart had placed him directly behind her. They had worked together on group projects. He had learned to relax around her, and they had started to talk regularly and make jokes. She had turned out to be cooler than he had hoped. They were actually becoming friends. So there was no reason for his heart to pound just because she was dressed up like Cleopatra.

A graded test sat on top of his test, a circled 96 in red ink proclaiming his success. Tests waited on the other empty desks as well. Cole tried not to spy on the other scores, but he couldn't help noticing that his neighbors got a 72 and an 88.

Jenna turned and looked at him. She wore a wig of limp black hair with ruler-straight bangs. Dramatic makeup accentuated her eyes. A golden circlet with a snake at the front served as her crown. "What are you?" she asked. "A dead scarecrow?"

"Close," Cole replied. "I'm a scarecrow that got used for target practice."

"Are those real arrows?"

"Yeah, but I broke off the tips. Halloween or not, I figured they would send me home if I brought sharp arrows to school."

"You aced another test. I thought scarecrows weren't supposed to have brains."

"I wasn't a scarecrow yesterday. I like your costume."

"Do you know who I am?"

Cole scrunched his face, as if she had stumped him. "A ghost?"

Jenna rolled her eyes. "You know, right?"

He nodded. "You're one of the most famous ladies in history. Queen Elizabeth."

"Wrong country."

"I'm kidding. Cleopatra."

"Wrong again. Are you even trying?"

"Seriously? I thought I knew it for sure."

"I'm Cleopatra's twin sister."

"You got me."

"Maybe I should have come as Dorothy all shot up with arrows," Jenna said. "Then we would have matched."

"We could have been the sadder ending to *The Wizard of Oz*."

"The ending where the wizard turns out to be Robin Hood."

Laini Palmer sat in the desk next to Jenna's. She was

dressed as the Statue of Liberty. Jenna turned and started talking to her.

Cole glanced at the clock. There were still a few minutes before class would begin. Jenna had a habit of arriving by the first bell, and Cole had coincidentally developed the same habit. More kids were coming in: a zombie, a vampire fairy, a rock star, an army guy. Kevin Murdock wore no costume. Neither did Sheila Jones.

When Jenna had finished talking to Laini, Cole tapped her shoulder. "Have you heard about that new haunted house?"

"On Wilson Avenue?" Jenna asked. "People keep talking about it. I've never really been scared by Halloween decorations. I always know they're fake."

"The guy who just moved in there supposedly did effects for Hollywood," Cole replied. "I heard that some of the stuff in his spook alley is real. Like, live bats and tarantulas and amputated body parts from hospitals."

"I guess that might be freaky," Jenna admitted. "I'd have to see it to believe it."

"It's supposed to be free. Are you going trick-or-treating?"

"Yeah, with Lacie and Sarah. You?"

"I was planning to go around with Dalton." He was relieved she would be out hunting candy as well.

"Do you know the address?" Jenna asked.

"For the haunted house? I wrote it down."

"We should check it out. Want to meet up around seven?"

Cole tried to keep his expression casual. "Where?"

"Do you know that old guy's house on the corner, with the huge flagpole?"

"Sure." Everybody in the area knew that house. It was one story, but the flagpole was basically a skyscraper. The old guy looked like a veteran. He raised and lowered the flag every morning and night. "Meet there?"

"Bring the address."

Cole retrieved a notebook from his backpack and opened it. While he looked for his homework, his mind strayed. He had never hung out with Jenna after school, but it wasn't like they were going on a date. They would just be part of a group of kids checking to see if a spook alley was actually cool.

Mr. Brock started class a few moments later. He was dressed as a cowboy with chaps, a big hat, and a sheriff's badge. The outfit made it tough to take him seriously.

Cole walked along the street beside Dalton, one foot on the curb, the other in the gutter. He was still a scarecrow bristling with arrows. The straw poking out from his neck kept tickling the bottom of his chin. Dalton remained a gloomy clown.

"She wanted to meet at the flagpole?" Dalton verified.

"Just near the house," Cole said. "Not on his lawn."

Dalton pulled back the sleeve of his coat and checked his watch. "We're going to be early."

"Only a little."

"Are you nervous?"

Cole shot him a scowl. "I'm not afraid of haunted houses."

"I don't mean the spook alley," Dalton clarified. "Haven't you always sort of liked——"

"No, Dalton, come on," Cole interrupted. "Be serious. It isn't like that. We're friends."

Dalton bobbed his eyebrows up and down. "My parents say they started out as friends."

"Gross, knock it off." Cole couldn't let Dalton say or do anything that might make Jenna suspect he thought she was cute. "I should have never told you I used to like her. That was forever ago. We're just doing this for fun."

Dalton squinted up ahead. "Looks like a big group."

He was right. They found Jenna waiting with seven other kids—three of them boys. She was still dressed like Cleopatra.

"Here they are," Jenna announced. "We can go now."

"I have the address," Cole offered.

"I know where it is," Blake said. "I went by earlier tonight."

"What's it like?" Dalton asked.

"I didn't go inside," Blake replied. "I just live nearby."

Cole knew Blake from school. He was the kind of guy who liked to take charge and talked a lot. He always wanted to be goalie at recess, even though he wasn't that good.

As they started walking, Blake took the lead. Cole fell in beside Jenna. "So what's your name?" Cole asked.

"Huh?" she replied. "Cleopatra?"

"No, you're her twin."

"Right. Want to guess?"

"Irma?"

"That doesn't sound very Egyptian."

"Queen Tut?"

"Sure, let's go with that." Jenna laughed lightly, then strayed over to her friend Sarah and started talking. Cole fell back to walk with Dalton.

"Do you think the spook alley will actually be freaky?" Dalton asked.

"It better be," Cole said. "I have my hopes up."

Blake set a quick pace. They marched briskly, passing a herd of little kids with plastic superhero faces. Most of the houses had halfhearted decorations. Some had none. A few had really elaborate jack-o'-lanterns that must have been carved using patterns.

Dalton elbowed Cole and nodded toward a doorway. A portly witch was handing out full-size Twix bars to a group of little kids.

"It's okay," Cole said, hefting his pillowcase. "We already made a good haul."

"Not much full-size candy," Dalton pointed out.

"A few little Twixes are just as good," Cole said, unsure about whether he had any in his bag.

"I heard they have some real cadavers," Blake was explaining. "Dead bodies donated to science but stolen to use as decorations."

"Think that's true?" Dalton wondered.

"I doubt it," Cole replied. "The guy would end up in jail."

"What do you know about it?" Blake challenged. "Have you been stealing corpses?"

"Nope," Cole said. "Your mom was too broke to hire me."

Everyone laughed at that one, and Blake had no reply. Cole had always been good at comebacks. It was his best defense mechanism and usually kept other kids from bothering him.

As they continued down the street, Cole tried to think

of an excuse to walk alongside Jenna. Unfortunately, she now had Lacie on one side and Sarah on the other. Cole had spoken with Jenna enough to feel fairly natural around her. Sarah and Lacie were a different story. He couldn't work up the nerve to barge in and hijack their conversation. Every possible comment that came to mind seemed clumsy and forced. At least Dalton was getting plenty of proof that he and Jenna were only friends.

Cole paid attention to the route. Part of him hoped Blake would lead them the wrong way, but he made no mistakes. When the spook alley house came into view, Blake displayed it to the others as if he had decorated it personally.

The house looked decent on the outside. Much better than average. A few fake ravens perched on the roof. Webby curtains hung from the rain gutters. One of the jack-o'-lanterns puked seeds and pulp all over the sidewalk. The lawn had lots of cardboard headstones, with an occasional plastic hand or leg poking up through the grass.

"Pretty good," Dalton conceded.

"I don't know," Cole said. "After all the buildup, I was expecting granite tombstones with actual human skeletons. Maybe some ghost holograms."

"The best stuff might be inside," Dalton said.

"We'll see," Cole replied. He paused, studying the details. Why did he feel so disappointed? Why did he care about the impressiveness of the decorations? Because he had talked Jenna into coming here. If the haunted house was cool, he might get some reflected glory. If it was weak, she would have gone out of her way for nothing. Was that really it?

Maybe he was just frustrated that he had hardly talked to her.

Blake led the way to the door. He knocked while the other nine kids mobbed the porch. A guy with long hair and a stubbly beard answered. He had a cleaver through his head, with plenty of blood draining from the wound.

"He must be the special-effects pro," Dalton murmured.

"I don't know," Cole said. "It's pretty gory, but not the ultimate."

The fatally injured man stepped away from the door to invite them in. A strobe light flashed nonstop. Dry-ice smoke drifted across the floor. Tinfoil coated the walls, reflecting the pulsing light. There were webs and skulls and candelabras. A knight in full armor came toward them, raising a huge sword. The strobe light made his movements jerky. A couple of the girls screamed.

The knight lowered his sword. He moved around a little more, mostly from side to side, trying to milk the moment, but he was less menacing because he had failed to pursue his attack. Seeming to realize he was no longer very threatening, the knight started doing robotic dance moves. A few of the kids laughed.

Cole frowned, feeling even more disappointed. "Why did everyone build this up so much?" he asked Dalton.

"What were you expecting?" Dalton replied.

Cole shrugged. "Rabid wolves fighting to the death."

"It's not bad," Dalton consoled.

"Too much hype," Cole replied. "My expectations were through the roof." Turning, he found Jenna beside him. "Are you terrified?"

"Not really," she said, looking around appraisingly. "I don't see any body parts. They did a good job, though."

The clunky knight was retreating to his hiding place. The cleaver guy started distributing candy—miniatures, but he gave everybody two or three.

Then an older kid with messy hair wandered into the hall. He was skinny, probably around college age. He wore jeans and an orange T-shirt that said BOO in huge black letters. Otherwise he had no costume.

"Was this scary enough?" he asked nonchalantly.

A couple of the girls said yes. Most of the kids were silent. Cole felt like it would be rude to tell the truth.

The Boo guy folded his skinny arms across his chest. "Some of you don't look very frightened. Anybody want to see the really scary part?"

He acted serious, but it also could have been a setup for some corny joke.

"Sure," Cole volunteered. Jenna and a bunch of the others chimed in as well.

The Boo guy stared at them like he was a general and this new batch of troops might not be up to his standards. "All right, if you say so. Fair warning: If any of this other stuff was freaky at all, don't come."

Two of the girls started shaking their heads and backing toward the door. One of them turned and buried her head against Stuart Fulsom. Stu left with them.

"Check out Stu," Cole muttered to Dalton. "He thinks he's Dr. Love."

"Why would those girls have come in the first place if

11

they didn't want to get freaked out?" Dalton complained.

Cole shrugged. If Jenna had wanted to bail, would he have left with her? Maybe if she had buried her head against his chest, trembling with worry . . .

The remaining seven kids followed the Boo guy. He led them through a regular kitchen to a white door with a plain brass knob. "It's down in the basement. I won't be coming. You sure you want to go? It's really messed up."

Blake opened the door and led the way down. Cole and Dalton shared a glance. They had come this far. No way were they wimping out now. None of the others chickened out either.

SPOOK ALLEY

Cole followed Jenna down into the dark basement. Not far beyond the foot of the creaky stairs, black curtains ran from the floor to the ceiling on all sides, concealing most of the room. The only light leaked from an old lantern on a low stool. Grimy and rusty, it looked like a relic from the Old West.

Dalton tugged on Cole's sleeve. Dramatic shadows fell across his face, making his frowning clown makeup look eerie. A painted tear sparkled on one cheek, the glitter in it barely reflecting the lantern's glow.

"That guy locked the door," Dalton whispered. He had been the last one down the stairs.

"What?"

"The Boo shirt guy. When he shut the door, I heard it click, so I checked. We're locked down here."

Sighing, Cole glanced up the stairs. "He probably just did it to add suspense."

"I don't like it," Dalton insisted.

Cole had been friends with Dalton since moving to Mesa, Arizona, from Boise in first grade. They liked a lot of the same books and video games. They both played soccer and liked riding their bikes. But Dalton tended to get easily stressed.

Cole recalled a time at the movies when Dalton accidentally left his ticket stub in the restroom before the show. Dalton had spent the rest of the time freaking out that the movie police were going to catch him without it and accuse him of theater hopping. He finally went and confessed to a worker about his lost stub. Of course the guy told him not to worry about it.

"It's just for effect," Cole assured his friend. "They're trying to make it scarier."

Dalton shook his head. "He did it quietly. I barely heard it. What kind of effect does it have when nobody hears it?"

"You heard it. You checked. You're scared. Seems like they're experts."

"Or psychopaths."

The five other kids were milling around at the bottom of the stairs. Blake had crouched to inspect the lantern. Stepping away from the light, he tugged at one of the black curtains. "This way."

As he pulled the drapery aside, Blake revealed a large man. Lantern light reflected off a mostly bald head with a bristly fringe around the sides. His wide, flat nose topped a drooping handlebar mustache. A fragile bone protruded from one earlobe. His overalls looked homemade, sloppily patched together from rough material. Curly hair sprouted from his thick bare shoulders.

Most of the kids jumped or stepped back. Lacie shrieked. The bulky stranger grinned at the reaction. Two of his teeth looked like they were made of dull gray metal.

"Ready to be scared?" he asked, eyes eager. His voice had a vaguely Southern twang. He rubbed his meaty hands together.

Cole glanced at Dalton. Maybe his friend had been right. He didn't like the idea of being locked down here with this weirdo.

"Who are you?" Jenna asked.

"Me?" the man replied, squinting at her. "You came here to be frightened, am I wrong?"

"That's right," Blake said.

The big stranger leered. "I'll make sure you get what you came for. I'll take you around, be certain you behave. You mustn't touch anything."

Dalton stepped closer to Cole. Jenna held hands with Chelsea.

"They call me Ham," the man said, picking up the lantern. He reeked of dust and sweat. "Tonight I will guide you to terrors like you have never known. Sure you want to keep going?"

"The door is locked," Dalton said weakly, twitching his chin toward the stairs.

Ham glared at Dalton. "Then you'd better stay with me." The big man held the curtain aside. Blake led the way through. Cole and Dalton brought up the rear.

Cole was one of the shorter kids in his grade, as was Dalton. They barely came up to Ham's chest. After they had moved beyond the curtain, Ham let it fall.

More dark curtains created a perimeter around the next space. Bones lay on the floor, some a little yellowed, some cracked or chipped. Human bones mingled with strange animal bones. To one side of the space rested a skull that was the size of a shopping cart and had a pair of thick broken tusks. It couldn't be real. The giant skull didn't match any animal Cole could picture, not even prehistoric ones. But it looked just as genuine as the other bones, which probably meant they were all fake.

Blake picked up what looked like an arm bone. "This feels realistic," he said.

"Real as you are," Ham replied.

"Run!" a young voice screamed, coming from somewhere behind the curtains to the left. "It's almost too late. Run for it! This isn't a——"

The voice was abruptly cut off.

Ham grinned. "You weren't supposed to hear that. Pay it no mind."

Dalton gave Cole a worried look. Cole had to admit the warning was a nice touch. It had sounded sincere. And Ham was unsettling. He seemed a little off—not very bright, big, creepy-looking, maybe not totally sane. He was the perfect pick to host a scary tour. Could he be a professional actor?

The curtains at the far side of the area parted, and a short swarthy woman emerged. She had a stocky build and wispy black whiskers above the sides of her mouth. Strands of gray highlighted her tangled black hair. Her clothes looked like layers of tattered rags.

"Last group," the woman announced, her eyes on Ham. "Ansel wants to get gone."

"Ansel is the boss," Ham replied.

The woman turned her attention to the visitors. "You kids came here to be scared. What do you know of fear? What do you know about hardship? You come from a soft, fat world full of soft, fat communities that breed soft, fat children. What kind of world celebrates bleakness on its holidays? A world that knows no bleakness. A world where bleakness has become a novelty."

"Is this going to be educational?" Blake sighed with despair.

The woman smiled. "I expect it might be very educational. You came here for thrills, boy, and thrills you will have."

"I hope so," Blake said. "These bones are about as scary as a museum."

"If you had any sense, the bones would scare you plenty," the woman said. "The bones are a warning. The bones are trophies. You came here to feel fear, and it is only fair you should be rewarded. Fear can be relative. What frightens one may not frighten another. Take this hunter roach, for example."

She held up a mottled brown cockroach the size of a bar of soap. The roach squirmed and hissed, legs wriggling. A pair of long antennae swiveled and twitched. As she held it, the roach curled its head to repeatedly strike at her thumb.

"See it biting me?" the woman asked. "On the prairie, you either build up a tolerance to the venom, or you die. Would any of you care to hold it?"

Nobody volunteered.

The woman shrugged. "To you this critter might seem scary. And maybe it should, because its venom would burn and fester beneath your skin. Might even kill you. But to me it's a snack." She popped the cockroach into her mouth and chewed. Cole heard it crunching. Black juice dribbled from one corner of her lips. She wiped it away with the back of her hand, leaving a faint smeared stain. Cole glanced over at Dalton, who made a gagging face. Lacie and Sarah turned away, murmuring hysterically to each other. The woman's eyes were on Blake. "Scared yet?"

"A little," Blake admitted. "But that was more gross than scary."

The woman gave a small smile. "You have no idea what lies beyond those curtains. You are all in quite a predicament. Would it scare you to know that your time in this world is over? Would it scare you to know that you will never see your families again? Would it scare you to know that all your plans and expectations for what your lives would hold became irrelevant when you walked down those stairs?"

"That isn't funny," Jenna said. "Halloween or not, you shouldn't make those kinds of jokes."

Cole agreed with Jenna. With those threats, the woman was crossing a line that should not be crossed. The locked door and the creepiness of Ham and the shouted warning and the eating of the bug were adding up in ways he didn't like. They really might be in trouble. If it was all a trick, it was working.

The woman nodded. "You're catching on. None of this is

funny. You belong to us now. You kids want to be scared?" She raised her voice. "Time to pack up! Tear down the drapes! Let's round up these stragglers and get gone!"

Many of the black curtains began to fall, torn down or hurled aside. Various men were revealed. A muscular redhead in a leather vest and buckskin trousers clutched a short metal rod. A pale, lanky man with white hair bared teeth that had been filed down to cruel triangles. A short Asian man in robes and a tightly wrapped turban held a net and a wooden pole. And a person with the head of a wolf and golden fur flexed fingers tipped with claws. If it was a costume, it was the best one Cole had ever seen.

A few other men were in view, but Cole found his attention straying past the grubby assortment of villains. His eyes went to the cages. Beyond the curtains, on both sides of the room, were cages packed with kids in Halloween costumes. The kids were seated, subdued, defeated.

Part of Cole still hoped this was all an elaborate hoax. If this was just part of the spook alley, then the creators had succeeded, because he felt certain that he and his friends were in genuine danger—that the men advancing on them were not actors in costumes, they were real criminals. The captives in the cages were definitely kids from the neighborhood. Cole recognized a few of them.

The men charged forward. The redhead seized Blake by the back of the neck and hurled him to the ground. Ham was reaching for Jenna.

That was all Cole needed to see. If these guys were getting physical, this was officially real. Stepping toward Ham, Cole swung his candy bag at the lantern as if he were trying to knock it out of a ballpark. The casing shattered with a flash, plunging the room into darkness.

Somebody jostled roughly into him, and Cole went down. He could see nothing. People were screaming. He rose, staggering blindly toward where he thought the stairs would be. Somebody had to get away. If these were kidnappers, somebody had to make it to the police before the situation turned even uglier.

Cole found himself tangled in curtains. Yanking desperately, he pulled them down. Instead of falling and letting him pass, the drapes landed on him. He tried to keep moving forward, but he hurried straight into a wall and fell.

A moment later a light came on. Instinctively, Cole held still. He was hidden beneath the fallen curtains. He heard orders being shouted. More lights were lit.

Moving slowly, Cole peeked out from under the edge of the drapery. An overhead electric light was on, along with three glowing lanterns. He had run exactly the wrong way. He was on the far side of the room, away from the stairs that led up to the kitchen. His friends were being manhandled into cages.

The stocky woman stood conversing with a lean man in a wide-brimmed hat and a long weathered duster. He held a sickle in one veiny hand.

Ham tromped up the stairs. He knocked on the door three times, hard enough to make it shake. The Boo guy opened it.

"We're done," Ham said.

"Good," Boo replied. "Great. I take it you're satisfied?"

"You did your part." Ham grunted, handing over a bulging sack. Boo accepted it. When he reached inside, Cole heard the unmistakable clink and rattle of coins. From his position on the floor, where he had slightly tented the curtain so he could peer out, Cole caught a glint of gold as Boo removed a few coins from the sack, weighing them in his hand.

"Do you need anything else from us?" Boo asked.

Ham looked back at the lean man in the duster, who shook his head. "Just get far away from here. After that, rest easy. Nobody will be able to follow us. Nobody will see these kids again. They'll soon be forgotten."

Boo hefted the bag of coins in a sort of salute. "A pleasure. Safe travels. Happy Halloween." He closed the door.

Ham came back down the stairs. He and the redhead wrestled the lid off a manhole cover in the center of the room. The pale man with the funky teeth walked over to one of the cages, keys in hand.

The lean man in the wide-brimmed hat held up a hand, and the room went silent. "Smart children," he said in a parched voice, not much more than a stage whisper. "You behaved well. Most of you kept silent as directed. Those who did not suffered as promised. We do not wish to harm you. This will be orderly. You will pay if you try something. We will make an example of you. We are your masters now. Treat us with due respect, and we will deal with you fairly." He motioned with his sickle for the pale man to proceed.

The cage opened. Kids filed out. They all wore iron collars.

Their legs were chained together. Cole guessed they were mostly between fifth and seventh grades. He saw no really little ones. One boy dressed as a pirate was gagged and had a huge bruise on his cheek that did not seem to be part of his costume.

The kids were paraded over to the open manhole. Ham went down first, slowly disappearing as he descended an unseen ladder. Before his head vanished, he paused. "When the rungs stop, just drop," he said. Then his head was gone.

The first kid, a girl with sparkly horns and a red cape, paused at the brink. "Down there?"

"Go," the pale man urged. "You're worth more alive, but we can make use of more bones."

She turned. It seemed awkward for her to get started with her ankles chained together. She crouched and started down.

Cole slowly let the edge of the curtain fall, closing off his view. He had ended up near a far corner of the room. There were fallen curtains everywhere, resting in lumpy piles. If he kept still, they might miss him. Unless they picked up the curtains before they left.

Where could the manhole lead? Were there big sewer tunnels running under Mesa? Apparently, they at least had some under this neighborhood. Maybe they would surface inside a warehouse where semitrailers stood waiting. Maybe the trucks would head over the border along some secret route. Anything seemed possible.

Occasionally a kid would protest from down in the manhole. The men up top would growl at him or her to drop. Cole heard several echoing screams trail off ominously.

These criminals were kidnapping dozens of people. They were taking Dalton. They were taking Jenna. He had to do something.

But he had to be smart. If he emerged now, he would get caught. Once they were gone, he could probably climb the stairs, break down the door, and go to the police. Would it be too late? Would the cops be able to follow the kidnappers through the sewers? If alerted quickly, would the authorities be able to guess where these men might be headed? What about Boo? Had he already left with the other spook alley workers? Or would they all be there, waiting for him?

Cole wished he had a cell phone. His parents had decided he was too young to need one. If they could see him now, he suspected they might rethink their policy.

He lay with his chin on the cement floor. The heavy drapes were making him sweat. His heart thudded in his chest.

Cole peeked again. Now that the kids understood the drill, the procession into the manhole was going fast.

He closed his peephole. Nobody was looking his way. Nobody was talking about a kid gone missing. One of the men was gathering up bones, but nobody was gathering curtains.

How could somebody kidnap this many people? It should be national news! There had to be more than forty kids. The whole town would be in an uproar! The whole *country* would demand answers!

Raising the edge of the curtain, Cole watched as the last

kids descended into the hole. Jenna was among them. Dalton was already gone. Cole had missed it. Some of the men had gone down as well.

The man in the wide-brimmed hat checked an old-fashioned pocket watch. "The way will close in less than ten minutes."

"Excellent timing, Ansel," the woman said. "This was a good plan."

"Think we found what we were looking for?" Ansel asked.

"Impossible to tell on this side," the woman replied. "But it's a large sample. I expect we have what we need. It should add up to quite a take."

"It's too early to count money," Ansel said. "Slaves captured are not slaves delivered. We sank most of our funds into this operation. I'll celebrate when the cargo has been sold."

Men tossed bones down the manhole. Cole did not hear them landing. Lastly, the redhead and a scarred man with long blond hair lowered the great skull down the hole, disappearing with it.

Soon only Ansel and the woman remained. Ansel's eyes swept the room. Cole felt the urge to lower the edge of the curtain, but he realized that a hasty movement might draw the eye. He held still, trusting that his face was tucked far enough back into the shadows to escape observation.

"Are we finished?" the woman asked.

Ansel checked his pocket watch. "Just over six minutes left." He gazed around the room again. "Doesn't matter how we leave the place. Nobody can follow us. We're done here."

She climbed down the manhole, and he followed. "Do we cover it?" her voice asked from out of sight.

"No need."

Cole waited. The room became silent. Were they really gone? Seemed like it. What would change in six minutes? Were they bombing the sewer tunnel? Closing it off somehow? Were they really going to sell all those kids into slavery?

In a far corner of the room a little girl crawled out from under a heap of curtains. She was small and skinny, with wavy auburn hair and freckles. She was dressed as an angel. Her wings had crumpled, and her tinsel halo was askew.

The girl looked around furtively. She approached the manhole cautiously and peered down. Then she turned for the stairs.

"Hey," Cole called.

The girl whirled and jumped, her face contorting with fear. Cole came out from under his curtains. She stared at him in shock and wonder, as if he must be a mirage. "You hid too?" she asked.

"By accident," Cole said. "I got lucky."

"I was part of a big group," the girl explained. "I ran for the corner and hid behind the curtains. Nobody noticed me. When the curtains came down, they covered me. I watched three groups get nabbed after I came here. You were with the last group."

"Right," Cole said.

"I wanted to warn you guys, but it was too late. They would have gotten me too."

"Once we came down the stairs, we were doomed," Cole said. "My friend heard them lock the door. He had a bad feeling about it, but I ignored him. And now . . ." He gestured at the hole.

"What do we do?" the girl asked.

Cole shrugged. "I don't know. You don't have a phone, do you?"

She shook her head.

"It sounded like they sent away the guys upstairs."

The girl nodded.

Cole looked at the manhole. "They didn't think they could be followed."

"I didn't understand why not," the girl said. "A lot of what they said didn't make sense. Where could they sell kids as slaves?"

"Some foreign country, I guess," Cole said. He walked to the open manhole and stared down. Rungs descended as far as he could see, which was not very far. It got dark quickly.

"Look," Cole said. "Why don't you go for help? Call the police. I'll go down and see if I can figure out where they're going."

"They'll catch you," the girl warned, her eyes wide. "They're fast and strong. You should come with me."

Cole folded his arms across his chest. She might be right. Then again, she was probably scared and wanted company. The kidnappers had seemed confident of escape. They had a ton of kids! They had Dalton! They had Jenna! "I'll be careful. I'll follow at a distance. I won't get too close."

The girl shrugged. "Up to you."

Cole looked around the room. There were a couple of windows on one side. "Don't go up the stairs. Use the windows. Break the glass if you have to, and run."

"Good idea," she agreed. "In case those other guys haven't left yet."

"What's your name?" Cole asked.

"I'm Delaney."

"I'm Cole Randolph. Tell the police where I went. Tell them they have to hurry."

She nodded and ran over to one of the windows. Cole started down the hole. If he stepped lightly, the metal rungs were reasonably quiet. Of course, for anybody staring up from the bottom he was probably silhouetted against the light above. But the kidnappers hadn't seemed like they intended to wait around. Besides, they had brought lanterns down with them. If they were still within view, he would see their lights below instead of the darkness.

Cole heard nothing as he descended. The space around him grew black. He looked up at the circle of light above him.

Suddenly his foot couldn't find the next rung. He looked down and kicked around. There was nothing. The rungs simply stopped.

The kidnappers had told everyone to jump from the last rung. They had all come down here. The drop had to be relatively safe. How far would he fall? He could only see shapeless blackness below.

Cole peered up at the circle of light again. It wasn't too

late to head back up. But what if he saw something that could save everybody? The license plate of a truck, or the tunnel the kidnappers took. If they had lights and he was in darkness, they would be easy to follow and he would be hard to see. He had to try. He couldn't desert his best friend and the prettiest girl he knew.

He tried not to imagine Jenna hugging him and calling him her hero. The thought embarrassed him, but it also helped confirm his decision.

Leaning away from the rungs, Cole dropped into the darkness.

CHAPTER

3

RESCUE

Cole was braced to land within a few feet, but instead he kept falling through darkness, picking up speed. Air whistled past him. With growing alarm he tried to prepare for a serious impact. Intuition suggested he might want to keep his body loose. Had the others who climbed down here all died? Was he about to join a pile of corpses? Could there be water at the bottom? With water he might fare better if he kept his body rigid and entered straight.

His speed kept increasing. He tucked his arms against his chest. At this velocity, simply clipping the wall would cause major injuries. Could there be an airbag at the bottom? If so, he should probably land on his back. He could hardly believe how far he was falling! He was going to die! Even if water waited at the bottom, nobody could survive a drop like this.

Glancing up he saw only darkness. Same when he looked down. His speed was no longer increasing. Only the air rushing by confirmed he remained in motion. Then the air stopped rushing, as if he were falling through nothing.

For a moment he became so violently nauseated that he lost all awareness of his other senses. It felt like his stomach was being folded inside out. He clenched his teeth to avoid releasing a stream of vomit.

The nausea departed as quickly as it had arrived. He felt dizzy. A severe ache blossomed behind the midpoint of his forehead.

It took a moment for Cole to realize that he was no longer falling. He was seated on the ground. When had he landed? Dimly realizing that his eyes were closed, he opened them.

He was seated on scorched dirt, encircled by a symmetrical ring of twelve stone pillars. Sparse brush grew here and there, as if the land lacked the fertility to support abundant weeds. Uneven brown plains extended in all directions. Near and far, lonely trees grew at random, like the haphazard survivors of a plague-ravaged forest. The sun had set, bathing the lonely prairie in soft twilight.

The kidnappers were not far off, backlit by the glowing horizon, loading the kids into horse-drawn cages. In the foreground, between two of the pillars, a hooded figure faced away from Cole, observing the activity.

Cole could hardly believe he was uninjured. A fall like he had experienced should have pulverized his bones. Apparently, none of the others had been hurt either. He could see the muscular redhead and the scarred blond man lugging the huge skull between them.

The brown landscape was unfamiliar. Cole knew of nowhere near his town where the terrain looked like this. He had never seen this ring of tall gray pillars. He looked up.

There was only sky. How could dropping down a manhole deposit him on a barren prairie? Yet here he sat. Something weird had happened, something inexplicable.

Holding his breath and staying low, Cole scuttled sideways, hoping to take cover behind one of the pillars. As he got closer, he noticed the pillar was textured like bark, and in a flash he realized the pillars were petrified trees.

On the far side of the fossilized tree, Cole sat with his back to the stone. The petrified trunk was wide enough to conceal him. If nobody came to this side of the tree circle, he might not be discovered. But then what? How had he gotten here? How could he get back to the manhole and the basement?

Motion off to one side caught his eye. The hooded, robed figure had moved into view. The person continued to stare toward the kidnappers, but he clearly addressed Cole. "You are a surprise." The male voice was somewhat deep, the words enunciated clearly, the tone neither menacing nor friendly.

"Please don't give me away," Cole asked quietly.

"The slavers have their quarry," the man said, still not looking at him. "They told me not to expect anyone else. The way closed right after you came through."

"What way?" Cole asked. "Where am I?"

"Far from home." There was a hint of pity behind the words. "You have crossed over to the Outskirts."

"The outskirts of where?"

"A difficult question. The outskirts of everywhere, perhaps. Certainly the outskirts of the world you know. This is an in-between place."

The man was showing no hostility. He showed no fear of the kidnappers, either. He stood in plain sight. Cole felt wary, but he needed information. "How do I get back?"

"You don't. It is hard to find the Outskirts, but much harder to truly leave."

"Who are you?"

"I am a Wayminder. I help control access to the Outskirts."

"Can't you send me home? And my friends, too? Those guys kidnapped them."

"I will not be able to open a way here for months. I have overtaxed my influence in this place. Others of my order would be able to accomplish the feat sooner. The slavers paid me well to open this way."

"You opened it for them?" Cole sputtered, unable to hide his anger.

"Harvesting slaves from outside the boundaries is no crime," the Wayminder said. "Not anymore. The High King of the five kingdoms supports it."

"What if I pay you?" Cole asked. "You know, like the slavers did. Could you open a way for me?"

"Not in this location for some time," the Wayminder said. "Elsewhere, perhaps. But your problem involves more than simply opening a way. Once you have come to the Outskirts, you will inevitably be drawn back here. The pull is considerably stronger if this is your birthplace, but once you have visited, all roads tend to lead you back."

Cole could hardly believe what he was hearing. "So even if I make it home, I'll end up here again?"

"Most likely within hours of your departure."

"This can't be happening."

"I sympathize with your disorientation. Be grateful that you did not come here as a slave."

"They took my friends. I wanted to help them."

"Your friends are beyond any aid you could offer. They have been claimed by the slavers. They will be sold."

Cole was nervous about the next question. He worried that mentioning his vulnerability could end the unspoken truce, but he needed to know what the Wayminder intended to do with him. "You're not going to turn me over to them?"

"I am no slaver, and I no longer work for the slavers. They paid me to open a way. I performed my duty. I held the way open for the agreed duration. Now the way is closed. Our arrangement was specific and temporary. You came through on your own. They presently have no claim on you. Nor do I. But if they catch you unmarked, they can take ownership of you."

"Unmarked?"

"Slaves bear a mark. The freeborn bear a different mark. Without a mark, the slavers could still claim you. Not all slaves hail from outside our boundaries."

"Can I get marked as free?" Cole asked.

"Yes."

"Where?"

"Many places, none of them close at hand. The nearest would probably be the village of Keeva. You would present yourself to a needle master. Any unmarked person can request a freemark. Naturally, you would have to avoid any slavers on your way there. Until you bear a freemark, any slaver given half a chance would promptly label you as their property."

"My friends will all be slaves?"

"If the slavers brought your friends here, their fates are sealed."

Cole tried to digest the information. He had thought he was following his friends into a sewer. Getting stranded in a desolate, magical prairie was a lot more than he had bargained for. Had he really left the world he knew behind? Was he really stuck here? If so, should he abandon his friends and run off to a village to get a mark that would protect him from slavery? If he fled, would he ever find his friends again?

"Will you help me?" Cole asked.

"I won't turn you in," the Wayminder replied. "I have no reason to do you harm. It costs me little to answer a question or two. But you will have to make your own way. Traveling with an unmarked person is a dangerous business. I have my own affairs to worry about."

"I need to save my friends," Cole said.

"Do not cross slavers," the Wayminder warned. "They are already marking the slaves. Your friends are now their property. If you free them, you would be committing a crime. And you would not succeed. These slavers know their trade. If you try to help your friends, you will join them. Wait until darkness falls or the slave wagons roll away, then take your chances on the prairie."

"Could you help me get to that town?"

"Keeva? You're on your own, friend. I need to move. If I tarry much longer, I will arouse their suspicions." Holding both hands behind his back, the Wayminder pointed in a certain direction. "The village is that way. Avoid people. It will be a tough walk, but less arduous than a life of slavery. Good luck."

The Wayminder strolled out of view. Cole had never gotten a good look at his face. There had been no eye contact. All he knew was that the Wayminder was reasonably tall and that his hands had been a chocolate brown.

The light was gradually fading. Cole could hear the blurred murmur of distant conversation. He heard horses and an occasional clanging. What should he do? If he was marked a free person, could he someday find his friends and free them? How big was the Outskirts? If he lost sight of the slavers, what were the chances of ever finding them again?

The Wayminder had warned him against a rescue. But maybe the Wayminder was overcautious. He hadn't seemed like the type to stick his neck out for others.

With his back to the petrified trunk, knees bent, Cole hugged his shins. He had no idea how to survive in the wild. Wandering the barren prairie alone, he might die of thirst or starvation before ever finding a village. If he could rescue Dalton, Jenna, and maybe some of the others, they could set off together. Even if he failed and got caught, at least he would be with his friends. And he would have some protection from the wilderness. Maybe he could escape later.

But Cole had not been caught yet. If he was careful, maybe he really could save everyone. He had to think positively.

The light faded. Bright stars adorned the moonless sky. He was no astronomer, but the swirling bands of dense stars above him were unmistakably grouped in different patterns than the stars back home. Camping in the desert, his dad had once pointed out the Milky Way. The crowded strips of stars above him seemed like multiple Milky Ways, curved galactic arms stretching across the firmament. Several stars glowed in brighter shades of blue and red than he had ever seen.

The only other light came from a number of campfires among the wagons. Using the dark night as cover, Cole crept closer to the camp. By the dancing firelight, he could see the kids in the cages, still in their Halloween costumes. The girls had been separated from the boys. Some were trying to sleep. Others moped, slumping against the bars. A few conversed quietly. He saw Jenna whispering to Sarah. In a different cage, Dalton rested his forehead against his folded hands.

Dalton had noticed the locked door after they had descended the stairs. He had wanted to leave. Not only had Cole shrugged off his friend's concerns, he had suggested the haunted house to Dalton and Jenna in the first place. He had sentenced his friends to slavery. He had to save them.

Not all the wagons looked like cages. Some were more like coaches. A couple looked almost like portable houses, with humble decorations and quaint windows in the sides.

Cole waited. A single sentry circled the camp, strolling through the gloom beyond the firelight. The first sentry had been the scarred man with blond hair. Now it was Ham. Nobody else seemed concerned about security. Cole watched as the slavers joked and ate. He never glimpsed Ansel, but he saw the woman go in and out of one of the homier-looking wagons. Maybe she had been talking with him. The other kidnappers were all present, except the guy with the head of a wolf. In addition, Cole noticed at least four men he had not seen earlier. They must have stayed behind with the wagons.

The slavers eventually bedded down—some in wagons, some under wagons, some on the open ground. Most of the kids fell asleep. But not all. Dalton leaned against the bars of his cage, staring vacantly at the dwindling light of the nearest campfire. The sight made Cole blink away tears. His friend did not deserve to be chained up in a portable cage like a circus animal.

The camp fell silent. The muscular redhead took over as sentry. He paced around in lazy circles, eyes studying the empty night. Empty except for Cole, huddled in a low depression at what he hoped was a safe distance.

Cole tried to form a plan. It was hard from this far. Presumably, the cages were locked. He had seen no keys. Nobody had gone in or out of the cages since he had started spying on the camp.

He couldn't do anything from where he was hiding. He needed to either risk moving in closer or try his luck finding the village of Keeva. Looking away from the campfires, Cole considered the empty gloom of the prairie. He could not wander off into the night alone and abandon his friends. It was his fault they were stuck here.

Cole waited for the sentry to walk around to the far side of the camp, then hurriedly approached in a crouch. He raced for the cage that held Dalton. His friend and a couple of other boys perked up as they saw him coming. Cole had carefully observed that none of the kidnappers had crawled under that particular wagon to sleep. With a finger to his lips, he dove into the concealing shadows.

"Cole?" Dalton whispered in disbelief.

Cole could barely hear his friend, but he still worried the greeting had been too loud. He had to respond. He needed info. But he waited a moment to be sure the camp remained still.

Sitting up, Cole put his mouth near one of the cracks in the plank floor of the cage. "I came through to this place on my own. I'm here to bust you out. Are the cages locked?"

"Yes," Dalton whispered through the same crack. "Ham has the key. The guy who first greeted us in the basement."

"I remember him," Cole said. Ham had gone into one of the coaches. "I saw where he went to sleep. I'll try to steal the key."

"Are you nuts?" Dalton asked.

"Not so loud," Cole urged.

"They'll catch you, too. You should run for it."

"No," another voice chimed in. "Get us out."

"Shut it," a third voice whispered urgently.

The boys above fell silent. Cole heard footsteps approaching. His body went rigid. He tried to breathe silently. Boots and legs became visible.

"What's all the commotion?" the redhead inquired in a rough whisper.

"Nothing," one of the boys answered.

"They were trying to take my coat," Dalton improvised quietly.

"Keep it down or I'll confiscate it," the redhead threatened. "It's time to sleep."

"Just wait until my dad catches up," one of the boys said. "He's a cop."

The redhead gave a weary chuckle. "There is no way from there to here. Your parents won't even remember you. No more noise. I don't want to come over here again."

"Sorry," Dalton said.

"Don't apologize," the redhead said. "Just stop talking."

"Excuse me," a girl called softly from a neighboring wagon.

"That goes for all of you," the redhead snapped, barely maintaining his whisper.

"I just thought you might want to know about the boy hiding under the wagon," the girl replied.

Cole felt like he had suddenly been immersed in ice water.

The boots shuffled. "What?"

"Ansel told us we would be punished for not telling what we know," the girl said. "A boy under that wagon is planning an escape."

The redhead crouched and met eyes with Cole. "Well, who have we here?"

Cole tried to force words from his throat. It took a second. "Me? I'm a free citizen looking for work."

"Free, you say?" The man chuckled. "I can see your wrist, lad. Free for the moment perhaps. Not for long."

CHAPTER
4

BONDMARK

Cole knew he had to get away, but for a moment the shock of discovery held him paralyzed. His only chance was to run. They were on an empty prairie at night. If he went far enough, fast enough, maybe the kidnappers would lose him.

When the crouching redhead reached under the wagon, Cole rolled the opposite way. Springing to his feet, he took off, passing other wagons and jumping a sleeping figure bundled in a worn blanket.

"Intruder!" went up the alarm from the redhead. "On your feet! Intruder! Don't let him get away!"

The shouted words fed Cole's panic. Men all around the encampment cast aside their covers and scrambled to their feet. Racing toward the open prairie, Cole saw two men running parallel to him and a little ahead, gradually converging. Both were faster than him. If he kept going straight, they would have him, so he abruptly doubled back, hoping to streak through the camp and shake them in the confusion.

The change in direction only revealed the redhead coming at him from behind, along with several others. Lacking better options, Cole swerved toward the nearest wagon, grabbed the bars, and climbed on top. The fingers of the redhead brushed his heel but failed to grab him.

Crouched atop the wooden roof of the wagon, Cole couldn't see his pursuers, but he could hear them coming from all directions. Cole had never been the fastest runner, but he was a confident climber. Heights had never bothered him. There was another wagon parked not too far away. With a running start, he jumped to the next roof, barely clearing the gap.

"He's moving!" shouted a gruff voice.

Cole ran across the wagon and leaped to the roof of another, landing in a sprawl, one cheek against the splintery wood. Rising to his knees, he realized that he had reached the end of the line. Unless he turned around, there was no other wagon within range.

"Still on the move!" a voice boomed. "He's on this one!"

If he stayed put, they would take him. Cole ran and jumped from the roof as far as he could. As the ground rushed up to greet him, he saw men coming at him from off to one side. Cole tried to land running but flopped painfully forward into the dirt instead, the impact jarring his bones. Driven by adrenalized panic, he scrambled to his feet just in time for a large body to tackle him from behind.

All the air whooshed from his lungs as Cole was pinned beneath the bulk of a large man who stank of leather and sweat. Cole squirmed, but calloused hands held him firmly.

Dirt filled his mouth, and a thorny weed prickled against his temple. Other men gathered around him.

Then the men hushed one another. A light approached, accompanied by footsteps. Craning his neck, Cole saw Ansel, a lantern in one hand. He wore his wide-brimmed hat, a long underwear shirt, pants with suspenders, and a dusty pair of boots. In his other hand he held a sickle. Cole closed his eyes, dread coiling inside.

The boots halted a pace away from Cole's face. "What have we here?" that dry voice asked.

Cole opened his eyes and kept silent.

"Found him under a wagon," the redhead reported. "Must've slipped into camp."

Ansel crouched down, setting the lantern on the ground. The nearby brightness made it hard to see Ansel's face. "Time to fess up, Scarecrow. Slipped into camp from where?"

"Just passing through," Cole tried.

"One of the girls said he was planning an escape," the redhead volunteered.

"She ratted him out?" Ansel asked.

"Sure did," the redhead said.

Ansel nodded. "Good for her. She might make a go of it here. That little darling deserves a reward. We have any of those cookies left? The frosted ones?"

"A few," a voice answered.

"She gets them all," Ansel said. "Give her the royal treatment the rest of the way to Five Roads. First served, largest helpings, front wagon—whatever we can do to make her comfortable."

Cole hoped the cookies would give her food poisoning. But he kept his mouth shut.

Ansel stood, picking up the lantern. "Let him up."

The man let go of Cole and got off him. A rough hand grabbed him by the collar and hoisted him to his feet. Ansel studied him through eyes so narrow, they almost looked closed.

"Were you planning to steal my slaves, Scarecrow?"

Cole glanced at the sickle—the wicked curve of the blade, the sharp point. He wasn't sure what this guy wanted to hear. "You took my friends."

"You're from over there," Ansel said. "From outside. You came through with us. How'd you slip away?"

Cole didn't want to tell Ansel that he had come through after them. The Wayminder had helped him, and Cole worried the truth might get him in trouble. "In the confusion, I hid behind one of the stone trees."

Ansel glanced at his men. "I'm less than overjoyed to hear that. We had people in place to prevent that kind of sloppiness as we welcomed you to your new home."

"Where are we?"

Ansel grinned. Not a happy grin. It was the grin of a killer who knew the police would never find the body. "That's the question, now, isn't it? See, we're not in Arizona anymore. We're not on Earth. I'm no astronomer, but this might not even be the same universe as Earth. We're in the Outskirts. Junction, specifically, between the five kingdoms."

"And that means you can kidnap people?"

Ansel glanced at his men. "Scarecrow has the right

43

questions." The lantern swung a little, squeaking. "In Arizona, yes, I stole your friends, and in those parts they might find me guilty. Your problem is, we're not there no more. Once we reached the Outskirts and marked those kids, they became our property according to the law of the land here. And by trying to take my property, Scarecrow, well, you made yourself a criminal."

Cole felt sick. How could they accuse him of wrongdoing for trying to help his kidnapped friends? Everything was upside down. "I don't know the laws here."

Ansel chuckled, and his grin almost became sincere. "Wouldn't that be nice, fellas, if you only had to keep the laws you knew about? I'd spend my life traveling, and I'd stay as ignorant as possible." He eyed Cole up and down. "You working alone?"

Cole almost laughed. "You guys better watch it. My backup will be here any second."

Ansel became expressionless in a scary way. "That wasn't an answer. One more try. You working alone?"

Cole nodded. "Yeah. I'm alone. Nobody else got away."

"If you lie to me . . . that'll be it."

"I'm not lying." They stared at each other in silence for a moment. "What are you going to do with me?"

The grin returned, cunning this time. "You tell me, Scarecrow."

Cole swallowed. All eyes watched him expectantly. "I become a slave?"

Ansel held his sickle higher, his eyes caressing the blade. "My vote was to take away your hands and feet as an example.

Slavers can't have people swiping their merchandise. Bad for business. But . . . Scarecrow . . . you caught me in a good mood. How often does that happen, fellas?"

All the other men found someplace else to look.

Ansel stepped closer to Cole. "Notice how they don't answer? Well, that's your answer. But we made a fine haul tonight, best in a long while, so I'm going to grant your wish and take you as a slave." He raised his voice, calling over his shoulder. "Secha? Tag him! He'll walk behind the rear wagon tomorrow. No food or water. We'll let him keep his extremities, but that don't mean we got to coddle the boy. Show's over. Now let's get settled again. We start our march in the morning."

Ansel retreated several paces, boots crunching over the dry ground. The woman who had eaten the cockroach approached with a lantern of her own. She held it out toward Cole. "You're the one that swung your bag at the lantern."

Cole nodded.

She gave him a penetrating stare. Cole glanced away.

"Look me in the eye, young man," Secha said.

He stared at her. She leaned in close, never breaking eye contact. Her fingers contorted into weird positions. Then she examined his hands front and back.

"Worst of the lot," she said. "No shaping potential at all. The High King won't pay a lead ringer for this one."

Ansel shook his head. "Had I known that, I would have made an example of him."

"Still could," Secha said over her shoulder.

"Nah, I already passed judgment. Following the wagon will suffice." Ansel walked off.

"Be glad I'm not in charge," Secha told Cole. "I would have fed you to Carnag."

"What's Carnag?" Cole asked.

The men guarding him chuckled at his ignorance.

Secha frowned. "Depends who you ask. The reports are mixed. But consensus has it that Carnag is a monster like we've never seen anywhere in the five kingdoms. People are scared. We're not too far from Sambria, where the monster has been prowling."

"You're right," Cole said. "I'm glad you're not in charge."

"Let's get the bondmark on you so I can turn in," Secha said. "Hold out your hand."

Cole briefly considered resistance. But two men stood right behind him. For all he knew, if he made a fuss, Ansel would return with his sickle. Cole extended his left hand.

Secha produced a drawstring bag and opened the mouth. The third finger on her left hand had an extra long nail. She dipped it into the bag.

"Hold still," she told Cole, then turned to one of the men. "Help him."

One of the slavers grabbed Cole's arm just above the wrist. The other man braced himself against Cole from behind. Cole clenched his teeth. If they were holding him like this, it meant the mark was going to hurt. He tried to ready himself for the pain.

When her fingernail touched his wrist, it felt extremely hot and cold at the same time. He wanted to yank his hand away, but the brawny redhead held him tightly. Secha moved her lips as she traced a simple pattern with her fingernail.

Then she backed away. The bondmark she had drawn blazed an angry red. It still felt hot and cold, though not as intensely as when her nail was in contact with his skin.

"Try not to touch it," Secha advised. "You'll slow the healing." She turned and strode away.

With a viselike hand on his shoulder, the redhead marched Cole over to the rear of one of the cages and chained him to it with a tight manacle on his unmarked wrist.

"Not a sound," the redhead threatened. "We'll reorganize the slaves according to value in the morning. The best go up front. You'll walk behind the last wagon. Better sleep. Long day tomorrow."

The redhead walked away. Cole didn't know any of the kids in this wagon. They were pretending to be asleep, but he had seen two of them peek at him.

Cole got down on the ground. He had no blanket. The earth was lumpy and hard. The chain wasn't long enough to let his hand rest on the ground, and his wrist dangled about four inches up.

He couldn't see Dalton or Jenna. Their wagons were lost in shadows, and he had no desire to draw more attention to himself by calling out to them.

The night grew quiet again except for the pop and crackle of the campfires. Less than half an hour ago, Cole had watched the camp from a distance. Many options had been open to him. He wished he could rewind time and do it over again, but it was too late. Now he was a slave like the others.

What kind of slave would he be? Would he labor in mines,

busting open rocks with a pickax? Would he row slave ships? Would he work farms? Would he fight in a gladiator arena? All of the above? None? He expected he would have answers sooner than he wanted. Cole closed his eyes and tried to relax, but sleep was a long time coming.

CHAPTER
5

CARAVAN

The next day got worse with every step. Chained to the rear wagon, Cole had more dust to deal with than any other member of the procession. The kids in the cages got dusty as well, but at least they could turn their backs to it. Cole found that by staying really close to his wagon, squinting his eyes, keeping his head down, and covering his nose and mouth with his unchained hand, he could avoid enough of the dust to remain on his feet. Some stretches of the way proved dustier than others.

Most of the time he had to maintain a fast walk to keep up with the wagon. The mounted guards wouldn't let him hold the bars of the cage, but he stayed close enough to touch them. At a certain distance from the wagon, the chain would help pull him along, but it also threatened to tug him off balance. Up inclines, the wagon went slower; down slopes, a little faster. The land remained more or less level, without any major hills or valleys.

By the time they broke for lunch, Cole was hungrier and

thirstier than he could remember ever feeling. His crusty mouth tasted like he had tried to eat the prairie.

The wagons formed up into a loose circle. He sat alone while the others ate, his body and legs exhausted. How was he supposed to keep going without food and water? Maybe that was the idea. Maybe he would end up getting dragged to death.

Most of the kids in the wagon avoided eye contact with him. Nobody tried to toss him any food. He couldn't really blame them. They didn't want to end up chained beside him. It was hard to watch them eat and drink. They only had bread and water, but to Cole it seemed like a feast.

Dalton and Jenna were in two of the farthest wagons. He told himself they would try to sneak him food if they weren't so distant. They kept looking his way, so he did his best to act content. He even managed some smiles.

When the wagons started rolling again, Cole's legs were stiff and cramped. Maybe resting hadn't been a great idea. Cole began to wonder if he could last until the end of the day. He didn't look at the guards. He didn't watch the kids in the cage. He didn't check the sun. Head down, he just kept trudging forward.

The afternoon grew warmer. Sweat soaked his scarecrow costume. He had gotten rid of the straw and the arrows, but he wished the sleeves were shorter. At least his hat kept the sun off his face and neck. The inside of his mouth became desiccated. His tongue felt swollen. When he tried to open his mouth, his lips stuck together.

As evening approached, he often stumbled and sometimes

fell. If he didn't get up right away, the chain towed him forward. Once, he let the chain drag him a good distance, hoping it might rest his legs. The manacle hurt his wrist terribly, and he soon realized that if he didn't stay on his feet, the front side of his body would become one huge scab.

While the sunset faded, his head pounded painfully. His tongue felt like an old sponge that had become rigid. No strength remained in his rubbery legs, but he trudged onward, because the alternative was worse.

When the wagon came to a halt, Cole collapsed and promptly lost consciousness. He awoke with Ham trickling water into his mouth from a canteen, a little at a time. Warm and metallic, it still somehow managed to taste heavenly. A little food followed—fragments of bread, accompanied by some more water.

"Learn your lesson yet?" Ham asked when Cole met his gaze.

Not trusting his voice, Cole nodded.

"Want to join the rest of the slaves in the wagon?" Ham asked.

"Yes, please," Cole croaked.

"Boss asked after you," Ham said. "I told him you might not last another day on foot."

Cole nodded. Ham was probably right.

"Boss never goes easy on thieves," Ham said. "But you only tried. You never got away with nothing. And you're his now. Boss likes to turn a profit when he can. Nobody buys dead slaves. I expect he'll load you in a cage."

"Hope so," Cole managed. Ham gave him a little more water.

"You'll sleep chained here tonight," Ham said. "Get some shut-eye."

As Ham walked away, Cole slumped down and closed his eyes. The ground was lumpy, the camp was noisy, but falling asleep was no problem.

In the cool twilight before dawn, Ham used a key to unfasten the manacle. Cole tenderly rubbed where his wrist had been scraped and bruised. He stood unsteadily, his legs stiff and sore. Following instructions, he entered the rear wagon's cage. Breakfast consisted of a crumbly biscuit and a strip of tough dried meat. He drank gritty water from a dirty tin cup, then collected and ate all the crumbs shed by the biscuit.

After the wagon started rolling, Cole curled up and slept, heedless of the jolts and vibrations of the uneven terrain. When he woke, all horizons were a bright orange, as if multiple suns were rising in every direction.

"What's with the sky?" he asked.

"Been that way for hours," a girl said quietly. She wore bloody scrubs, as if she came from a horribly botched surgery.

"Where are they taking us?" Cole asked.

"Someplace to sell us," the girl said. "I guess some of the kids are going to the king or something. They kept talking about shaping potential."

"Shhh," hissed a boy dressed like a commando. "We're not supposed to talk."

Surgeon girl looked guilty. Cole glanced around but didn't see anyone who was likely to overhear them. A couple of the men roved up and down the caravan on horseback, however none were currently nearby. The wagon was noisy, and the driver didn't seem to be paying attention. Still, Cole could understand commando boy not wanting to make a bad situation worse. The eight kids in this cage had all watched him stumble along behind the wagon yesterday. None would be eager to risk trying it.

Cole settled back and gazed at the sky through the bars. There had been a sun yesterday, so what was with the weird lighting? Surgeon girl must have been mistaken. The sky couldn't have been like this for hours.

But as the wagon rumbled onward, the sky stayed the same, as if the sun were about to rise or had recently set in all directions. The other kids all kept their heads down. No one tried to whisper to anyone else.

Leaning against the bars with his back to the dust, Cole thought about home. His mom and dad were probably out of their minds. Even his sister, Chelsea, was probably worried.

And he wasn't the only person missing. All the parents had to be freaking out. That many kids disappearing without a trace would make the news for sure. Cole had never heard a story to top it.

The redheaded guard had thought their parents would forget them. Maybe people in this weird place would let their kids disappear without a fight. Obviously the guard had no idea how things worked in America.

Cole hoped the little angel girl had made it to the police. Assuming she had, there was no way even the best detective could follow their trail to another dimension. Her story would just make the disappearances more mysterious.

Looking around at the barren prairie and glancing ahead at the other kids locked up like circus animals, Cole realized he might never make it home. If he did, according to the Wayminder he wouldn't get to stay there.

What had been his last words to his family? He clearly recalled his final remark to his sister. Chelsea was two years older and considered herself an expert on maturity. Just before he left to meet up with Dalton, she had been getting dressed up for a Halloween party. As he was leaving, she informed him how immature he was for going trick-or-treating. He told her she looked like something Halloween had thrown up.

He felt bad for it now, although it was better than having no comeback. He wondered if Chelsea would think disappearing forever was immature.

His last words to his mom were assurances he would be home by nine thirty. His dad had asked him to take out the trash, and he had promised to do it later. He hadn't lied to them on purpose.

Maybe he would see them again. But somehow, as he rattled along a lonely prairie in a world where a stationary sunrise glowed in all directions, he had a hard time believing it.

He tried to look ahead and spot Dalton or Jenna, but with so much dust, and with the wagons in single file, he could seldom see much beyond the wagon in front of him. He wondered if they were looking for him.

Brown prairie, more or less level, stretched in all directions. Cole saw weeds and brush and some isolated trees, but not much else. He decided that if he'd wanted to be bored by nature, he had come to the right place.

Staring down at the floorboards of the cage, Cole noticed where somebody had carved a happy face into the wood. It was simple—a circle with two dots for eyes and a curved smile. The circle was imperfect, but not bad considering it had been scratched into wood.

The face struck him as odd. "Who would draw a smiley face while riding in a slave wagon?" he muttered.

"Somebody who wanted company," the happy face answered in a friendly voice. "The miles go by faster when you have a buddy." The mouth didn't open when it spoke, but it quivered.

Cole jumped in surprise. He glanced over at the other kids in the wagon. Nobody was paying attention to him. He stared at the smiley face. "Did you just talk?" he whispered.

"Sure did," the face answered, mouth trembling again. "I'm happy as a clam to meet a nice guy like you."

The voice wasn't very loud and sounded like a young boy.

Cole rubbed his face with both hands. Was he dreaming? Hallucinating? Surgeon girl was sitting closest to him. He crawled over to her and tapped her shoulder. "Check something for me."

"What?" she asked, glancing around for guards.

Cole had already looked. One rider was way behind them, and two others roved much farther up the line of wagons. He motioned her over to the happy face. She followed uncertainly. "Say something to her," Cole instructed.

"Today is the bestest day ever to make a new friend," the cheerful face said.

The girl blinked, then looked at Cole in surprise. "How'd you do that? Are you a ventriloquist?"

"Yeah," Cole said. "Cool trick, right?"

She rolled her eyes. "What's the matter with you? Does this seem like a good time for jokes?" She scooted back to her former position.

Cole hunched down with his head near the happy face. He put his hand up to cover his lips. "Do you mind talking quietly?"

"Not a smidge," the face said at a lower volume, although still chipper. "I'm just glad as can be to have a new pal."

"What are you?" Cole asked. "How are you talking?"

"I'm a semblance, silly. I was shaped to talk."

"A what?"

"I was made by Liam, the superdy-duperest shaper in all the land. After he was taken as a slave, he made me to keep him company. When he got sold, he left me here to cheer up anyone who talked to me. Feeling better yet?"

Cole could hardly believe he was talking to a magical happy face. It seemed even weirder to him than slave traders from another world. The little guy was so enthusiastic, Cole couldn't help feeling a bit better. "Yeah, actually. Do you have a name?"

"Happy."

"I'm Cole. Can you see me?"

"Sure, silly billy. I can see up your nostrils."

Cole stifled a chuckle. He glanced at the other kids, but they all sat with their heads bowed, wrapped up in their fears.

"Does it hurt if people step on you?"

"Not a bit. You stepped on me when you came in here."

"Sorry."

"No harm done. You have a good sole."

Cole smiled for Happy's benefit. "You said the kid who made you was a shaper. Did he shape you with a knife?"

"No, silly, with his shaping."

"What? Like magic?"

"Kind of, I guess. Life is magical."

"He brought you to life?"

"Not really. I'm a semblance. I seem alive, don't I?" The face gave a squeaky giggle.

"Did Liam program your words?"

"I just say what I say, Liam showed me the way, in this cage I will stay, while you're here, we should play."

Cole wondered whether Liam or the little face had created the rhyme. "Do you feel alive?"

"I love to talk, especially with a special new friend."

The face seemed mostly designed to act friendly. Cole wanted to check if it could tell him anything useful. "Why is the sky like this? Why does it look like sunrise everywhere?"

"We're lucky it's a duskday—not too hot, not too cold. It's nice to feel glad about the weather."

"Are there lots of duskdays here?"

"They come and go. It depends. Are you from outside?"

"Outside of this place? I'm from Earth. These guys kidnapped my friends."

"Don't let greedy slavers keep you down. Whenever you fall, remember to bounce!"

"Listen, Happy. Can you help me get out of here?"

"I'd surely help if I could. I'm just a face on some wood."

Cole glanced around to make sure nobody was noticing his conversation. No guards were near, and the other kids still ignored him. "You've been here a long time. Maybe you know something that could help me."

"You bet I do," Happy chirped. "Here's a good one: If at first you don't succeed, another chance is all you need!"

"I mean info about the slavers," Cole said. "Or about this wagon. Secrets that might be useful to help me get away."

Happy giggled nervously. "Don't try to get away. It makes them very grumpy. You'll get to leave when they sell you."

"Where will they sell me?"

"The slave market at Five Roads."

"What kind of people might buy me?"

"The kind with money, silly. The kind who need slaves."

"What sort of work will I do?"

"You never know, but you can always hope for the best. You might get to do something really amazing!"

Happy didn't seem like a fountain of useful information. "Let me see if I've got this straight. You're saying I should never stop chasing that rainbow?"

The smile widened. "That's the spirit! Follow a star! Keep your chin up and you'll go far."

"Do the slavers know about you?"

"The Shaper does, Secha. She told Ansel. They spoke with me one night. I'm tricky to remove, so they let me be."

"Secha is a Shaper?" Cole asked.

Happy giggled. "She marked you, didn't she?"

Cole remembered her tracing on his wrist with her fingernail. He looked at the maroon mark. "Does it talk?"

Happy laughed hard. "Your bondmark? That isn't even a semblance!"

"Why would it be tricky for them to remove you?"

"Liam wanted me to stick. If I get destroyed or removed, I take shape elsewhere on the wagon. They'd have to scrap the whole wagon to get rid of me."

"Can you move on your own?" Cole wondered.

One of the eyes flattened in a wink. "Just a little."

Cole traced the circle of the happy face with his fingertip. Happy laughed as if it tickled. How could such a thing have been created? "What else can shapers do?"

"It depends."

"Depends on what?"

"On what they want to make, silly! And whether they can."

Cole sighed. Happy was cheerful, and it was unbelievable he existed, but prying anything useful from him was exasperating.

"Do you know any secrets that will help me survive here?" Cole asked.

"They're not secrets," Happy said. "Enjoy the beauty of the sky and keep a twinkle in your eye."

The wagons came to a stop.

Cole sat up, looking around. He couldn't see the front of the procession. "What's going on?"

"We stopped," Happy said. "Seems early for lunch."

When they had stopped to eat in the past, the wagons had formed a circle. This time they remained in a line. Was there an obstacle up at the front? Cole couldn't tell.

After some time Ansel walked away with a man Cole hadn't seen before into a field off to one side. The man was shorter than Ansel, with graying hair and bushy sideburns. He used a cane and walked with a limp. They headed out far enough to be visible from all wagons at once, then turned to face the caravan.

"We've met a customer by chance on the road," Ansel announced, his parched voice even more gravelly when he raised it. "This gentleman works north of here with the Sky Raiders at the Brink. Those names won't mean much to you newcomers, but the Raiders have a heavy need for slave labor, in part because the life expectancy for a new slave among them is around two weeks."

This caused a stir among the caged trick-or-treaters. Ansel waited for the murmuring to die down.

"Our customer was returning from a supply run," Ansel said, "but figured he should take advantage of our encounter by gaining an extra pair of hands. The wagons headed for the royal palace are naturally off limits. Otherwise he can have his pick. Since the slave who goes with him will probably perish shortly, I mentioned the new boy who caused a ruckus the other night. Due to my soft spot for obedience, I denied him Tracy, who pointed out the clumsy thief."

Ansel then led the man directly to Cole's wagon. As they approached, the other kids in the cage crowded away from Cole.

If this stranger bought him, how would he ever find Dalton, Jenna, and the others from his neighborhood? Then again, they would probably all get sold to different places anyhow. At least this guy seemed kind of old and not too quick on his feet. There might come a chance to escape.

The potential buyer stepped forward and looked up at Cole through the bars. "You're the boy who caused the commotion?" His clearly enunciated words made him seem professorial. Or maybe it was the slightly battered top hat in his hand.

"Yeah," Cole replied.

"Any physical handicaps? Chronic illnesses?"

"I'm healthy. A little hungry."

"We feed them twice what most slaves get," Ansel inserted. "They're in prime condition, fresh from a prosperous world."

The man nodded, eyes still on Cole. "How well do you handle heights?"

Cole wondered whether he should lie. Maybe a fear of heights would disqualify him from the dangerous work Ansel had mentioned. But the buyer looked and acted nice, which was more than Cole could say for the slavers. He decided to see where honesty would lead him. "I'm not scared of heights."

The man shifted his stance. "How do you feel when standing near a high brink?"

"Doesn't bother me," Cole said. "Never has."

The man turned to Ansel. "Easy as that. I'll take him."

THE BRINK

The quick decision surprised Cole. The buyer turned away, and a tall, muscled stranger came into view, glaring at Cole distrustfully. So much for making an easy escape from the old limping guy. He should have guessed the buyer would have help.

On his way out of the cage, Cole leaned close to surgeon girl. "If you get lonely, talk to the happy face."

She looked at him like he was crazy.

Cole hopped down to where the tall stranger awaited him. "This way," the man said, pointing toward the front of the caravan. He had a familiar reddish mark on his wrist.

"Are you a slave too?" Cole asked.

The man cuffed Cole on the ear, hard enough to knock him to the ground. Cole stayed down for a moment, the side of his head smarting and his mind buzzing with anger.

"Don't speak unless spoken to," the man said. "Up."

Cole got to his feet. The kids in the slave wagons watched him with wide eyes. Without an audience, he would have gone quietly. But he didn't want all those kids to see him offering no resistance to a bully. It set a bad precedent.

So he turned and kicked at the side of the stranger's knee as hard as he could. Crouching, the man swiveled, caught Cole's ankle in one hand, and then swept his other foot out from under him with a brisk kick.

Cole's back hit the ground first with a flat slap, and he found himself unable to breathe. Rolling onto his side, he shuddered as he tried to get his paralyzed lungs to kick into gear. He needed air but couldn't inhale. Then the paralysis passed, and he was breathing again. He gratefully took several deep breaths.

"You have any fight left in you?" the tall stranger asked. "I could do this all day."

Cole rocked into a sitting position. A glance at the wagon showed the occupants all pointedly looking elsewhere. He had taught them that defiance led to pain and failure. Not exactly the lesson he'd had in mind.

Cole got up and brushed himself off. The tall guard gestured for him to proceed. "Bye, Happy," Cole called toward the cage.

"Bye" came a faint, high-pitched reply.

Cole noticed several heads in the cage swivel toward the floor.

Well ahead of them now, the buyer limped beside Ansel toward a group of burdened mules at the front of the caravan. "Those your mules?" Cole asked.

The man cuffed Cole on the other ear, not as hard as last time, but enough to make him stagger. "You learn slower than most dogs."

"You didn't hit me for saying good-bye," Cole replied.

"I'm not that heartless," the man said. "No more out of you."

Cole watched the wagons as he walked. He saw Jenna, her Cleopatra costume filthy and bedraggled. Cole forced a smile and gave her a wave.

"You were brave to come for us," Jenna called. "Tracy deserves to be run over by every wagon in the line!"

The other kids in her cage distanced themselves from her. She stood by the bars defiantly.

"They're taking my wagon to the High King," Jenna called. "Whatever that means."

"This isn't over," Cole promised, ducking just in time to feel the man's hand whoosh over his head. He had swung hard that time. Cole sprang to the side, barely avoiding a kick, then ran ahead toward the mules.

Something struck the back of his head and sent him tumbling. It was hard to tell whether it had been a fist, a rock, or a club, but it hurt plenty. Cole curled up, cradling his sore skull, worried that more blows might rain down. When none came, he risked a peek. The big man stood over him, frowning, arms folded beneath his chest.

"I misspoke," the man said. "I'm not willing to do this all day. Act up again, and we'll have to cart you to the Brink in a wheelbarrow. On your feet."

Head still throbbing, Cole rose to find Dalton staring at him from behind nearby bars. Heavily powdered by dust and with his frowning makeup smudged and faded, his friend looked like the saddest clown ever. Dalton cautiously shook his head, warning Cole not to speak.

Cole nodded at his friend and mouthed, *I'll find you.*

Dalton waved, tears brimming in his eyes. "We're going to the king too," Dalton said softly, barely loud enough to hear.

Cole looked away. Would he really find them? Or was this the last time he would see anyone from his world? He had been mostly trying to give Dalton a little hope, but he found that he really meant his words. Maybe he would lead a slave revolt. Maybe he would sneak away on his own. It was hard to guess what opportunities he would find, but he silently vowed never to stop watching for a chance to escape and to find his friends.

When Cole reached the mules, the buyer already sat astride a horse. A long-haired man with a shiny burn scar on his chin rode beside him. "Come here, slave," the professorial man invited.

Cole approached the man on the horse.

"I heard you sassing Vidal," the man said. "Don't speak to your betters unless we ask you a question. Is that hard to grasp?"

"I'm a quick learner," Cole said. "All it usually takes is a concussion or two."

The man looked beyond Cole and held up a hand to stay Vidal. "The slave was answering a question." The man returned his gaze to Cole. "A little spirit might serve you well at the Brink. A lot will serve you ill. You're not from here, so our treatment of slaves might seem barbaric, but you had better get used to it. Even if I don't personally cherish certain aspects of slavery, we're teaching you the order of things for your own good. I'm Durny, this is Ed, and we have some riding ahead of us. You're now the property of Adam Jones, owner of the Cliffside Salvage Yard and leader of the Sky Raiders. Don't make problems, or you'll pay dearly. Understood?"

"I get it," Cole said.

Durny looked to Vidal. "Put him on Maribel. Our business here is done."

By his sixth day of riding, Cole had grown accustomed to Maribel. In spite of her burden, she and the other eleven mules plodded tirelessly forward from daybreak to nightfall. Normal suns had crossed the sky ever since the duskday ended, and today was no exception.

Cole had found the ride lonely. The men tended to converse when he was out of earshot. They only addressed him directly with basic instructions. He had to unpack and brush the mules at night and get them ready to travel every morning.

The cold treatment wore on Cole. He had never felt like such an outcast. After having been marked, chained up, caged, and now ignored as if he was less than a person, Cole had to fight worries that his life was over. He began to doubt whether he would have another happy day.

Today they had started early, in the gray chill before sunrise. Durny had explained that the Brink was dangerous at night and that a long ride should get them to their destination before sunset.

As the day progressed, Cole tried to enjoy the scenery. At least the land had grown more interesting, with ridges, hills, and ravines. Grasses and brush grew everywhere, along with numerous bushes and occasional stands of tall trees. He saw rabbits and squirrels, and occasionally glimpsed deer or foxes.

Cole kept an eye on the sun as it began to sink. Durny had made a point throughout the day of hurrying the mules along, not wanting to end up near the Brink after dark. The sun was less than an hour away from setting when Durny dropped back to ride beside Cole.

"Come with me, slave," he said. "Let Ed and Vidal tend the mules for a spell."

Durny dismounted and Cole did likewise. Durny motioned for him to follow, then led him onto a trail and up a rise. Up ahead the trail came to a sudden end at what was clearly a precipice.

Durny nudged Cole's shoulder with the back of his hand. "You claimed not to mind edges. Why not give that one a try?"

Cole crept to where the ground stopped, and then he leaned forward to look down the cliff.

And down.

And down.

He had never seen anything like it.

He wasn't looking down at the ground in the distance. He was looking down at sky that darkened toward purple the farther he peered.

Durny came up beside him. "Welcome to the Brink."

"Permission to speak?"

"Granted."

"Where's the bottom?"

Durny shrugged. "Far as anyone can tell, there is no bottom. Expeditions have explored by climbing and flying. No one who ever returned has seen where the cliff bottoms out. It seems to go down beyond infinity."

"It's like the end of the world," Cole said, staring out at the emptiness.

"Exactly."

Cole glanced at Durny. "The world can't just end."

"This one does. At least in this direction. The Brink doesn't go all the way around the Outskirts, at least as far as we've been able to determine." He waved a hand to the right. "Go far enough in that direction and you'll reach the Eastern Cloudwall. Can't go over it, can't slide under it, can't dodge around it. Of those who have tried to go through it, none have returned. Same story with the Western Cloudwall, if you follow the Brink in the other direction. What lies behind or within the cloudwalls none can tell, for they cannot be breached by land or air. Notice anything else out there? Look closely."

Scanning outward from the Brink, all Cole saw were sky and some clouds, the same view he got if he looked up. Wait, on one of the smaller clouds, in the distance, he observed the distinct shape of a castle with several towers.

"That cloud looks just like a castle," he said, pointing.

"That *is* a castle," Durny replied.

"It can't be," Cole said. "It's floating."

"Once again, welcome to the Brink."

Cole gave Durny a suspicious stare. "You have to be kidding. This place might be weird, but not that weird."

Durny reached inside his coat and removed a collapsible brass spyglass. Extending it, he raised it to one eye and focused it before passing it to Cole.

Since the spyglass was powerful, it took Cole a frustrating moment to line it up with the castle. Sure enough, the structure appeared to be made of stone, inexplicably resting on a wisp of cloud with nothing but blue sky all around. It had battlements, banners, towers, windows—even a visible drawbridge.

Cole lowered the spyglass. "How is it possible?"

"Specifically, I have no answer," Durny said. "Generally, we're in Sambria. This part of the Outskirts is the most susceptible to deliberate physical tampering. Some things I have seen shaped here make me wonder whether anything is impossible."

"I've heard about shaping," Cole said. "What is it? Like magic?"

Durny harrumphed. "Any phenomenon we don't understand seems like magic. To a primitive culture, fire might seem like magic. This spyglass certainly would."

"Shaping is science?"

"Not exactly. It's . . . the ability to rearrange things and to imbue them with new qualities. Some people have a knack for it. I have a share of the talent myself. No matter how much talent you have, it's easier to shape material here in Sambria."

Cole gazed out across the gulf of sky. "Somebody shaped that castle?"

"Nobody knows who shapes the castles," Durny said

thoughtfully. "They appear out of the Westtern Cloudwall and drift across into the Eastern Cloudwall. Today is a quiet day. You can often see a dozen or more from a single spot. While the castles migrate from one cloudwall to the other, we salvage what we can."

"Wait," Cole said in disbelief. "The Sky Raiders raid the castles?"

"You're catching on," Durny approved. "And you'll be helping us."

"How do you get to them? Planes? Helicopters?"

"Skycraft. Flying ships."

"How do they fly?"

Durny glanced toward the sun. "Last question. We need to get indoors before dark. Near the base of the castles are suspensors, commonly called floatstones. They keep the castles aloft. We harvest them from time to time and use them in the construction of skycraft."

Cole could not believe what he was hearing and seeing. But it was hard to argue with the sight of the castle in the distance. After all, he had crossed over to a mysterious world through a manhole in a spook alley, and he had held a conversation with a happy face. "The job is dangerous? Raiding the castles?"

Durny gave a snort. "I said no more questions, but what do you think? Now come—let's go meet your owner."

CHAPTER

— 7 —

SKYPORT

Skyport, as Durny named it, came into view just before the sun dipped below the horizon. The Brink was ragged and far from level. They had not paralleled the edge long before finding a shallow basin that looked like half a valley because it ended so abruptly. Skyport was nestled down at the bottom.

Constructed from stone and heavy timbers, the sprawling main building perched right at the edge of the Brink. Several balconies and porches projected out over the drop. To Cole, the structure looked one medium-size earthquake away from tumbling off the end of the world.

There were several smaller outbuildings scattered around, including a stable and a modest barn. A tall wall enclosed a huge area behind the main building, which Cole assumed was the Cliffside Salvage Yard. Between the distance, the bad lighting, and the height of the surrounding barrier, Cole couldn't tell what was inside.

A bell clanged as Durny led the mule train down the

gentle slope to Skyport. Men and teens hustled out to help unpack the mules. The people wore odd clothing. One burly man sported a furry vest. Another had a T-shirt featuring fried-egg eyes above a bacon smile. One of the teens wore a dark-blue military jacket glittering with medals.

Unsure how to contribute, Cole stood off to the side as Durny gave instructions. He noticed men standing guard around the perimeter of the buildings. There were lots of people here and not much cover on the surrounding slopes. Making an escape would be tricky. He couldn't afford to blow it, so he would get to know the area first. If he kept his eyes open, sooner or later the right opportunity would arise.

Before long, Durny came over to him. "This way, slave. Time to meet your master."

Cole followed Durny up wooden steps to a porch. He noticed an ivory rocking chair, a silk hammock, a chest made of solid iron, and a hairy creature, with a head at either end, inside a cage.

There was no time to consider these sights, because Durny pushed through the door into a busy common room. Most everyone was male—the youngest around Cole's age; the oldest, gray-haired or bald. Some of them were eating, some played cards, others sat talking. Slave marks abounded.

Durny led the way to a beefy man with a graying beard and long curly hair, who sat on a cushioned, elaborate throne carved from translucent jade. The magnificent seat would have looked out of place in the saloon-type atmosphere if not for the other odd treasures scattered around the room—a gleaming stack of gold bars, a platinum sarcophagus studded with jewels, an ornate harpsichord, and a stuffed creature much larger and fiercer-looking than any bear.

"It's about time!" the man boomed. "No more sending our top shaper away on elongafied excursions. Did you see Carnag?"

"No. Saw some refugees. Reports have it well into Sambria, near Riverton."

"I keep hearing the most outlandish stories. If it heads this way, we'll help it off the Brink. The trading went well?"

"Very well," Durny said. "I even acquired some new blood."

"Are they vending slaves in Mariston these days?"

"We crossed the path of a caravan."

"You only bought one?"

"I'd used up most of my cash fund, but he's an interesting candidate. Fresh from Earth."

The man on the throne shifted his attention to Cole. "How'd you end up here?"

"Slavers kidnapped my friends," Cole explained. "I wanted to help them."

"You came through on your own?" Durny asked.

Cole decided there probably wasn't much reason to hide that detail anymore. "Yeah. I followed them through. I wanted to rescue my friends. You can guess how well it went."

"You got nabbed." The man on the throne chuckled, slapping his thigh. "Steep price to pay for helping your mates. Unfortuitous. Well, if a bondmark is your fate, you've landed at the right place."

"Ansel didn't mention you came here voluntarily," Durny said.

"I didn't tell him," Cole replied.

Durny nodded thoughtfully, then glanced at the man on the throne. "The lad doesn't mind an edge."

"I would hope not," the man blustered. "You have a name?"

"I'm Cole."

"Adam Jones. I'm the greedy bone-picker who runs this operation. I answer to 'Your Majesty,' 'Your Excellentness,' and 'Adam.' We'll call you Cole until you earn something better." Adam looked at Durny. "Did you explain the way of things here?"

"The boy needed to learn his new station," Durny said.

"Ah, sensible—new slave and whatnot." Adam focused back on Cole. "A slave won't find a deal like working as a Sky Raider in most corners of the Outskirts. I was once a slave too. Most of us were. You won't get typical treatment here. Not from us." His eyes grew serious. "You're lucky. You only had the littlemost taste of slave life. Be glad you'll never really know what you're missing."

Cole nodded.

"You're new, so you'll have to pay your dues, take some ribbing, perform some distasteful chores. But you won't always be the greenest recruit at Skyport. The more seniority you gain, the better it gets. You can even earn your freedom. The catch? You might die tomorrow."

Cole had been feeling better until that final statement. "Really?"

"Sky Raiders risk their lives on every mission," Adam

said. "For the first season or two, you'll serve as a scout, risking your neck more than anyone. Being careful, smart, and quick can help you survive. Still, part of it is the luck of the draw. We lost a good young scout last week."

"Who?" Durny asked.

"Fiddler."

Durny made a pained expression. "Too bad."

"Lively boy of fourteen," Adam continued. "He'd almost earned his way out of scout service. Takes fifty missions. He was four short. Fiddler came up against something no man could have outrun. His death showed the crew that an unfightable predator occupied the castle. His sacrifice saved lives. It's noble work. We always need more scouts." Adam winked. "And now we have one."

Cole felt sick with dread. Heights were one thing. Monstrous predators like the stuffed superbear in the corner were another. "Do I have to?"

Adam laughed heartily. "What a question! Nobody would volunteer as a scout. You're a slave until you work it off. This is how you start. There are no other choices. Last long enough, and someday you could become a partner, wealthy and comfortable. Until then, you'll do your part to embiggen the organization."

Cole nodded grimly, trying not to let his terror show. "What are my chances?"

Adam looked at him skeptically. "You want a straight answer?"

"I don't know."

Adam exploded with laughter. "You'll be fine! There's

nothing to worry about. One day it'll be you sitting on this throne."

Cole frowned. "Wait. Give it to me straight."

Adam shrugged. "More than half our scouts survive their first ten missions. Maybe one in twenty survive all fifty. But the odds of coming home the first time are reasonable!"

"I start tomorrow?"

Adam nodded. "Today was slow out there, which often-times means the next day will be busy. I'll want a report about your first outing."

"How can I prepare?"

"There's a proper attitude!" Adam said. "Durny, you've earned a rest. Have Mira show him about, get him equipped, give him some tips. And have her dig up some decent clothes. The boy looks like a storm-blown scarecrow."

Cole almost explained his costume, but Adam seemed through talking to him. Durny ushered him away and began asking people if they had seen Mira.

Before long, Cole found himself facing a girl nearly his height. She wore boots, corduroy pants, a collared shirt, and suspenders printed with shamrocks. Her brown hair was chopped short. She wasn't very clean, but that couldn't hide her pretty gray eyes and cute face.

"Find some new monster bait?" she asked Durny.

"Go easy," Durny said. "Boy's had a rough week. Mira, this is Cole. He'll be raiding tomorrow. He needs to learn the ropes."

Mira gave Cole a once-over. "Let me guess. He needs clothes, too."

"He's all yours."

Durny moved away.

"Not a lot of girls here," Cole said.

"We have more than you see topside," she said. "Most of the girls stay below."

"In the basement?"

"In the caves. This whole section of the cliff is honeycombed with them. That's why they built here. We're right above them."

"It's a big building," Cole said.

"Big enough for most everyone to have a room topside. But some prefer the caves. When a storm comes, everyone prefers the caves."

"You get bad storms?"

"It doesn't get much worse than a castle landing on you."

"Has that happened?"

"They've had close calls. Some damage. No direct hits."

Cole regarded Mira pensively. "Have you been here long?"

"A couple of years."

"Really? You must have been young when you came here." She shrugged. "I'm about eleven."

"'About'?"

"I'm an orphan. Nobody knows when my birthday is."

She didn't seem to be asking for pity, so Cole tried not to give it. "Are you going to help me survive tomorrow?"

"Survival is up to you. I can help you get your stuff."

A boy, maybe a year older than Cole, chummily clapped Mira on the back. "Did you finally find a boyfriend?" he asked.

Her shoulders hunched uncomfortably until he removed his hand. "No, but I already have a boy-enemy."

"Nice," he said, smiling. He stood a few inches taller than Cole, with a bronze complexion and dark hair. He held out his hand. "I'm Jace."

Cole shook it. "Cole."

"You're my new best friend."

"How come?"

"With Fiddler gone, it was my turn to scout tomorrow."

"Glad I could help," Cole said.

"If you get an easy one, we aren't friends anymore. If you get killed, I'll love you forever."

"Buzz off," Mira said. "I need to show him the place."

"Listen to everything she says," Jace advised. "Then do the opposite."

Mira punched at him, but Jace dodged away.

"Come on," Mira said.

Cole followed her out of the common room and down a wide hall. They turned corners, passed some doors, then went down a flight of stairs.

"Where are you from?" Mira asked.

"Earth," Cole said.

"You're from outside? How long have you been here?"

"About a week."

For the first time he saw a flash of real sympathy in her face. She stopped walking. "A week?"

"My friends got kidnapped by slavers. I followed them through to try to help them."

"You came through on your own?" She sounded impressed.

"I had no idea where I was going. I got caught. Then Durny bought me."

She gave a little nod. "Do you know what the Sky Raiders do?"

"They raid the floating castles. That's all I know."

"This is a salvage operation," Mira explained. "There's nothing alive in those castles. Not truly. Just semblances. Some are big and dangerous, some seem like people, but none are really living. Most of the semblances disintegrate if you bring them back here, just like the floatstones if they head inland. Everything else holds together just fine. It's all ownerless and headed for the Eastern Cloudwall, never to be seen again. So the Sky Raiders take what they can. We keep certain valuables, but most of it goes to the salvage yard. People come from all over the Outskirts to buy our finds."

"Sometimes the semblances are dangerous?"

Mira huffed. "Up in the castles, they seem plenty real. Some castles are empty. Some are deadly. If nothing gets taken, it doesn't count as a mission, so make sure something gets back to the ship every time, even if it's just a floatstone."

"Got it. I don't want to end up doing more than fifty missions."

"Right."

Cole cleared his throat. "So I'm the bait. For the semblances."

"More or less. Nobody wants to see you fail. They'll scope out the castle before they send you down. They'll be ready to lend a hand if possible. And we'll equip you."

She opened a door to a room full of clothes. "Your outfit is about function, not fashion. You want clothes that let you move freely, have enough pockets, and maybe give a little protection. Put tough material over your knees and elbows."

The room contained a bizarre variety of clothing—tunics, long underwear, embroidered robes, a sequin cape, a medieval breastplate, turbans, a trench coat, a pliable cloak as clear as glass, grass skirts, a football helmet, garlands, beaded vests, and togas. Cole fingered a fringed buckskin jacket, like the kind Davy Crockett might wear. "Where did all of this come from?"

"You get one guess."

"The castles?" Cole picked up the football helmet by the face mask. "Do you even play football here?"

"Is that a game?"

He set it down. "Do the castles come from my world?"

"Do you have floating castles on Earth?"

"No," Cole said. "But we have a lot of this stuff. Like that T-shirt over there. It's for a movie called *Medal of Shame*. It doesn't belong here."

"Nothing *belongs* in the castles," Mira said. "It's why they're worth raiding. You never know what you might find. It might be valuable or useful. It might be garbage. But it's there for the taking."

"If you don't get killed."

"You're catching on."

Cole picked up the breastplate. It was heavier than he had expected.

"First and last, worry about speed," Mira advised. "If things go wrong, you'll survive by escaping."

Cole put down the piece of armor. He decided the

football helmet would be cumbersome as well, limiting his vision. He grabbed a shirt and pants that looked about the right size. He tried on some different shoes until he found a match. At the end he added the buckskin jacket, even though it was a little too large.

"If anything doesn't fit right, just come back and trade," Mira said. "This other room is more important." She led him to the next door in the hall. "You get to pick one special item crafted by our shapers. Durny leads them these days. Don't try to take more than one. If you get caught sneaking more, you'll be in big trouble. These items are hard to make and usually get lost when a scout . . . doesn't survive. So they can't afford more than one per scout. Same rule applies to most in a raiding party."

Arranged on racks and shelves, weapons and gear filled the room. Cole saw swords, axes, spears, javelins, bows, arrows, crossbows, slings, maces, war hammers, knives, and throwing stars. He also noticed ropes, packs, shields, bottles, compasses, spyglasses, and all sorts of knickknacks ranging from figurines to shells.

"What should I pick?" Cole asked.

"You want something shaped," she replied. "Many of the items here have special properties. Take some of the best ropes for example: a Winding Rope will tie itself around things, a Climbing Rope can stand up straight like a pole without any support, and a Slithering Rope will track and bind a target."

"No way," Cole said. "Seriously?"

"Get used to the unbelievable," Mira replied. "You'll find plenty of it in the castles."

"I don't know anything about this place," Cole admitted. "You should probably choose for me."

"I always bring a Jumping Sword," Mira said.

"You've scouted?"

"The scouts aren't the only ones who get to bring something," Mira said. "I did scout a little when I first came here, but then I showed some potential as a shaper."

"You're a shaper?"

She gave an embarrassed smile. "Barely. Not a good one. But since I've learned a few little tricks, they don't want to waste me as a scout."

"Like how I'm going to get wasted," Cole said.

"Don't think that way," Mira said. "You need to get cocky about it. The cocky ones last longer. Some even make it to fifty."

"I'll aim for a hundred."

"That's the spirit."

"What does the Jumping Sword do?"

Mira retrieved a short sword and unsheathed it. "It's a weapon, obviously." She sheathed it and set it down. "When you point it at something and shout 'away,' it'll pull you in that direction. Hard. You can jump really far with it, but you have to be careful, because there is no guarantee of a soft landing."

"Jumping far is important?" Cole asked.

"Escape is important," Mira corrected. "You can jump into a lifeboat from a distance in an emergency. The Jumping Sword is a specialty of Durny's. He makes more of them than any other item. They're the most popular choice."

"Does it always let you jump the same distance?"

"No. It depends what you point it at. You don't have to point it perfectly. The sword seems to get what you mean. But it has limits. Point it at the top of a tall tower, and you'll only make it partway there and then fall to your death."

"Sounds like just what I need."

She gave him an annoyed look. "It isn't very safe, but neither is exploring these castles. The Jumping Sword is powerful and useful."

"Does Jace use it?"

She shook her head. "He has this golden rope. It can do everything the other ropes can, and more."

"Should I consider one of those?"

"You can't. There's only one. Jace found it himself. You can keep anything you find if you claim it as your one special item."

Cole thought about that. "What if I find a huge diamond?"

"You could keep it instead of the Jumping Sword or whatever. Personally, I'd rather survive than have a sparkly rock."

"Good point," Cole said. When he made his escape from Skyport, the Jumping Sword would come in handy. "I'll take a Jumping Sword."

"Smart choice." She handed him the sheathed sword. "Are you tired?"

"Yeah."

"We'll track down some food and then help you find a bunk. Would you mind taking Fiddler's old one?"

The idea of sleeping in a dead kid's bed wasn't his favorite. But he supposed a lot of the beds around here probably belonged to someone who had died at one time or another. "I guess not."

"It'll be less musty than the alternatives. You'll be in with Jace, Slider, and Twitch."

She started leading him toward the stairs. He caught her arm. She looked back at him, irritated and a little curious.

"Before we head back, do you have any tips?"

She considered the question. "Things tend to go bad right after you set foot on castle grounds or just after you enter a building. Always have an escape plan. Fighting is a last resort. It's usually the last thing you do before you die."

"Should I practice with the sword?"

"You could. I wouldn't. Every time you jump with it is dangerous, so it's better to save it for emergencies. It'll work how I said."

"Okay. Thanks."

Her eyes softened. "Don't thank me. This might feel like good treatment after a slave caravan, but no worries. Tomorrow will remind you where you rank."

CHAPTER

8

SKY RAIDERS

A vast cavern in the side of the cliff served as a landing bay for three big skycraft. Constructed out of dark wood, they looked vaguely like old pirate ships, though broader and flatter, with a pair of modest masts and no sails. Each had three lifeboats—one on each side and one at the back.

Jace led Cole toward the skycraft called *Domingo*, where several men were gathering. Morning light streamed through the open side of the cavern. Out in the blue sky, Cole could see numerous castles hovering.

"Lots of castles," Cole mentioned.

"We usually have a crowded day after a quiet one," Jace said. "That's good news. Two other companies compete with us—the Cloud Skimmers and the Airmen. On a busy day like today we probably won't have much competition."

At the gangplank to the *Domingo*, a middle-aged man with unruly brown hair greeted Cole. "You're Cole, the new scout," he said, extending a hand.

Cole shook it. "Yes."

"I'm Captain Post. Jumping Sword. Savvy choice." He handed Cole a cord with a little cylindrical container dangling from it.

"What's this?" Cole asked, accepting it.

"A poison capsule," the captain said. "Have they discussed falling?"

"No."

He jerked a thumb at the sky. "We don't know if you'd ever land. Could be you'd fall until you starved. As a courtesy, we provide the capsule."

Cole examined the container more closely.

"Top unscrews from the bottom," Jace explained. "It's airtight. The poison reeks, which wrecks any chance to use it as a weapon. They trust slaves here more than most places, but not enough to arm us for an assassination."

"Put it on," the captain said. "We all wear one."

Cole fought down a feeling of dread as he slipped the cord over his head. He hated the idea of carrying something meant to end his own life.

"This way," the captain said, leading Cole to a battered bin beside the gangplank. He selected a medium-size backpack from among others. "If you fall, this parachute is your best friend. Give the cord a sharp tug, and we'll try to get a craft under you. The skycraft can only descend so far, but if you pull the cord quickly, you'll have a chance."

"Good to know," Cole said, shrugging into the backpack. Jace helped him adjust the straps over his buckskin jacket.

"Jace is here to coach you," the captain said. "Listen

to him. He's a survivor." The captain moved away, giving orders to a group of men.

"Some scouts skip the parachute," Jace said. "They don't want the extra weight slowing them down."

"Do you use one?"

"Always. The risk of a fall is real."

"How many missions have you done?" Cole asked.

"The next will be my thirtieth."

"More than halfway there."

Jace gave him a rough shove. "You trying to jinx me? Never talk about how many you have left. Only what you've done."

"Sorry," Cole said, feeling off-balance. "I didn't know."

"You've got all fifty left," Jace said. "All fifty. Now we're even. Apology accepted. Looks like they're ready for you."

About twenty men, including Captain Post, had lined up along the gangplank. The captain signaled for Cole to come aboard. As Cole walked up the gangway, every man in the line shook his hand and thanked him for his service. There were no grins or jeers. They were serious. It made Cole's stomach knot. These men were paying their last respects.

Cole was the first aboard, with Jace right behind him. The other men followed, moving to their stations. Jace led Cole to a bench near the front of the skycraft. Cole noticed that it was bolted to the deck.

"Freaked out yet?" Jace asked.

"Kind of," Cole said. "That felt like a funeral."

"It's all you'll get," Jace said. "If you don't make it, they'll either leave your body on the castle, and it'll drift off into the cloudwall, or you get buried in the air—the bottomless grave. There's never a body to bring back."

"Fun to think about," Cole said, straining to sound brave.

"You get used to it," Jace said. "If you live long enough."

"You should become a motivational speaker."

Jace grinned.

The skycraft drifted up and forward, not like a plane taking off, but like a weak helium balloon in a soft breeze. "Smooth," Cole said.

"Most of the time," Jace agreed. "The helmsman is back there."

Cole followed his finger to where a man stood on a raised platform behind a large wooden wheel. A pair of tall levers jutted up from the deck, one on each side of him.

As the *Domingo* coasted out into the glare of the rising sun, Cole shielded his eyes. The day was clear and cool, and they floated along serenely, like how it might feel to travel by blimp.

"Can we stand at the railing?" Cole asked.

"Sure."

They rose. Cole felt a little unsteady walking with the deck shifting underfoot, but it could have been worse. Once his hands were on the railing, he felt plenty secure. Scanning from one side of the sky to the other, he counted at least thirty castles, some at higher altitudes than others, some larger, all slowly drifting west to east.

"What exactly do I do?" he wondered.

"They'll take you down in a lifeboat," Jace said. "You'll climb down a ladder. Usually nothing much happens until you set foot on castle grounds. Sometimes that alerts the semblances and they come running. Other times nothing happens until you enter a building, or trigger a response some other way. Sometimes the castle is empty—easy pickings. Your job is to scout to see if anything is worth taking and to check for threats."

"If I get attacked?"

"Run for it," Jace said. "Get back to the lifeboat. They'll try to help, but they won't set it down. Once you're safe, they'll assess whether the threat is worth challenging. The guys in the lifeboat will bring weapons. The main ship has two ballistae—see over there?"

Cole saw what looked like a giant crossbow on the deck near the railing.

"They'll mount that up and get it ready before you go down," Jace said. "People will be covering you. We all want you to make it. And you have your Jumping Sword."

"Did you bring your golden rope?" Cole asked.

"Did Mira tell you about that?" Jace produced a golden string, maybe a foot long. He noticed Cole's perplexed stare. "It gets bigger."

"She said it can do all sorts of things."

"It can," Jace said. "It was a lucky find. But a Jumping Sword has advantages too. I know some guys who did all fifty missions with a Jumping Sword, including some dicey ones."

"How often does it get dicey?"

"Roughly? I guess one in three missions amounts to nothing. The rest are at least annoying. Maybe one in eight will give you nightmares. That's not exact. It depends on your luck."

"Define 'annoying.'"

"Am I a dictionary? You know, you eventually have to run for it, but you know you'll probably make it."

"That's just annoying?"

"Yeah, at least compared to the worst days."

"What kind of stuff can happen?"

Jace ran a hand through his hair. "I've done this a lot, and you just have to be ready for anything. Once, a whole castle exploded, took out an entire skycraft. That was before my time. Nobody made it back. Some of the guys at Skyport saw it through their telescopes. The semblances might want to talk. Some are friendly or at least reasonable. Sometimes they'll treat you like a guest. They might act nice, then try to backstab you. There can be monsters, traps, bees, poisonous gas, archers, fireballs—you name it. Anything."

Cole didn't feel very reassured to know there were millions of ways he might die. He hoped Jace didn't notice how tightly he was squeezing the railing. Still gliding smoothly, the skycraft sped up enough that wind ruffled his hair.

"Do you know where we're going?" Cole asked, looking out at the castles. The nearest one was horribly ruined. The next nearest was made mostly out of logs, giving it the appearance of an elaborate frontier fort.

"Not even the captain knows yet," Jace said. "The spotters are checking our prospects. Badly ruined castles are almost always empty and have nothing worth taking. We wouldn't go to one like that unless it was the only option. There have been too many bad experiences with castles that look really dark and scary, so we avoid those. Same with any metal ones.

It isn't an exact science. They're looking for something promising—not too menacing, in decent shape, maybe with some hints of wealth."

"What if one of the other salvagers wants the same castle?"

"You'll plant a flag claiming it for the Sky Raiders first thing," Jace said. "We're all good about honoring claims. Saves a lot of violence."

The skycraft went into a long bank, then straightened out. "Looks like we have a prospect," Jace said, eyes forward. "See the one we're heading for? They'll take a closer look, then if they're still feeling good about it, they'll send out a lifeboat."

On the way there, they passed a castle that looked to be made entirely from white styrofoam and duct tape. Another one that was not so near seemed like a natural formation of orange and yellow sandstone rather than something constructed. A few others in various states of disrepair looked more traditional. One floated along upside down.

Sooner than Cole liked, the skycraft turned in a wide circle around a solid gray castle, old but undamaged. The high wall had sturdy towers at intervals, and enclosed a big courtyard with a few smaller structures. The drawbridge was raised. The tallest towers belonged to the main building, which seemed to have been built more for intimidation than for beauty. In one corner of the courtyard, Cole observed a gallows and a guillotine. The sight made him shiver.

There was no sign of life on the walls or the towers, but

down in the courtyard figures moved about. It was tough to see many details, but they walked purposefully, weaving among one another. Nobody sat or stood idle.

After the *Domingo* circled the castle twice, the captain, with two other men, approached Cole. "All we see are women on the move," the captain said. "There's an unnatural pattern to their activities. They could be drones, all but mindless. Or they could be dangerous. That's for you to find out, Cole. The brothers, Jed and Eli, will pilot the lifeboat."

The pair bore a strong resemblance to each other, though Eli was a little taller and broader through the shoulders. Eli had a longbow and Jed held a crossbow. They looked to be in their thirties.

"We'll get you there and bring you back," Eli said.

"Unless you don't," Jace added.

Jed smiled ruefully. "Unless we don't. Come on."

They led Cole to the rear of the skycraft, where they climbed into a lifeboat with the name *Okie Dokie* stenciled on the side. Jed squatted at the back, near the tiller and a pair of levers. Cole got situated beside Eli.

"Remember to shout if you use the sword," Jace advised. "It might not respond if you say 'away' too softly. It's a safety measure."

"Got it," Cole said, stomach fluttering, hands trembling.

"Die bravely," Jace said.

"Die bravely," the captain and several others echoed.

Cole glanced nervously at Eli.

"It's unlucky to wish you good luck," Eli explained. "We use 'die bravely' instead."

"Thanks," Cole said to the people on deck, with a little wave.

When the lifeboat lurched into the air, Cole caught hold of the side. It flew quite a bit faster than the *Domingo* and also rocked a lot more.

"The lifeboat is more of a ride," Jed said with a laugh.

Cole watched as Jed worked the controls. The tiller swayed the boat from side to side. One lever tipped the nose up and down, the other adjusted their speed. Cole felt amusement-park tingles with every motion Jed made.

"We'll drop you in the middle of the yard," Eli said. "Just climb down the ladder. If you step on the ground and a monster bursts out of hiding, get right back on the ladder and we'll soar away. Otherwise, we'll hover above, helping to spot trouble, ready to swoop in if you need us. Understood?"

Cole watched the castle walls drawing near. His mouth was dry. "Yeah."

"You never know," Eli said. "There might be no trouble at all."

"Castle is in good repair," Jed said.

"Right," said Eli.

"And it's big. And we can see semblances."

"We can always hope for the best."

Jed shrugged.

As the lifeboat breezed over the outer wall, Eli leaned forward. "Busy, busy."

Along the edges of the courtyard, doors opened and closed. Older women entered, exited, and crossed the yard, dressed in plain dresses and shawls.

The lifeboat slowed, hovering.

Dozens of women strode this way and that. None were young enough to be called middle-aged, but none were bent with extreme age, either. Some were empty-handed, some held buckets or brooms. None spoke or looked at one another, their expressions neutral.

"What do you think?" Jed asked.

"Let's watch them," Eli replied.

Although they were constantly coming and going, the number of women in the yard stayed at around three dozen. None of them gazed up at the lifeboat.

"What do you think, Cole?" Eli asked.

"Creepy."

"I'll grant you that," Eli said. "Let's see if this shakes them up." He tossed a rope ladder over the side. It unrolled, the end dangling a couple of feet above the surface of the yard.

The women took no notice of it.

"They don't act too alert," Eli said. "It might mean there is no predator here. They would make easy prey."

"They could be the predators," Jed said. "You never know."

"Only one way to find out," Eli said, patting Cole on the shoulder. "You ready?"

No part of Cole felt ready. His heart was pounding and his skin felt clammy. Managing a nod, he put a leg over the side and started down the flimsy ladder.

CHAPTER
9

SCOUT

The ladder swung and twisted as Cole descended one rung at a time. Holding the flag made the climb tricky. A few rungs from the bottom he paused to study the women. Though not identical, they resembled one another—grayish complexions, neutral expressions, creased faces, bony builds, medium height, hair in buns, faded dresses, dark shawls.

He could find no differences between them and real people, except for their uninterested attitudes. Nobody glanced his way. Nobody paused. Nobody smiled. Instead each woman walked briskly about her business.

Cole stepped down to the bottom rung. He had been warned more than once that trouble tended to happen when you first reached the castle. What if this was it? What if he didn't make it back? Nobody would ever know what happened to him—not his parents and not his friends. He wondered if Jenna and Dalton believed he would come for them. He wondered if they would forgive him if he never showed up. Wherever they were, he hoped they weren't on dangerous missions, being used as monster bait.

Taking a deep breath, Cole checked the position of his sword. Keeping one hand on the ladder, he stepped down onto the paving stones of the courtyard.

Every woman immediately stopped. With chilling synchronization, they turned and stared directly at him.

Chills washed across Cole's shoulders and down his back. Frozen with surreal horror, he stared back.

As the moment stretched out, he wanted to race back up the ladder. But some instinctive part of him worried that as soon as he moved, they would rush him. He didn't breathe.

One woman bustled toward him, her footfalls noisy in the silent yard. She peered nervously over her shoulder more than once. The others remained still, solemn eyes boring into Cole. The oncoming woman removed her shawl. When she reached him, she wrapped it around his shoulders and fastened it below his neck with a clasp.

As if responding to some invisible signal, the other women turned and continued about their business. One moment he had their full attention, the next he was utterly forgotten.

Remembering the flag in his hand, Cole set it on the ground. It stood upright despite lacking a base.

The woman without her shawl held out a hand to Cole. "This way," she urged. "We haven't much time."

"Why?" he asked.

"Not here," she said, anxious eyes checking the area.

"Indoors." Her agitation was convincing. Supposedly, she wasn't alive, but there was nothing phony about her appearance or demeanor. It was in the details—the redness at the corners of her eyes, the faint gloss of sweat on her forehead, the loose skin of her neck, the spots on the back of her hands, the ragged tips of her fingernails.

Cole took her hand and let her lead him away from the ladder. She placed her other arm around his shoulders protectively. Women marched past on either side, going about their errands without a flicker of interest in what was happening around them. But they had to be aware. He had stopped traffic when he first stepped off the ladder.

The woman kept her head down and walked swiftly. It didn't seem like she meant him any harm. If anything, he thought she was trying to help. But he stayed ready, in case she turned on him.

Cole noticed fossils embedded in the paving stones—mostly leaves, bugs, and fish. As they neared the castle, he saw similar fossils preserved in the wall.

The woman led him to a minor door into the main castle. They entered a corridor and passed another woman on her way out.

"What's your name?" Cole asked quietly.

"Not yet," she said, giving his hand a squeeze. They moved down the hall, then through a door into a storage room. Releasing him, she shut the door behind them. "Merva."

"I'm Cole. What's going on?"

"We have no time. It's expecting me. We can't break routine. It must be cleaned. You must come."

"What's expecting you? Come where?"

She took his hand again. "Keep near me. Move how I move. Say nothing."

He resisted her pull. "Wait. You have to tell me what's going on."

Her grip tightened, and her face became agonized. "There's not time. It'll kill us all!"

Cole let her lead him from the room. She increased her pace to a fast trot. They passed a few other women in dresses and shawls.

This was happening too quickly. Cole had no idea where they were going or what they would face when they got there. He had lost all control of the situation. Merva's desperation had vanished when they exited the storage room, but the glimpse of her terror had left him even more deeply unnerved. At least nothing had attacked them yet. Maybe Merva knew what she was doing.

He tried to keep an eye out for valuables. The halls were mostly bare. What furniture he saw looked simple.

They started down a dim, winding staircase. Women climbed up from below, passing them without a glance.

The stairs deposited them into a long, cavernous room, comparable to a subway station. A single creature filled the chamber—a nightmarish cross between a centipede and a scorpion. Armored by a glossy black shell, the monster was the size of a train. It had five sets of claws, each pincer larger than a minivan. Hundreds of legs supported the long, segmented body. The gargantuan tail curled up toward the ceiling, a vicious-looking stinger at the tip.

Anchored to rings in the floor, thick chains crisscrossed each segment of its body. Women bustled everywhere, cleaning the creature with rags, mops, brooms, chisels, and sponges.

The sheer scale of the monster left Cole stunned. The busy women looked like insects by comparison. No wonder Merva had worried about making it angry.

Cole realized he was in way over his head. His best chance of survival was probably to follow Merva's instructions. She seemed to think there was a chance of keeping the monster calm. After a brief hesitation at his first sight of the colossal scorpipede, he stayed close to her, carefully matching her pace and posture. She no longer hurried. He tried to breathe quietly.

She led him to a wall where she retrieved a large iron crowbar. Cole reached for one as well, but she waved him off, pointing at hers. Apparently she wanted them to share.

Merva walked along the huge body of the scorpipede. Each segment was several paces long and more than three times taller than Cole. She stopped where the casing of one segment overlapped the next, and started chiseling at the gap between them. With her eyes, Merva told Cole to help. Placing his hands on the crowbar, he assisted as they chipped away material from the slick surface of the shell.

A ripple ran along the body of the scorpipede, making some of the chains squeal. The nearest pincers scissored opened and closed a few times, prompting some of the women to momentarily back away.

Merva wedged the crowbar deeper between the segments

and scraped harder. Cole helped her push, lever, and pull.

The scorpipede shuddered. Cole felt the sharp vibrations through the crowbar. Then came a screeching roar that was high and low at the same time. The penetrating noise thrummed in his bones and teeth.

The room went still. In unison, all the women besides Merva dropped their tools. Brushes, gaffs, crowbars, poles, mops, and brooms clattered to the floor. As one, the women turned to stare at Merva.

All color draining from her face, Merva brushed Cole's hands from the crowbar. "It knows," she murmured.

Merva glanced down at the shawl he wore and then around at the women. Cole suddenly realized that the attention was on her because she lacked her shawl. Her expression became blank, her voice monotone. "It knows I tried to conceal you. You might as well try to run."

As Cole took his first step away from the scorpipede, the creature reared up, mighty chains snapping like threads and whipping around violently. More than one woman went flying, but the others didn't scatter. They held still, watching Merva.

Glancing back, Cole saw the tail lash down, spearing Merva with the stinger. He skidded to a halt. The stinger withdrew and stabbed another woman with merciless precision. Merva stayed on her feet for a moment, eyes distant, then collapsed.

Cole felt horrified, but there was nothing he could do to help her. If he didn't get away soon, he would be next. As the segmented body bucked and squirmed, giant claws clamped other women. None cried out or tried to escape.

Focusing on the stairway, Cole yanked out his sword. The floor trembled with the thrashing of the scorpipede. The castle walls groaned. The whole place might come down on him any second, if the stinger didn't pierce him first. Pointing his sword at the base of the stairs, Cole yelled, "Away!"

The sword pulled his body from the floor. Holding tightly, he sped forward at a low trajectory, never more than a few feet high. As his destination approached, Cole realized he would be crushed against the stone steps. But the sword decelerated enough at the last moment that instead of impacting with backbreaking force, he almost stayed on his feet, and tumbled into the steps jarringly instead of fatally.

The scorpipede screech-roared again. Driven by terror, Cole rose and dashed up the steps. He had hurt one hand trying to catch himself, and a shoulder and knee had taken harsh blows, but there was no time to really recognize the pain.

The stairway seemed longer going up than coming down. His thighs burned with exertion. The stairway rumbled and then quaked. Cole could hear stones falling.

He considered using his sword to climb faster, but since the stairway spiraled, he could never point it very far ahead, and little leaps didn't seem worth the risk of falling. Beyond the top of the stairs, Cole tried to retrace the route to the courtyard. The dim corridors all looked alike, and soon he knew he had lost his way. He stayed at a full sprint, hoping that he wasn't going in circles. The castle continued to shake in response to an ominous rumble in the foundation.

Finally Cole saw a promising door at the end of a hall up

ahead. It was not where he had entered, but it opened onto the courtyard. The lifeboat was in the air at the far side, ladder still dangling.

"I need out!" Cole screamed, rushing forward. The lifeboat banked and came his way.

Cole considered using the sword, but he would have to leap across almost the whole courtyard. He wasn't sure if it would pull him that far and wasn't sure he could catch hold of the ladder if it did. Instead he held the Jumping Sword ready and ran hard.

As the lifeboat came closer, the enormous scorpipede erupted from the ground between them, its shiny black body stretching skyward like a fairy-tale beanstalk, multiple sets of pincers grasping toward the little skycraft. Huge blocks of stone fountained like confetti and crashed down in all directions. Cole dodged a large one before the quaking ground dropped him to his knees.

For a moment the bulk of the creature completely obscured the lifeboat. Gritty dust hung in the air. A screeching roar saturated Cole's eardrums. By the time Cole saw the lifeboat again, it was curving up and away from the castle, passing beyond the wall, well out of jumping range.

He had missed his ride.

A lonely sense of doom smothered him.

His fate was sealed.

The towering scorpipede swiveled, then started to curl back on itself in Cole's direction. Relatively small mouthparts clicked open and closed, eager little mandibles. The body continued to emerge from the hole it had created.

Last would come the tail and the evil stinger.

From high above, an arrow the size of a javelin lanced down. It hit the glossy carapace and rebounded harmlessly. The attack did no damage, but the scorpipede reared back in that direction to investigate.

The oversized arrow must have come from the ballista aboard the *Domingo*. They were still trying to help him!

Cole scrambled to his feet. Maybe the lifeboat would come back around. He had to buy himself time. Nobody would be able to save him if he let fifty tons of ugly mash him into paste.

His only hope was the Jumping Sword. He scanned the courtyard, then noticed the balconies jutting from a pair of the castle's tallest towers.

With another ear-rending screech, the scorpipede swung back his way. Cole pointed his sword toward some bushes at the base of one of the towers and shouted, "Away!"

He was attempting to jump farther than his previous leap. As the sword pulled him forward, the acceleration took his breath away. He skimmed over the ground at a speed that should have led to death by road rash, but again the sword slowed somewhat at the end. His feet hit the ground an instant before his momentum heaved him into a bush.

After coming to rest, Cole realized that he was uninjured. Twigs snapped and leaves rustled as he extracted himself from the foliage. He got to his feet in time to see the tail of the scorpipede slither out of the hole and then curve up into the air, poised to sting. The monster scuttled his way.

Cole aimed his sword at a balcony high above him. If he failed to reach it, the fall would surely kill him. "Away!"

He had only jumped low before. This time he felt like a superhero taking flight. Air rushed by as he rocketed upward. He realized that somehow the sword exerted a pull on his whole body. If he had to trust only the strength of his grip to keep hold of an object accelerating so rapidly, he never would have managed to do it.

Cole reached the balcony at the peak of his jump, allowing him to land lightly. After his ground-skimming leaps, the soft landing was a welcome relief.

The stinger-tipped tail rose up higher than the balcony, then blurred forward, punching a hole in the wall a few feet away. Shattered bits of stone peppered him as Cole fell flat. The stinger retracted and exploded up through the bottom of the balcony, missing him by inches. The balcony rocked and made horrible cracking sounds. The scorpipede might be striking blindly, but it wouldn't have to wait long for results.

Rising, Cole pointed his sword toward the neighboring tower and as he sprang, he yelled, "Away!" Roller-coaster sensations surged through him as he soared across the intervening space and up to another balcony, again landing gently at the apex of his flight.

The scorpipede let out another screech-roar, the tail flailing down below. He had traveled higher than it could reach. Cole looked hopefully for the lifeboat, but saw nothing. The scorpipede started climbing straight up the tower wall.

Pointing his sword at a higher balcony across the way, Cole said his word and jumped again. Once again he landed smoothly. A glance down showed the scorpipede climbing fast.

There was no time to really strategize, but a rough plan flashed through his mind. When he got to the top, hopefully the lifeboat would be within range. He would either make a final jump to his rescuers or get trapped by the scorpipede with no escape.

If he leaped to the other tower with this next jump, he would be back on the same tower the scorpipede was climbing. But it was also the tower closest to the edge of the castle, which would allow Jed to steer the lifeboat within range at minimal risk.

Extending his sword, Cole jumped up to the flat roof of the opposite tower, landing in a crouch. Battlements surrounded the top like blunt teeth. Cole looked frantically in all directions. The *Domingo* hovered high above. Other castles floated in the distance.

When he saw the lifeboat, his heart sank.

It was swinging around to come his way, but it was too far out and much too low. They must not have spotted him climbing until a moment ago. Cole decided he could buy a little time by jumping back across to the roof of the neighboring tower before the scorpipede arrived. As he raised his sword, the tail shot up in his way.

Cole hesitated. With the scorpipede crawling up the tower, he would be in full view when he jumped. The tail would skewer him. The head of the scorpipede loomed into view, its weight crushing battlements as it leaned toward him. The tower shuddered as the scorpipede heaved more of itself to the top. The lifeboat would not be within jumping range in time.

But if he waited, he was dead.

Running away from the scorpipede, Cole jabbed his sword diagonally up and away from the tower, shouted "away," and leaped with everything he had. He launched into his biggest jump yet, testing the sword's limits. He heard the tail strike the castle behind him, and the scorpipede gave a furious cry.

Still curving upward, Cole saw the castle wall pass underneath him. His trajectory carried him well beyond the edge of the cloud at the castle's base. As he lost his forward momentum and plunged downward, all he saw beneath him was endless sky, dropping away to immeasurable purple depths.

The shawl flapped above him, held in place only by the clasp at his neck. Fumbling desperately, it took Cole a panicky moment to find his rip cord. He was falling almost straight down by the time he gave it a sharp tug. The parachute blossomed up above him, jerking him as it interrupted his descent.

As he slowed, the shawl draped down over his head. He pulled it off and tucked it under one arm. His heart was still racing. Down between his feet yawned such endless nothing that it gave him shivers.

Above and behind him, the scorpipede let out another screech-roar. It was loud even at this distance.

"We've got you!" called a voice from below and off to one side.

The lifeboat appeared beneath him, falling with him to catch him softly. Eli steadied his landing, sat him down, and began pulling in the parachute as it went limp. He bundled it expertly.

Cole sat in shocked silence as the *Okie Dokie* climbed. He had hoped they would get to him before he dropped below where the skycraft could descend. And they had. He had made it.

He couldn't believe he was alive. He had been so close to dying that at some level he had known he was only prolonging the inevitable. But now he was safe.

Eli and Jed stayed silent, and so did he. They rose toward the *Domingo*, glided up above it, then landed on the deck at the rear.

"Quite a performance," Captain Post greeted as Cole clambered out of the lifeboat.

Cole tried to muster a smile. "I thought I was dead."

Jace came up and gave him a big hug. "You're officially my best friend."

"That was a bad one?" Cole asked hopefully.

"Terrible," Jace conceded. "You shouldn't have survived."

"One down," Cole said shakily.

"Weeeell," Jace replied, stretching the word out. "You have to bring something back for it to count."

Cole paused and then gave a single chuckle. "I forgot to even think about that."

"What have you there?" the captain asked.

"It has to be something valuable," Jace explained hesitantly. "Something we would salvage on purpose."

The captain took the shawl from Cole, shook it out, and held it up. "It's less than we would normally accept. But that was a brutal first outing." He eyed the shawl more closely. "It's in good condition. And it might have useful properties—the other semblances ignored you once you put it on. If nothing else, I know a woman who might thank us for this. Granted, it's a bit more effort than one would normally make to acquire a wrap, but we'll count the mission valid."

Cole slumped with relief.

"Nice job, rookie," Jace said with a jeering smile. "Only forty-nine to go!"

CHAPTER
10

STARRY NIGHT

A falling star blazed diagonally across the sky, a searing ember of white-gold brilliance with a long tail. After flaring bright enough to cast shadows and make Cole squint, the meteor shrank to a spark, vanishing before it reached the horizon.

Cole's eyes needed a moment to adjust so he could get back to enjoying the sky. Several of the stars were brighter than any he had seen in Arizona. There was more variety in color as well, particularly in shades of red and blue. He could make out the little spiral smudges of distant galaxies, and cloudy patches of light that were either nebulae or dense clusters of faraway stars.

Stranger than anything was the rising moon. It wasn't like the moon back home. It was smaller, dimmer, bluer, and more translucent, almost like a glowing ball of ice. He wondered why he hadn't noticed the difference before.

"You shouldn't be out after dark without a good reason," a voice said from behind.

Cole glanced back to find Mira coming toward him across the back porch. "I'm not far from the door. There's a wall around the whole area."

"Even the yard can be dangerous once the sun goes down."

"I needed some time alone."

"There are places in the caves," she said.

"Not with stars," he replied.

Mira stood next to where he sat on the porch steps. "True." She stared out at the dark salvage yard.

Cole had wanted some alone time, but he found himself glad for the company. He hadn't spoken to Mira since she'd equipped him the night before. "I just saw a shooting star," Cole said. "A bright one."

"We have a beautiful sky," Mira said wistfully.

"It's different from the one on Earth."

"People from outside always comment on it. At least the observant ones do."

"The moon is really different."

She gave a faint smile. "That isn't our most common moon. It's Naori, the Shiver Moon. We only see it now and then."

"That makes sense," Cole said. "I think one of your more regular moons is more like ours."

"Light can partially pass through Naori, so it's always full," she said. "They make a big deal about it in Necronum."

"How many different moons do you have here?"

"At least twenty," Mira said.

"Are they ever all up at once?"

"I've never seen more than five at the same time. Sometimes there are none."

Cole reconsidered the glittering sky. "You guys must have complicated calendars."

"There are no really reliable calendars," she said. "There isn't much of a pattern to the moons or the stars. You can never be sure what sky you'll get. The years tend to be around three hundred and fifty days, but the seasons are haphazard. It can be summer for a hundred days, autumn for twelve, winter for forty, spring for two hundred, then summer for twenty, and on and on without any kind of pattern. The days aren't trustworthy either. We measure hours, but only to track how many have passed since sunrise. First hour, second hour, and so on. Then we start counting again from sunset. Most days are around twelve hours, followed by twelve hours of night. Without warning, they can be as short as four, or as long as thirty, though the extremes aren't common."

"Wow," Cole said. "Do you have more than one sun?"

"Almost always just one. It usually rises in the east and sets in the west. Sometimes we have duskdays, when the sun seems to be rising in all directions but never does."

"I saw one of those."

"That's right. We had one not too long ago."

Cole scanned the salvage yard, cluttered with bizarre, shadowy shapes, great and small. Among the discernible objects were statues, potted trees, cages, wicker baskets, outdoor furniture, coiled chains, a huge barbershop pole, a battered jukebox, a canoe, an old-fashioned bicycle with a huge front wheel, and a shantytown of sheds, large and small, that probably housed more fragile treasures. The yard was still, the night cool. The door into Skyport was only a few steps away. It was hard to believe he was in any danger.

"You shouldn't lurk out here," Mira said. "They're still talking about your escape from the centipede. You ought to soak it up."

"Scorpipede," Cole corrected. "At least, that was how I thought of it. Part scorpion. It had claws."

"Whatever," Mira said. "You should come enjoy the attention. These men have seen it all. They're not easy to impress, especially on a first outing."

"I should be dead," Cole said, suddenly fighting a hard lump in his throat. "This lady . . . she protected me. The scorpipede . . ." He couldn't continue speaking and keep it together, so he stopped.

"One of the semblances?" Mira asked.

Cole nodded, not trusting his voice.

Mira crouched beside him and put a hand on his shoulder. "You're sweet, but you can't let that get to you. She wasn't real. None of them were. They're just puppets. Dangerous, lifelike, but puppets."

"She gave me her shawl to help hide me. She seemed so real, Mira. Perfectly real."

"Some do. It's an illusion. They're just temporary. If you had brought her back here, she would have dissolved into dust. Only some of the simplest ones have any chance of surviving outside the castles. That lady didn't die. She wasn't alive. She was heading for nothingness in a day or two, when the castle vanishes into the cloudwall."

Cole stared down at his hands. The guilt had gnawed at him all day, but Mira's explanation helped. "One mission down."

"At least the other one was more fruitful."

Cole smiled at her wordplay. One of his bunkmates, a boy called Twitch, had scouted today for another Sky Raider ship, the *Borrower*. They had found what looked like a village of big, fancy gazebos. The woodwork was all fragile and ornate, but the raiders were most interested in the extensive gardens, especially the fruit trees. At a signal from the *Borrower*, the *Domingo* had joined in reaping the harvest.

The only obstacles had been a few giant carnivorous weeds. Since the weeds were stationary, they were easily avoided once you knew to watch for them. Both ships had spent the day off-loading fruit of all description. Some were familiar, including oranges, lemons, bananas, plums, apricots, apples, pears, and kiwis. Other varieties had looked foreign—fruit protected by stinging tendrils, fruit that grew in clusters like grapes but had thick rinds, fruit they had to chisel out of the trunks like tumors.

"We brought a lot of food," Cole said.

"We never go hungry here. Some food comes from the castles. Plus, traders go out of their way to bring us goods. They know we can pay or barter."

Cole looked around. "It doesn't seem dangerous out here."

Mira shrugged. "It's safer inside the walls of the salvage yard than out in the open. But just because you don't get killed tonight doesn't mean you won't get ambushed tomorrow. Bad things come up from lower down the cliffs at night. We seal the caves carefully. We have some tricks that help keep the night stalkers away from Skyport. But it can get plenty dangerous. A lot of people have disappeared because they braved the Brink at night."

Her words made Cole less comfortable. Certain pockets of shadow suddenly seemed more suspicious. Had one of the sculptures shifted position a little?

"Maybe we should go in," Cole suggested, standing.

"You go ahead," Mira said, stepping out into the yard, head craned back to take in the sky. "I just need a minute to unwind after——"

She froze and said nothing more.

"After what? Mira?"

She looked at him, and for an instant he saw unbridled panic in her eyes.

"Are you all right?" Cole asked, looking up for signs of danger. All he saw were stars. What was he missing?

"I'm fine," Mira insisted with an uncomfortable smile. "I just . . . I remembered something I forgot to do. Something important. I'll come in with you."

"Are you sure?" Cole asked. "For a second there, you looked like you'd seen a ghost."

She gave a feeble smile. "Life of a slave. I forgot to do a chore that could get me in trouble."

"Need help?"

He followed her through a doorway into a hall. She closed the sturdy door and locked it in three places. "I should do it on my own. Thanks, though. You've had a busy day. Go get some rest."

Cole watched her walk away. He had a strong suspicion that she wasn't being completely honest with him. While looking up, she had seen something that scared her, and then tried to mask her reaction. Could it have been a winged creature? Did the night stalkers fly? Maybe she'd glimpsed a threat lurking on the roof?

He looked back at the door. He could peek out to see if something had entered the yard. No, if some monster had scared her that badly, he didn't want to take the risk.

But why would she try to cover up something like that? If she had seen a monster coming for them, why not grab him and race indoors? Why be secretive? Why make up an excuse?

Maybe her excuse was real. He supposed an important task left undone could explain her reaction. Looking at the sky might have reminded her. Or it might have been a coincidence.

Avoiding the boisterous commotion of the common area, Cole made his way to his room. He had already eaten, and decided he would take Mira's advice and get some rest.

The narrow bunk room had a high ceiling and a pair of stacked bunks on either side. Cole found Twitch seated on a bottom bunk. His head jerked up, as if Cole had startled him, blue eyes wide and round. The short, skinny boy had a young face. He couldn't be older than ten.

"I didn't know you were in here," Cole said. He hadn't spoken much with him besides a quick introduction the night before.

Twitch licked his lips. "All the people can be . . . a little much. Do you need the room?"

"Not for anything special. I was just getting tired." Cole had been assigned the bunk above Twitch, across from Slider.

"Don't let me stop you. I can dim the lamp." Twitch hopped out of bed and crossed to the oil lantern.

"Nice job finding all that fruit."

Twitch gave a weak chuckle. "Don't thank me for the fruit. Spotters handled that. Thank me for almost getting eaten by a plant. I barely got out of the way in time." The lantern dimmed.

"Those things were scary."

"They weren't too bad once you knew what they looked like and could keep out of range."

"But you had to find out the hard way." Cole opened the trunk he had inherited and started changing into his sleeping clothes.

Twitch went back to sit on his bed. "A crazy part of me almost wishes the weeds got me."

"What?"

"Just to end the suspense. It's too much. If something is going to get me sooner or later, sooner might be a mercy."

"Don't think like that," Cole said. "You have to aim for fifty."

"I've done sixteen missions. I don't want to even think about fifty. That isn't the end, you know. After fifty, the danger isn't gone. The scouts aren't the only raiders who have accidents. The other jobs are only a little safer."

"Well, you've done fifteen more than me." Cole stashed his clothes into his trunk. "Is Twitch your real name?"

"Ruben."

"Why do they call you Twitch?"

"Very funny."

"No, I'm serious."

He studied Cole as if measuring his sincerity. "I'm kind of jumpy. I guess I flinch a lot. That kind of thing. Some of

116

them think I scout too slowly. If they don't like it, they're welcome to take my place."

"Nothing wrong with being careful."

"That's what I say! It's *my* neck I'm risking. I do it how I do it. Helped save me from those killer plants."

"What item do you use? Jumping Sword?"

Twitch gave him a suspicious look. "Drop the act. Who put you up to this? Slider?"

"What do you mean?"

Twitch considered him. "Nobody knows what item I picked. I've never used it. Some of the other scouts are always trying to find out."

"Why the mystery?"

"It's not their business. I have little enough privacy. They know my birthmarks and the color of my underwear. My item is mine." He shared a sneaky smile. "Not knowing drives Slider nuts."

The door opened and Jace peeked in. "There you are! Man of the hour." He came inside. "Already going to bed?"

"Long day," Cole said.

"Busy night, too," Jace replied.

"What do you mean?"

He wore a teasing grin. "I noticed you hanging out with Mira in the yard. Starry night, Shiver Moon . . . pretty romantic."

"Stop it," Cole said. "I just wanted some fresh air. She came out to warn me it could be dangerous."

"She came back in a hurry," Jace said. "Seemed kind of flustered. Maybe somebody was putting on the moves?"

"What? No way! She just forgot something she had to do."

Jace nodded knowingly. "Right. You're good."

It frustrated Cole that Jace kept after him. Why did he care so much? "Wait a minute," Cole said. "How do you know everything she was up to? Were you following her?"

"I just pay attention," he said, sounding a little defensive.

"We weren't by the common room." Understanding dawned. "Oh, I get it, *you* like her."

Twitch looked intently at Cole and gave a little shake of his head.

Jace exhaled sharply. "Whatever. In her dreams."

He was trying to act tough, but he couldn't hide that Cole had gotten to him. Twitch's anxiousness confirmed it. "How else could you know we were out there together?" Cole pressed. "You really were following her! Were you up on the roof?"

The guilt was written all over his face. "Shut up, Cole."

Cole made his voice dreamy. "I bet you wish *you* were with her under the stars. Sailing in a lifeboat, putting flowers in her hair."

"Keep your messed-up daydreams to yourself," Jace almost shouted, his eyes darting to Twitch.

"I wasn't the one tailing her," Cole pointed out.

Jace's face went rigid. It took him a moment to speak. When he did, his voice was barely under control. "She's one of the few people in this place who is actually nice. Actually a *good* person. I watch out for her a little. Don't try to make it sound like I . . . You don't want me to hate you, Cole. You really don't. Watch it."

Cole knew he shouldn't, but he couldn't resist. "I'm sure you'll do plenty of watching for both of us."

Jace's hand strayed to his pocket. He glanced at Twitch again, who had his head down as if wishing he could disappear.

"I'm just messing with you," Cole said, trying to lighten the mood.

"You're right about that," Jace replied. "I hope you think it's worth it."

Cole felt bad for teasing him so hard. Jace was really fuming. "Thanks for the tips today."

"Want a new tip? Stay out of my way."

"We sleep in the same room."

"Then borrow a lesson from Twitch and keep your head down." He turned and walked out, leaving the door open.

After a quiet moment, Twitch went and closed it.

"What was that about?" Cole asked.

"You're not very careful," Twitch replied.

"Neither was he."

"He's not new. I'd watch my step. Jace is probably the best scout we have. He's the last kid I'd want to cross."

"Does he have a crush on Mira?"

"We should forget about it. But what do you think?"

It seemed pretty obvious, especially since he had been so touchy about the subject. Cole considered how he would feel if somebody had caught on that he liked Jenna and kept pestering him about it. "I'll try to make it up to him."

"That'll just remind him. The smart move would be to follow instructions. Keep your head down and let it blow over."

CHAPTER
11

PROVING GROUND

One week later, Cole boarded the *Domingo* for his fifth scouting mission. As a rule, the captains tried not to assign any scout more than three missions in a week, but that courtesy was getting harder to honor since two scouts had died over the last five days. Cole hadn't really known either of the boys.

He couldn't help wondering whether other slaves from the caravan of trick-or-treaters would end up at Skyport. According to Twitch, Adam Jones seldom sent buyers to Five Roads to make purchases. Certain slave brokers made acquisitions there and brought likely candidates directly to Skyport. Part of him didn't want any members of the caravan to end up at Skyport, but a more secret part hoped for it, just so he could see someone from his world and feel a little less alone.

Dalton and Jenna had been selected to go to the king, so even if people from his caravan ended up here, they wouldn't be the ones he was most anxious to see. He tried to be happy for them. Hopefully, serving the king would be safer than raiding sky castles.

None of the three missions since the scorpipede had been as harrowing as his first outing. The worst had involved headless semblances chasing him through mazelike ruins around a single tall tower. The entire area had been slanted about ten degrees from level. Not exactly a day at the beach, but the Jumping Sword had kept him out of their clutches.

He had made little progress on an escape plan. His superiors kept him busy. If he wasn't trying to stay alive as a scout, then he was doing chores. Skyport was isolated, and a runaway could be tracked down by a mounted militia armed with special items. But Cole had noticed that as people earned more trust here, they were occasionally included in groups that traveled away from the Brink on Skyport business. That gave him something to daydream about while he searched for other opportunities to escape.

As he advanced up the gangway one handshake at a time, Cole found Mira and Durny in line to thank him. She wore a Jumping Sword at her waist. Cole wanted to ask why she had come aboard, but stopped himself. He had taken Twitch's advice about not antagonizing Jace, and a part of that had included avoiding Mira. She had made no effort to seek him out, either. Jace still wasn't acting very friendly, but at least he had stopped giving Cole angry looks.

Because Cole had been avoiding Mira, shaking her hand made him uncomfortable. He accepted her thanks with a nod. It was peculiar to have Durny along as well, since he spent most of his time in his workshop, shaping objects and training apprentices.

Handshakes finished, Cole went and sat on his usual

bench while the other men took up their stations. Mira and Durny joined him.

"Where have you been hiding out?" Mira asked.

Trying to act casual, Cole shrugged. "I wondered the same thing. I haven't seen you around."

"I've practiced a lot with Durny this week."

"What brings you guys onboard?" Cole asked.

"We mean to harvest floatstones," Durny said.

"Durny wants to teach me how to extract them," Mira clarified.

"Dangerous work," Durny said. "Remove the wrong floatstone and an entire castle might collapse."

"Why risk it?" Cole asked. The Sky Raiders had three major skycraft—two for active missions, and a third held in reserve.

"No immediate purpose," Durny said. "Educational reasons, mostly."

"The raiders don't have any floatstones stockpiled," Mira said. "So they always come in handy."

"Valid point," Durny agreed. "No matter how carefully the captains fly, skycraft eventually get lost or damaged."

Cole scrunched his eyebrows. "If they need floatstones to make the skycraft, and they use skycraft to get the floatstones, where did the first floatstones come from?"

Durny tapped his temple. "A thinker, this one. It isn't documented. Presumably, some bold shapers made it out to the castles using balloons or gliders."

Cole nodded.

As the *Domingo* drifted out of the landing bay, Cole went

to the railing so he could watch the sky. Near and far, high and low, white, billowy clouds obstructed his line of sight. Their shapes and textures were so clearly defined that they looked almost solid. He counted five castles, but the plentiful clouds most likely concealed many others.

Mira joined him at the railing. "Much cloudier and they might not have flown today."

"Does it sometimes get foggy?"

"It can. Or stormy. Either way, the skycraft stay grounded."

"I'm surprised there isn't a castle on each one."

"The castles don't sit on clouds," Mira said. "The floatstones hold them up. Clouds just form around the foundations. I don't know why."

They stood together in silence as the *Domingo* weaved among the slowly shifting clouds. Castles regularly came in and out of view.

"Did Jace give you a hard time?" Mira asked.

Cole looked at her sharply. "What?"

"He got the idea in his head that you'd upset me," she said. "He kept bugging me about it. I told him he was wrong, but it can be hard to get through to him. He tries to be protective."

Cole wondered if he should mention that Jace had a huge crush on her. If Jace ever found out, he would go nuclear. It wasn't worth more trouble. Mira probably already knew. "He's fine. It's no big deal."

Mira nodded. She glanced at the clouds. "You nervous?"

"About the castle? Of course."

"As bad as the first time?"

"Different. At least I know the drill. Then again, I also have a better idea of how bad it can get."

The *Domingo* started circling a complex of buildings connected by wide patios. The stately structures were made of white stone and featured lots of grooved pillars. Water splashed in numerous marble fountains. The only greenery came from a few narrow lawns and some neatly squared hedges. Fires burned in large kettles, in suspended bowls, and on platters held by statues. Cole could smell the smoke.

"Die bravely," Mira said as the captain approached.

"I like this prospect," Captain Post said. "So do the spotters. Go have a closer look."

"Should I take the shawl?" Cole asked.

Captain Post had kept Merva's shawl. He had sent out some scouts wearing it to see if it helped conceal them from semblances. If it had turned out to be powerful, he'd meant to make it a special item. That didn't seem to be the case. "It didn't stop those headless fiends from chasing you. I haven't seen it do anything."

"It might have only worked at the castle where you found it," Mira chimed in. "Some items are like that."

"I've used it every time," Cole said. "I wouldn't mind."

"Take it, then," the captain said. "Nothing wrong with a lucky token or two." He went and retrieved it from a nearby bin. "Keep it if you'd like."

"Thanks."

Cole fastened the clasp around his neck and then climbed into the *Okie Dokie* with Jed and Eli. They had ferried him on every scouting mission so far. They nodded in greeting. No words were exchanged as Jed guided the lifeboat into the sky.

"Any preference to where we put you down?" Jed asked.

While Cole studied the collection of buildings and patios, a man emerged from between the columns of one of the largest buildings and started down broad steps toward a fountain. Dressed like a Roman soldier, he wore a breastplate molded to his powerful torso and carried a hefty sword in one hand. Shielding his eyes, he looked up at the lifeboat.

"Think he's trouble?" Cole asked.

"That knife looks a little big for dicing vegetables," Eli observed.

"He sees us," Cole said. "Might as well put me down near him."

"You got it," Jed replied.

The soldier waited as the boat came to a halt above him. Eli threw out the rope ladder. Cole climbed down, flag in hand. The man watched him silently. He made no threatening gesture. Still, when Cole reached the bottom, he felt hesitant to step off. The soldier only stood a few paces away.

"Mind if I join you?" Cole asked.

"Up to you," the man said. His wild hair hung almost to his shoulders. A jewel gleamed in one earlobe. Complex bindings held his sandals in place and were partly hidden beneath his metal shin guards.

Cole planted the flag by dropping it to the ground, then drew his sword. "I don't want to fight you."

"I wouldn't want to fight me either."

Cole stepped down. The man watched him curiously. Cole stayed ready to jump.

"Explain the flag," the man said.

"It's just a signal," Cole replied. "Proof I came here."

"State your business," the soldier said. His voice was manly and resonant, but not unfriendly.

"I'm a scout," Cole said.

"A scout has no business here," he said. "This is a place for heroes."

"Are you a hero?"

"I am Lyrus. The vital question is, are you a hero?"

"What if I'm not?"

"Then you had better hurry back up that ladder."

"I have a sword," Cole said, holding it up.

Lyrus rolled his eyes. "Is that little thing your best argument?"

"I fought a scorpipede."

"That's more promising. What's a scorpipede? Was it big?"

"Huge. Longer than most of these buildings."

Lyrus brightened. "Did you slay it?"

"Um, no, but it didn't kill me, either."

"Did you wound it?"

"Not really. I mostly ran from it."

Lyrus looked disappointed.

"But I got away," Cole added. "It was a good chase."

"Were you rescuing somebody?"

"No."

"Hunting treasure?"

"Sort of."

"What did you claim?"

"Just this shawl," Cole said, tugging on it.

"Hmmm," Lyrus said. "Why the shawl? Can it turn you into a bat? Make you invisible?"

"No," Cole said. "I don't think it does much."

Lyrus frowned thoughtfully. "Yet here you are."

"Why is this place for heroes?" Cole asked.

Lyrus looked upon his surroundings with pride. "Parona is a sacred proving ground."

"Heroes train here?"

Lyrus gave him half a grin. "Lessons are for elsewhere. This is no school. Champions come here to test themselves."

Cole considered the area more cautiously. "How are they tested?"

"It depends how they choose."

"Can they die?"

"Wouldn't be much of a trial if they couldn't. Are you staying or going?"

"I can still go?"

"I suppose. I'm the wrong person to ask. I don't understand how cowards think."

"Ouch! Are you daring me?"

"I'm stating a fact. I've never run from a fight or backed down from a challenge. Nor will I ever. But that is me. I see no valor in forcing a coward to prove himself when he would rather flee. Do you?"

"No."

Lyrus gave a nod. "The man unwilling to brave the test has already shown himself to be much more craven than the man who fails."

Cole couldn't help feeling offended. "What if I didn't

come here to be tested? Heroes only need to be brave when there's a good reason. It would be stupid to risk your life without a purpose."

Lyrus sighed. "Every coward has his excuses."

"What are the tests?"

"The only way to find out is to try one."

"What do I get if I pass?"

"Confirmation of your heroic status."

"Like what? A certificate?"

"You get to keep a weapon from the arms room, a work of art from the gallery, and an item from the treasure house."

Cole glanced up at the lifeboat. "Can I tell you why I'm here and get your advice?"

"If you wish."

"We're salvagers. We want to take some stuff before this place is destroyed. Would each person have to pass a test to take something?"

Lyrus paused. "There are five trials prepared."

"What if we pass all five?"

"Then . . . I would arrange for more."

"Would you have time?"

Lyrus scowled in thought.

"This place will only be around for a day or two," Cole pointed out.

"Nonsense."

"You know we're floating in the sky."

"Nonsense."

Cole glanced upward. "I came here in a flying ship. Look around."

"Non—" Lyrus began, but then stopped himself. He squinted up at the *Okie Dokie*. He surveyed the area. "I feel . . . odd." He rubbed his eyes. "It's hard to explain." He scanned the area some more. "How have I missed so much?" He folded his arms. "It's as though I'm not supposed to recognize what I'm seeing. I'm not supposed to pay attention." He gave a sheepish smile. "I never thought about whether Parona was in the sky or not. I didn't stop to consider the odd manner of your arrival. Yet I see it all now, and no matter what impulses compel me otherwise, I cannot unsee it. I never run. I never hide. Not from anything."

Cole felt bad for the big soldier. He knew he had just messed with his head.

Lyrus glowered at the ground. "You call yourself a salvager. You claim that Parona will be destroyed?"

"This is a castle floating in the sky. You came out of a cloudwall. You're heading for another cloudwall. You'll never come back."

Closing his eyes, Lyrus rubbed his temples. He gritted his teeth. "Where do I come from?" he muttered. "I can't recall where I come from."

"You've probably existed for less than a day," Cole said. "Nobody really knows how you were made."

"Nor do I," Lyrus said. His eyes widened. "No! No, no, no! You speak the truth! I'm a fraud!"

Cole was ready to run. The soldier didn't seem very stable.

"I had no idea," Lyrus said, a little calmer. "I have no past. It seemed I did, before I gave it my attention, but as I examine myself honestly, I have no history. No childhood. No memories before this place. I pose as an expert on heroism, yet I have accomplished nothing."

Cole stared at the soldier. He seemed more perplexed than angry or sad.

"Would you mind if we took some stuff?" Cole attempted. "That way, part of Parona can live on."

Lyrus examined his sword. He stared down at himself, stroking his breastplate with one hand. "I look real enough." He met eyes with Cole. "Real as you."

Cole wasn't sure how to respond.

The soldier looked up at the *Okie Dokie* and beyond to the *Domingo*. "There are fine treasures here. I understand why you salvagers took an interest. But I cannot allow you to take anything without first passing a test."

Cole sagged a little. Lyrus had been sounding so reasonable. "Why not?"

The soldier straightened. "It is my duty. It is my purpose."

"Why is it your duty?" Cole pressed. "Who gave you the duty?"

Eyes squeezed shut, Lyrus bowed his head. "I have no answer."

"Can't you just drop the act?" Cole asked.

"I'm here to test heroes."

"What gives you the right to test anyone?"

Lyrus sheathed his sword. "This is my purpose. I may have no past, but I am still Lyrus. I am not deaf to your request. I can be reasonable. I don't want the treasures of Parona to head needlessly into oblivion. There may be some room for bargaining. But a test must be passed."

"We're not heroes," Cole said. "My job is to run from danger, not to fight it."

"If only," Lyrus began, and then he looked like he was choking.

"Are you okay?" Cole checked.

The big soldier nodded and steadied himself. "Perhaps," he started again, then couldn't finish.

"You can't tell me," Cole realized.

Lyrus nodded.

"You want to help me?"

"Yes."

Cole had a devious thought. "Don't run away from this. Don't back down. If you want to help, there must be a way around it."

The soldier's expression grew intent and serious. His lips moved as if to speak several times before he said, "I'm chilly."

"What?"

Lyrus gave him a level gaze. "You don't know what you have. I'm chilly." His eyes dropped a little.

Cole fingered his shawl. "This?"

Lyrus trembled but said nothing.

Cole sheathed the sword and unclasped the shawl. Lyrus knelt, and Cole put the shawl over his shoulders, clasping it.

"Is that better?" Cole asked.

Lyrus smiled. "Much better."

"Why?"

"The cloak makes a semblance obey whoever puts it on them."

Cole blinked. "You know you're a semblance?"

"Not until you gave me the cloak. It freed me to know what I had to know in order to serve you. Whoever made me caused me to ignore my true nature. You were helping me catch glimpses, but now I see plainly. Until you gave me the cloak, I didn't realize I had been fabricated. This is common with semblances. We play a role without much self-reflection. It helps us seem more authentic."

"Who made you?" Cole asked, wondering if he could answer now.

Lyrus furrowed his brow. "I still don't know. I'd tell you if I did. I've never met my maker. I sprang into being along with Parona not long ago."

"A semblance gave me this shawl. How could she take it off if it controlled her?"

Folding his arms, Lyrus paused before answering. "In a place like Parona, we semblances form a system. Some semblances are allowed more leeway than others. The semblance you encountered must have had the freedom to decide how best to preserve the system. I myself enjoy similar freedoms."

The explanation matched Merva's behavior. It clarified why she might have been the only one to offer him her shawl. "Wait. You wanted me to give you the shawl so you could help me?"

"I've become more self-aware than my creator expected," Lyrus said. "After you helped me recognize my origin, I turned my bravery against the cognitive limits my shaper had placed on me. The effort opened my eyes to many things, but there were some mental boundaries I couldn't cross. I recognized what your shawl could do when I first saw you. It was why I asked about it—to see if you were aware. Without the shawl, my options were limited. But with it, more becomes possible. To be honest, helping you was only a small portion of my intent."

"Then why point out the shawl?"

Lyrus stood tall. "I want the chance to prove my worth. If you command it, I'll take the test for you. I'll serve as your champion."

CHAPTER

—— 12 ——

HEROICS

"You can take the test?" Cole asked.

"I can with the shawl," Lyrus replied. "If you wish."

"You want to?"

"I am Lyrus. The instant I realized I was unproven, I craved nothing more than this opportunity."

"If you pass the test, we can have the treasure?"

Lyrus drummed his fingers against his breastplate. "It will require bargaining."

"Can't I just order you to give us the treasure?"

"You could. But regardless of how you command me, I cannot force the other semblances of Parona to let you claim any rewards unless a test has been completed. Even with my full cooperation, if you try to take treasure without completing a test, the full defenses of Parona will engage, including the catapults and the ferocious beasts. However, if we strike a bargain, with me speaking for all Parona . . ."

"So let's bargain," Cole said.

"Allow me to remove the shawl so I can act as the guardian

of Parona. Our bargain would not be binding to the others if I were under your control during the negotiation."

"How do I know you'll put the shawl back on?"

"You have my word."

Cole thought about that. The soldier was still wearing the shawl, so he had to obey orders. "I command you to tell me if you can lie to me."

"I cannot lie. With or without the shawl, I keep my word. I want to bargain so I can face the trial for you and earn you access to our treasures."

"All right," Cole said. "Take off the shawl."

Lyrus removed the shawl and draped it over one arm. "You wish to bargain for full access to our treasures?"

"They won't do anyone much good if they're destroyed."

"True. I need your name."

"Cole."

"What are the chances of other heroes coming here before Parona is no more?"

"None," Cole said. "Only salvagers can reach you. And we run if things get bad."

"Very well. With little chance of another hero visiting, and with Parona facing destruction, on behalf of all the guardians who dwell here, I will make a deal that grants the crew of your airship full access to our treasures—on one condition."

"What?"

"You must pledge that, along with my other responsibilities, I can remain a protector of Parona whether or not I am wearing the shawl."

Cole hesitated. "Would that mean you would stop protecting me?"

"No matter what happens, I vow to fight to the death to protect you. Remaining a protector of Parona would not enable me to alter any agreement we make. But I cannot allow your crew full access unless I know someone will be able to act in the interests of Parona. Otherwise, by the terms of this arrangement, Parona will be left unguarded."

"You won't attack any of us?"

"I pledge that I will not attack you or your crewmates. As promised, I would defend you."

"What about the other semblances?"

"The other semblances will not be able to attack you for coming here or for taking anything. They must honor this agreement. I speak for all Parona."

Cole felt satisfied that Lyrus was being straightforward. "What is the agreement exactly?"

"If you pass one of the tests, using whatever aid is at your disposal, the treasures of Parona will be yours for the taking. After a single trial is won, the guardians of our treasure cannot move against you or your crewmates for setting foot here or for removing anything."

"Including the floatstones," Cole verified.

"Anything."

"And you'll help me pass the test."

"I have sworn it."

"Deal."

"Including my condition?"

"Yes. You'll still be the protector of Parona."

Lyrus gave a single slow nod. "The bargain is struck. I can now put on the shawl if you desire."

"Sure."

Grinning, Lyrus clasped the shawl around his neck. "Come, young salvager. Let's select a trial."

Cole followed Lyrus up broad, shallow steps into one of the larger buildings. The rectangular structure contained a single room with no walls—just columns on all sides and a roof overhead. At one end of the room, on a platform, sat five large bowls in a row.

Lyrus took a torch from a sconce and led Cole to the row of bowls. "Choose which I should light."

"Don't you know what test you want?"

"I know which trial pertains to each bowl. I know which fight would be easiest. But only a coward would deliberately pick the easiest. I yearn for the hardest fight—Gromar the cyclops. But is that fair to you? I would be more likely to fail. As your champion, it would be selfish to select Gromar. So I will abide by your choice."

Cole considered the five bowls. They appeared identical. "Second from the left," he said, pointing.

"Ah," Lyrus said weightily. He walked forward and dipped the torch into the bowl. Crimson flames rose up, red as blood. "Harano the Lion. I should have known this would be my trial. It will be a good fight. Be ready to flee. I will get no second chance against this opponent."

Lyrus led Cole to a large empty square surrounded by eight buildings. Looking up, Cole saw the *Okie Dokie* following at a distance. He cupped a hand beside his mouth. "If he loses, I'll need to get out of here fast!"

Eli gave a thumbs-up.

Lyrus directed Cole with a gesture. "Wait on the perimeter." He proceeded to the middle of the square, drew his sword, and raised his voice. "Harano, come forth! Slay me if you can."

From one of the buildings surrounding the square, there emerged a huge lion with red-gold fur and a mane that matched the bloodred flames in the bowl. Cole felt an instinctive terror. No fences divided him from this alpha predator. He drew his Jumping Sword.

Head high, advancing with lazy grace, the lion ambled into the square on large paws. The tufted tail swished. On all fours, Harano stood as tall as Lyrus. As the giant cat drew near, the soldier coiled into a fighting stance, sword held ready.

The lion roared, the mighty challenge echoing across Parona. Cole felt the hair on his neck and arms stand up. He glanced at the lifeboat. It hovered just within jumping distance.

Lyrus didn't waver. "Come, Harano," he invited. "Measure yourself against me."

The lion rushed Lyrus with sudden speed. Cole flinched. Harano sprang. Lyrus stepped forward, crouching, and thrust his blade upward. The oversized lion slammed into the soldier, hurling him backward. Both flopped to the ground. Cole heard armor scraping against paving stones.

Man and beast lay still for a few heartbeats. Then Lyrus arose. Bracing one foot against the lion's shaggy head, he removed his sword, yanking it out from under the jaw.

As Lyrus cleaned the sword by wiping it against the luxurious mane, Cole approached cautiously. "Are you all right?"

Lyrus turned and flashed a wide smile. "Now I have a memory worth owning."

"That was incredible."

"I felt alive for the first time. Thank you for that gift. The trial has been won. Our defenses are no longer engaged. You and your comrades are welcome to off-load our treasures."

All three lifeboats shuttled workers down from the *Domingo*. Still wearing the shawl, Lyrus showed them where they could find the armaments, the artwork, and the treasure. While the lifeboats waited in the square where Lyrus had defeated Harano, the raiders began collecting valuables.

Helped by his cane, Durny approached Cole with Mira at his side. "Fine work, Cole. I take it the shawl helped convince that soldier to fight for you?"

"It made him obey me," Cole said. "But I didn't trick him. He wanted me to have control. He wanted to fight. He wanted to prove himself."

"Did you know the shawl could do that?"

"Not until he told me," Cole said. "Lyrus thought he was an expert on heroes. As we spoke, he realized he was a semblance and that he hadn't ever done anything heroic. He hinted about the shawl so he could have his chance."

Durny clapped Cole on the shoulder. "Impressive job. Much better to fight with your head than with your hands. Would you care to help us seek out floatstones?"

"Sure. What can I do?"

"Go get my tools from Rowly. That should include a mattock, a pry bar, a hammer, a chisel, and two spades. Bring them and catch up with us."

"Good job, Cole," Mira said.

"Thanks." As Cole turned to find Rowly, his cheeks felt hot. He suspected he was blushing.

A pair of men slowly descended the steps from one of the buildings, holding a huge silver harp between them. Setting it down, they paused to rest. Another man clutched a jeweled scepter in one hand and an ornately framed mirror in the other. A fourth man struggled to carry a stone bust.

Cole spotted Rowly over by the lifeboat called the *Charmer*. He was a round, balding man who wore spectacles. Beyond Rowly, Cole noticed Lyrus climbing the steps to the building where they had lit Harano's flame.

Why would Lyrus go there?

Frowning, Cole trotted past Rowly, then increased his pace to a jog to catch up to Lyrus. As he hurried up the broad, shallow steps, Cole told himself that he was probably worrying about nothing. At the top of the steps, he looked through the columns to where Lyrus stood across the room, torch in hand, lighting a fourth bowl.

"What are you doing?" Cole yelled, racing into the room.

Lyrus turned. The bowl that had held the red flame was empty. The other four bowls burned green, blue, gray, and black.

"You granted me the right to remain a protector of Parona," he said.

"You promised to defend me!"

"I will. To the death, if necessary."

"You promised the guardians wouldn't attack us if we came for the treasure!"

"Only the dishonorable would break a vow. I pledged they would not attack you for coming here or for taking anything. And they won't. They'll attack because, in my role as protector of Parona, I have begun four trials. True to my word, I will strive to defend you. This proving ground deserves to fulfill its purpose." He grinned. "And I deserve a final chance to test my skills."

Lyrus started running for the square.

"I command you to stop!" Cole called.

"You pledged I could act in my role of protector," Lyrus called back. "I do not release you from that promise."

Cole felt sick and horrified. He had been played! Lyrus was getting everything he wanted—another chance to fight for glory while making sure Parona tested any visitors. The soldier was running toward the square. Where the lifeboats were. Where the creatures would emerge.

Cole ran hard, yelling at the top of his voice. "Watch out! Emergency! Get to the boats! Take off!"

Some of the raiders moved toward Lyrus as the soldier dashed into the square, shawl flapping behind him. The warrior paid them no mind, calling in a mighty voice, "Skelock, Rulad, Nimbia, and Gromar, come forth!"

Creatures emerged from buildings on three sides of the square: a black rhino, horn lowered, charging hard; a spider bigger than a lifeboat, gray and hairy; a huge green serpent with a head the size of a barrel; and a muscular cyclops that was more than twice the height of a man. Lyrus held his sword high. "Come, Rulad; come, Skelock; come, Nimbia and Gromar! Defeat me if you can!"

The creatures converged on Lyrus. The rhino reached him first, but the soldier sprang aside and brought his sword down in a vicious sweep, nearly decapitating the beast. The enormous serpent came next, rearing up high above Lyrus, staying beyond the reach of his sword.

The discordant clang of a dropped harp roused Cole from watching the fight. The men with the harp had abandoned the instrument and were now climbing inside a lifeboat. Two of the boats lifted off the ground. Other empty-handed raiders came racing from a couple of the buildings. A few of them jumped into the last boat as it took off.

When Cole looked back to the fight, the towering cyclops was ignoring Lyrus and charging toward the lifeboats, as was the supersized tarantula. The snake shifted sinuously, head jerking from one position to another, trying to strike, but Lyrus kept his sword in the way. The warrior tried to press forward, but the snake kept sliding back, giving him ground.

An oversized arrow streaked down from above, piercing the center of the tarantula and poking out its other side. The hairy spider clenched into a quivering ball.

An instant after the javelin skewered the spider, catapults appeared all around Parona, rising as hatches opened on rooftops and patios. Without anyone apparently operating them, the catapults launched balls of flaming pitch at the *Domingo*. The skycraft lurched up and away from Parona, but not before a pair of fires started on the hull.

Club raised to strike, the cyclops closed in on the lifeboats. A few arrows from the boats flew at the brute, lodging in its hairy clothes. One sank into its shoulder. The cyclops didn't seem to mind.

As all three lifeboats banked up and away, the catapults swiveled to target them. The cyclops jumped and swung its club, just missing the lowest boat. Two men who had been dashing for the boats tried to reverse their direction and make for the buildings, but the cyclops chased them down, crushing one with a downward blow and then swatting the other man a ridiculous distance through the air, his body landing in a crumpled heap.

Lyrus sprinted at the snake. Its mouth gaped wide, showing slender fangs bigger than bananas. While gliding away on writhing coils, the serpent struck at the soldier repeatedly and got slashed with every attack. Then the tail whipped around the warrior's legs, and the massive snake encircled him, closing from all directions, wrapping him up while striking furiously.

The cyclops ran toward Cole, and he realized that his moment as a bystander was over. It was all happening so quickly, and he felt so much responsibility, that he had nearly forgotten he needed to escape as well.

Raising his sword toward the nearest lifeboat, Cole shouted, "Away!" He soared upward at the same time as many spheres of flaming pitch. One fireball passed close enough for him to feel its hot backwash. The fiery projectiles missed the boat, and Cole landed neatly inside. The boat contained Jed, Eli, and two others, along with a few treasures.

"They'll skin us if we leave Durny!" Eli yelled.

Jed turned the boat and swooped lower. "We're going to get roasted," he grumbled.

"Give him one chance," Eli insisted.

Cole leaned over the side, peering ahead. He had nearly forgotten Durny and Mira! They had gone off on their own.

Mira and the older man were running away from the lifeboat down a paved lane between two buildings. Durny moved as best he could on his bad leg, stabbing the ground with his cane. The spider was chasing them, the ballista's arrow protruding from its body. Cole thought it had been a lethal shot. Apparently not.

The speedy tarantula gained rapidly. Durny was a poor sprinter. Mira stayed near him, urging him on. He waved for her to run ahead.

Another volley of fiery pitch blazed into the air. Jed dipped the lifeboat down and to the side as several blistering projectiles roared past. One of the lifeboats that had managed to climb high took a direct hit and burst apart. Cole glimpsed burning bodies falling amid shattered wood. The boat had passed beyond the borders of Parona, so none of the people or debris hit the ground.

The *Okie Dokie* was gaining on Durny and Mira. Cole's attention returned to them in time to see the tarantula leap forward. It landed on Durny, and a furry leg clipped Mira as well, sending her to the ground, the Jumping Sword clattering from her grasp. The tarantula tilted down, as if biting Durny.

The shaper cried out, and the tarantula tore in half, black

gore erupting in all directions. Advancing faster than Cole had ever seen a lifeboat move, Jed brought the boat in low. Eli leaned over the side and reached a hand for Durny. Their fingers brushed, and Eli shouted in frustration.

Cole looked back at Mira and Durny, both of them drenched in spider juice. Club held high, the cyclops was charging at them. Mira crawled toward her Jumping Sword, but it was clear the cyclops would reach her first.

"Go," Eli growled. "They're lost."

The cyclops was only a few paces away from Mira and Durny. They were going to be pulverized.

Without time to think or plan, Cole aimed his sword at the head of the cyclops. "Away!"

Cole sprang from the lifeboat and sailed toward the one-eyed giant. Air rushed over him as he rocketed toward his target. Oblivious to the incoming threat, the cyclops glared down at Mira and Durny. The sword slowed Cole a little as he neared the brutish head. Straining forward, he stabbed the center of the cyclops's big blue eye, the momentum of the jump adding considerable power to his thrust. The sword disappeared, and so did his arm—all the way up to the elbow. It felt as if he had punched a deep bowl of warm pudding.

The cyclops collapsed beneath him, landing on its back. Cole kept hold of the sword through the jolting impact. Stunned, he lay atop the fallen giant, watching thick blood well from the ruined eye. He was alive. The cyclops was not.

CHAPTER
13

FLOATSTONES

The sword did not come out easily, but with effort, Cole wrenched it free. Rattled, he slid off the cyclops and stumbled away from the fallen brute, arm and sword red and dripping.

He found Mira on her feet, soaked in black gore, sword in hand, her expression a mask of disbelief. "Cole?"

Beyond her, the *Okie Dokie* had flown past the edge of Parona, diving now instead of climbing as another barrage of flaming pitch flared toward it. Their ride sank out of view.

Cole turned away from her, eyes scouring the empty lane. "There's a snake."

"Snake?" Durny moaned.

"Durny?" Mira called.

"Are you all right?" Cole asked in surprise.

"What snake?" Durny demanded.

"A gigantic one," Cole said. "Last I saw, it was killing Lyrus."

Mira crouched beside Durny. "Are you hurt? Can you get up?"

Biting his lower lip, he gave his head a little shake. "I doubt it. Give me a moment." He closed his eyes and began rubbing his torso while muttering quietly.

"What's he doing?" Cole whispered.

"Trying to heal himself with shaping," Mira said. "Not usually smart. It must be bad."

Cole looked down the lane both ways. "The snake is big. And fast. We can't fight it." He glanced up. "It could come at us from a roof."

"Durny?" Mira asked.

"I won't make it," he panted. "Use me as bait. Cole, when it consumes me, strike at it from hiding. Take off the head."

"No," Mira insisted. "If you die, we'll die. They left us."

"They may return," Durny said.

"Not unless the catapults run out of ammo," Cole said. "I saw one lifeboat go down. The *Domingo* was on fire."

Durny looked at the sky. Only a strip of partly clouded blue was visible because of the buildings on either side. The *Domingo* and the lifeboats were out of sight. "You're probably right. We're on our own. And we're too vulnerable here. We should get indoors. You'll have to drag me."

"Aaaargh!" yelled a voice from down the lane. Armor scraped and dented, Lyrus had stumbled into view. He staggered toward them. "Who killed Gromar?"

"What about the snake?" Cole called.

"I dispatched Nimbia," Lyrus declared, "though she did herself proud."

"The snake is dead?" Mira asked.

"Headless and squirming."

"Is that the last of the guardians?" Cole asked.

"The catapults will continue to defend Parona until the end," Lyrus said. "I did not activate them. When your ship fired upon Skelock, the response was unavoidable. You had permission to come here and remove treasure, not to attack from the sky."

"Can you shut down the catapults?" Durny wondered.

"They're beyond my control."

"Will the catapults shoot at us?" Cole asked.

"Only if you're airborne."

As the warrior neared them, Cole saw large wide-spaced punctures in his breastplate. Blood flowed from the holes. "You're injured," Cole said.

"I'm dying," Lyrus gasped. "I won't last much longer." He lifted his chin. "But I vowed to protect you until the end." When he reached the cyclops, the soldier kicked its head. "I wanted to measure myself against Gromar. Who slew him?"

"Cole," Mira said.

"You?" Lyrus shouted.

Cole held up the gory sword.

"With that tiny blade?"

Cole nodded.

"I misjudged you," Lyrus said. "I'm most impressed."

"Come here," Durny said.

"I obey Cole," Lyrus said.

"Do it," Cole said.

Lyrus went and knelt beside Durny. The warrior eyed the two mangled halves of the tarantula. "How was this accomplished?"

"I'm a shaper," Durny said. "Semblances are somewhat vulnerable to me. With the spider on top of me, I put everything I had into parting it. I've never accomplished such a feat before. It took a lot out of me."

"How badly are you hurt?" Cole asked.

"It landed right on me," Durny said. "My spine is broken. I have crushed organs. It also bit me twice. I neutralized the toxin and reshaped my insides to buy some time. I succeeded, but the actions I took guaranteed that my injuries will be fatal."

"I don't have much longer myself," Lyrus said.

"Cole," Durny spat. "Ask him if he harbors any other plans that could directly or indirectly harm you or Mira in any way."

Cole wished he had used that question earlier. "Do you?"

"I have no such plans," Lyrus said. "My duty as protector of Parona is complete. All defenses have already been engaged, and of course I will honor my pledge to personally do you no harm."

"You won't send any more tests our way?" Cole pressed.

"None," the soldier answered.

"Give me your hand," Durny said. After a nod from Cole, Lyrus complied. Durny closed his eyes, and beads of sweat appeared on his brow. His lips moved without sound.

The soldier's eyes widened. "What have you done?"

"I quelled the venom, closed some wounds, and patched some damaged bones," Durny said, releasing his hand. "It's much easier to tinker with a semblance than a living being. Parona will not outlast you."

"What now?" Mira asked.

"The catapults are no longer firing," Durny said, eyes on Lyrus.

"They cease operating when no targets are within range," the soldier said.

"Will they start again if a skycraft approaches?" Durny asked.

"They're active now. They'll target all newcomers."

"How much ammunition do the catapults have?"

"Enough to fire continually until Parona disappears."

"Is there any chance of Captain Post trying to rescue us?" Cole asked.

Durny closed his eyes. "Not under these circumstances. Few castles resist airborne intruders. This one resists them staunchly. The Sky Raiders don't want to lose their most skilled shaper, but they wouldn't send rescuers against defenses like this, not for anyone, not even for Adam."

Cole looked at Mira. Were they doomed? Would they drift away into the cloudwall to be destroyed with the rest of Parona? "There must be something we can do."

Durny opened his eyes. "Of course there is. I'm holding on to life for a reason. We must construct our own skycraft. It will require a minimum of five floatstones. Seven would be preferable. And we'll need something to serve as the vessel itself."

"We could use your help," Cole told Lyrus.

"You'll have it," the soldier said.

"I don't suppose you retrieved any of my tools?" Durny asked Cole.

"They were in one of the lifeboats that got away," he said.

"Which lifeboat didn't make it?" Mira wondered.

"The *Melody* got tagged by a catapult," Cole said. "It blew apart. The men fell."

"Did the debris land on Parona?" Durny asked hopefully.

"No, it missed."

Durny frowned. "This mission is our biggest disaster in years."

Cole felt terrible. "I really blew it."

"This isn't your fault," Durny said. "You've helped us more than duty demanded. All raiders know the risks. I interviewed Lyrus, as did Rowly. We failed to ask the right question. Your champion hid his intentions well."

"I grieve for your losses," Lyrus said. "I was doing my duty."

Durny studied Lyrus. "How well do you know Parona?"

"Almost as if we were one and the same."

"Could you help us locate seven of the most available floatstones? The nodes that keep Parona aloft? We need to extract them with a minimum of digging and without bringing buildings down on top of us."

"We can access some in the catacombs," Lyrus said. "Six for certain, as long as we harvest them from different areas. The seventh would start to make things unstable."

"I can manage with five," Durny said. "I'll need to be carried. I'm paralyzed from the waist down, and Mira lacks the know-how to extract floatstones on her own."

Lyrus scooped Durny from the ground, cradling the injured shaper in his arms. The soldier looked to Cole.

"Take us to the first floatstone," Cole ordered.

The soldier started walking. Cole and Mira followed.

"Pray that Parona drifts slowly today," Durny said. "And pray I'm wrong about the look of these clouds."

By the time they had extracted the fifth floatstone, night had fallen, and rain poured down on Parona. None of the fires had gone out in any of the torches, bowls, kettles, or platters scattered throughout Parona, whether indoors or outdoors. Droplets spat and hissed as they came into contact with the open flames.

The wind had risen, blowing the raindrops diagonally. No stars were visible. The temperature had fallen considerably.

Cole had felt useless while they hunted for floatstones. The catacombs beneath Parona connected into an elaborate labyrinth, allowing his group to move from one floatstone to the next without returning to the surface. Along most of the webby, convoluted corridors, skulls, partial skeletons, and other strange bones were embedded into the waxy walls. At each extraction site, Lyrus would strip away wax, fungi, and filth until he had laid bare the stone wall or floor. Mira gave Durny some support, but he did the heavy work, dividing the stone with his mind and holding it open while Mira pulled out the floatstone, then sealing the stone back up again as best he could.

Each floatstone was a mirrorlike disk with rounded edges, no bigger than a dinner plate, maybe three or four inches thick. Cole's job was to carry them. When he let go of a floatstone, it hovered in place, perfectly stationary. The floatstones resisted movement. He learned that they offered less resistance when he moved them slowly.

After helping Mira collect the fifth floatstone, Durny had slumped back, his pale face gaunt and slick with sweat. Cole doubted whether he could have extracted seven of these even if they had been readily available.

They had emerged from the catacombs some time ago. Durny rested on the floor, eyes closed, his breathing shallow but steady. They were waiting for Lyrus to return with something they could use as a skycraft. All the buildings were sparsely furnished, and so much of Parona was made of stone that they had yet to come across anything suitable. The soldier had assured them that he had some ideas.

"What a mess." Cole sighed, staring beyond the colonnade to the steam hissing up from the rain-lashed fires spaced about the patio. "I'm so sorry."

"You saved my life," Mira said. "Durny's, too."

"Whatever. If you say so."

He felt her hand on his shoulder. "Why'd you do it?" she asked earnestly. "Why risk your life for me? You were in a lifeboat. You could have escaped."

Cole turned. She looked perplexed. He had asked himself the same question a couple of times while they roamed the catacombs seeking floatstones. He felt a little guilty about the chance he had taken. After all, Jenna and Dalton needed his help too. If he got himself killed, who would rescue them? "I didn't want to see you get squished. It would have been my fault."

She shook her head. "We're slaves, Cole. You came here

153

because they forced you. If you want to place blame, give it to the owners of the Sky Raiders. No matter what goes wrong, you don't deserve any of it."

"Maybe you're right," Cole said. "Still, I couldn't watch you get killed. I just couldn't. I saw it coming. I saw a chance to stop it, so I tried. There wasn't time to think it through. I can hardly believe it worked."

"Well, it was the bravest thing anyone has ever done for me. And the least expected. Thank you." She leaned in and gave him a quick kiss on the cheek.

Cole suddenly found it difficult to breathe properly. He had never felt more self-conscious, or more pleased. He told his mouth not to spread into a big goofy smile, but the muscles in his cheeks wouldn't listen.

"Aha!" Lyrus called. "To the victor go the spoils!"

Flustered, Cole tried not to look surprised and embarrassed. The brawny soldier was dragging something into the room. Maybe he was talking about the potential skycraft he had found. "What?"

"You saved a damsel in distress," Lyrus said. "I may never have that pleasure. You speak like a coward but act like a hero. I can respect that."

Lyrus set down the box. It was a large coffin in the traditional shape, widening to accommodate the shoulders, then narrowing toward the feet, like an elongated hexagon. Except it seemed to be built for an eight-foot-tall occupant.

"Where'd you find that?" Cole asked.

"In one of the crypts. There were plenty of smaller ones.

You should have seen the skeleton. It had the head of a bull. A minotaur, most like."

Mira ran a hand along the side of the open box. "Feels sturdy. It hasn't rotted."

"I hope it serves," Lyrus said.

Mira gently shook Durny. The shaper smacked his lips and opened his eyes. He looked over at the coffin, then propped himself up on one elbow and squinted intently. "Oh dear. A bit morbid, isn't it? But it will have to suffice." He looked to Lyrus. "How much time do we have?"

"The storm has hastened our progress," the soldier replied. "Not more than two hours."

Durny sighed. "I had hoped the children could wait for the storm to relent before departing. We'll have to work quickly, and you two will have to risk the turbulent air."

"Won't you come with us?" Mira pleaded.

"There would be no sense in it," Durny insisted. "It'll take the last of my vitality to make this skyworthy on such a short schedule. I won't last many more hours. Better for me to bow out gracefully than spend my final moments as deadweight."

"You have to try," Mira said. "Maybe they can heal you. Maybe—"

Durny held out a hand. "Please don't weary me further. We have no time to waste. You don't understand the damage inside of me. I shaped myself in unnatural ways. It bought me some extra hours of life, but nobody could heal me now. I have no desire to die—there is simply no way around it. Give me the floatstones. Cole, might I have a private word with you?"

"Sure," Cole said.

While Mira and Lyrus moved to the far side of the room, Cole crouched down beside Durny. "You must look after her," the older man whispered urgently.

"I'll try," Cole said.

"I can't explain everything, for it isn't my place, but there is much more to that girl than meets the eye. My mission in life has been to protect her. My role as shaper for the Sky Raiders was merely a cover for that vital purpose. But I will no longer be able to watch over her. This is a terrible time for me to leave her. She will be unacceptably vulnerable without me. The others at Skyport won't shield her as I have. None know her value. You must keep her safe at all cost."

His intensity left Cole surprised. He knew Mira was Durny's apprentice, but he hadn't realized the old guy felt so strongly about her. "Are you related?"

"Not by blood," Durny said. "I have no right to tell you more. My life ends here, tonight. Promise me you'll watch over her."

Cole wasn't sure he could watch out for *himself* in a place like Skyport. But he liked Mira, and Durny needed assurance. "I'll do my best. I promise."

Durny looked relieved. He nodded slowly. "You're a good lad. Thank you for coming back for her. Protect her with that same courage, and she will be in good hands." He raised his voice. "We're done. Cole, why don't you go claim some weapons or treasure? I would have private words with Mira."

CHAPTER
—— 14 ——

STORM BLOWN

Following instructions from Durny, Lyrus turned the coffin on its side near him. Then the soldier led Cole away.

"Durny is meeting his end bravely," Lyrus said.

"He'd be fine if it wasn't for you," Cole replied.

"Did I bring him here? Did I bring you? This is a proving ground for heroes."

"Just doing your job, right? You picked a bad time to be so good at it."

"I gave you what help I could."

"I'm surprised you beat that snake. It looked like it had you."

"It did have me," Lyrus said. "In the end I took its head, but not before it did fatal damage. Had Durny not restored me, I would be dead. In truth, my contest with Nimbia ended as a draw. What surprised me was you besting Gromar."

Cole had cleaned his sword, but the sleeve of his buckskin jacket remained crusted with dried blood. "It surprised me too."

"You proved yourself," Lyrus said. "You deserve to be rewarded. What manner of prizes would you prefer?"

"Do you have any special weapons?" Cole asked. "You know, that are shaped to do useful things? Or treasures with secret abilities, like my cloak?"

"You're wise to ask. There are three such items: a painting that foretells the next day's weather, a jewel that will always return to the first person who kisses it, and a bow that requires no arrows. They were prepared to reward discerning eyes, but you asked, and I wear your shawl, so I would be glad to give them to you."

Using the catacombs to avoid the rain, they visited three different treasure rooms, all lit by candles and torches. Lyrus carefully wrapped the painting in cloth. Cole kissed the jewel as soon as he claimed it. After receiving the bow, he tested it by pulling the string. Once the string was back far enough, an arrow appeared.

Lyrus took custody of the painting and the bow, freeing Cole to collect other treasures. He tried to choose items that might make the Sky Raiders happy, including a small heavy chest loaded with jewels and gold coins. He put rings on every finger and wore several pendants. Lyrus also recommended a pair of hooded cloaks to help against the rain. It was hard for Cole to tear himself away from investigating the treasure hoards, but Lyrus finally informed him that they had less than half an hour before Parona would reach the cloudwall.

Upon returning to where they had left Durny and Mira, Cole found Durny facedown on the floor. Mira knelt at his side. By the torchlight in the room, Cole could see the shiny tracks of tears on her cheeks. Her eyes were puffy and red. "He's gone."

"I'm sorry," Cole said.

"Did he finish the skycraft?" Lyrus asked.

"He died as he finished it," Mira said. "He warned me that he might. We can't steer it, but that shouldn't be necessary. The coffin will fly itself to the salvage yard. It was the safest destination he could give us. The cliffside entrances will be sealed at night."

"You should depart," Lyrus said. "Time runs short."

"Do you want to come with us?" Cole asked.

"I would not survive the journey," Lyrus said. "Better that I remain here where I belong."

"Durny told me we should launch the boat from the edge of Parona," Mira said.

"He was right," Lyrus agreed. "Once you're airborne, the catapults will target you. The storm should wreak havoc with their aim, but why take needless risks?"

"Seriously?" Cole snapped. "That's your advice? You just fought monsters on purpose!"

Lyrus shrugged. "She's a maiden. And you can't fight a ball of flame. Cole, I should return your shawl."

"Let's wait until we take off," Cole said. "Just to be safe."

"Very well."

They situated the items they were taking into the coffin. Cole and Mira put on their cloaks. Lyrus picked up one side of the coffin and dragged it out into the rain. Cole followed, the rain pattering against his hood. The wind gusted hard enough to make the walk laborious.

"Not the night I'd choose to go flying in a minotaur's coffin," Cole said to Mira, speaking loudly to be heard over the storm.

"I've had some bad days with the Sky Raiders," Mira said. "But this one takes the prize."

They followed Lyrus until he left the coffin at the edge of a patio and stepped back. Beyond where the patio ended, the night was impenetrably dark.

"What now?" Cole asked.

Mira stepped inside the coffin. "We get in and I tell it to go."

Cole got in as well. The coffin was fairly deep, which offered some security, but the only things to really hold on to were the sides. It was like sitting in a primitive canoe.

"Would you like the shawl now?" Lyrus asked.

"Yes, please," Cole replied.

The soldier removed the shawl, handed it over, and stepped back. "Luck be with you."

"Die bravely," Mira said.

"Die bravely," Cole repeated.

Lyrus straightened to full attention. "Count on it. Live well."

"Skyport!" Mira yelled.

The coffin lurched forward. Cole gripped the sides tightly. The improvised skycraft flew swiftly, rocking, bucking, and fishtailing as it was buffeted by the swirling wind.

The catapults started firing. Comets of flame illuminated the darkness, though no shot came close to them. Three more volleys were launched, each more hopeless than the last. Soon all light from the fires of Parona were lost behind them.

Only the dark tempest remained.

Between their speed and the gusting wind, rain whipped Cole violently. Tucking his head down, he braced himself against the sides of the coffin. He felt like a paper airplane in a tornado. Sometimes the coffin lurched forward, sometimes it stalled, sometimes it dove, sometimes it climbed, and sometimes it spun. Often it tipped almost sideways, though never upside down. There was no predicting how it would move, so Cole hung on with all his strength.

Cole measured time by each second that he didn't go flying freely into the storm, plummeting toward forever, surrounded by raindrops. There was no lightning or thunder, but the wind raged, and the rain seemed determined to drown him.

He had no chance to exchange words with Mira. She sat close enough that he occasionally bumped against her, which served as his only clue that he was not alone in the coffin.

As their wild flight stretched on and on, Cole began to doubt whether they would ever reach their destination. There was no way to gauge if the skycraft was moving in the right direction. They could be blown farther off course with every gust. All he could do was hold tight as the coffin reared, plunged, turned, twisted, pitched, heaved, shook, wobbled, jerked, slowed, accelerated, and curveted.

His hands grew numb from the cold. In spite of his cloak, his clothes were drenched. His muscles ached from the strain of holding on. His body throbbed from the constant jarring. He shifted a bit, trying to find new ways to brace himself.

The storm refused to relent. There was no shelter. The merciless fury was all around them. Time lost all meaning.

Cole stopped hoping that it would ever end. He just held on.

He didn't know they had reached their destination until the coffin thumped down in the salvage yard. Looking around, he could see the lit windows of Skyport perhaps fifty yards away. The rain still bucketed down, and the wind continued to howl.

Mira kept her head down.

"We're here!" Cole called.

She looked up, then shakily climbed out of the coffin. "We have to get indoors."

Cole took the time to collect his shawl and the bow. He had made sure to sit on them.

He checked the coffin for the other items he had brought. It was too dark to be sure, but it looked like everything else was gone, including the chest of coins and the enchanted painting.

Cole followed Mira through the gloomy, wet salvage yard, shoes squelching in muddy puddles as he navigated around sheds and other shadowy obstacles. When they reached the porch, he tossed the bow and the shawl underneath it while Mira climbed the steps. He had worked hard for them and was in no hurry to give them away.

He caught up to Mira as she pounded on the door. "It's locked," she told him as he approached.

At least on the porch they were out of the rain, though the wind clawed at them. Cole was about to tell her nobody would be able to hear them over the storm when the locks started to disengage. Eli opened the door.

"We'd all lost hope!" he exclaimed with a grin, stepping aside so they could enter. "Durny?"

Mira shook her head. "Just us."

His face fell a little. Then he swatted Cole with the back of his hand. "Did you have a nice landing on that cyclops?"

"Nicer for me than for it," Cole said.

Eli shook his head. "You're absolutely mad. But here you are. The Maker protects fools and children. Adam will want to see you. He had some of us waiting up, in case you showed."

Eli led them to the common area where Adam sat on his jade throne. The warm air made Cole more conscious of how wet and cold he was.

"Oh ho!" Adam bellowed. "The castaways return! I had a feeling you might resurface. Is the shaper with you?"

"He didn't make it," Eli reported.

Adam scowled. "What? The man built a skycraft, then forgot to board?"

"He died making it," Mira said. "He was crushed by a huge spider. It took all he had to last as long as he did."

Adam banged a fist on the arm of his throne. "This is why you don't send your best shaper to collect floatstones. We have three less capable men who could have handled that errand. But given a full year and a death threat, not one of them could produce a Jumping Sword. Shame on me for letting Durny talk me into it. Anything can happen out there. You two look like drowned kittens. You're otherwise unwounded?"

"We're all right," Cole said.

"Must have been a white-knuckle ride." Adam chuckled. "I can hardly imagine. How'd you navigate back here?"

"Durny rigged the coffin to find the salvage yard," Mira said.

Adam shook his head. "That man has forgotten more about shaping than most will ever know. A corpse box, you say? Not the friendliest omen."

"It's out in the yard," Cole said.

"You bring back any goods?" Adam wondered.

Cole tried not to dwell on the bow and shawl he had chucked under the porch. "We tried. I think most of it fell out. It's dark out there."

"You have some jewelry," Adam noted.

Cole grinned sheepishly. "That's right." He had forgotten the pendants and the rings. He started taking them off.

"Princely adornments. The two lifeboats that survived also off-loaded some nice finds. We'll fly the *Vulture* while we make repairs to the *Domingo*. If nothing else, your bone-holder should have some floatstones we can salvage. Cole, I understand you went back to help Durny and Mira after boarding a lifeboat."

"He saved us," Mira said. "The spider left us stunned, and a cyclops would have finished us. Cole killed it."

"Not a bright move," Adam said. "Most days, that would lead to three corpses instead of two. But it's the kind of stupidity I can admire."

"Thanks," Cole said. "I think."

Adam winked. "You two had a tough night. Take the day off tomorrow, and I mean completely—no chores, no responsibilities. Go dry off and get some sleep."

Chapter
— 15 —

MIRA

Cole could sense the sunlight through his eyelids. The sleep felt so good that he didn't want to wake, but he peeked with one eye, then the other.

Daylight poured through the window. The room was empty. The other bunks were made.

Jace's bunk had been empty when Cole came to bed the night before. The two other boys had been asleep. After putting on dry clothes and curling up under his covers, Cole had slept undisturbed.

He kicked his legs over the side of his bunk and dropped to the floor. Cole hadn't had a true day off since arriving at Skyport. When he wasn't out on a scouting mission, there had been chores to learn and perform. He hardly knew what he would do with a whole day to relax, but breakfast seemed like a sensible start.

In the kitchen, he scraped the bottom of a vat and ladled sticky porridge into a bowl. He grabbed some fruit as well—an apple and some sort of purple citrus. Fruit had been abundant lately.

Cole took his time eating. The common area was deserted. Outside, the sun glared across a blue sky as if the storm had never happened. The *Borrower* and the *Vulture* were probably out raiding.

The purple citrus fruit turned out to be the best part of the meal. Cole went and grabbed a second one. As he walked back to his room, Mira caught up to him from behind.

"Good morning," she said. "You slept late."

"Maybe I've been up for hours," Cole said.

"Nope. I looked in at you a few times. We need to talk."

She sounded serious. Cole tried to think what he might have done wrong. Did she know about the bow and shawl under the porch? He hadn't taken the time to hide them well. "What's up?"

Mira stepped closer and lowered her voice. "We mustn't be overheard. Come with me."

She led the way down multiple stairways, beyond the basement and into the caves. Although the floors, ceilings, and walls were natural stone, the addition of wooden walkways and steps made travel more convenient. Some areas of the caves had so many rugs, tapestries, and furnishings that Cole could almost forget he was underground.

A narrow offshoot branched from one of the main walkways. At the end they came to a door. Mira paused. "This is my room."

"Not many doors down here," Cole observed.

"True. Durny got this room for me. It's isolated. I don't bring anyone inside." She took out a key, unlocked the door, and entered. "Come on."

Cole followed her in and then stopped in his tracks.

The room was amazing.

A huge canopied bed with silky covers and mounds of pillows stood out the most. Other furniture included an ornate desk, two fancy sofas, a pair of stately armchairs, and a wooden table with matching benches. Beautiful paintings hung on the walls, some wider than his outstretched arms. Fine rugs softened the floor. Statues of animals prowled on shelves and crouched in corners. Crystal lamps made everything bright.

"How'd you get all this great stuff?"

"I made it," Mira said.

"What?"

"I wove the rugs, painted the pictures, sculpted the animals, and built the furniture."

Cole took a closer look at a painting. It showed a flying tiger swooping over a pond near a fanciful castle, its reflection somewhat blurred in the rippling water. The image looked beyond professional. "No way. You're messing with me."

"I'll take that as a compliment," Mira said. "Please don't mention the crafts I have in here. Durny tried to hide my talents, or Adam would have had me slaving every day as an artisan."

"You're serious? You built that bed?"

"Sheets, pillows, everything. Durny lent me some help. I used a little shaping."

Cole chewed on his bottom lip. "If there was shaping involved, I might start to believe you."

She sighed despairingly. "If you find *that* hard to believe, just wait."

"I almost forgot," Cole said. "There's more. What do you want to tell me?"

"Have a seat," Mira invited, sitting down on one of the sofas. Mira was normally so confident, but right now she seemed a little fidgety.

The two sofas were at right angles to each other. Cole sat on the near side of the other one.

"I have . . . some secrets."

"Okay," Cole said patiently. "The first step to telling secrets is admitting that you have them."

Mira looked down. "My secrets could be dangerous, Cole. They could get you into trouble."

"This place is nothing but trouble. What's a little more? We've been through some harsh stuff already."

She looked at him intently. "I know. It's why I know I can trust you. I have to be careful about who I trust. At Parona, you didn't have to risk your life for me, but you did. I don't think anything less would let me confide in you. Without Durny, I need somebody on my side. Before he died, he told me it should be you. I think he was right."

"He asked me to look out for you," Cole said. "When we talked in private."

"Should I tell you?"

"You have to now. I'm too curious."

"It's not just gossip," she warned. "These secrets matter. People have died because of them."

Cole thought about that. His life was already nightmarishly hard. Did he really want more danger? Mira obviously needed him. How bad could it be? "Go ahead."

She gave a nervous giggle. "I've never talked about this with anyone who didn't already know most of the story. You're so new here. I hardly know where to begin."

"Just go for it."

"Do you know about Junction? The High Shaper?"

"Is he like the High King?"

"Yes," Mira said. "The High Shaper is the High King."

"Then I know he took some of my friends as slaves," Cole said bitterly.

"Really?" Mira asked.

"Remember? I came here because my friends were kidnapped."

"Right. But how do you know they were going to the High King?"

"After I was captured, this woman examined me. She said I had no shaping potential. But some of the others—the ones with potential—were set aside for the High King. That included Dalton and Jenna, two of my best friends."

"Hmmm," Mira said. "He must need more slaves with shaping talent. That could be good and bad for your friends."

"How come?"

"Slaves who can shape get the best treatment. And if they're going to be slaves, the royal palace is more comfortable than most places they could be working. But the High King is a maniac. Anyone who works near him is in danger."

"What do you mean?" Cole asked.

"It ties directly into my secret. What do you know about how the five kingdoms are governed?"

"Nothing. I don't even really know what they are."

She nodded. "There are five major kingdoms in the Outskirts: Sambria, where we are now; Necronum; Elloweer; Zeropolis; and Creon. Junction lies more or less between the kingdoms. It's the capital of the Outskirts. The five kingdoms used to be governed by five Grand Shapers. The High Shaper ranked above them all and lived in Junction City. Together they formed the Governing Council, and they ruled the Outskirts as a group. Except, around sixty years ago, the High Shaper decided he wanted all the power for himself. The Grand Shaper of Zeropolis became his puppet, and the other four went into hiding."

"Is this the secret?"

"This is the background. You don't know any of this, do you?"

"No. Who is the High Shaper now?"

"The same guy," Mira said. "The more advanced shapers have ways to slow the aging process. They can live for hundreds of years."

"The Grand Shapers are really powerful?"

"They're usually the best of the best."

"So what does this have to do with you?"

"I'm getting there. More than sixty years ago, the High Shaper lived with his wife and five daughters. The five girls all showed promise as shapers. Their father, not so much. Although he came from a long line of shapers, and married a woman who was a powerful shaper, he held his position more by pedigree and political games than by talent. Anyhow, one day, there was a terrible accident, and all his daughters died."

"What happened?"

"Their carriage went off a bridge into a raging river. It was huge news throughout the Outskirts. All the kingdoms mourned. But I know some secrets about the accident. Secrets that involve the High Shaper. Things he would do anything to cover up."

"Was he involved?"

Mira stared at Cole in silence. "We're talking about the most powerful person in all of the Outskirts. And yes, he was behind the accident. He planned it."

"His own daughters?" Cole asked.

"I don't think he ever saw them as daughters," Mira said. "Rivals would be more accurate."

"The guy killed his own kids?" Cole exclaimed. "And he got away with it?"

"He still rules the Outskirts," Mira said. "Almost nobody knows what really happened. The High King is ruthless and selfish. He destroyed his own family to get what he wanted. The more his power grows, the more people are seeing that side of him. And his power keeps growing every year. Every day."

"My friends went to that guy?" Cole asked, feeling ill.

"Hopefully, they won't work with him directly," Mira said. "There's more to the secret, but I shouldn't share too much yet. The more you know, the more danger you're in. The High Shaper has killed to keep these secrets and wouldn't hesitate to kill again. But I wanted you to know enough to appreciate the seriousness of my situation."

"How did you learn this stuff?" Cole asked.

"My mother is close to the High Shaper," Mira said. "I

used to live in his palace. She still does. If I say much more, I'll end up telling you everything. My mother sent me away for my safety and then sent Durny to watch over me."

"Were you and your mother slaves?"

"We weren't slaves," Mira said. "I got marked as part of my cover, to help me hide. But whatever the reasons behind my bondmark, having it makes me as much a slave as you or anyone."

Cole rubbed the arm of the sofa. If Mira was willing to become a slave in order to hide, that alone proved her desperation. "Why tell me?"

After glancing at her door, Mira lowered her voice. "Because Durny and I were planning an escape."

"From Skyport?"

She nodded.

"How come?"

"My mom uses a special signal to let me know when trouble is coming," Mira said. "The signal can also guide messengers to me. But she only uses it for emergencies. The signal showed up recently, and Durny decided we needed to relocate."

"What signal?" Cole asked. "What kind of danger is coming?"

Mira studied Cole. "You can't leak a word of this. To anyone. *Ever.*"

"I promise," Cole said.

"My mom is a shaper. She can put a special star in the sky, right above me. Not a bright one, but it has a distinct pinkish tint."

"Wait," Cole said. "She can make a star?"

"She doesn't create an actual star. That wouldn't even be useful since the sky changes so much. Think of it as the illusion of a star, high up so it blends with the night sky. The first and only time she did it, my star stayed right above me until Durny found me, then it went away."

"Could enemies follow the star to you?"

"If they knew what to look for. That's why the secret mustn't get out. Without help, somebody would have to know the stars really well to even notice it. My star is a distinct color, but pretty faint. Almost nobody really studies the stars here because the night sky behaves so strangely. It would be tricky to single out a new star in all the chaos. Even if a few people noticed the new fixed star, unless they understood what the star meant, there would be no reason for them to follow it and get directly under it."

"Does your mom know Durny died? Will she send someone else to help you?"

Mira gripped the edge of the sofa. "The signal came before Durny died. I can't imagine Mother knows I lost my protector. It's possible the star is leading a messenger to me. But it might only be a warning. In all my years, the one reason she ever put my star in the sky was to guide Durny to me. That was it. But seven nights ago, my star appeared again."

"Wait a minute," Cole said. "Is that what you saw? You know, when we were out in the yard by the porch?"

"It was tough to cover up my surprise. I check the stars every night, just in case. There's never anything there, but I still check. The last thing I expected was to see my little star above me. It scared me."

"And Durny decided you should run."

"Yes. In a way, the star caused his death. The star is probably more than a warning, since it has remained in the sky. A warning would only have stayed for a night or two. But since the star moves with me, a messenger could follow us wherever we went. After I told Durny about the star, he wanted to gather some floatstones to make a skycraft."

"Why not just steal a lifeboat?" Cole wondered.

"Runaway slaves get treated harshly," Mira said. "The Sky Raiders would be angry enough without us stealing from them. According to our plan, while collecting floatstones, Durny would have smuggled some extras. He would have assembled the skycraft outside of Skyport so we could leave at any time. We would have flown our little skycraft to the end of the Brink, near one of the cloudwalls, let it fall off the edge once we were done with it, and headed inland on foot. We would have disappeared without a trace."

Cole leaned forward on the couch. "Do you still want to make a run for it?"

"I don't *want* to escape," she said. "It's incredibly risky. The Sky Raiders will come after me and punish me if they catch me. But my mother's warning was as clear last night as the first, and it wouldn't be there if this wasn't something important. If I run off, I might avoid the danger, and the messenger should still be able to find me."

"What if it's just an important message? What if there's no big threat?"

"Then I don't need to run. But the message almost certainly means horrible trouble. Probably life or death. I can't risk standing still. Durny stalled too long already trying to get permission to personally gather floatstones."

Cole considered all she was telling him. He could think of only one reason she would reveal so much. "Are you asking me to run away with you?"

She stared at him. "I've already waited for too long. I need to leave. The only questions are when, and how, and whether you want to come with me."

Cole buried his face in his hands. This was a lot to digest. He had wanted to escape ever since he came here. He needed to go find his friends. It would be great to have company—especially someone who knew a lot about the Outskirts. And Mira apparently knew how he could find the High King.

"If we get away, could you show me how to find my friends?" Cole asked.

"I could tell you the way to Junction City," Mira said. "But you'd be crazy to try to take slaves from the High King on your own." Mira lowered her voice. "I know people who want to see the High King fall. People who could help you find your friends. People who could give you a chance to succeed."

"Really?" Cole asked, not daring to believe her.

"I want the High Shaper to lose his throne," Mira whispered. "If we can get away, I'll help you get the aid you need."

Cole was so relieved that he wanted to hug her. This was better than he could have hoped! The thought that he might not have to rescue his friends alone and unguided lifted an oppressive weight from him.

But they hadn't escaped yet. Mira had people after her, and they were both marked slaves. How far could they get without being discovered?

"How do you think we should do it?" Cole asked.

"You'll come?" The hopeful relief in her voice helped cement his resolve.

"As long as we put together a decent plan."

"You don't have to let me drag you into this. The coming danger probably isn't a threat to you unless you're with me."

"Good point. You're on your own."

She stared at him uncomfortably. "I understand."

He grinned. "I'm joking. It's just funny that you're asking for help and trying to talk me out of it at the same time. Mira, I'd do anything to save my friends. If I can help you, too, that's even better."

"We can definitely help each other," Mira said. "But even though I'll try to help, don't forget that getting involved with me could get you killed. The High Shaper hates me, and he hates the people I know who might help you. The secrets I know are dangerous to him. If you get mixed up with me, he'll end up hating you, too."

"I kind of hope he does," Cole said. "He took my friends as slaves. I'm not a fan."

Mira took a deep breath. "Okay. So we're going to escape together."

"The question is how."

"That's where it gets complicated. On foot, leaving at night would be reckless this close to the Brink, but we'll get noticed quickly if we sneak away during the day. Whether we take off on foot, or even if we steal horses, they'll be after us in no time. I don't think we'd make it."

"Can we steal a skycraft?"

"You need to wear an operator's stone to steer one," Mira said. "Otherwise it won't respond. I know where Durny hid a few in case we needed a lifeboat in an emergency. But taking one will make the Sky Raiders doubly mad at us. They'll know how we got away, and they'll hunt us relentlessly."

"What if you mess with the coffin?" Cole suggested. "Could you make it so you could steer it?"

"I could try." Mira sighed. "I'm not sure I could pull it off. I haven't done anything like that on my own before. I'm sure the other shapers have already taken the floatstones to use for a new lifeboat. Adam will want to replace the one we lost as quickly as possible."

Cole folded his hands. "They'll be plenty mad at us for leaving. If stealing a lifeboat helps our chances of getting away, I think we should risk making them even madder."

Mira nodded. "That makes sense. It's probably our only realistic option."

"When were you thinking of going?"

She grimaced. "Soon. Probably early tomorrow morning, after they open up the landing bay but before any skycraft head out. They're quick to seal the bay when the skycraft return at the end of the day."

"They'll chase us," Cole said. "The skycraft can't fly far over land, right?"

"A few hundred yards at best," Mira said. "The float-stones only work in the sky beyond the Brink."

"Tomorrow?"

After glancing cautiously at the door, Mira gave a serious nod. "Tomorrow."

MESSENGER

A stranger came through the front door while Cole was snacking in the common area. Twitch sat nearby, elbows on the table, gnawing at a large beef rib. Mira ate fruit on the other side of the room.

Cole had been watching everyone eat and talk with a strange sense of distance. This would be his last day here. In the morning he and Mira would make a run for it. No more meals prepared for him. No more Twitch or Jace or Adam or any of the other people. Also, no more salvaging missions where he risked death on a regular basis. And he'd finally get a real chance to find Dalton and Jenna. If he ended up back here, he and Mira would have failed, and who knew what punishments might await?

A pair of salvagers escorted the stranger. He wore dark jeans, dusty boots, and a gray leather jacket with black stripes down the sleeves. As the stranger considered the room, he showed relaxed interest rather than fear. He was of medium height, with his hair cropped short and stubble on his chin and cheeks. He might have been as young as thirty, but probably closer to forty.

Many had paused eating to watch as the stranger was escorted to where Adam sat on his jade throne. "Who is this?" Adam asked.

"He wants to see you," said one of his escorts.

"I don't know this guy," Adam said. "You looking to join us?"

"No," the man said.

"Buyers talk to Rowly or Hollis. Traders talk to Finch."

"I need to speak with *you*," the man said. He gave the room a sweeping glance. "In private."

"Ha!" Adam shouted, slapping his hand on the arm of his throne. "We all hold shares of this business, friend, or we all will if we live long enough, so what you'd say to one, you can say to all."

"How democratic," the man said without approval. "Look, my news isn't fit for all ears."

Adam narrowed his eyes. "What's your name, stranger?"

"Joe MacFarland."

"You from Zeropolis?"

"What gave it away?"

"Besides your clothes, your attitude, and the weapon tucked away near your left armpit? Joe, you're far from home, so I'll cut you a break. These people flirt with death on a regular basis. Your message won't rattle anyone half as much as you think. Enough treadmilling. Let's have it."

Joe sighed. "There's a large detachment from the Junction Legion heading this way. They want to seize one of your slaves."

Cole met eyes with Mira from across the room. They

looked away from each other hurriedly. It didn't have to be her, did it? But the High Shaper lived in Junction, and her mother had sent a warning.

"Legionnaires?" Adam asked incredulously. "Nobody is going to waltz in here and dance away with one of my slaves. The High Shaper is one of my top customers."

"The High Shaper wants this slave much more than he wants your trinkets," Joe said. "We're talking about four hundred trained soldiers."

"Four hundred?" Adam blustered. "Do you know what it would take to send four hundred legionnaires from Junction to the Brink? Most of the land between us is empty!"

"I counted," Joe said calmly. "The High Shaper isn't playing games. They'd burn your operation to the ground to get what they want."

"I'd like to see them try," Adam said staunchly.

Several voices around the room lent support.

"Do nothing, and they'll take what they came for," Joe warned. "You can't guess the value of this person. Let me smuggle the slave away from here. If they search the place and their quarry is gone, that should mark the end of your troubles." Looking around, he hesitated. "Can't we finish this in private?"

"Search our place?" Adam complained. "Listen, friend. Nobody crosses the High Shaper. He's bad news to his enemies. I get that. But the Brink is the edge of the map, a long way from anywhere, and this operation has been running for hundreds of years. I don't care how many men they have, we're not going to let anyone push us around, especially not in our home. What sort of scam are you running? Smells like you're the shyster after one of my slaves."

"No con," Joe said. "I'm not after handouts. I'll pay you twice the fair value for the slave. You'll be out nothing. But the legion will be here soon. If we're to have a chance, we need to go."

"Which slave are we discussing?" Adam asked. "Nearly all of us were slaves at some point. You here for me?"

Joe gave a rueful glance around the room. "That detail can only be shared in private. The information is dangerous to anyone who hears it."

Adam folded his hands. "Then I fail to see why I should hurry to lend an ear."

Joe sighed. "You'll be dealing with the issue soon enough. The legion isn't far behind me. Delay, and your options will shrink. You'll end up betraying one of your own. Do you want the High Shaper to prove that he can take whatever he wishes from you? They'll be diplomatic at first, but one way or another, they'll claim their prize."

"What slave?" one of the raiders asked.

"Out with it," another demanded.

Hands on his hips, Joe shook his head and stared at the floor.

"Is this about Cole?" Adam guessed. "He's our newest acquisition."

All eyes turned to Cole, who shrank down in his seat. Joe followed their gazes to him and gave a little huff. "I'm not telling. I don't want to be mysterious or difficult. It would just be safer for everyone if we settle this quietly."

Adam put his boots up on a footstool. "You're failing at mysterious, but you're overskilled at difficult. We all know one another here, Joe. If someone vanishes, everybody in this room will realize who departed."

"Not immediately," Joe said. "And they won't know why. We need all the time and secrecy we can get."

Adam scowled. "Who would the High Shaper care about? Is it Durny? Our lead shaper? If so, you're too late. He's beyond all reach."

"Not him," Joe affirmed.

Cole avoided looking at Mira. He felt sick with worry. They had to be talking about her.

Adam raised his voice. "Any sign of legionnaires?"

"We've seen hints of a big group approaching," a voice answered near the door. "Really big. Thought it might be a herd of buffalo. Could be riders. If so, it's lots of them."

"Hundreds of them," Joe added.

Adam stood up. He was taller than Joe, with a thicker build. "I'm not sure whether you're trying to solve our problem, cause it, or just profit by it."

"I can make it all clear in private," Joe insisted.

"I'll tell the others, soon as we're done."

"I'm willing to take that chance."

Adam considered him shrewdly.

"Incoming riders" came a shout from outside. "Three legionnaires."

"We're out of time," Joe said urgently.

"Advance party," Adam said. "Might be wise to hear both sides of this."

"They'll lie," Joe said. "They'll pressure you. Lend an ear, and you'll end by handing over the slave."

Pounding hoofbeats approached outside. Everyone turned their attention to the door.

"You skipped your chance to state your side," Adam said.

Joe stepped close to Adam and whispered something. The men escorting Joe moved to intervene. Eyes widening, Adam lifted a hand to stop his men from interfering. Adam whispered something back. The stranger whispered something else.

"You want to hide?" Adam asked.

"Only if you give me the slave."

Adam furrowed his brow.

The hoofbeats stopped near the door. Joe stepped away, taking a seat at a table. Adam returned to his throne. A man in a dark-blue uniform with gold trim came through the door, followed by two others, all three striding confidently. They each wore swords at their hips and held helmets under their arms.

"Captain Scott Pickett looking for Adam Jones," the legionnaire in front announced. He had a small neatly trimmed mustache. His sweaty hair was plastered to his head from wearing the helmet.

"You found me, Pickett," Adam said. "I don't know your face. What brings you to the edge of the world?"

"An errand of small weight to you but of great import to our leaders," Pickett said. "Might we confer in private?"

"We conduct our business publicly around here," Adam said. "Most of those present share ownership in the operation."

"As you will," Pickett said efficiently. He seemed slightly unsettled, but he kept his gaze on Adam. "A slave was stolen some time ago from the High King. His Majesty would like her returned. We have traced her to this location. At present, we do not hold you at fault in the matter—you would not have known she was stolen property."

Cole refused to let himself look at Mira. She had told him she wasn't a slave before she left the High Shaper. The soldier must be lying to get what he wanted.

Shooting a quick glance at Joe, Adam shifted in his seat. "All the slaves here are bought and paid for."

Pickett nodded briskly. "Understood. Considering the inconvenience, we will offer you five times her value."

Adam whistled softly. "Slaves don't come cheap. If she's already the High Shaper's property, why offer so much?"

"She is dear to the High King, and he wants the matter resolved."

"You have her papers?"

"The matter is . . . delicate," Pickett hedged.

"Surely you have proof of ownership."

"You have the word of the legion and of the High King."

Adam rubbed his mouth. "If you can spare five times her value, surely you could offer ten."

Pickett paused. "I expect that could be arranged."

Cole squeezed the edge of the table where he sat. Was Adam going to bargain with him? If so, Mira needed to run for it immediately.

"I see," Adam said. "And if ten, why not a hundred?"

"Now let's not—"

Adam held up a finger in protest. "The High Shaper has deep pockets, the matter is sensitive, and I'm a broker of rare valuables. Why not a thousand?"

Pickett straightened, his expression hardening. "Do not imagine you can abuse the legion, sir. The High King would prefer this to be handled with civility. He appreciates the value of your operation. But he will not hesitate to take what belongs to him. Commander Rainier is coming with a number of men."

"Four hundred?"

"At least."

Adam narrowed his eyes. "Why send so many men for a single slave you can't prove you own?"

"We're not just here for the slave," Pickett said. "We're also on our way to deal with Carnag."

"Carnag?" Adam repeated. "The High King is finally getting involved?"

Pickett ran a hand through his hair. "The reports about the monster are most disturbing. We've seen some oddities across the five kingdoms, but never anything quite like this. It's emptying towns quicker than a plague. Local militia and small groups of legionnaires haven't even been able to get reliable information."

Frowning, Adam stared at Pickett. "Who is the slave?"

"She presently goes by Mira."

Unlike the rest of the room, Cole didn't swivel to stare at his friend. The revelation came as no shock. At least now he knew for sure.

Jace sprang to his feet. "Mira? What do you want with Mira?"

Pickett looked from Mira to Jace. "I want nothing. I'm under orders. None of you know this slave. Not really. She is here under false pretenses. The High King will have his property returned."

In the distance, Cole heard the drumming of many hooves. Others in the room seemed to notice the rumble as well. All else was quiet for a moment as they listened.

Pickett cleared his throat into his gloved fist. "Please believe me that this business will conclude much more pleasantly if we resolve the matter before Commander Rainier arrives."

Cole risked a glance at Mira. Her eyes were wide. She looked panicked and uncertain. The situation was unraveling. They had to get away. What could he do?

"The girl has some shaping skills," Adam said. "It makes her natural value at least five times more than a talentless slave."

"Understood."

"And you'll give us ten times her value?"

"Fifty times the value of a common slave? I suspect that could be arranged."

"You suspect or you're sure? Are you empowered to negotiate or not?"

Picket rubbed his mustache. "Very well. If it will settle the matter without a disturbance, done."

Cole got up and started toward the hall to the back door. If he skirted the walls, keeping away from the center of the room, he might be able to slip away unnoticed. Twitch looked at him questioningly, but Cole subtly waved away the attention. A few other men glanced his way, but most kept their eyes on the negotiation.

Adam rubbed his hands together. "That's a generous offer. Seems almost too good to be true. Deals seldom are. Makes me wonder what I'm missing."

"The High King wants the girl and would prefer to have the matter settled quietly," Pickett replied. "Even so, you have my best offer. I won't agree to more."

Cole reached the hall to the back door. He turned his back to the negotiation and started down the corridor. Just a few more steps and he would pass out of view from the common area.

"Where do you think you're going, boy?" Pickett asked sharply.

Cole froze. Trying to stay composed, he turned to find the legionnaire staring at him, along with everyone else in the room.

"I have to pee," Cole apologized. "I was trying to hold it. When you have to, you have to." Forcing a small smile, he crossed his legs.

Pickett waved a dismissive hand. "Fine. Be quick about it."

Cole hurried down the hall and broke into a sprint once he knew he was out of sight. He raced out the back door and heard the thunder of approaching horses much more clearly. The legion wasn't at their doorstep yet, but judging from the sound, it would only be a minute or two before the first soldiers arrived.

He found the bow and the shawl under the deck right where he had left them. Would he really shoot those soldiers?

For Mira, if he had to, yeah, maybe. There might be a big army coming, but Cole doubted their horses could fly. Mira had to get aboard a skycraft.

Items in hand, Cole rushed through other halls to reach his room. If they were going to try to get away, he needed his gear. He strapped on the Jumping Sword as he exited and then settled the shawl over his shoulders. He returned to the common room from the hall that led to the stairs to the skycraft hanger. The drumming of hooves was slowing down right outside.

On his feet now, Adam was shaking hands with Pickett. "You've purchased one very expensive slave," Adam said.

"You drive a hard bargain," Pickett replied.

Releasing his hand, Adam shrugged. "It's how we scrape by."

Nobody had noticed Cole return. Was he really going to do this? Adam had sold Mira. Any second, more soldiers would enter. Cole didn't want to see her get captured, and he couldn't lose his one link to finding his friends. It was now or never.

Heart pounding, Cole raised his bow and pulled the string back until an arrow appeared. Keeping the feathers near his cheek, he pointed the arrow at Pickett. Nobody was looking his way.

"Not so fast!" Cole yelled.

That got their attention.

Pickett and the two other legionnaires placed their hands on the hilts of their swords. Pickett glared at Adam. "What is this?"

Adam raised both hands. "Not my doing. That boy is a slave, not an owner. He'll wish he was never born after we disarm him. The girl is yours. If she runs, we'll help give chase. You've got too many comrades out there. I don't want the deal spoiled."

On the far side of the room, the front door opened, revealing a sea of legionnaires. Beyond the mob pressing toward the doorway, Cole could see others on horseback, some dismounting. The first couple of legionnaires stepped through.

"Now, Mira!" Cole called. "Time to go."

Chapter

— 17 —

FLIGHT

For a moment all was still. The legionnaires at the front door halted. Cole was undoubtedly the center of attention—some of it confused, much of it angry.

Then Mira lunged from her seat and the spell was broken.

Pickett and his two comrades drew their swords and rushed forward in a crouch, using the raiders at the tables as shields. The legionnaires at the door drew their weapons and burst in as well.

Joe sprang from his chair and tackled Pickett hard. Leaping up, Joe produced a silver tube and pointed it at one of the other legionnaires. When nothing happened, he slapped it, then pointed it again.

One of the legionnaires was moving quickly enough to cut off Mira's escape. Cole pivoted and prepared to release his arrow.

Before he let it fly, a golden lash snapped forward, coiling around the legionnaire's boots and jerking him into the air. The lash flung the soldier brutally against a wooden support beam, and he folded with a loud grunt and crumpled to the floor. Jace held the other end of the golden rope.

Mira raced past Cole, who held his position, bow bent, covering her escape. Jace whipped a second legionnaire in the face with his golden lash, and diving over a table, Joe blindsided the stunned soldier.

"Don't spoil this, men!" Adam bellowed. "After her!"

All around the room, raiders sprang to their feet. Many shuffled toward Cole. Another large group headed for the hall to the back door. Cole noticed Pickett slip into that hall, ahead of the mass of raiders.

Outrunning the other raiders, Jace and Twitch dashed by Cole. "Let's get her out of here," Jace gasped without slowing.

Sidestepping so he could face backward, Cole retreated, arrow nocked and ready. The oncoming raiders collided with one another as they crammed from the wide room into the bottleneck of the hallway. Some stumbled and fell, further clogging the passage. Jostling one another, they grimaced and elbowed and made slow progress. Eli was among the foremost. Giving Cole a meaningful look, he motioned for him to run.

Suddenly Cole got it. The raiders hadn't turned into clumsy fools. They were deliberately blocking the hallways to give him a chance.

Turning, he sprinted down the hall until he reached the stairs to the caves. Bounding down recklessly, he followed the only underground route he knew well—the way to the landing bay. He could hear people running ahead of him—probably Jace and Twitch.

Why had the raiders decided to help them? Would they keep the halls plugged for long? He had no answers, but he knew that if Mira didn't get in the air quickly, she probably wouldn't get the chance. It was well into the afternoon. The salvaging parties had all returned. Would the landing bay be sealed? If so, could they open it?

While making his way toward the hangar, Cole heard footfalls behind him. Glancing back, he saw Mira. He slowed to let her catch up.

"Why are you behind me?" he asked.

"I had to swing by my room," she said breathlessly, reaching him and then passing him. "We need an operator's stone to fly a lifeboat." He saw that she had grabbed her Jumping Sword as well.

Cole ran hard. Keeping up with Mira was a challenge. Her full sprint was a little faster than his.

They burst through the entrance to the landing bay to find all the cliffside exits closed. The hangar was sealed up tight, the three big skycraft looming in the lamplight.

Jace was yelling at an older guy named Martin.

"Adam will have your head if you don't open it now!" Jace cried. "It's a Situation Spoiled. He said it twice."

"And if you're lying?" Martin replied.

"Then we'll be the ones in hot water!" Jace shouted.

"He's not lying," Twitch said.

"I have a stone," Mira called, drawing her Jumping Sword and leaping aboard the *Vulture*.

Keeping hold of one end, Jace threw his golden rope toward the *Vulture*. Uncoiling, it stretched out longer than

Cole had seen it reach before, and the far end snaked around the mast. The rope then abruptly shortened, lifting Jace off his feet and pulling him aboard. After he landed on the deck, the rope unraveled from the mast.

Cole didn't hear footsteps until just before Captain Pickett burst into the landing bay, sword in hand. Whirling, Cole pulled the arrow back and aimed low, at the legionnaire's legs. Less than ten feet separated Cole from the officer. As Cole released, Pickett dodged sideways, and the arrow streaked past him.

Pickett lunged forward and Cole skipped away, yanking the bowstring back until another arrow appeared. Pickett charged straight, Cole released the arrow, and it pierced the officer's thigh. Cole scurried aside as Pickett went to the ground with an anguished growl. Nobody came racing into the room behind him. For now, the legionnaire was alone.

Drawing his Jumping Sword, Cole pointed it at the deck of the *Vulture* and shouted, "Away!" As usual, the leap made his insides flutter. He held tightly to the sword as it hauled him up, over the railing, and onto the deck where he landed in a stumble. Twitch ran aboard the *Vulture* using the gangplank.

Mira and Jace were climbing into a lifeboat called the *Fair-Weather Friend*. Turning a wheel set against the wall, Martin began opening one of the smaller cliffside exits, not much bigger than a typical garage door. Late-afternoon daylight streamed into the hangar, outshining the lamps.

Cole hurried to the lifeboat. Jace sat in the rear by the tiller. A smooth, dark stone hung from a chain around his neck. He gave Cole a flat stare. "You coming?"

Twitch reached the lifeboat and jumped in as Cole hopped inside.

"You sure, Twitch?" Jace asked.

"I'm with you," he responded.

"Hurry!" Pickett cried out. "They're aboard the *Vulture*!"

Jace grabbed the tiller and tugged one of the levers. The lifeboat lurched forward, rocking Cole back. He clung desperately to the gunwale as the boat tilted enough to almost dump him over the side. After rearing up too steeply, the *Fair-Weather Friend* leveled out and dipped its nose toward the cliffside opening.

Legionnaires streamed into the room, swords drawn, some bearing bows. From his position on the floor, Pickett gestured manically at the fleeing lifeboat.

"Stop them!" Pickett cried. "Close the hatch!"

Several of the other legionnaires forcefully repeated the command as they raced toward the widening exit. Cole slouched down as arrows hissed into the air, some striking the stern of the lifeboat near Jace.

"You out of arrows?" Jace asked Cole, the skycraft wobbling as he tried to crouch and steer at the same time.

Cole wasn't anxious to raise his head, but some shots at the legionnaires would force them to take cover and slow their attack. He sat up, pulled back his bowstring, and sent an arrow toward the soldiers, then repeated the action again and again, a new arrow appearing every time. Keeping low, Cole took little aim, focusing instead on speed and on not getting shot. An arrow whistled past, almost close enough to scratch him, and he ducked down again. More arrows thumped against the hull.

"Hold your fire!" Pickett called, his voice strained. "You might hit the girl. Block their escape!"

To Cole's horror, he saw Martin slumped against the wall, pierced by three arrows. Mouth open, head lolling, the raider looked up at them blankly, one of his hands twitching. The lifeboat had almost reached the exit! The hatch hadn't been raised very much, and many legionnaires were charging their way. It would be close.

"Heads down," Jace ordered as the lifeboat rasped through the gap, the keel scraping the landing bay door.

After ducking, Cole looked back to see legionnaires appear in the cliffside opening. As the *Fair-Weather Friend* climbed away from the landing bay at full speed, Cole released arrow after arrow back at the opening, forcing the soldiers to stand aside. They got off a few arrows, but none hit the lifeboat.

"We're leveling off?" Cole asked.

"If we climb too fast, the cavalry will use us for target practice," Jace replied. "We'll go higher once we're farther from the Brink."

"Of course today has to be clear," Twitch grumbled.

Cole looked around. The sun was dropping toward the dark mass of the Western Cloudwall. The only normal clouds were high and wispy. The castles were few and distant. "Not many places to hide."

"How long before they come after us?" Mira asked.

"They'll demand skycraft," Jace said. "Adam is in no position to deny them. He'll stall a little, but not for long. Situation Spoiled doesn't call for direct resistance."

"They'll also track us from the cliff top," Twitch said. "Even at top speed, a lifeboat can't outpace a horse."

"Maybe not at full gallop," Jace said, "but a horse can't gallop forever."

"The legion has good horses," Twitch said. "They can probably gallop long enough to keep us from landing on the Brink before they have the skycraft after us. Even if we get ahead of them, on a day like today they'll see where we return to the cliff and track us down."

"If we're doomed, why'd you come?" Jace snapped in frustration.

Twitch gave a little shrug. "I'm done with Skyport. We risk our lives on every mission. This seemed dangerous, but I'll take one big risk over all the missions I have left. If we can stay free until nightfall, we might slip away into the darkness."

The lifeboat was climbing again. Skyport shrank behind them, the horses and the legionnaires becoming an army of ants. With the fresh breeze in his face and the warm sun about to set, Cole could almost forget they were still in danger.

"What are our assets?" Jace asked. "I have my rope. Mira and Cole have their Jumping Swords. Where'd you score the bow, Cole?"

"On our last mission," Cole said. "I stashed it away in case I needed it."

Jace whistled. "That could have gotten you in deep trouble. I won't complain, though. How long until it runs out of arrows?"

"Supposedly, never."

"That'll be useful if they get close," Jace said. "You have rotten aim, but you can make up for it with volume. By the way, when a guy is coming for you, don't shoot at his legs. If it's worth shooting him, it's worth shooting him dead. Aim for the middle of his chest. Trying to wing an enemy will get you killed."

"I didn't want to kill the guy just for doing his job," Cole said, a little embarrassed by the reprimand.

"His job was to kill you," Jace said. "They obviously want Mira alive, but they'd take out the rest of us without losing any sleep."

"He's right, Cole," Twitch said. "The legion plays for keeps."

"How about you, Twitch?" Jace asked. "What do you have that might help us?"

"Nice try," Twitch said.

"It's not a game anymore," Jace insisted. "Tell us."

"It was never a game," Twitch replied, wringing his fingers. "I kept my special item secret before, and I'll keep it secret now. Knowing what it is won't affect our plans. You'll find out if I have to use it."

"Can it camouflage us?" Jace asked. "Make us invisible? Knock a skycraft out of the air?"

"If I could do something like that, I'd tell you. My secret won't affect our strategy."

"What *is* our strategy?" Mira asked. "Try to evade them until it gets dark? Hope for a moonless night?"

"The landing bay is opening up," Cole said, eyes on the cliff. "All three of the big entrances."

Jace nodded. "We'll head as far away from the Brink as

we can. A lifeboat is a bit faster than the big skycraft. We'll veer toward the Eastern Cloudwall. It's almost twice as far from us as the Western Cloudwall, so we'll have more room to maneuver. Plus, there are more castles that way."

"How many do you count east of us?" Twitch asked.

"Five," Jace replied.

"Six," Twitch said, pointing. "You probably missed that little one down low."

Jace leaned eastward and squinted. "You're right, I missed that one. Not that it matters. It's almost to the cloud-wall. We couldn't get there before it vanishes."

"Do you think we could hide out at one of the castles?" Cole asked.

"Might be worth a try as a last resort," Mira said. "The problem is that any castle safe enough to hide us will probably be easy to attack. We could end up cornered."

"If they have a bunch of skycraft, they might corner us in the air," Cole said. "Maybe one of the castles has defenses, like the catapults at Parona."

"It might be worth checking out," Jace said. "But only because we have so few options."

"This won't be easy," Mira said. "I'm sorry."

"You didn't make us come," Jace said.

"Why'd you stick your neck out for me?" Mira asked.

Jace shrugged, looking away from her. "They had no proof you belonged to them. It made me mad to think of them taking you away."

Cole wondered if Mira really didn't get how much Jace liked her. She seemed oblivious.

"It made you mad, so you attacked legionnaires and ran away with us?" Mira asked.

"I have a bad temper," Jace mumbled.

"Did you really used to belong to the High Shaper?" Twitch asked.

"Who are you to probe at secrets?" Mira complained.

Blinking rapidly, Twitch gave a nervous chuckle. "I'm one of the guys who ran away with you and might get killed for it. I'm just wondering if their claim is legit."

"The High Shaper knows me," Mira said. "I was never his slave. I shouldn't say more. It could put you in even greater danger."

"Here come the skycraft," Cole said, watching as the *Vulture*, the *Borrower*, and the even the damaged *Domingo* glided out of the landing bay openings and away from the cliff.

"We're in hot water already," Jace said. "We'll probably end up captured, falling, or dead. What's the Big Shaper's attachment to you?"

"It's complicated," Mira said. "I'm not really a slave. The mark is real, but it's a cover. Durny was helping me hide. Is that enough?"

"I guess, if it's all you want to spill," Jace said. "Did you know that guy from Zeropolis? Joe?"

"I've never seen him before," Mira said, glancing at Cole. "I think he knows who I am."

"I hope so." Jace chuckled. "He probably got himself killed for you." He paused. "The High Shaper sent four hundred legionnaires to track you down. That's the craziest part. Why would he do that for anyone?"

"It was for Carnag, too," Mira reminded him.

"Right, but the Brink is a good distance out of the way," Jace said. "They could have sent a smaller group. But all four hundred came. Why?"

"Good question," Twitch murmured, biting his thumbnail.

Mira looked at them. "The visit from the legion means I'm in serious trouble. The less you get involved, the better. My secret isn't fun. It would make you targets for the rest of your lives."

"We'll probably get killed, anyway," Jace said. "It would be nice to know why."

Mira sighed. "Okay. Here's the short version. The High Shaper is a monster. I know some things about the death of his five daughters. He planned it. He got away with murder. I even have proof. He would do anything to keep that secret."

"You're serious," Jace said, astonished.

She nodded. "Four-hundred-legionnaires serious."

Everyone kept silent for a long moment.

"The skycraft are spreading out," Twitch reported. "They've deployed all the lifeboats. While heading this way, they're also cutting off any retreat to the Brink."

"Can we just keep flying away from the Brink?" Cole asked. "It looks like it goes forever."

"It might," Jace said darkly. "We can't. If we get far enough from the Brink, the sky won't hold us anymore. The same thing happens if we go too high, too low, or inland. It doesn't change all at once. We'll feel the boat start to slip when we get too far out, beyond where any of the castles go, near where the cloudwalls end."

"The cloudwalls end?" Cole exclaimed. "Can we go around them?"

"The skycraft won't work that far out," Twitch said. "There's no way over, under, or around them."

Cole frowned. "We're boxed in."

"Pretty much," Jace agreed.

"Think we can dodge them until dark?" Cole wondered.

Jace stared at the oncoming skycraft. "We're about to find out."

CLOUDWALL

As the sun sank into the Western Cloudwall, Jace tried to keep the *Fair-Weather Friend* away from the oncoming swarm of skycraft, which included the three large vessels, along with seven lifeboats. The plan to escape the legion by skycraft looked worse and worse as the persistent armada cut off any attempt to double back, herding them away from the Brink and toward the dead end of the Eastern Cloudwall.

From what Cole could see, the skycraft mostly contained uniformed legionnaires, with raiders at the controls and also manning some of the weapons on the larger vessels. The pursuing skycraft moved with ruthless coordination, climbing when they rose, dropping when they dived, crowding them toward a corner with no escape.

Cole and the others had checked the castles they could reach ahead of the other skycraft. One had been crafted out of black metal and looked like a certain death trap. Another had crumbled to ruins, offering scant cover. A third was made of crystal, again leaving nowhere to hide. With the skycraft hounding them relentlessly, there was no time to plan. They could only flee and pray for darkness.

The *Fair-Weather Friend* swerved farther away from the Brink and began to shudder. It dropped jerkily, leaning hard to the right. Jace curved the little craft back toward the distant Brink. "If we go any farther out, we'll fall."

Cole looked back at where the sun had disappeared behind the Western Cloudwall. That side of the sky remained bright red and orange. It would still be close to an hour before the true darkness of night. He glanced at the other skycraft drawing nearer, leaving no room for evasion.

"They've got us," Cole said. "We don't have enough room to run until it gets dark. We have to try to break through them."

Jace shook his head. "If we charge between them, they'll just close in from all sides. We'll get swarmed. They have grappling hooks and plenty of weapons. We don't stand a chance of getting past them."

"He's right," Twitch said, licking his lips. "Avoiding risk is my specialty. Charging through them won't work."

The Eastern Cloudwall loomed closer than ever. Impenetrably dark and unnaturally flat, the cloudbank stretched high and low, left and right. Cole squeezed his bow. None of the other skycraft were close enough to hit with an arrow yet, but the nearest weren't out of range by much. "We've got maybe ten more minutes of running room."

"Twitch," Jace said. "What else can we try?"

"They want Mira," Twitch said, tapping his fingers rapidly against his knee. "Maybe we can bluff. If we threaten to fly into the cloudwall, they might back off."

"Try to stall them until it gets dark?" Mira asked.

"It's worth a shot," Jace said. "Unless anybody has another idea."

Cole could see no other solution. If they tried to fly through their pursuers, they wouldn't succeed. If they tried to fight, it would be even worse. The only option was to keep flying toward the cloudwall.

"What if they call our bluff?" Cole worried.

Jace frowned. "We'll have no escape. If they ignore the bluff, and we don't fly into the cloudwall, they'll swoop in and take us in seconds."

"It's a pretty weak option if we're not willing to follow through," Twitch said.

"If we fly into the cloudwall, we'll be killed," Cole said. "At least if they capture us, we'll have a chance to live."

"I might live," Mira said. "For a while. As a prisoner. They'll want to question me—try to confirm what I know and who I've told. You guys are runaway slaves. Jace hurt some soldiers. Cole shot an officer. You all helped me. They know I could have shared my secret. They'll execute you."

"We don't *know* that going into the cloudwall will kill us," Twitch said slowly. "We just know that nobody has returned."

"Now you're talking crazy," Jace said.

"Am I?" Twitch replied, tapping his knuckles together. "They won't follow us in there. We could just go in a little, barely out of sight. My instincts feel better about that than letting them have us."

"We bluff first, though," Cole clarified.

"Of course," Mira said. "But if they keep coming anyway, we take cover in the cloudwall. And if we can't get back out, we try to survive it."

Jace chuckled bitterly. "If you're going to die, you might as well be doing something really, really stupid."

Cole peered over the side of the lifeboat at the infinite drop. None of them had parachutes—there hadn't been time to grab them. He gazed ahead at the imposing cloudwall. What dangers was it hiding? Would it grind them to atoms? Did it house deadly monsters? Or was there some other explanation for why people never returned? Could it be a one-way portal to some other place?

As the cloudwall drew near, the other skycraft closed in. Cole kept his bow ready. The *Vulture* was probably within range now, as were two of the lifeboats. But many of the legionnaires had bows. If everyone started shooting, Cole doubted whether he and his friends would survive.

Mira stood up. "Back away from us!" she shouted. "Leave us alone or we'll enter the cloudwall!"

A man on the *Vulture* raised his voice to answer. He had gray hair and a prominent nose. "We would rather take you alive, child, but we can't help it if you destroy yourself. Do what you must."

"Take us in," Mira muttered. "Hurry."

"You sure?" Jace whispered back. "Even if they kill the rest of us, you might still live."

"I'm not so sure," Mira said. "I'll take my chances with the cloudwall. Don't let them get too close. Go for it."

Fingers tight on his bow, Cole glanced over at the

cloudwall. It was less than a minute away. The closer they got to the foggy barrier, the clearer it became that the wall wasn't perfectly flat—some indistinct mistiness on the surface caught the glow of the sunset. Did that mean there might be a hazy space before the true cloudwall began, a place where they could hide?

"Don't be fools!" the man from the *Vulture* cried. "You don't want to suffer a horrible death in that darkness. Mira, if you come to me, I will spare the three slaves who aided you."

"I don't believe you," Mira yelled back.

"I am Commander Rainier, highest-ranked officer of the legion," the man replied loudly. "It is well within my power to make this deal. I swear by my office and by my good name, before all witnesses present, that your three companions will be returned to their master unharmed if you end this folly and turn yourself in."

Arms hugging her chest, Mira glanced down at the others.

"Don't give in for me," Jace said, still guiding the lifeboat at full speed toward the cloudwall.

"Me either," Cole said, unsure whether he fully meant it.

"Up to you," Twitch said.

Mira scrunched her eyebrows and stared down. "I'm willing to chance it, but it's not fair to force you three into this."

"He's pulling your strings," Jace said. "Don't let him use us against you. If you give up because of me, I swear I'll jump. Plus, he could be lying. Who knows? Maybe we'll survive the cloudwall. Forget about us. Do what you want to do."

"No thanks!" Mira called.

"Stop them!" Commander Rainier roared. "Stop them at all costs!"

Grappling hooks came flying through the air, three from the *Vulture*, one from a lifeboat. One grapnel missed. Jace kicked another that would have landed in the stern, knocking it away. Two fell inside the lifeboat and pulled tight against the side, instantly slowing them and causing them to turn.

Dropping his bow and drawing his Jumping Sword, Cole severed one of the lines attached to the grapnel. Mira cut the other one.

All the vessels converged at top speed. More grappling hooks came flying. Cole batted one out of the air with his sword. Twitch nimbly caught another and tossed it aside. A few fell short. When one caught hold of the lifeboat again, Mira promptly slashed the line.

"Fools!" Commander Rainier shouted.

Glancing over his shoulder, Cole saw the murky surface of the cloudwall perhaps five seconds away. Was this how he would die? Would it hurt? Would he even know he had been killed? He had to hope that they could duck out of sight and lurk at the edge of the cloudbank until nightfall.

Cole looked back at the *Vulture*, where Commander Rainier had a hand extended toward them, face distorted with panic and anger. He realized that with his Jumping Sword, the *Vulture* was comfortably within range. What if he took his chances with the legionnaires? No, that wouldn't end well. Having lost Mira, they would make an example of him.

Mira and Twitch pulled Cole down. Only then did he

realize that the others were no longer standing. They were bracing themselves. Sheathing his sword, he followed their example.

"Hold on!" Jace yelled. "Here we go!"

The prow of the *Fair-Weather Friend* nosed into the mist. Everything became hazy. Cole could hardly see Mira beside him. A moment later, damp darkness completely enveloped them. Looking back, Cole could no longer see outside the cloudwall. He couldn't even see his own hands.

"Turn!" Twitch urged in the darkness. "Slow down! We mustn't go in too far."

"I'm trying," Jace replied, voice strained. "It won't respond."

Their speed was increasing. Damp air whistled by them. The lifeboat lurched and shuddered.

"Hang on!" Mira said.

Gripping the side of the lifeboat, Cole stayed low and wedged himself into the most secure position he could manage. The wind became a moist gale, roaring in his ears. The lifeboat rattled, jerked, and jolted. He was on a nightmare bobsled ride without a track or a finish line.

What if he fell? Would he tumble through damp darkness until he starved? Would his fate be any different if he held on?

The lifeboat whooshed onward. It didn't feel like they were turning much. Cole only saw black. His clothes and hair became soaked by the mist. He thought he heard Jace shouting, but the words were lost in the gale. The *Fair-Weather Friend* quaked and groaned.

And then the cloudy darkness lifted, though the lifeboat did not slow down.

Eyes squinted against the damp wind, Cole glimpsed a distant castle in the twilight, surrounded by wide grounds with walls and fences, fountains and statues, lawns and trees.

His eyes registered the encouraging sight in a flash before the nose of the lifeboat dipped down toward a swirling funnel that yawned larger than a football stadium. It was like beholding the inside of a tornado—the howling suction whirled down, down, down into infinite darkness. Wispy streams of vapor from the rear of the cloudwall flowed into the chaotic funnel, along with the *Fair-Weather Friend*.

Jace was on his feet, wrenching at the controls. "It won't budge!" he yelled in frustration, face flushed with effort.

Rocketing faster than ever, the lifeboat reached the rim of the funnel and began circling down into the enormous mouth. Looking around frantically, Cole saw no escape. They were already too low to view the castle. With each revolution, the lifeboat sank deeper into the funnel. Despite the immense size of their circular path, they streaked fast enough to feel the mighty g-forces of the constant turn.

Mira yelled something, and Jace shouted something else, all words lost in the cacophony of swirling air and water. Other objects descended with them, hugging the blurred walls of the endless vortex—a damaged wagon, an embroidered carpet, a stuffed tiger, an irregular jumble of timbers, a copper birdbath. Some of the debris seemed to hold steady or even rise, but the lifeboat was definitely in a downward spiral.

With no warning, the *Fair-Weather Friend* rammed into a huge church bell, which crumpled the prow and produced a mellow *gong*. The impact sent Jace over the side of the lifeboat, tumbling into the gloomy throat of the funnel.

Twitch immediately leaped from the boat, wings appearing on his back. He dove after Jace, reaching him just before he joined the frenetic wall of the vortex. Wings fluttering, gradually losing altitude, Twitch toted Jace toward the center of the funnel. The lifeboat rapidly left the two boys behind as it continued with the wild swirl of the maelstrom.

"Did you see that?" Cole yelled to Mira.

She either didn't hear him or couldn't understand. She was shouting something and pointing at the bottom of the boat. Cole followed her finger to where a split in the hull was trembling and widening.

"Oh no," he managed before the *Fair-Weather Friend* split down the middle, the two halves flying apart. For a moment he glided through the air, his bow hovering in front of him. He snatched it an instant before plunging into the seething motion of the vortex's wall.

All breath was ripped from him. When he tried to inhale, vapor blasted into his nostrils, making him cough and choke. He flipped end over end, like a surfer who had wiped out on a tsunami. The tumult was deafening, the wind and water blinding. No motion he made mattered—he was at the complete mercy of the vast whirlwind.

Clamping a hand over his nose and mouth, Cole managed to filter the tumultuous air enough to gasp quick breaths. He had no sense of where he was in relation to the others or to anything else. All he knew was that he was moving very fast. If he collided with a church bell or part of the lifeboat, that would be the end.

He became entangled in the mesh of a net. It was all around him and constricted abruptly. Upon tightening, the net pulled him away from the wall of the whirlwind, out into the central void.

Swinging like a pendulum, Cole stared in confusion down the turbulent vortex at the fathomless well of darkness below. The noise was tremendous, a banshee choir that made his chest throb and his head vibrate. This was no mere tornado, no simple whirlpool, no common hurricane. This was the cosmic drain that would suck all reality into everlasting nothingness.

Looking up, Cole found that his net dangled from an insectile flying machine. Somewhat like a honeybee, and somewhat like a beetle, the wings of the machine moved in a barely discernable blur. Although crafted out of silvery metal, a mosaic of snail shells, colored glass, and macaroni decorated much of its surface.

Craning his neck as the net continued to rock, Cole found that three other flying machines had collected Mira, Jace, and Twitch, each in their own nets. Empty nets hung from an extra pair of flying machines. The machines weren't much larger than a person. Cole saw no sign of anyone piloting or otherwise controlling them. Except for the wings, the machines didn't seem particularly lifelike. The eyes were brass rings.

After gathering in the middle of the vortex, the flying machines rose together. Cole's companions looked uncomfortable in their nets—Mira lay curled on her back, Twitch was folded on his side, and Jace was struggling to flip himself right-side up.

Cole realized that he was partly upside down himself, with a lot of his weight on his left shoulder and side. Clawing at the net, he tried to right himself. His efforts made him sway, but yielded little result because the net was too confining for much movement.

Though awkwardly positioned, the others seemed glad to see one another. They had to be surprised to be alive. Cole sure was. That tumble into the whirlwind had felt like the end. He tried to ask what was going on, and they shouted things as well, but nothing could be heard over the ferocious howl of the vortex.

The flying machines gradually levitated above the mouth of the maelstrom. They rose straight for some time before moving away from the cloudwall. Above them, stars appeared in the fading twilight. Beyond the frenzied mouth of the whirlwind, the castle reappeared, several of the windows lit, but many more of them dark.

Who lived in the castle? Was it the people who controlled the flying machines? Whoever they were, they couldn't be worse than death by vortex, could they?

The flying machines moved toward the castle, flying lower as the spacious grounds approached. The landscape reminded Cole of the Brink—cloud and downward glimpses of sky until the ground suddenly began.

As the tumult of the whirlwind receded, Cole called out to Mira again. "Where are we?"

She met his eyes uncertainly. "We're off the map. This shouldn't be here." Even though she was yelling, he could barely hear her.

Jace gestured for them to look ahead.

On a wide lawn below waited a human figure surrounded by a group of crude, thick-limbed giants. As they drew nearer, it became clear that the figure was a woman and the giants were made of sharp, eroded stone, the sort found by the seaside. The giants formed an orderly ring, and the flying machines hovered into the center of the circle.

In unison, the flying machines dropped their nets. Cole fell a few feet, landing awkwardly on his side on the close-trimmed grass. He started scrabbling with the net, trying to find a way out.

"Keep still," the woman demanded in a hard voice. She walked closer, hands behind her waist. Her hair was tied back tightly, her features harsh, with dramatic eyebrows and a defined jawline. Sleek black boots rose almost to her knees, and a long, slender sword hung at her side. "This is a private estate. Outsiders are not welcome. Your lives depend on the answers to two questions: Who are you, and what are you doing here?"

CHAPTER
— 19 —

ASIA AND LIAM

Cole stared up at the woman through the netting. How should he answer? He hesitated, as did the others. She stopped right in front of him, glaring down.

"Don't lie," she said humorlessly. "I'll know. Spit it out."

"I'm Cole," he said. "I'm not from here. The Outskirts, I mean. I came here to help my friends who got kidnapped, but I was taken as a slave and sold to the Sky Raiders. I was escaping from them with some friends."

"You," she said, approaching Twitch, "are not as you appear."

Cole noticed that his wings were gone. Had that been his special item? Wings?

"I'm not," Twitch said. "I'm from Elloweer. I was taken as a slave as well."

"How did you revert to your true form?" she pressed.

"I have a ring," he said.

"And you?" she asked Jace.

"Why do you care?" Jace replied.

"You're all trespassers," she barked. "I handle any intruders."

"You have a name?" Jace asked.

"I have three—Judge, Jury, and Executioner. Answer me or perish. Who are you? Why did you come here?"

Jace gave a reluctant sigh. "I've been a slave since I can remember. I never knew my parents. I was sold to the Sky Raiders because my owners hated me. I was escaping with these guys."

"Escaping into the cloudwall? Do you know nothing?"

"We were cornered," Jace said.

She gave a single nod and walked to Mira. "And you?"

"You can probably guess by now," Mira said.

"I cannot," the woman said. "You are not as you appear. There is a potent shaping bound to you. Something I can't readily identify. And I sense a degree of power in you as well."

"Are you a shaper?"

A slight sneer curled her lip. "You've never met my equal."

"I do a little shaping," Mira said. "Maybe that's what you're sensing."

"Evade my questions at your peril," the woman said, snapping her fingers.

One of the stony giants stomped forward and raised a misshapen fist above Mira. The big rocky limb was large enough to flatten half of her with one blow.

Jace's golden rope flashed out from his net, coiling around the woman's throat. "Call it off," he growled.

A young man swooshed into view, standing on a silver disk the size of a manhole cover. Not older than twenty, he had boyish features and mischievous eyes. He wore a fuzzy brown jacket and alligator-skin boots, and he held what looked like silver salt shakers in each hand. Knees slightly bent, he hovered perhaps ten feet off the ground, although the disk had no visible means of propulsion.

"That's enough," the young man said in a friendly tone. Pointing at the rope, it unraveled from the woman's throat and fell limply to the grass. Chopping a hand toward the stone giant, it turned to cardboard and staggered back a few paces.

Glowering, the woman turned to the newcomer. "This is none of your affair."

"I did make the fliers," the young man corrected. "And I overheard the conversation."

Jace kept flicking his wrist, but his golden rope didn't respond any differently than an ordinary rope would. "What did you do to it?"

"I cut it off from you," the young man said offhandedly. "Don't worry. If we like you, I can set things right. It's a pretty cool rendering. You got it from a sky castle?"

"You're ruining the interrogation," the woman seethed.

"Be honest, Asia," the young man said. "The interrogation was getting messy."

"I was about to sever the rope—"

"Which would have wrecked it," the young man inserted.

"I had the situation under—"

"Asia, a simple thank you would—"

"What have I told you about using my name in front of outsiders?"

"Maybe it was your *codename*," he said with a wink.

Cole tried to stifle a laugh.

The young man on the disk glanced his way. "They can't be all bad. This one even has a sense of humor—and that's while lying in a net after nearly getting drawn into a terminal void."

The muscles in her jaw clenching, Asia took a controlled breath. "Let me do my job."

"What about our new captain of the guard?" he asked.

"I sent him to fetch reinforcements," Asia said. "He's all right for monitoring semblances, but these are our first living intruders in ages."

The young man waved a hand at them. "They're escaped slaves. It fits. It rings true."

"We have to verify—"

"They're obviously not the vanguard of a conquering army."

"They could be spies."

The young man paused. "True."

"We have hundreds of legionnaires coming this way," Asia said.

He cocked his head thoughtfully. "Also true."

"We can't risk exposure."

The young man faced them. "I'm Liam. Are any of you spies? Answer out loud."

"No," Cole said.

The others said the same, their answers overlapping.

"What about you?" Liam casually asked Mira. "You really are linked to a very unusual shaping. What's the story?"

"What is this?" Cole asked. "Good cop, bad cop?"

"What?" the young man exclaimed, leaning back and covering his eyes. "You know about good cop, bad cop! Who told you? Asia, he knows!"

Asia faced the young man imploringly. "Would you please just let me—"

"Pound them into the lawn?" the young man interrupted. He stopped, as if considering. "They might make decent fertilizer . . . but no, I think we've heard enough. We'll let You Know Who be the final judge."

"You want to bring possible spies before You Know Who?"

"If they're spies, then we'll turn them into fertilizer. No, better—we'll make wishes and chuck them into the terminal void."

"And if her peculiar shaping is letting the girl communicate beyond the cloudwall?" Asia pressed.

"Have you sensed transmissions from any of them?"

"The shaping has strange connections beyond her," Asia said.

"Right, but no communication," he said. "They're not spies. If they are, he'll figure it out, and we'll punish them. I'll take the blame."

Asia sighed in defeat. "Why do I put up with you?"

"Because it isn't your choice," he said.

"You've got that right," she huffed.

Liam faced Cole and his friends. "If you'll hand over any weapons, renderings, or enhanced objects, I'll untangle you from those nets."

"What if we refuse?" Jace asked.

"Don't worry," Liam said. "If he likes you, you'll get it all back. I don't even want any of your . . . Well, I kind of want the rope, but I'll get over it. Come on, let's have the stuff. It's getting late."

He was right. Only the last traces of twilight remained in the sky above. Many stars were out now.

Cole was having trouble unsheathing his Jumping Sword. "This is sort of hard with the nets."

"Valid point," Liam agreed. "Promise you'll be cool about it? Without the nets, if you try something, we'll have to sick the grunts on you." He pointed to the cardboard giant, and it turned back to wave-worn stone.

"We'll behave," Cole said.

"What about you, rope boy?" Liam asked.

"If you don't mess with us, I won't mess with you," Jace pledged.

"I guess that's fair. Promise? Double-dog promise?"

"I think that's 'double-dog *dare you*,'" Cole put in.

Liam looked at him in surprise. "You're right. What's a really strong promise?"

"'Cross your heart and hope to die,'" Cole said.

"Oh, I like that," Liam replied. Looking at Asia, he jerked his head toward Cole. "This one could be useful."

She rolled her eyes.

"Do you all swear to be good?" Liam asked. "Cross your hearts and hope to die? I need verbal confirmation."

They all agreed.

Liam waved a hand, and the nets blew free of them, becoming gaseous and quickly dispersing in the air.

"You're good," Mira said.

Liam shrugged. "I'm not completely useless. Let's have those items."

Cole handed over his shawl, his bow, and his sword to Liam.

Twitch hesitated with his ring. "This means a lot to me."

"I'll take good care of it," Liam assured him. "I wouldn't even have a use for it. I'm not from Elloweer."

Twitch handed it over. Jace gave up his inert rope. Mira surrendered her Jumping Sword.

Liam returned to Cole. "You still have something small."

"I forgot," Cole said, taking the jewel he had gotten in Parona from his pocket.

Liam held it up and scrutinized it. "Never mind. It's not worth the trouble to keep it with me." He handed it back. "You hold on to it. Or don't. Either way, you won't lose it."

"Here he comes," Asia said.

Cole looked beyond her to where a large warrior led a group of others in full armor across the lawn. Even though it was dim, Cole recognized the leader. "Lyrus?"

The big warrior increased his pace to a jog. "Cole? Is that you?"

Liam looked befuddled. "You two know each other?"

"We've met," Cole said.

Lyrus hustled forward and gave Cole a small bow. "I am astonished. How did you come here?"

"Through the cloudwall," Cole said.

"You know them?" Asia asked. "Are they Sky Raiders?"

"Salvagers, yes," Lyrus said. "And Cole is a proven hero."

"Anything suspicious about them?" Asia inquired.

Lyrus shook his head. "I have only met Cole and Mira, but I believe they have good characters. Cole helped me awaken to my true nature."

"Why aren't you dead?" Cole asked.

"I was resigned to my demise," Lyrus said. "But I was rescued. They fully healed my injuries."

"Lots of semblances slide into the terminal void," Liam said. "We can lend a hand to only a small fraction of them. Our master sensed that Lyrus was unusually self-aware. We rescued him and decided he would be a good fit as captain of the guard."

"Can we please take this reunion to the castle?" Asia begged.

Liam touched his forehead and gave a quick bow. "As you wish. Follow me!" Tilting on his disk, he took off at a speed none of them could possibly match. His flying insects buzzed after him, rapidly falling behind.

"Stay with me," Asia grumbled. "Judgment has yet to be passed on you. We're off to meet the master."

DECLAN

The castle swept up from the ground, its unusual architecture dominated by concave curves. Smooth walls sloped inward before flaring outward as they rose. The towers tapered, then widened toward the top. The subtle hourglass theme was echoed on the battlements and in the windows.

Cole spent most of the long walk in silence. Lyrus had been reluctant to converse, explaining that, technically, Cole was a prisoner until the master decided otherwise. Whenever Cole spoke to his friends, Asia stayed nearby, obviously listening.

Left to his thoughts, Cole wondered about the identity of the person whom Asia, Liam, and Lyrus served. If the master were an enemy of the legion, hopefully he or she would be on their side. But not necessarily. The master could simply be a recluse who hated all trespassers. Obviously, the master wanted to stay hidden. Otherwise why live behind the cloudwall with lots of guards and a giant whirlwind to vacuum away any visitors?

The castle grounds had little light, and though the stars were bright, no moon was in view, making it hard to discern the hedges, lawns, trees, and fountains, except as vague forms in the dimness. The castle was easier to observe, thanks to lights in the windows and fires on the walls.

Full night had fallen by the time they reached the huge gates. As they neared the sloping walls, the gates swung open and a portcullis cranked upward. The group passed into a large courtyard lit by elaborate fountains of water and flame. Wavering shadows and splashes of light danced on the soaring walls. Heavily armed figures clanked around the area, armor glinting in the firelight.

As Asia led them toward the main castle doors, they opened and a figure emerged, head wreathed by curly brown hair, his body husky but not flabby. He wore a green robe and sandals, and he looked to be in his thirties.

"Welcome," the man said with a graceful half bow. "It has been too long since we have enjoyed the company of visitors."

"Don't play host to prisoners, Jamar," Asia scolded.

He raised his eyebrows. "Prisoners, are they? That isn't how Liam told it."

"Since when has Liam known anything besides shaping?" Asia challenged.

Jamar gave an apologetic smile to the group. "Asia takes the defense of this castle very seriously." He eyed Cole and the others in turn. "The day may come when we are indebted to her wariness, but I suspect that will not be today. The master will have the final word. He is aware of your presence and wishes to meet with you at once."

Jamar stepped aside, and Asia motioned for Mira to enter. Cole passed through the door after her, entering a grand hall many stories high, with stairs at the far end and tiers of balconies and galleries along the walls. Glowing globes spaced about the chamber provided steady luminance. Crystal trees with stained-glass leaves transformed much of the hall into a sparkling grove.

Not far from Jamar stood a dozen figures made of white wax, humanoid in size and form but faceless and smooth, like some department store mannequins Cole had once seen. Though they were all different sizes and builds, each one wore a green robe and carried some kind of weapon—a sword, a spear, or a knife. They generally held still, but a few of them shifted, revealing that they could move. One took a moment to stretch, arms raised, back arched.

"Look at this place," Jace exclaimed breathlessly, eyes wide.

There was a lot to take in. Expertly carved marble statues filled alcoves. Frescoes decorated the ceiling, mosaics enlivened the floors, and tapestries brightened the walls. Gilded accents and enormous jewels embellished the railings and the furniture.

Leaving their other escorts outside, Asia joined them in the castle. She addressed Jamar. "Where will the master receive them?"

"In the Silent Hall," he said.

She raised an eyebrow. "Does he want us present?"

"Only at first."

Asia shook her head. "He grows reckless."

Jamar gave her a chiding look. "He is the master. Our place is not to question him."

"My place is to protect him," Asia said firmly.

"Not here," Jamar corrected. "You control the external defenses. I manage affairs within these walls."

"Where does that leave Liam?" asked a deep female voice. A giant pig made of stuffed quilts waddled into the hall from a neighboring room, short legs laboring below a rotund body. Even though it was bulky and ungainly, it was quite tall. Cole would have to jump to touch the quilted animal's snout.

"In charge of the skies and the spies," Asia answered. "Is he coming?"

"He's working," the patchwork pig explained.

"Is any of this work happening in bed?" Asia asked skeptically. "With the lights off? While he snores?"

"Maybe a little," the pig replied. "He sent me as his representative to help transport our guests."

Cole met eyes with Mira. He had to glance away for fear her expression would make him laugh. The pig was pretty ridiculous.

Asia exhaled venomously. "They're not our guests yet. They're potential enemies. I shouldn't be surprised that Liam can't be bothered."

"He bothered to send me," the pig said.

"The master is waiting," Jamar reminded everyone.

The quilted pig knelt down. "I'm Lola. Climb aboard, if you please."

Jace folded his arms across his chest. "I keep waiting for this to get less weird, and it keeps not happening."

Cole had to agree. He had witnessed some bizarre sights in the sky castles, but he doubted whether anything could have prepared him for a ride on the back of a quilted pig through the most opulent palace he had ever seen.

"We're with talented shapers," Mira said, patting Jace's elbow. "They can produce all sorts of strange semblances."

"I'm with the boy on this one," Asia said. "Liam shows little restraint with his imagination."

"I'm right here," the pig said.

"And you're charming," Jamar said. "A cozy, swinish pillow."

"That's a little better." Lola sniffed. "You kids climb aboard before my feelings take another beating."

Grabbing fistfuls of fabric, Cole scrambled up the side of the pig, pressing into her soft side with his knees and feet. It was like climbing a beanbag the size of a haystack. Once on top, he spread his legs wide to straddle the broad back just behind the head. Though understuffed enough to be cushy, the pig still felt relatively stable. The four of them fit on her without any trouble—Cole in the front, Mira kneeling behind him, then Jace, and Twitch in the rear. They would have had to squish together to add another rider.

"Comfortable?" Asia asked, her voice oozing sarcasm.

Cole rubbed his palms over the fabric in front of him. "Actually, yeah. What's this material? It's really soft, almost silky."

"The boy has good taste," the pig said.

"Let's get this over with," Asia grumbled.

Jamar and Asia led them away from the cavernous hall.

The pig swayed as she waddled, but Cole felt reasonably secure. They moved through a room filled with musical instruments, including drums the size of hot tubs and a gleaming pipe organ that took up most of one wall. They passed through tinkling curtains made of long strands of tiny bells into a chilly room where everything was carved out of ice—the furniture, the statues, the fireplace, even the rugs.

"Yep," Jace muttered. "Weirder and weirder."

"Cool, though," Cole said, his breath pluming out in front of him.

After more chiming curtains, they entered a spacious ballroom with a polished wooden floor and a gargantuan chandelier. Jamar waved an arm, and the center of the floor melted away to reveal a broad stairway going down and out of view.

"Whoa!" Cole called as the pig toddled to the top of the stairs. On the level floor the pig was fine, but Cole was worried about tipping forward down the incline. "Should we hop off here?"

"Don't worry," the pig said. "Stairs are a specialty of mine."

Lola leaned forward and started sliding on her belly. Gripping with his legs as best as he could and grabbing on to handfuls of fabric, Cole leaned back as they started down, tingles rushing through him. Once they were moving, the ride was surprisingly quick and smooth. After reaching the foot of the stairs, the pig kept sliding for a little ways along the polished marble corridor at the bottom.

"We lost Twitch," Jace said.

Cole looked back. Twitch was nowhere in sight.

"He slid off my backside at the top of the stairs," the pig said. "He'll have to take the slow way with the others."

After a few moments, Twitch came into view, walking down the stairs beside Jamar, Asia, and four of the waxy, robed guards. He waved sheepishly when he saw the others looking back at him.

"You should have stayed on," Mira called. "It was fun."

"I'm not big on unnecessary risk," he answered.

When the others caught up, Lola crouched down and let Twitch climb back on. Jamar led the way forward.

At the end of the hall waited a large carved door. As they approached, it opened, and they passed through into a long chamber. Two rows of pillars supported the high, arched ceiling. The pillars were carved like stacked heads, and every head had four faces, one on each side. Black veins swirled through the red marble floor, and dark draperies softened the walls.

In the middle of the chamber sat a small old man on a modest chair. He stood as they entered, using a cane in each hand. The pig stopped ten paces from him and crouched down.

"Should we get off?" Jace asked.

"Yes," Lola replied.

They all slid down the same side. The marble floor was hard and smooth underfoot. The quilted pig backed away.

The little man walked forward a few steps, relying heavily on his canes. He was almost bald, with a thin fringe of white around the sides of his lightly spotted head. His features disguised by wrinkles, he looked frail, like he belonged in a hospital gown. Instead, he wore a plain green sweater and brown trousers. The slippers on his feet left a clear view of his pale, bony ankles.

The old man paused. "Would you close the door, Jamar?" His voice lacked vitality.

The door swung shut.

The old man smiled awkwardly. He had very even teeth. "Well, you have uncovered our little secret, haven't you? Happens on occasion, but not often, not often."

He seemed to be waiting for them to respond.

"Are you the master?" Mira asked.

His smile widened, and he gave a weak chuckle. "I suppose so, especially if we're still keeping this secretive. Welcome to Cloudvale, one of the least publicized hideaways in the five kingdoms. It's a small province, but it's free. We'd prefer to keep it that way."

"We're not spies," Cole said.

"Now that I see you, I suspect that's true," the old man said, his smile fading a little. "The only one of you with the potential to transmit information out of here is definitely not allied with the High Shaper. Do you three boys know who you're escorting?"

"We know enough," Jace said.

"How much?" the old man asked Mira.

"Not everything," Mira said. "You know who I am?"

"Yes," he said. "How much do you trust them?"

"As much as I can trust anyone. They've all risked their lives for me."

He nodded. "Have you figured out who I am?"

"I think so," she answered.

He lifted one of his canes momentarily to point at her. "Out with it, then, young lady. Who am I?"

"You're Declan Pierce, the Grand Shaper of Sambria."

His smile grew wide again, eyes crinkling. "Guilty. Guilty as charged. Do you mean to continue in the company of these three boys?"

Cole watched Mira, as did Jace and Twitch. She considered them. "You don't have to stay with me. Trouble will follow wherever I go."

"I'm not going to leave you unprotected," Jace said.

"Me neither," Cole seconded.

"We've come this far," Twitch added.

Mira faced Declan. "Then, yes, they'll remain with me."

"Would you like them to share in our counsel?" Declan asked. "It would mean revealing your identity."

"Yes," Mira said.

His smile vanished. "Leave us, Asia, Jamar. Lola, tell your maker to take a greater interest in current events."

"Are you sure, sire?" Asia asked.

Annoyance flickered across Declan's features. "We have sensitive matters to discuss. We're not just meeting here because I adore drafty underground theatricality. You'll be included when the time is right. Look to our defenses. We must stay on high alert going forward. That is all."

The doors opened. Jamar exited with his wax people. Asia walked out beside the pig, and the doors swung shut.

Declan made his way back to the chair using his canes.

Once in his seat again, he wiped perspiration from his brow, breathing shallowly. "I feel terrible sitting while you stand."

"It's fine," Cole said.

"It's rude," Declan replied. "Old bones. Can't be helped. Well, could have been helped, perhaps, with better planning. I didn't anticipate visitors, and we need utter silence."

"Can't you just shape us some chairs?" Jace asked.

"Elsewhere, yes. But I mustn't risk shaping in here. Any new shaping I perform could disturb the balance that keeps this room inscrutable from the outside."

"We can't be heard?" Mira asked.

"We probably couldn't be overheard anywhere in Cloudvale, but this room makes it certain that nobody will eavesdrop. Young lady, it's time to reveal your true identity. Would you like to do the honors, or should I?"

"Go ahead," Mira said politely.

"The five daughters of Stafford Pemberton, High Shaper over the five kingdoms, were Elegance, Honor, Constance, Miracle, and Destiny. He never had a male heir. The girls supposedly died in an accident more than sixty years ago. Except they didn't. They lived."

"How do you know that?" Mira asked.

"Harmony has been in touch," Declan said. "Stafford faked their deaths so he could hold them prisoner. He had somehow stolen their powers, but he needed them alive or he would lose his newfound talents. So a carriage dramatically plunged into a roiling river, and even as he locked his daughters away in a dungeon, the High Shaper pretended to mourn with the rest of us."

"When he took their shaping abilities, the girls stopped aging," Mira said. "The process wasn't merely slowed—they are all as young today as the day their father betrayed them."

"Their mother, Harmony, got wise to the plot and helped her daughters escape," Declan continued. "The five royal princesses hide in exile to this very hour—Elegance, Honor, Constance, Miracle, and Destiny. Some of them may not even bother to use clever aliases."

As the realization hit, Cole felt like the breath had been knocked out of him. It took him a moment to speak. "You're Miracle."

Mira raised her eyebrows. "I used a less obvious name for the first twenty years in hiding. With my family, I had always gone by Mira. As time passed, people forgot about my death. If I had survived, I should have been an adult. Instead, I was a slave girl. I stayed far from anyone who might have remembered my face. Regaining my true nickname never caused any problems."

"No way," Jace said. "You're really Princess Miracle?"

She flashed an awkward smile and nodded.

"They call those five princesses the lost treasure of Junction," Twitch said. "Everyone knows the story. They were all amazing shapers. After they vanished, the High King was never the same."

Declan gave a sour chuckle. "Too true. He had taken their gifts, and with that new power, he found the courage to show his true colors."

"I can hardly believe it," Twitch said, dropping to one knee. "I should have been more respectful. I should have——"

"No," Mira interrupted. "Get up. None of that. You've all been exactly what I need. Real friends in a time of hardship."

Cole squinted at her as he did a quick calculation. "You're in your seventies?"

"No, I'm eleven," Mira said, her cheeks flushing. "I've just been eleven for a really long time."

"Your nickname should be 'Granny,'" Jace said.

"Ha-ha," Mira replied. "I'm not an adult who looks like a kid. I'm a kid who never became an adult. Years going by isn't the same as aging. I don't change. I've always been treated like I'm eleven. I've always looked eleven. I've never really felt any older than that."

"But you've lived for so long," Twitch said.

"I'm sure I know more than a normal eleven-year-old," she said. "I just don't feel older. How could I? I've never *been* older."

"You must have watched other people get old," Cole said.

Mira brushed some stray hairs from her eyes. "Not for long. We moved a lot. Looking back is weird. I was ten so long ago. It's been forever since I've seen anyone in my family. I saw Durny age, though, since he stayed with me."

"Durny was your bodyguard?" Jace asked.

"My second protector. The first, Roderick, eventually got old and died. Even though we moved around, my mother has a way to find me. Many shapers have specialties. My mother has two—visions and the stars. Those abilities complement each other. She can find her daughters wherever we roam. She sent Durny to me after she sensed that Roderick had died."

"You know," Declan said, "I met your older sisters once—Elegance and Honor. They were quite young at the time. It was during my last visit to Junction, when I was first beginning to suspect that your father was not to be trusted. I should have given more serious heed to my instincts."

"How did you recognize Mira?" Jace asked.

"I understand a thing or two about shaping, boy," Declan said. "I can sense the power of a shaper. Her power has been stripped from her, and it is connected to a gathering mass of shaping energy elsewhere in Sambria. But a lesser portion of her gift is slowly returning to her. Only one girl in all the Outskirts would fully match that description." His expression softened. "You poor child. You have endured some trying years. Sadly, I fear it will only get worse from here."

"What should I do?" Mira asked.

"That's the question. You shouldn't stay here, and you shouldn't go either, yet we have to do something. How much do you know about what your father did to you?"

"I know he took my power," she said. "I still don't understand how."

"You're not alone there," Declan assured her. "It defies all knowledge of shaping."

"I know I stopped aging," Mira went on. "I know my power has slowly started coming back. And now Father has sent hundreds of legionnaires after me."

"You know so little?" Declan asked, his voice sad. "We definitely need to talk."

Twitch sat down on the floor, legs crossed. Cole did likewise, followed by Jace.

"I apologize again for the seating arrangements," Declan said.

"This isn't bad," Cole assured him.

Declan shook his head. "Chilly and hard."

"What can you tell me about my father?" Mira asked, not sitting, eyes intense.

"Not everything," Declan said. "But I can shed some light on a few matters. Please, have a seat. This may take some time."

CHAPTER
21

ANSWERS

"How often do you corresponded with Harmony?" Declan asked after Mira sat.

"Mother only contacts me indirectly," Mira said.

"No messages?" Declan verified.

"Not really. She recently tried. She has a signal for when danger is coming. It can also lead messengers or new protectors to me."

"Where is your current protector?"

"He just died. We got into trouble at a sky castle. Mother had sent her warning signal, so he was trying to collect floatstones to make a skycraft for our escape from Skyport, but he got killed. Then today, a messenger arrived right before a large group of legionnaires. I never got the message. I can only assume it was a warning that my father had found me. I wouldn't have escaped Skyport without help from my friends."

"These boys stepped in," Declan said, sizing them up. "I take it you have names?"

"Jace."

"I'm Cole."

"They call me Twitch."

"Three young slaves escaped from the Sky Raiders," Declan said. "Not the most likely escorts for a princess of the highest royal family in the five kingdoms. Were you all born in Sambria?"

"I was," Jace said. "I've been a slave since I can remember."

"I was born in Elloweer," Twitch said.

"I'm from Earth," Cole said.

"Liam mentioned you," Declan told Cole. "How did you arrive here?"

"Slave traders took my friends. I came here to help them but got caught."

"You arrived voluntarily?" Declan asked.

"Nobody forced me," Cole said. "I didn't really know what I was getting into."

"Interesting. A newly minted slave, I take it?"

"Just a couple of weeks. Two of my closest friends were taken to be slaves of the High King. Mira promised to help me find them."

"And I'll keep that promise," Mira assured him.

The old man gave half a smile. "We will converse later, young man." He studied Mira. "What do you know about all that has transpired since you went into hiding?"

"I know the basics," Mira said. "We tried to stay informed. Father drove the Grand Shapers into exile. All except Paulus, who joined him. He set up governors to replace the Grand Shapers in the other four kingdoms."

"Correct," Declan approved. "Your father tries to pretend the Grand Shapers surrendered our posts willingly. That we retired."

"People don't believe that nonsense," Jace said.

"You might be surprised," Declan said. "As time goes by, it becomes easier to accept the claims of the current government, the one right in front of you, the one controlling the present. For example, the governors Stafford established have now taken to calling themselves kings. Even the Grand Shapers seldom emphasized that title."

"How did you end up here?" Mira asked.

Declan looked around, as if reminding himself of his surroundings. "I knew of this place before your father moved to unseat me. More than any feature in Sambria, the cloudwalls have always fascinated me. As I made a study of them, I discovered this space behind the Eastern Cloudwall. I managed to access it by a roundabout fashion and decided it might prove a refuge in time of peril. When Stafford came after me, I fled here with some key members of my household and a pair of my most promising pupils. And here we have stayed, biding our time. All you see here, we shaped from scratch."

"Were Asia, Jamar, and Liam with you from the start?" Cole asked.

"Asia and Jamar. Liam came later. All have great potential and significant ability, but none are ready to assume my duties as Grand Shaper. Asia is too harsh, and her shaping skills too narrow. Jamar is too interested in pleasing others. And Liam, the most gifted by far, is also the least serious. I'm not sure he will ever learn to focus, to plan, to lead."

"Sounds like you want to retire," Jace said.

Declan chuckled wheezily. "Look at me! I was never a strong man. My body is shutting down. I've lived far more than my share of years; many regular life spans. Even my mind shows signs of flagging. Let's see, we have Cole, like the fuel. Twitch, like his mannerisms. And, I'm sorry, you are?"

"Jace."

"Yes, of course. But it escaped me. Not long ago I could have learned a hundred names once and repeated them back a week later. My short-term memory begins to wane. I've held this post for too long, but how am I supposed to find and train a worthy successor from here? My refuge is also my prison. I would like nothing more than to be Grand Shaper emeritus. But reality doesn't always align with our preferences."

"How many other people live here?" Mira asked.

Declan blinked at her. "Actual people? You've met them all. Me, Jamar, Asia, and Liam. The rest are semblances."

"What about the others you brought with you?" Jace asked.

"The people who came with me have passed away," Declan said. "Only those with potent shaping skills can slow the aging process, as my apprentices have. With clearer foresight I might have brought more couples, but there was little time. One couple formed from those I brought, but they were unable to have offspring. The last of my regular staff passed on almost ten years ago."

"Others must have come through the cloudwall," Twitch said.

"The last explorers we know of came here more than fifty years ago," Declan said. "We only rescued three out of the dozens aboard the large skycraft. Liam wasn't with us yet, so our flying semblances were much less sophisticated. The trio we rescued have since died."

"When did Liam get here?" Cole asked.

Declan folded his hands and frowned, making him look like an elderly hospital patient who didn't like what he'd been served for lunch. "Liam came looking for me almost twenty years ago, and he found his way here in the same way I did, through the Boomerang Forest."

"Why was he looking for you?" Mira asked. "Was he a messenger?"

"No," Declan said. "He was a young, powerful shaper in search of a teacher. He had been taken as a slave but used his shaping to escape."

"Wait a minute," Cole said. "Liam? Did he make a talking happy face on a slave wagon?"

"Possibly," Declan said. "He had great talent at a tender age. I have done my best to instruct him, though our styles are very different. Much of what he does can't be taught or learned. He shapes by instinct. But I'm rambling. The old man's curse. You get lonely and your mind gets lazy, and you ramble. The topic should be Miracle and her father, Stafford Pemberton."

"What can you tell me?" Mira asked.

"Until you girls were divided from your powers, I had never imagined such a feat was possible. When Harmony first told me, I scarcely believed her. Though your father comes from a line of skilled shapers, the talent apparently skipped a generation. I had the opportunity to assess him when he was young. He had ordinary shaping ability, nothing more. But what might I have missed? I had no idea the shaping power itself could be manipulated, so in his case, I may not have known what to look for."

"I never saw him do much shaping," Mira said. "I learned from my mother and from private tutors."

"Stafford was not gifted in the traditional ways," Declan said. "That much I can confirm. Yet he hid his mediocrity well, mostly by avoiding chances to shape in public. By all reports, each of his daughters and his wife were easily his superior. I know from experience that Harmony, Elegance, and Honor all practically glowed with ability. Conclusion? Either your father has unique talent, or he has access to arcane knowledge otherwise lost to the rest of us."

"Have you any idea where he could have learned something like that?" Mira asked.

Declan gave a little shrug. "Here we enter the realm of conjecture. There are whispers of his elite Enforcers, claims that they possess unusual shaping skills. Do they all share the same secret? I have some talent with every known aspect of shaping, yet after learning that it was possible, I have utterly failed to touch the shaping power itself to any degree, despite years of study and effort. Stafford is either vastly my superior, or else he knows some technique that eludes me."

"Have you talked to other Grand Shapers?" Mira wondered. "Perhaps the key lies with some other discipline."

Declan rubbed the end of his cane. "Possible. The way shaping works in each kingdom is unique. The shaping in Creon is almost unrecognizable from the shaping here. I have only risked communication with Harmony. I'm not sure how to reach the others. None of us are eager to expose ourselves by reaching out too boldly. Honestly, despite the differences, I fail to see how the shaping styles in Zeropolis, Elloweer, Creon, or Necronum could take hold of the shaping ability any more than the shaping we practice here in Sambria."

"Then what do we do?" Mira asked.

"Keep your eyes open and your wits about you," Declan suggested. "There has to be an answer to this riddle. Learning how your powers were taken could prove vital to fighting back."

Mira huffed cynically. "It might be too late to fight back. I'd settle for avoiding him."

"I understand," Declan said. "Your father has more control over the Outskirts than any ruler in memory. I've hidden here for years—studying, planning, scheming, and taking little action. But an old man can dream."

"After all this time, why are my powers returning?" Mira wondered.

Declan smiled, creases radiating from his eyes. He pointed at her, the finger gnarled and bony. "Now we shift to the most important topic. Have you regained many of your former abilities?"

"Just a little," Mira said. "Only the most basic shaping. Nothing like before my powers were taken."

"And you were just beginning to tap your potential," Declan said. "Your father has been using your combined powers to assert dominance over the five kingdoms. After you five disappeared, he began to gradually reveal his new abilities. There was no reason for most to suspect he had not enjoyed such power all along. Who would dare oppose a man who was not only High Shaper, not only commander of the legion, but also adept in all five major styles of shaping? He has dealt harshly with any who opposed him. Except now— word has it that his abilities are suddenly waning."

"Why?" Mira asked.

"Whatever unorthodox shaping bound your skills to him is unraveling," Declan said. "But only a fraction of the power is returning to you. Most of it is gathering elsewhere in Sambria."

"To someone else?" Mira asked angrily.

"Evidently not," Declan said. "Liam and I have carefully traced the connections. Your power is running wild, Mira. On its own. Somehow, it is evolving into a mighty semblance."

"What?" Mira exclaimed.

"I know," Declan said, both palms raised, the skin there the smoothest and youngest-looking on his body. "It's unprecedented. But your power has organized itself into some kind of entity."

"Father stealing my power is one thing," Mira said. "But how can my power exist outside of a person?"

"It remains connected to you. After all, it is your power. If you perish, it will perish with you. For this reason, your father meant to hold you prisoner, not kill you. Had you died, Stafford would have lost that portion of your ability he stole. The same is true now, except your power is operating independently."

"How can my power have a mind of its own?" Mira asked.

Declan spread his hands. "I don't know how the separation was accomplished in the first place, so it is difficult to speculate about what is going on. I assume it relates to how we develop a mind for a semblance. Perhaps some aspect of your father has united with your power and changed it into something new. Perhaps dividing you from your talent eventually allowed it to shape itself. I can only guess. What we know for sure is that your power was recently wreaking havoc outside the town of Alvindale."

"What was it doing?" Cole asked.

"No witnesses who got close escaped to tell the tale," Declan said. "Same with the semblances Liam sent to spy— many failed to return. Those that came back brought only anecdotes. The people are calling it Carnag."

"What?" Mira exclaimed. "Carnag is my shaping power?"

"You've heard of it?" Declan asked.

"Everyone has heard of it!" Mira said. "Sambria is in an uproar!"

"I suppose they would be," Declan muttered. "There are dozens of incorrect origin stories. Accounts from a distance are unanimous that your power is leveling homes, scattering herds, tearing down trees, and erratically reshaping the countryside. Many people have disappeared."

Mira held a hand over her mouth. She looked stricken. "It's because of me? I'm hurting people? I'm wrecking communities? My power is out there causing harm, just like my power helped my father take control of the five kingdoms."

"It's involuntary," Declan soothed.

"Maybe, but it's still *my* fault."

"Your father caused it. Not you."

"If I were dead, this wouldn't be happening."

Declan raised his eyes and shook his head. "Why are the young so dramatic? And so rash?"

Mira looked irritated. "How should I feel?"

"You should think," Declan said. "Solve the problem. Don't leap to suicide as the best option."

"Are there other options?" Mira asked.

"I should hope so," Declan said. "There is a great deal of energy involved. Not passive energy that you could potentially summon. Active energy is out there, interacting with the world. Your power is free from any physical limitations your mind or body would have imposed. It's pure, unrestrained, and volatile. Cut off that energy from its source, and we could have a disaster of epic proportions. Killing yourself would certainly destroy your power. The question then becomes how much of Sambria would be destroyed along with it."

"It would explode?" Jace asked.

"Or worse," Declan said. "That much unrestrained power wouldn't go quietly."

"Then what can I do?" Mira pressed.

Declan placed his palms together, tapping his fingers. "Here is where we must make some choices. Your father is desperate to reclaim you and your sisters. He wants to regain your powers, and he certainly doesn't want you using your powers against him. Maybe he knows your powers are gathering outside of you, maybe not."

"He sent hundreds of soldiers for her," Cole pointed out. "They spoke about going after Carnag afterward."

Declan gazed at Mira. "Your father was searching for you before now. But perhaps not desperately. He had your powers, you were out of the picture, and it had been smooth sailing for decades. His situation was not particularly urgent. It would have been safer to have you under lock and key, but it wasn't essential. However, with his stolen talents fading, matters have changed. Going forward, all of his resources will be turned toward finding you and your sisters."

"Where can she hide?" Jace demanded.

Declan spread his hands again. "This is one of the best hiding spots in the five kingdoms. Unfortunately, the legion saw you come here. A portion of Mira's power remains with her father. It continues to seep away, but it is there. While any of her power remains with him, he knows that she lives. He will not rest until he finds where she went."

"Which will lead him to you," Mira said.

Declan shared a tight smile. "Some legionnaires will undoubtedly come through the cloudwall, probably not long after daybreak. They will all die. Everything that comes through the cloudwall is drawn into the void. It was expertly designed to that end. We can intervene by entering the vortex from our side, but of course we won't rescue our enemies."

"Did you design it?" Twitch asked.

Declan's answering laughter degenerated into a hoarse cough. He hawked up some phlegm, shakily produced a bag, and spat into it. "If I could have produced the terminal void, I would fear no being in the Outskirts or beyond. I have no idea who designed the Eastern Cloudwall and the void, or the Western Cloudwall with its staggering output. I cannot comprehend the mind that conceived the possibility let alone executed it."

"Could that person be hiding behind the Western Cloudwall?" Cole asked.

"Very doubtful," Declan said. "I studied the Western Cloudwall for years, and there is no way behind or inside of it without being destroyed by the creative furnace that generates the castles. The cloudwalls have existed for all of recorded history. I suspect their creator designed them to be self-sustaining."

Jace cleared his throat. "If everyone who comes here gets sucked into the vortex, maybe Mira should stay."

Declan frowned and shook his head. "The legionnaires who brave the cloudwall will fail. But there is another way. Cloudvale is no island in the sky. This is a peninsula, jutting out from the Brink. Access is difficult, but I came here, as did Liam. Now that Stafford knows where to look, his people will find a way in."

Mira winced. "I'm sorry to bring this trouble to you."

"Can't be helped," Declan said. "It wasn't deliberate. Your father was bound to catch up to us. This hiding place would not have concealed us forever. There are powerful shapers aiding Stafford. There are spies and mercenaries. Not only does he have the legion at his disposal, but also his secret police, the Enforcers. It was only a matter of time before his full attention turned to finding me."

"Where should I go?" Mira asked.

Declan sighed, his eyes sad. "Stay here, and they will

corner you and take you. Run, and sooner or later, they will catch you. I suggest you take the offensive. Track down your power."

"The power that's running wild?" Jace checked. "The power that leaves no living witnesses?"

"*Her* power," Declan said. "This could be the chance you've been waiting for, Mira. Reclaim your power. Help your sisters reclaim theirs. I can't risk more communication with your mother, not with all eyes turned my way, but from what I understand, I believe this is what she would want. It won't be enough to run from Stafford. It won't suffice to hide. You have to beat him."

Mira returned Declan's gaze. "How do I get my power back?"

"I'm not sure," Declan said with a faint scowl. "I don't understand how it was taken. I don't fully grasp how it is acting independently. But I do know that it is *your* power. It cannot survive without you. So defeat it. Make it submit to you. If you must, kill the form it has taken. Exert mastery over your power, and it should return to you."

"How do we know you're not just telling her what's best for you?" Jace challenged. "If she leaves, it will draw the attention away from here. Once she's back out there, they'll question whether she ever made it through the cloudwall. Maybe she snuck around it somehow, or hid in it temporarily, like we were planning to do. Then Mira attacks her power. If she defeats it, great. If it kills her, it destroys itself. Either way, for you, problem solved."

Declan gave Mira a small smile. "Keep this one close. He

clearly has your best interests at heart. The advice I shared does benefit me as well. That doesn't make it insincere guidance. Heed as much of it as you choose. Your path is not mine to walk."

"How would we leave?" Mira asked.

"That part will not be hard," Declan said. "Liam will show you the way. And I will lend what aid I can to your quest. Why not sleep on it tonight? Decide in the morning."

"All right," Mira said. "Thank you for your hospitality."

"I wish I could do more to ease your burdens," Declan said. He tapped one of his canes against the floor, and the door to the chamber swung open. "Go and rest. Jamar awaits without and will see you to your rooms."

"Thanks," Cole added to the mumbled gratitude of Jace and Twitch. He wondered how well they would sleep with so much to think about.

CHAPTER
22

VISITORS

In Cole's room, every item of furniture balanced on a single leg. Not just the chairs and the table, but even the couch and the bed. He figured this was a way for a shaper to show off.

Supported by a slender central rod, the queen-size bed looked especially precarious. Cole tested it by leaning against the thick mattress and shaking it roughly. Though it swayed a little, the bed seemed improbably stable.

Cole sat down on a chair with a single leg. It wasn't connected to the ground—he had checked by moving it around. But when seated in the chair, no matter how hard he tipped his body, it refused to fall over.

Somebody knocked on his door. As he crossed the room, he wondered if it was Mira, wanting to talk about the choice she had to make. He still couldn't believe that she was a princess.

He opened the door and found Jace standing there. The other boy looked tired. His torn sleeve had grass stains on it. "Hey," he said.

"What's up?"

"Can we talk for a minute?" Cole backed away, and Jace entered, looking around the room. "Everything's on one leg?"

"And it doesn't fall over," Cole said.

"Everything in my room is edible."

"Do you usually taste furniture?"

"Jamar told me."

"Is it good?"

"Not really. The curtains aren't bad. Look. We need to talk about tomorrow."

"Okay," Cole said. "Want to sit?"

"I'm fine. In the morning, Mira will start hunting her power."

"She told you?"

"She didn't have to. I can tell. You heard Declan. It's really her only choice."

"Maybe she'll make a run for it."

Jace shook his head. "No way. Declan told her she might be able to get her power back. And that she can stop it from hurting people. And that it's a better strategy than running or hiding. I saw her face. She'll follow his advice."

Cole paused. "I guess we'll have to go with her."

"Not necessarily," Jace said slowly. "I won't leave her. But you don't have to stick around. She'll have help. You're not from here. This isn't your battle."

Cole frowned. Jace was giving him an out. Did he want one? Kind of. How were they supposed to beat some huge creature made of pure shaping power? Cole didn't want to let Mira down, but he was also worried about finding Dalton and

Jenna and figuring out how they could get home. It sounded like Declan might have some ideas that could steer him in the right direction. He would make sure to bring it up tomorrow.

Jace had never been particularly nice to him. What was he up to?

"You don't want me around?" Cole asked.

"I don't really care," Jace said, although it sounded like maybe he did. "It's up to you. I'm just saying you don't have to feel trapped."

"What about Twitch?"

"I talked to him already," Jace said. "He's not too excited about it, but it looks like he's coming, more out of duty than anything. He doesn't want the High Shaper to get away with what he did. But I think partly he doesn't want to be on his own as a runaway slave with the legion and the Sky Raiders on his tail. If you go your own way, there's a chance he'd join you."

"You just want to be alone with her," Cole realized.

Jace reddened. "What are you talking about?"

"I can't believe it," Cole said. "Even after all this, you're mostly worried about your crush."

Jace took a deep, angry breath. "Don't try to push your feelings onto me. Just because—"

"*My* feelings? Are you serious?"

"Cole, don't mess with me about this."

"I might have to if you're trying to talk me out of coming."

"This isn't up to me. The choice is yours. I'm just not sure I'd try to force my way into a situation where I wasn't wanted."

"What?" Cole exclaimed. "You get that she was going

to leave with me. We were going to sneak away tomorrow morning. Then the legion showed up."

Jace grew very still. "You're such a liar."

"Why do you think she knew about my friends who the High King enslaved? She was going to help me find them. You heard us talking about it. Go ask her."

Jace looked away, his lips twisting. He flexed his fingers. "This is hilarious. What are you saying? That I'm the intruder?"

"No. I'm saying that Mira and I were going to run away and help each other. She told me her secret because I saved her life. She decided she could trust me."

Jace gave a stiff nod. "Then you want to come?"

"Not really," Cole said. "I don't know how we're going to beat that creature. If it kills her, sounds like we'll get to see what explosions look like up close."

"It'll have to go through me first," Jace said.

"I get it. You're brave. You really are. She's lucky to have you. She needs all the help she can get. Working together got us this far."

"You're coming, then?"

Cole thought about it. Did he want to abandon Mira to her problems? She was the only real friend he had made in the Outskirts. And Jace and Twitch were the next closest. Could he leave Mira to their care? He had promised Durny to look after her, but Mira had told him he could go. Did he want to be on the run alone? Not really. But what about Jenna? What about Dalton?

"I don't know," Cole said. "My friends have nobody help-ing them."

"Right," Jace said. "So what does that mean?"

"It means I need more information. I want to hear what Declan knows. My friends really need me."

"Got it. Good to know where we rank."

"Weren't you just trying to get rid of me?"

"Maybe. Cole, I don't like her how you think. We just found out she's more than any of us have a right to dream about. She's a real friend. I appreciate her. It's not like . . . I just don't want anything to happen to her."

"Okay."

"You better not say anything."

"I get it," Cole said. "I won't."

Jace looked calmer. "All right. See you in the morning." He let himself out.

Cole walked over and flopped onto the bed. After all they had been through today, he could hardly believe that Jace wanted to add more drama. Jace obviously had it bad for Mira, but so what? They all had way bigger problems for now.

Cole buried his face in a pillow. Was he really going to ditch Mira? Maybe . . . if it meant saving Jenna and Dalton. But what if they were fine? What if they were becoming good shapers? What if they *liked* working in a palace? Thinking about the decision made him ache with doubt.

There was another knock at the door. Cole sat up. Could it be Mira this time? Or was Jace coming back with more inspirational thoughts?

Cole crossed to the door and opened it to find Liam waiting on the other side. "May I come in?"

"Sure," Cole said, stepping back.

Liam entered. He wore loose blue pajamas. It was the first time Cole had seen him not on his disk. "I did this room," Liam said.

"It's weird," Cole replied.

"Thank you. Mind if I sit?"

"No."

Liam plopped down on the couch, making it wobble. "How is Happy?"

"The face on the wagon? That *was* you!"

"One of my early semblances," Liam said. "I was glad to hear he's still out there. I wonder how many people have found him over the years."

"He still talks about you."

"And here we are talking about him. Did he cheer you up?"

"Actually he did. I was having a bad day."

"Anyone in that wagon is having a bad day."

"True." Cole sat down on a chair near the couch. "Did Declan tell you about our conversation?"

"No, I spied."

"What? I thought nobody could spy on that room."

"Nobody can penetrate it from the outside. I had Lola the Pig leave behind a tiny rendering. It sent vibrations to an earpiece that I wore. Nobody else could have overheard. I take a greater interest in current events than Declan realizes."

"Then you heard about Mira," Cole said.

"Miracle, yes," Liam said. "I suspected her identity when I first saw her up close and noticed the powerful shaping keeping her from her abilities. I've been helping Declan track the embodiment of her powers. It's such a puzzle. Even right there in front of me, I still had no idea how they did it. Amazing work, really."

"No fun for her," Cole said.

Liam pointed at Cole's chair, and it toppled over sideways. "Don't be a downer. Of course it's no fun for her. It's still incredible."

Cole had managed to break his fall with his hands. "Thanks for that."

"I try to teach little lessons wherever I go," Liam said. He waved a hand at his couch, and the support vanished. Rather than fall, the couch started floating gently.

"Why are you here?" Cole asked, shifting into a kneeling position.

"That's deep," Liam said. "I'm not sure I have enough focus to answer."

"You heard what Declan said about you," Cole realized.

Liam gave a little shrug. "At least when he talks behind my back, he sticks to the same things he says to my face. It's actually kind of admirable."

"Do you lack focus?"

"Absolutely. He was telling the truth. I'm not very serious. But I'm not sure it's as big a weakness as he thinks. Get too serious and you freeze up. I may lack focus, but some important things catch my interest."

"Like what?"

"Flashing lights. Dominoes. Pinball."

"Pinball has flashing lights," Cole said.

Liam grinned. "I'm sensing a pattern."

"You guys have pinball?"

"In Zeropolis," Liam said. "I went there as a slave. We know about a lot of stuff from your world. Most of us have our roots there. I notice many things from your world on the castles when they head down the void. I'm not sure how the items get there."

Cole stood up. "Would you fix my chair?"

Liam snapped his fingers and the chair lurched upright. "You must hate it here."

"I don't know," Cole said, sitting gingerly, making sure the chair would hold him again.

"They enslaved you!" Liam said. "Not a great way to encourage tourism."

"How did you end up a slave?" Cole asked.

The couch had drifted up to the ceiling. Liam pushed off gently, and the couch glided lower. "I saved a bunch of orphans from a fire, and my freemark got charred. I was enslaved the next day while I was recovering."

"You're kidding."

"Yes. Ready for the truth? My parents sold me. Not my real parents. I never knew them. They supposedly died in a riot. The parents who raised me decided to sell me."

"Really?"

"Yes. We lived on the border between Junction and Sambria. My parents didn't like my shaping. They tried to get me to hide it. I didn't. It was the only thing I was good at! One day, I got sold, marked, and chucked into a slave wagon. Thanks, Mom! Thanks, Dad! Don't spend it all in one place!"

Liam talked like he was joking, but Cole heard real bitterness behind the words. "So you came here."

"Not right away," Liam said. "I had to escape first. And it took some effort to find Declan. Long, boring story."

"Was it hard to find your way in?"

"Much harder to get in than to get out. I found where Declan had entered and followed the faint path he left behind."

"Wait," Cole said. "Didn't he come here years before you?"

"The woods he came through make you turn around without knowing it. The Boomerang Forest. You walk in, stay on a straight course, and walk out the way you entered without ever turning."

"Really?"

"Yes. But Declan performed counter-shapings wherever the forest tried to turn him around. He adjusted certain places in the woods so he could move sideways or diagonally instead of backward. His shapings were left in place, and I followed them here."

"How do you like it?"

"Beats slavery. Beats parents who would sell me to slavers. I've learned a lot. It's kind of like a voluntary prison where I get to shape amazing things all the time. I won't stay here forever. Sounds like you four won't stay here past tomorrow."

Cole nodded. "Looks that way."

"You'll have fun," Liam said. "New experiences. Fighting a monster made of shaping power? Nobody has done that! Nobody can even guess what it would be like. The idea is revolutionary."

"Do you think we can survive it?"

Liam scrunched his face in thought. "I should probably make a tomb. You know, the kind of memorial they use when you can't retrieve the bodies? We can have the funeral before you leave. I could whip up some black clothes."

"Is it that bad?"

"Who knows? It's unprecedented. Sounded bad to me."

"Me too."

Liam fluttered his fingers and the couch drifted back to its former position. The single, slim support reappeared. "I should let you get some rest."

Liam stood and went to the door.

"Liam," Cole said, rising. "Why'd you come by?"

"I was curious about Happy. What a small world!"

"Is that all?"

"I couldn't sleep and felt a little bored."

"Okay," Cole said. "Good night."

"We'll keep watch tonight. You'll be safe. Try to settle down. You look like you've seen a ghost."

"I have. Mine."

Liam laughed. "Nice. I'm sorry you can't stick around." He walked out and snapped his fingers. The door banged shut.

Shedding his clothes, Cole crawled into bed. Liam was right about one thing at least: He needed sleep. Who knew when he would get a good rest again? Hugging a pillow against the side of his head, Cole tried not to obsess about what the next day would bring.

GIFTS

Breakfast was spectacular the next morning. Eggs had been prepared in numerous ways—scrambled, hard-boiled, soft-boiled, poached, fried, deviled, baked, and pickled. Thick strips of bacon glistened in their crinkly glory. Various kinds of toast and pastries vied for attention, along with butter, honey, and jam. A vat of oatmeal had been sweetened with berries and sugar. Pies bulged with spicy potatoes, veggies, eggs, and sausage. Milk was available, and fruit juice, and numerous hot drinks.

Cole felt a little like a death-row inmate at his last meal. They were fattening him up so he could go get eaten by Mira's rampaging powers.

Jace acted unconcerned. He tossed berries into the air and caught them in his mouth. Mira and Twitch were more subdued. Declan and Jamar ate with them—Declan nibbling at a dry piece of toast, Jamar tearing into the spiciest pie and the pickled eggs. Jamar's waxy white assistants served the food and drink.

Cole had awakened to find nice clothes—exactly his size—laid out for him. Jace and Twitch had new clothes as well. Mira wore a much more flattering outfit, including a thin silver necklace and sparkly hairpins.

Cole still wasn't sure precisely what he planned to do. He wanted to corner Declan for advice, but he felt awkward bringing it up during the meal. Unless Declan had compelling alternatives, Cole figured he would leave with the others, then possibly split off when they reached a road to Junction.

After breakfast, Declan stood, supporting himself against the table. "I take it you have decided how to proceed," he said to Mira.

"We're going to leave," Mira said. "I'm going after my powers. The others can join me or go their own way as they choose."

Cole and Twitch made quick eye contact. Cole wondered how much temptation Twitch felt to take his chances on his own.

"Very well," Declan said. "I expected as much. It's really the only option, given the circumstances. I won't send you away without aid. Most of the semblances and renderings we create here would only function in close proximity to the Brink. The atmosphere near the cloudwalls is much more generous for shaping than elsewhere in Sambria. Nevertheless, I have instructed each of my apprentices to provide an item to help you on your way. These gifts will function anywhere in Sambria. They all belong to Mira. Those who accompany her will benefit from them as well. Asia! Liam!"

Asia entered the room, followed by Lyrus, who carried a wicker basket. She gestured toward him, and the soldier upended the basket on the floor, revealing a tangle of chains and iron balls.

"I call this the Shaper's Flail," Asia said. "It responds to a few commands. Flail, ready!"

At those words, the chains became untangled. Five of the iron balls reared up into the air like serpents poised to strike, some higher than others, each attached to one of the thick-linked chains. One ball stayed on the ground. Each ball had to weigh twenty or thirty pounds, and each chain connected to a central iron ring.

"It also responds to commands like 'return,' which will send it back to the basket; 'follow,' which will make it trail along behind you; 'defend,' which will make it protect something or someone; and 'attack,' which you should only say if you really mean it. The word 'flail' must precede the command for it to work. Flail, return!"

In a clattering blur, the mass of chains and spheres sprang smoothly into the basket. Cole and Twitch shared a glance. The new weapon would definitely bring some added protection.

"The flail is linked to Mira and will only respond to her," Asia said. "She will guide it to targets with her thoughts and focus, but no effort will be required to determine how it attacks. The flail will also respond to the commands 'capture' and 'threaten.' As you might guess, don't try to capture anything delicate. It isn't a gentle rendering."

"Thank you, Asia," Declan said. "Jamar?"

The curly haired shaper stood and held up a red velvet

sack with a golden drawstring. "I harvested one of our most abundant natural resources for your use. Massive amounts of water vapor are drawn into the terminal void every day, which means the cloudwall is somehow being constantly replenished. This sack contains twenty thousand cubic yards of fog. It can empty in twenty seconds. Once empty, if you turn the bag inside out, it can swallow up to twenty thousand cubic yards of fog at the same rate. Use it over and over if desired."

"Are there commands?" Mira asked.

"'Empty slow,' 'empty medium,' 'empty fast,'" Jamar rattled off. "They work when the mouth of the sack is open. When inside out, 'fill slow,' 'fill medium,' and 'fill fast.' No need to make it complicated."

"Or useful," Liam said, entering the room on a hovering disk. "Unless they want to ruin an afternoon at a small beach."

"Perhaps they'll need to confuse their enemies," Jamar said.

"Can they see through the fog better than others?" Liam asked.

"They can release the fog behind themselves during an escape," Jamar said less patiently. "They could fill enemy barracks. Or obscure a courtyard."

"I guess it could come in handy," Liam allowed. "Asia's gift was as subtle as ever."

"I'm not sure subtlety will be their greatest need," Asia said.

"Well, I'll provide some, anyway." Liam whistled, and a bird flew to his shoulder—a white-and-gray cockatiel with a yellow crest and orange cheeks. "This is Mango."

"You're my new masters," the cockatiel said in an eager

voice, only vaguely birdlike. "I'll spy for you and do whatever else I can to keep you safe and informed."

"She'll answer to any of you," Liam said. "That way if Mira gets knocked unconscious or is otherwise indisposed, you can still give Mango orders. But if you split up, Mango will stay with Mira."

The cockatiel flitted from Liam's shoulder to Mira's. She stood about six inches tall, not counting the long tail feathers. The bird cocked her head and whistled. Mira petted it gently.

"Her wings feel strange," Mira said.

"Strange?" Mango challenged, ruffling her feathers.

Now that Mira mentioned it, as Cole leaned closer, the bird didn't look quite right. The texture of the feathers seemed too smooth and shiny.

"Mango is made from a light substance I designed," Liam said. "I call it ristofly. It makes her much more durable than if she were composed of flesh and actual feathers. She can fly faster and see better than most real birds. She doesn't need food or water, doesn't sleep, doesn't relieve herself, and can dwell underwater as easily as in the air."

"See how handy I am?" Mango said. "And you sum it up with 'strange.'"

"Sorry," Mira said. "I didn't mean any offense."

Asia exhaled derisively. "A semblance that requires apologies? Brilliant work, Liam. Very subtle."

"I'm plenty subtle," Mango snapped. The bird hopped close to Mira's ear. "I won't let anyone sneak up on you. I'll steer you away from danger. And you can command me to do just about anything. If I don't understand, I'll let you know."

"You made her in one night?" Mira asked Liam.

"Sort of," Liam replied. "I repurposed one of my best spy birds. But I completely reshaped and refined her, added some spunk."

"She's so lifelike," Mira said.

"Few shapers could manage such a creation," Declan said. "Flying semblances are hard. Personalities are harder. None of us can replicate lifelike humans and other beasts to match the ones the Western Cloudwall creates. Semblances like Lyrus are uniquely realistic."

"Could Lyrus come with us?" Cole asked.

"I would relish nothing more than an adventure," the soldier said.

"I'm aware," Declan replied. "But nothing we can do would allow you to leave here and survive. That aspect of you is beyond any of our abilities to tamper with. It would be like trying to shape an actual human—there is too much complexity to cause anything but disaster. The semblances from the sky castles can only survive on the castles or here on the peninsula."

"Then why can Mango come with us?" Cole asked.

"It is easier to make semblances out here beyond the Brink," Declan said. "Most of the semblances and renderings we create can't leave. But with effort, we can design semblances and renderings that could survive elsewhere in Sambria, just as most nonliving renderings from the sky castles can survive elsewhere."

"Forgive me if I spoke out of turn," Lyrus said, head bowed.

"I appreciate your enthusiasm," Declan said. "If I could

make a gift of you to help these young people on their way, I wouldn't hesitate."

"You've already done so much," Mira said. She made eye contact with Asia, Jamar, and Liam. "Thank you for the gifts."

"We're not done yet," Declan said, sounding mildly offended. "I haven't given you mine."

"There's more?" Mira asked.

"How about this for starters?" He waved an arm in a wide gesture and Cole felt his wrist tingle.

All four kids investigated the sensation. Cole saw that the mark tattooed there had changed.

Jace gasped. "It's a freemark," he said reverently.

"That's right," Declan said. "It would be difficult to go abroad marked as slaves."

"You can't change a bondmark!" Mira exclaimed.

Declan gave a small smile. "Most people can't. They're designed to be permanent. The shaper who developed them was a student of mine."

"Just like that," Twitch said, rubbing his wrist.

"It looks real," Jace marveled.

"It *is* real," Declan said. "Those new marks are indistinguishable from authentic freemarks. They have been reshaped. No traces of the original bondmarks remain. No shaper or needle master can claim otherwise."

"I can hardly believe it," Mira said.

"There's more," Declan said. "Join me outside."

Declan moved a finger and his chair hovered up and away from the table. Advancing at a pace that let the others keep up, he led the way to the courtyard. At first Jace didn't follow the others. It took a nudge from Cole to stop him from staring at his freemark.

Beyond the castle doors, an odd carriage awaited in the courtyard. The enclosed compartment rode on four wheels—not fancy, but clean and well crafted. At the front, instead of a horse, there stood a huge black brick with legs.

"An autocoach," Jace said.

"For us?" Mira asked hopefully.

"For you," Declan said. "I could have modified it to move faster. I could have made it more elaborate. But I thought it wiser to make it as typical as possible."

"Won't it raise suspicions to see four kids with their own autocoach?" Twitch asked. "Free or not."

"Astute," Declan said. "Wearing nice clothes will help, which is why we updated your wardrobes. The last part of my gift also tried to address that problem. Bertram?"

The door to the autocoach opened, and an old man with a close-cropped white beard leaned out. He was dressed in a slightly shabby, old-fashioned suit. "What was that? My hearing isn't so keen."

"State your business," Declan ordered.

The old man's eyes widened. "How's that? My business?" He absently patted his pockets. "Yes, well, if I wish to show my grandniece and grandnephews a bit of the countryside, I suppose it is my business. That's enough chatterboxing. I feel past my prime today, and my joints ache something terrible." Coughing, he closed the carriage door and leaned back out of view.

"That's quite a semblance," Mira said.

"Not my best work," Declan lamented. "Don't look to him for profound conversations. But Bertram should hold up well enough while you remain in Sambria. He won't leave the carriage unless forced, mostly because I doubt his authenticity can withstand close inspection. But he should serve to deflect attention if questions get asked about four youngsters traveling alone."

"Four kids and an old man," Cole muttered. "What if somebody decides to rob us?"

"We'll have our gear," Jace said. "Right?"

"Your items are already stowed in the autocoach," Liam said. "I strengthened the shaping of the Jumping Swords to help ensure they would hold up through Sambria. The other objects should continue to function very well."

"How's my rope?" Jace asked, an edge to his voice. "It wasn't working last I saw."

"It was still functional," Liam corrected. "I had merely severed its connection to you so it wouldn't respond to your commands."

"Will it now?" Jace asked.

"I restored the connection," Liam assured him. "You don't have to act so put out. I was doing you a favor. Asia would have cut the rope."

"The rope is tough to cut," Jace said.

"Maybe with normal weapons," Liam replied. "Asia's blade has a miraculous edge. It would have slashed through your rope like it was smoke, and your rendering would have been ruined, probably permanently."

"Then thanks, I guess," Jace mumbled.

"We've stored food and water in the autocoach as well," Asia said. "You'll find the food packed under the seats, and your gear in a compartment beneath the floor. We included some money to help you on your way. Bertram can assist if you have trouble finding anything. We suggest you leave now. The less time you allow the High Shaper to move his forces into the area, the better chance you'll have to make a clean getaway."

"The top speed of the autocoach is not impressive," Jamar said. "Compare it to a horse at an easy trot. But the autocoach can maintain that speed indefinitely. It needs no food, no water, no rest."

"So if we get chased, we might be in trouble," Cole said.

"If dangerous enemies are in close pursuit, you may have to abandon the vehicle," Asia said. "But the autocoach will only operate for Mira. This is standard enough that thieves will have little interest in the coach itself. Your belongings could be another story."

"Does it know where to go?" Mira asked.

"Unless you issue new instructions," Declan said, "the autocoach will take you to Middlebranch. Bertram can advise you about alternative routes and destinations. If you reach Middlebranch, seek out Gerta, a shaper. The locals call her 'the herb woman.' She could be a source of guidance. Most of my old colleagues are dead or in hiding. Gerta has no love for the High Shaper and is among the few from the old days who you can reliably find."

Mira nodded. "Thank you for everything. It's much more than we could have hoped for."

"I wish I could do more," Declan said. "For the first time in decades, your father has shown hints of vulnerability. He will move aggressively to reestablish the certainty of his reign. Evade him. Survive. Trust your instincts. Liam will catch up to instruct you about leaving Cloudvale."

Mira gave Declan a peck on the cheek, then started toward the autocoach. Jace had lifted the hatch in the floor and was examining his golden rope. Beside him, Twitch searched the compartment, probably looking for his ring.

Lingering behind, Cole studied the withered old man in the floating chair. Declan watched him expectantly.

"We need to talk before I leave," Cole said. "I'm not from here. Is there any chance of me ever getting home?"

Declan brought the chair close and spoke loud enough for Cole's ears only. "I was beginning to wonder whether you would seek my counsel. There are ways for you to return to your world. Staying there will be slippery. This is a question for the Wayminders of Creon."

"I briefly talked to a Wayminder," Cole said. "It was the guy the slavers hired to help them reach my world. He told me the same thing—that I could probably get home, but that it would be hard to stay. I came here so unexpectedly. I still don't really get where I am. What is the Outskirts? It's almost like a dream."

Declan gave a snort. "Almost, especially here in Sambria, where certain aspects of reality can be adjusted. I have studied this question, as have others. The most I know is that the Outskirts is an in-between place. One of the five kingdoms seems to lie between life and death, another between reality

271

and imagination, another has pockets outside the normal order of time and space, and another stretches the limits of technological innovation. As you noted, Sambria seems to lie between wakefulness and dreaming. Where else besides dreams can you rearrange the world according to your whims?"

Cole nodded. "Only here."

"Each kingdom has its own kind of shaping," Declan said. "Each has its own wonders and mysteries. I'll let you in on a Sambrian secret. It may only be the fancy of an old man, but I suspect that the Western Cloudwall taps into dreams to form the castles. Could be dreamers in your world, or ours, or both, or more worlds than we can guess. Troubled dreamers, it seems to me. Perhaps failed dreamers. Call it a hunch."

"That might explain why some of the castles have stuff from my world," Cole said.

"It could explain that and more," Declan agreed. "But the issue is mostly academic. Here is the lesson you must learn—the Outskirts may feel dreamlike at times, but this is no dream. In a dream, if you get into trouble, you can eventually wake up. You will not wake from this, Cole. If you get hurt, you will suffer. If you get killed, you will die."

"I believe it. I can tell the difference between being awake and being in a dream. I've slept and had dreams since I came here. I've been hungry and thirsty and tired and scared. None of that felt like a dream. Some things are unbelievably weird, but it's all way too real."

"That's right," Declan said.

"I'm worried about the other kids who came here

from my world," Cole explained. "Especially my two best friends."

"The pair who went to the High King as slaves," Declan said. "You're certain of their destination?"

"Some woman tested us for shaping potential," Cole said. "I had none. She called me the worst of the bunch. Kids with the most shaping ability were put into cages to go to the High King. That included my friends Jenna and Dalton."

"When we met, you mentioned you came to the Outskirts voluntarily," Declan said.

"Right," Cole said. "I didn't know where I was going, but nobody forced me. I was trying to help my friends."

"The slavers didn't know you came through on your own?"

Cole shook his head. "The Wayminder saw me after I came through and gave me a little help. I didn't want him to get in trouble, so I pretended I arrived with the others but slipped away."

Declan gave a frail chuckle. "That explains why you weren't sent to the High Shaper."

"What do you mean?"

"People who come to the Outskirts from your world tend to have more shaping potential than the average citizen born here, which explains why the slavers went to your world looking for slaves with shaping talent. People who come here voluntarily from your world, rather than by accident or compulsion, tend to have far greater ability than most."

"Then why didn't the woman see any shaping potential in me?" Cole asked. "When I came here, I didn't really know where I was going. Maybe that counts as ending up here by accident."

"No," Declan said. "If you followed the slavers, you purposely entered. You didn't blunder into it by happenstance. Unsure of where it would lead, you chose to follow them, and that is deliberate. The shaping power manifests differently for someone who chooses to come to the Outskirts. It's a rare occurrence."

"What makes it different?"

"You become much more likely to develop more than one kind of shaping talent, and those talents tend to be unusually strong. But the abilities take longer to show up. I don't currently see shaping potential in you. Not any. That is rare. Almost everyone has at least a little shaping talent. Having absolutely none is less common than having a lot. I expect that one day, you'll discover powerful skills."

"Really?" Cole said, excited by the thought of having ways to help his friends besides flying through the air with a sword. "How long will it take?"

Declan shrugged. "That's where it gets complicated. It could take years. Or it could never happen."

Cole's excitement dimmed. "Is there anything I can do to speed it up?"

"I'm unaware of any techniques that would hasten the process," Declan said. "But I do know this: If the slavers were looking for slaves with shaping potential, and they knew you came through voluntarily, and they saw that you displayed zero potential, you would have been their top pick."

"Even though I might be a dud?" Cole asked.

"They would gladly take that chance. According to the odds, your talents will show up eventually, and when they do, they'll be strong."

"But that potential doesn't help me much right now," Cole said.

"True," Declan said. "Perhaps not for a long time."

Straightening, Cole steeled himself. "With or without shaping powers, I need to help my friends. Do you know how I can find them?"

"If they went to Junction City, I could direct you there," Declan said. "So could Mira. Many people you would meet could point you in the right direction. But stealing a slave is a serious crime. According to the laws of the land, your friends legally belong to the High King. I don't expect you could free them on your own. Even if you managed it, I doubt you would remain free. You'd be caught and punished, as would they."

"You're saying there's nothing I can do?" Cole asked in frustration. "I have to try. It's my fault my friends are here in the first place. I took them to the place where they were kidnapped."

"Deliberately?" Declan asked.

"Not on purpose," Cole said. "But my friends got grabbed. The slavers only missed me by accident."

Declan pressed his fingertips together. "There may be ways for you to help your friends. However, if you go to Junction alone and try to free them, you will probably fail. Here is my advice: Stay close to Mira. If she defeats Carnag and reclaims her power, it will deal a major blow to the High

King. Mira could become the focal point of a revolution. Before Stafford claimed the throne, it was unlawful to go beyond the Outskirts to hunt slaves. The best way to free your friends would be to topple his regime."

"The High King made it legal to take slaves from Earth?" Cole asked.

"Before Stafford, that was always forbidden," Declan said. "The Outskirts has a long and unfortunate history of slavery, but at least there were limits. Believe it or not, the High Shaper before Stafford wanted to abolish slavery entirely. But Stafford pushed everything in the opposite direction. Now slavery thrives more than ever."

"My friends and I aren't the first people taken from my world as slaves?"

Declan shook his head. "Far from it."

"Then why haven't I heard of mass kidnappings?" Cole asked. "When the slavers came after me and my friends, they took dozens of kids. It should be major news."

"Ah," Declan said. "The Wayminder didn't explain it all to you."

"We only talked a little."

"Cole, when people travel from your world to ours, those who know and love them best remember them the least."

Back at the slave caravan, the redheaded guard had claimed that their parents wouldn't remember them. Cole had assumed the man had been exaggerating. It took him a moment to muster a reply. "My parents won't remember me?"

"Those who should remember you most will have

forgotten all about you," Declan confirmed. "They no longer know you exist."

"What about someone like my teacher?" Cole asked. "I'm on the class role. Won't she notice I'm missing when she takes attendance? She'll call my name. . . ."

"Your teacher won't notice," Declan said. "As people try to focus on you, they'll end up ignoring you. Evidence of your absence may remain, but people won't pay attention to it. Not your family. Not anyone."

Cole chewed his bottom lip. He and his friends were even more alone than he had realized. Nobody missed them. Nobody was looking for them. Getting home really was all up to him. And if they got home, what then? "Can it be fixed? Will they ever remember us?"

"Save that question for a Wayminder," Declan said. "I simply don't know."

Cole wanted to scream. What if he had permanently been wiped from the minds of his family? If he ever made it home, his life might never be the same. It was too awful to contemplate. He had to believe there was a way to repair the problem. "Why did the High Shaper expand slavery?"

"I can only guess, Cole," Declan said. "Maybe he likes the economics. Slaves increase many opportunities for the ruling class. Also, slaves from Earth are more likely to be strong shapers. I know he adores power."

"You're right about one thing," Cole said, anger smoldering inside. "The High King is my enemy. He ripped me and my friends from our lives. He's holding my best friends captive. But he's the king! How am I supposed to overthrow him?"

"You're not alone," Declan replied. "That's my point. You need support. A rebellion has been brewing for some time. The four exiled Grand Shapers all want to see Stafford fall. During his rise, he made many enemies. The return of his lost daughters could be the key to his ruin. Help Mira, and the chance to truly free your friends could follow. Even a failed rebellion could provide you with the help and the distraction you would need to liberate your friends."

Cole tried to sort through the pros and cons. Staying with Mira would mean delaying any rescue attempt. But if it improved his chances to succeed, it might be worth it. When he had tried to save his friends back at the caravan, he got caught in no time. He didn't want to repeat that mistake. Jenna and Dalton would probably be much harder to free from the royal palace. Once free, where would they run? Cole wasn't sure whether they could ever get home.

He looked over at the autocoach. He didn't want to abandon Mira. This gave him a real reason to stay with her. It would also give him time to see if he developed any shaping powers. If he could help Mira weaken the High King before he charged in to save his friends, maybe Mira and some of her allies could assist him in return.

Cole folded his arms. Did he want to go after his friends on his own? Or would he rather face Carnag with Mira? Either option could lead to failure. Either could get him killed. Neither path would be easy, but staying with Mira felt right.

"Sticking with Mira makes sense," Cole finally said.

"I agree," Declan said. "Your interests are aligned. You need each other. Help her succeed, and you'll triumph as well."

Cole was almost too scared to ask his next question. "What are our chances? Can we beat Carnag? Could we win a revolution?"

"Your chances are small," Declan said. "But great movements have started small before. Take it one step at a time. You have more power than you know. So does Mira."

Cole nodded pensively. He felt like he should keep Declan talking. There had to be more questions he could answer. Cole knew so little about the Outskirts, and Declan knew so much. But his friends were waiting in the autocoach, and the questions refused to form. "The Wayminders are in Creon?"

"And elsewhere," Declan said. "But they come from Creon. The least of them knows more about traveling beyond the five kingdoms than I do."

Cole searched his mind for anything else he should ask. He knew he would kick himself later. Nothing was coming, and they needed to hurry.

"I can see your anxiety," Declan said kindly. "Relax, my boy. You're here. You can't change that all at once. Take it one day at a time. Learn as you go. You have many knots to untie, but you won't unravel them all today. How well did you understand your old world? How it originated? Its deepest mysteries and secrets? I know the Outskirts feels foreign, but you don't need to understand everything about a world to live in it. Stay close to Mira. I wish you well."

"Thanks for the advice," Cole said. "Watch out for the bad guys."

Declan gave a small wave. "We always keep watch."

"Enjoy your quest," Lyrus said, placing a large hand on Cole's shoulder. "I envy you."

"Thanks, Lyrus. I'll try to be brave."

"I have no doubt," the warrior approved.

Feeling he had kept his friends waiting too long, Cole ran to the autocoach and jumped inside. He sat on the bench beside Twitch and Jace, opposite Mira and Bertram.

"Go," Mira said as she leaned forward and closed the door. Smoothly, the autocoach began to move.

CHAPTER

—— 24 ——

THE QUIET WOOD

"That was quite a talk with Declan," Jace said. "Have you decided when you're ditching us?"

Mira looked unsettled by the blunt question. Cole could tell she didn't want him to go. He wasn't eager to leave. But she had Jace and Twitch, while Dalton and Jenna had nobody.

"I'm with you guys at least until Carnag," Cole said. "My best chance to help Jenna and Dalton is to weaken the High King. And that means helping Mira. Let's get her powers back. We'll figure out our next move after that."

"There's no guarantee we'll defeat Carnag," Mira warned.

"I know," Cole said. "But I don't think I'll have much chance trying to take a couple of slaves from the High King on my own."

"That's true," Mira said.

"Your father made the laws that allowed those people to come for us," Cole said, trying not to let his tone get too heated. He was mad at her father, not Mira. The High King had wrecked her life too. "He owns my friends according to those laws. Declan wants us to overthrow him. I like that idea."

"It's hard to imagine," Mira said. "He's clever and brutal. Still, this could be the first step in that direction. When my mother sent us away, she promised that one day we would return and inherit all we lost."

"First things first," Jace said. "Let's try to escape in one piece."

When they reached the edge of Declan's sanctuary, Liam appeared in the window and asked Mira to halt the autocoach. The vehicle came to an even stop, and the kids climbed out. Ahead, the path disappeared into a mossy forest. Cole was surprised to see two other autocoaches behind them.

"What's with those?" Cole asked, nodding at the carriages.

"Declan had some extras on hand," Liam said. "He decided it might confuse your pursuers to send a pair of empty autocoaches in different directions. If you ever cross paths with one again, they will answer to Mira. Otherwise they'll loop through a long preset course."

"Smart," Twitch said, nodding in approval.

"He does have centuries of experience," Liam said. "I've sent Mango ahead. She will report back to you periodically, but especially if danger approaches."

"Any trick to these woods?" Jace asked.

"Not getting out," Liam said. "The autocoach will do the work. Don't let the easy exit fool you. If you try to backtrack to this place, with or without the autocoach, it'll just lead to frustration. You'd have a better chance braving the cloudwall again."

"Once was plenty," Mira said.

"After you're through, you'll notice the trees get bigger," Liam said. "That's the Quiet Wood. Don't speak until the trees get small. You might hear some strange sounds. Say nothing. Not to one another, not to any creatures you see, not to yourselves. The semblances who prowl the Quiet Wood are attracted to speech from nonsemblances. Talk, and they will hunt you down."

"You tell us this now?" Cole exclaimed.

"Now is when you need to know it," Liam replied calmly. "Why do you think I came to see you off? For a second farewell? In the direction you're heading, it'll take an hour or more to pass through the Quiet Wood. When the trees return to normal size, you're clear. You shouldn't have trouble if you keep silent. Most people stay well away for obvious reasons."

"What kind of semblances would attack?" Jace asked.

"Imagine giant bears that hunt in packs, and you'll have the basic idea," Liam replied.

"Are you serious?" Cole cried. "What's with this place?"

Liam looked taken aback. "Sambria is the result of centuries of shapers tampering with the environment. Some in big ways, others in small ones. Certain big changes fade, and some of the minor ones have greater impact over time. It's hard to predict. The Quiet Wood is neither the strangest nor the most perilous region of Sambria. Bertram will guide you around the worst areas. He'll take you on safe roads to Middlebranch. If something gets in your way, he'll improvise. Won't you, Bertram?"

"Not bad weather for an outing," the old man remarked

from the autocoach. "It's not every day I go for a ride with my young relatives."

"Not much personality," Liam whispered conspiratorially. "Declan tends to be more about function than ornamentation." He stopped whispering. "Bertram knows the geography. One perk of Sambria is that over the years, shapers have laid down many roads and paths, even through wild and otherwise inaccessible country."

"Any other hazards we should know about?" Twitch asked.

"Mountains of them," Liam said. "But who knows which ones you'll encounter? We don't have the weeks it would take to list them all. You have handy renderings and your common sense. Use them well." He elevated upon his disk. "I can't emphasize enough, no talking in the Quiet Wood. Remember that, and your trek should start out fine. Forget it, and you won't get a second chance."

"Thanks for everything," Mira said earnestly. "We came here expecting to die. We leave with a fighting chance."

"Good luck on your journey," Liam said, raising a hand in farewell. "Remember, if you get into horrible trouble and desperately need me, I'll be much too busy with my own problems!"

With that he sped off.

The four kids looked at one another. Jace and Cole burst out laughing.

"It may not be funny before long," Twitch mumbled.

Jace rubbed away his smile. "We might get into trouble, but it'll still be funny."

"We should go," Mira said, climbing back into the

autocoach. "Think you three can keep your lips sealed?"

"We'll see," Cole said. "Sometimes when it's really quiet, like during a test, or in the library, I get this urge to shout something just to break the silence and surprise everyone."

Mira assumed a patient expression. "Um, Cole, you're going to have to control that urge."

"I've never given in and shouted," Cole assured her. "And for the record, getting eaten by giant bears is the best reason I've ever had to keep my mouth shut."

"Should we stop talking now, you know, to be safe?" Twitch asked.

"We're not moving yet," Jace pointed out.

"Go ahead," Mira commanded.

The autocoach started rolling forward, accompanied by the soft clomping of the walking brick's strides. Now that he listened mindfully, Cole heard the other autocoaches following.

"We're moving now," Twitch observed.

"Then I agree we should shut up," Jace said.

"All in favor?" Cole asked, raising a hand.

The other three kids raised their hands. "Aye," Mira said.

"As long as I get the last word," Jace said.

"What if I want it?" Mira asked.

Jace gave a slow grin. "Then you'll have to take it."

"Maybe I will," Mira said.

"I will for sure," Jace said, his stare level.

"Guys, are you sure this is a good time to play chicken?" Cole asked. The autocoach was entering the forest.

"We have until the trees get big," Jace said.

"It's the Boomerang Forest first," Mira agreed.

"Any chance of getting slaughtered by giant bears is too big of a risk," Twitch said.

"Getting in on the contest too, Twitch?" Jace asked.

"Just trying to be the voice of reason," Twitch explained. "How about you guys say something at the same time? You can both have the last word!"

Jace shrugged. "Seems like a nice, reasonable, cowardly way to settle it. Count me out."

"Me too," Mira said. "You're not going to beat me."

Jace smirked. "I will if I'm willing to get eaten by bears."

"Are you?" Mira asked.

"Out of stubbornness?" Jace asked. "Sure, why not? I considered myself dead on my first sky castle mission. Helped my nerves. The rest of this is just borrowed time. A bonus."

Mira narrowed her eyes. "But things have changed. You're not a Sky Raider anymore."

Jace cocked his head, as if unsure he believed her. "The danger feels about the same. Or worse."

"What about that freemark?" Mira asked, glancing at his wrist.

Jace jerked a little, the comment cracking his facade. He rubbed his wrist and stared out the window. "You're right. That hasn't really sunk in yet." He glanced her way. "I guess . . . it would be stupid to throw my life away to win some little contest."

"Right?" Mira said appreciatively.

"Of course, if you're going to die . . . ," Jace said.

"Might as well be doing something stupid?" Mira finished. "The good stupid is the brave kind. When there's a real reason behind it. Bad stupid is everything else."

"The same is true for you," Jace said. "You're being just as obstinate. Just as dumb. So why do I have to back down?"

"To show you're the bigger person?" Mira tried.

"I don't get how losing makes me big," Jace said.

They were well into the woods now. Cole stared out the window. The path had become twisty. Did the trees look larger? A little, maybe. Not way bigger yet. How big had Liam meant?

"Guys," Cole said. "We're deep in the woods. The trees are looking bigger. This isn't funny anymore."

Jace smiled wide. "Wrong. It's just getting funny. Do you know what the punch line will be? I hear they look like huge bears."

"You're a riot," Mira said blandly.

"I'll die laughing," Jace said. "Go ahead, test me."

Cole felt like the situation was out of control. "Mira, this is crazy. Let him have the last word. Who cares? We have too much to do, too much real danger to survive. If he wants the prize of biggest nut job, let him have it."

Mira looked from Cole to Jace and back. The only sound was the gentle clomping of the walking brick. "No. He doesn't have to always get his way."

"I kind of do," Jace said. "Want to know the secret? You don't bluff."

Cole thought Jace had been kidding before, but something about the way he said it made him really wonder. Of course, that was probably the point. "Mira," Cole repeated.

"Cole's right," Twitch murmured.

"And the grasshopper is back in the contest!" Jace cried.

Twitch glared, lips compressed, but said no more.

Bertram leaned forward. "Might want to stop speaking now. Up ahead is a stretch where talking could prove problematic."

Everyone fell silent. Leaning out the window, Cole peered ahead. The path had mostly straightened. About a hundred yards forward on his side, partly obscured by lesser vegetation, he saw a soaring tree with a trunk wider than the autocoach. The path went right by it. He could glimpse others beyond.

"Big tree," Cole said, pulling back into the compartment. "Really big tree."

"Liam might just be messing with us," Jace said. "You know, playing a joke on the new guys."

"You know it's serious," Mira said.

"We'll find out soon," Jace said.

If Cole thought he could knock them unconscious, he would have. But Jace was bigger than him and already had his golden rope in hand. Cole considered getting out his Jumping Sword. He might need it when the bears showed up.

"Please, Mira," Cole urged.

"All right," she sighed, exasperated. "Fine. You win, Jace. Have your last word, and let's live to get killed in a more surprising way."

Jace's grin widened. He held out a hand to Mira and nodded once.

"That's it?" Mira asked.

Jace nodded again.

"You just wanted me to say that you could win," Mira said.

Jace gave a slower nod and pointed at her.

"You're so chivalrous," she said dryly.

Jace shrugged.

Cole made a zipping motion over his lips and then buttoned them. The others nodded.

Cole watched as they passed the first big tree. The trunks only grew thicker after that one. The path continued to wind. Some of the trees looked wider than Cole's house. The grooves in the bark were deep troughs. The path weaved a slalom course through the towering forest. Between the surreal trunks, fragile ferns grew among expanses of dark soil and mossy boulders. The colossal trees filtered the sunlight, transforming the world beneath their layers of unreachable limbs into a twilight realm.

The steady clomps of the walking brick provided the main sound. Faint clomping reached them from the trailing autocoaches. Despite the rough path that had grown weedy in places, the autocoach itself made little noise—a slight creak when they hit a bump was all. Otherwise the ride was surprisingly smooth and quiet, especially when Cole contrasted it against the jolting and rattling of his slave wagon.

The atmosphere under the trees felt close and silent, almost like all of nature had paused and was listening. Cole supposed it might feel that way because he knew about the giant bears.

As minutes passed, Cole relaxed enough to feel a small temptation to shout something. He tried to think what would be funny. "I win the contest!" was up there, but his favorite was "Bears are wimps!" Of course, he said nothing. Aside from wanting to live, any loud noise in these imposing woods would feel out of place, like screaming in a church.

He thought about his Jumping Sword, wishing he had retrieved it when he had the chance. Although, technically, it was only talking that would trigger the bears, he didn't want to risk the extra noise of digging through the storage compartment, just in case.

"Hello?" called a voice in the distance.

Cole looked across the coach at Mira. Her eyes were wide.

"Hello?" the voice called again. "Anyone?" It was a man, his voice muffled by the trees, like he might not be as far away as the first cry had sounded. What came to mind was some hunter or hiker who had lost his way.

Jace squeezed Cole's arm and shook his head sharply. Twitch brought an urgent finger to his lips. Mira nodded, both hands over her mouth.

Cole knew they were right. This had to be a trick. And besides, if it was real, the guy had already sealed his fate.

"Please!" the voice called again, a bit fainter, as if heading away from them. "Help! Somebody!"

Soon the woods were silent again. Cole watched and listened, wondering if he might notice a sign of one of the giant bears. He knew it would freak him out if he saw one, but he couldn't resist looking.

"Hello?" called a new person from the other side of the autocoach. This time it was a woman, her voice hoarse. "Anthony? Where are you? Say something!"

"I wanted to show my grandnephews some of the sights in Sambria," Bertram said. "My grandniece as well. No laws against that I hope!"

Cole went rigid at his words. Bertram was a semblance, so he was free to talk, but the unexpected response startled him. Jace was covering a laugh. Cole remained too tense to find it funny.

"Is somebody there?" the hoarse woman called out. "Please! I've lost the road!"

Mira was shaking her head. They were all in agreement to keep silent.

"Please, answer me!" the woman called, her ragged voice dripping with despair.

"I'm afraid we're just here on holiday," Bertram said brightly. "I'm getting on in years—call it a last hoorah."

"Please, help me! Someone! Anyone!"

"I'm not feeling my best today," Bertram apologized. "Better stay coach bound, I'm afraid. Aging joints and what have you."

The woman's pleadings faded behind them.

The trees remained enormous. They heard a couple more people calling for help, different voices, one male and one female, lost souls roaming the forest. The distant cries were faint enough that Cole partly wondered if his ears were playing tricks on him.

Finally the trees began to diminish in size. They were still huge, but most of the trunks were now smaller than the auto-coach, and none were as wide as a house. On Cole's side, a deer ambled beside them, keeping pace. Cole watched the graceful creature, wondering how long its curiosity would last.

"Greetings," the deer called to him in a male voice. "Are you good people lost?"

Cole watched the animal in stunned silence.

"Can you hear me?" the deer asked.

Cole looked at his companions. Twitch mimed buttoning his lips shut. Cole nodded.

"That isn't a very safe road," the deer called. "Where are you trying to go?"

Cole waved good-bye to the deer.

"Think you know these woods better than I do?" the deer asked, turning away. "Your funeral."

"One and one makes two," said a voice at the other side of the autocoach. Cole swiveled to see another deer. "Two and two makes . . ."

His mind automatically answered "four." But he kept his mouth shut.

"Row your boat, gently down the stream," the deer recited. "Merrily, for life is but a . . ."

He could hardly believe the deer was so blatantly trying to get them to say something. Twitch shooed the deer away with his hand, and it bounded off.

The autocoach rolled onward, and the trees continued to diminish until they resembled an ordinary forest. They passed a crossroads. Their autocoach went straight, but behind them, one of the autocoaches turned right; the other, left.

Cole and the others stayed silent for another long stretch. Finally Mira tapped Bertram and pantomimed talking.

"What's the trouble, my dear girl?" Bertram said. "I'm sorry, you'll have to speak up. My hearing isn't what it once was."

Leaning close to him, Mira whispered in his ear. Cole couldn't hear a word she said.

"Oh, yes, we're in the clear," Bertram replied. "Feel free to converse. After all, we're on holiday."

"That's a relief," Mira said.

"I was honestly ready for the two of you to get us killed back there," Twitch said. "I was set to fly away."

"Sometimes you have to stand up for what's right," Jace said.

Mira kicked at his shin from across the compartment. "You were like a spoiled kid who complained until he got the treat he wanted."

"What did that make you?" Jace asked, having twisted to avoid her foot.

"The adult who relented," Mira said.

"It worked out perfectly," Jace said. "I waited for you to give me what I wanted, but I let you be the nut job who got the last word."

Mira sprang out of her seat, crouching because of the coach's roof. She didn't kick him too hard, but this time it connected. Jace laughed along with the other boys.

Then Mango flew in the window and perched on Mira's shoulder. "Good, good," the bird approved. "You're having fun. I hate to spoil the mood, but we have company."

"What?" Mira asked, settling back in her seat, all playfulness gone.

"Legionnaires coming this way. On horseback. Lots of them."

ON THE RUN

"Legionnaires?" Cole exclaimed. "How many is lots?"

"One hundred and forty-four," Mango said. "They're west of us, coming this way in four equal groups, along four different routes."

Jace yanked open the hatch to the compartment where their gear was stashed. He handed Mira her Jumping Sword, then Cole his bow and his sword.

"How'd they find us so quickly?" Twitch asked.

"They haven't found you," Mango replied. "They've fanned out over a broad area. They're searching."

"They might suspect we ran off this way," Mira said. "Or they might just be checking everywhere. Either way, I guess they know we're alive."

"Like Declan warned us," Cole reminded her. "Your father must be able to feel that you haven't died. He must have told them."

"What matters is what we do now," Jace said, all business. "Mango, will they find us if we stay on our current path?"

Mango gently pecked at Mira's silver necklace while talking. "If they don't double back or change course, they'll overtake you before the end of the day."

"Can we go in other directions?" Mira asked.

"You could leave the autocoach," Mango said, nibbling at one of the pins in her hair. "They're sticking to the roads. But traveling cross-country on your own can be dangerous in Sambria, especially in a wild area like the north of the kingdom."

"We should stay with the coach until we know we're going to be found," Twitch said. "You can warn us when they get really close, right, Mango?"

"Yes, sirree," the bird replied.

"If they find an empty coach, they may heavily search the nearby area," Jace pointed out.

"I don't mean we should desert the coach a minute before they find us," Twitch clarified. "More like an hour before. The autocoach will travel a good distance before they find it, and we'll have time to get well away from the road."

"Good thinking," Cole approved.

"We want the autocoach as long as we can keep it," Mira said. "We'll be much slower on foot. And Mango is right. This part of Sambria is unsafe."

"Maybe we can use that to our advantage," Jace said. "Sort of like the cloudwall all over again. Is there anywhere we can go where the legionnaires won't want to follow? Someplace they would expect us to avoid? Especially if it's away from where they're headed."

Mango flapped her wings and gave a soft squawk. "There

are plenty of dangerous places. The legionnaires are west of you, some moving northeast, others southeast. Going west isn't an option right now, and I don't think you could get ahead of them cutting straight south. If you flee north, you'll end up back in the Quiet Wood, and eventually you'll get pinned against the Boomerang Forest. If you try to get around the Boomerang Forest to the east, you'll end up against the Brink."

"I don't mind the Quiet Wood," Jace said.

"But we don't want to get pinned with nowhere to run," Twitch said. "The Boomerang Wood is a dead end. With no skycraft, the Brink is too."

"For most of us," Mira said.

Twitch blushed. "We can talk about me later."

"The Brink continues east of the cloudwall?" Cole asked.

"Yes," Mira said. "The cloudwalls only mark off a portion of the Brink. The Boomerang Forest keeps people from looking behind the Eastern Cloudwall, just like the Briarlands keeps people away from the Western Cloudwall. But beyond the Boomerang Forest, the Brink keeps going. Floatstones don't work there, so having skycraft wouldn't matter."

"What else can we do, Mango?" Jace asked.

"You can run to the northeast," the cockatiel said. "That leads away from civilization and into some wild, dangerous territory. Plenty of places to get lost that way. Based on the current search pattern, they assume you're fleeing there."

Bertram cleared his throat noisily. "If they still want to reach Middlebranch and don't mind a risk, Brady's Wilderness would be an option."

"I've heard of that place," Jace said. "Isn't it trouble?"

"It's in the right direction," Mango said. "Mostly east, a little south. They won't expect you to risk going that way and won't be eager to chance it themselves. It has quite a reputation."

"I've heard of it too," Twitch said. "Seems like you only hear about the really bad places."

"You don't hear about the worst places," Mira said. "Nobody makes it back to spread the rumor. Didn't a shaper go nova there?"

"'Go nova'?" Cole asked.

"All shapers worry about going nova," Mira explained. "When gifted shapers overextend themselves, they can lose touch with what is real and what is a semblance. Greed or paranoia or insanity take over, and they shape uncontrollably, usually until they kill themselves in the process. Sometimes it leaves a big mess behind."

"What do we know about this place?" Cole wondered.

Mira shrugged. "I haven't heard much."

"Little is known," Mango said. "Story has it Brady was a young child who came here from outside. He had a lot of power and a child's mind. He shaped vividly but without control. This happened about forty years ago, and there has been no word of him since."

"A shaper that strong doesn't just disappear," Mira said. "He must have shaped something that killed him."

"Have you been there, Mango?" Twitch asked.

"Just the borders," Mango said. "People don't go there, so I've never monitored the area."

"Are there still roads?" Twitch inquired.

"Three roads," Bertram said. Cole noticed that the old semblance spoke with more clarity and authority when travel routes were involved. "Hard to guess their state of repair. We can hope they're passable. If so, it would prove a clever shortcut to Middlebranch."

"The soldiers don't seem to be headed that way?" Mira clarified.

"Not presently," Mango said. "There is no guarantee they won't change course."

"If the nearest soldiers turn toward it, would we arrive before them?" Twitch checked.

"Probably," Mango said. "Barely."

"I say we go for it," Jace said. "We can handle whatever some kid dreamed up."

"The place has a reputation for a reason," Twitch pointed out.

"And we've all survived some dicey sky castles," Jace said. "I'm not saying it'll be easy. But this is more our thing than fighting legionnaires. Think of it as a big castle."

"I hate the castles," Twitch said. "Why do you think I ran away?"

"You hate them," Jace said, "but you survived them. We have better gear than ever. We'll be working together. The legionnaires won't follow us in, especially if they have no idea we're in there."

"We can't let the legion find us," Mira said. "What do you think, Cole?"

Cole paused before answering. He certainly didn't want

to head to deadly shaping grounds that might feel like a giant sky castle. But he wanted to get caught by the legionnaires even less. "Are there other options like Brady's Wilderness?" Cole asked Mango.

"East of Cloudvale, the brink curves away more toward the north," Mango said. "So you could go northeast or east. That seems to be where the soldiers are heading, probably because it's the most sensible place to run. There are no decent hiding places that way unless you head off into the wild on foot. Even if you take the autocoach by the cleverest routes, if the legionnaires continue in that direction, they'll overtake you by tomorrow."

"It sounds like we should try the Brady place," Cole said.

"I don't love the idea," Twitch said. "But I agree."

"All right," Mira said. "Bertram? Can you take us to Brady's Wilderness?"

"Brady's Wilderness," Bertram said. "Then past there to Middlebranch, I gather?"

"Unless we're forced to turn aside," Mira said.

"I know how we'll go," Bertram said. "Let's hope the roads have held together enough for us to pass."

"I'll keep scouting," Mango said. "You'll hear from me if we need to rethink our maneuvers."

"Thanks, Mango," Mira said as the bird leaped from her shoulder, wings flapping, and disappeared out the window.

"Didn't take long for things to heat up," Cole grumbled.

"Did you think those legionnaires would disappear?" Jace asked.

"I hoped they'd look in the wrong place," Cole replied.

"It's easier to check the right place when you look everywhere," Twitch said.

They clomped along in silence for a moment. Cole glanced over at Twitch. "You never told us about the wings."

"Oh yeah," Jace agreed. "We have time now. You're from Elloweer? One of the natives?"

"I guess the secret is out," Twitch said with a nervous laugh. "I'm one of the grinaldi. People call us springers."

"Never heard of you," Jace said.

"Plenty of people don't know about the grinaldi. We're not numerous. We have wings, but we don't fly for long distances. The wings are used to enhance our hopping."

"How does the ring work?" Cole asked. "Did you bring it from Elloweer?"

"No," Twitch said. "If I had the ring, I doubt I would have been taken as a slave. I found the ring in the supply room at Skyport and chose it as my special item. I've never had to use it until yesterday."

"The ring shows his true form," Jace explained.

"Why aren't you always in your true form?" Cole asked.

"I sometimes forget that you're new here," Twitch said. "Elloweer is full of unusual beings. Some of them can't leave Elloweer. They come up against a barrier. Others, like me, change to human form if they leave."

"And the ring switches you back," Cole said.

"Rings like this are rare," Twitch said, holding it up. It was silver, with a strip of tiny blue gems all the way around. "They're crafted by Ellowine enchanters. I'm not sure how one ended up at Skyport, but there it was, so I claimed it."

Cole thought back to the slave wagons. "When the slavers were in my world taking my friends, one of them looked like a golden wolfman. I never saw him again."

"One of the lupians," Twitch said. "A warlike people. You don't see many with golden fur. He must have reverted to his true form in your world."

"Show us what you really look like," Jace said. "I never got a good look."

"Not when I was carrying you?" Twitch asked.

"My mind was on other things," Jace said.

"Mira told us her secrets," Twitch said. "We know where Cole comes from. But I don't know much about you, Jace. Why don't you tell us about your past, and then I'll show you my true form."

"Not much to tell," Jace said with a slightly uncomfortable smile. "I've been a slave all my life. Never knew my parents. I hated being controlled, and nobody could break me. I still found ways to have fun. And I worked really hard at not working hard. Owners got sick of me. I was traded a couple of times, and finally they sold me to the Sky Raiders. Best thing that ever happened to me. I could finally live. It was dangerous, but I could do my own thing most of the time. Okay, let's see your bug parts."

Twitch rubbed his lips, one of his eyelids fluttering. "Thanks for putting it so delicately." He unbuttoned his shirt and took it off. "My wings ripped the old one," he explained.

Twitch slid on his ring, and a pair of insectile antennae appeared high on his forehead. A quartet of translucent wings were now on his back, two on each side, like a dragonfly, but folded downward. Pulling up one pant leg, he revealed that his leg looked like it belonged to a giant grasshopper.

Cole flinched a little but tried to keep his expression composed. The bug legs were a little much.

"You're knees are backward," Jace said.

"From your anatomy, yes." Twitch laughed. "But I can jump, like, twenty times higher. And I can kind of fly. Although I may not look it, I'm also quite a bit stronger."

"Being human must feel so limiting," Mira said.

"It does," Twitch said, tapping his fingertips together in rapid succession. "It's part of the reason I'm so careful. Picture if you were suddenly weaker and slower and your Jumping Sword was malfunctioning."

"Were you a big risk taker back home?" Jace asked.

"I'm careful by nature," Twitch clarified. "Among my people, it's seen as a positive trait."

"They sound really exciting," Jace teased.

"We prefer quiet, happy lives," Twitch said, taking off the ring. The wings and antennae vanished. "But we don't always get what we want." He started putting his shirt back on.

"What about you, Cole?" Jace asked. "What was your life like before coming here?"

"Easy. Compared to this, I mean. My parents took care of most things. We have a nice house. My sister thinks she's awesome, but she's not too bad, especially compared to slavers and scorpipedes. I went to school. I played sports."

"Sounds like you were rich," Jace said.

"I didn't think so," Cole said. "Maybe compared to some people. We were about average."

"Did you ever get your hands dirty?" Jace asked. "Work in a mine? Or a field? Did you handle livestock? Build a house?"

"Nothing like that," Cole said. "Mostly just school and sports and goofing off."

"Rich must be average where you're from," Jace said. "Sign me up."

"I'd love to," Cole said. "Who knows if I'll ever make it back there?"

"One step at a time," Mira said. "Kind of like back at Skyport. First priority? Survive today. Second? Survive tomorrow."

"How long until Brady's Wilderness?" Twitch asked.

"Barring delays, we'll arrive tomorrow morning," Bertram said.

"Then I'm going to get comfortable," Jace said, snuggling into his corner of the coach. "Wake me if something tries to kill us."

CHAPTER
— 26 —

BRADY'S WILDERNESS

Chocolate chip cookies the size of hula hoops floating in a pond of milk gave Cole his first warning that something was out of the ordinary. He squinted out the window in the morning light. Bushes and small trees grew intermittently on the muddy bank beside the pond. Rocks and sticks littered the shore. Everything looked like a normal woodland pond except for the creamy white liquid and the huge, unmistakable chocolate chip cookies doubling as giant lily pads.

Twitch had curled up on the floor of the autocoach between the seats. Jace was wedged in his corner. Mira had her head on Bertram's lap. They all breathed like they were sleeping. The old semblance stared sedately out the window.

Cole had only dozed intermittently through the night. Despite the smooth ride, he had struggled to get comfortable sitting up. Mango had visited before sunrise to confirm that the legionnaires were veering north and south of them— not into Brady's Wilderness. Too anxious to sleep, Cole had stayed awake since the cockatiel's visit, watching for trouble.

"Guys," Cole said. "Check this out."

Mira popped up as if she hadn't been fully asleep. "What is it?"

Jace leaned forward blearily to look out Cole's window, then promptly snapped more awake. "Are those cookies?"

"And milk," Mira said.

Twitch sat up, stretching. Still on the floor, he was too low to see outside. "Everything all right?"

"Yep," Cole said. "Just a cookies-and-milk pond."

"I want one," Jace said. "Stop the coach."

"We have food," Mira said.

"Dried meat and biscuits," Jace said. "No cookies."

"They're probably stale," Cole said. "The milk has to be spoiled."

"It doesn't smell spoiled," Jace said. "This is shaping. The normal rules don't always apply."

"Could be a trap," Mira said.

"I'm just the guy to spring it," Jace said. "Remember that castle with the candy garden? Best day of my life."

"We're being chased," Mira said.

"We haven't stopped all night," Jace replied. "The bird told us we're ahead of them. It's time for breakfast."

"Okay," Mira said. "Stop."

The autocoach immediately responded.

"You'll be careful?" she asked.

"I'll dive blindfolded from the highest tree I can find." He opened the door and hopped down, golden rope in hand. "You coming, Cole?"

Cole fumbled for his sword. "Sure."

Mira placed a hand on his arm. "You don't have to go."

"Giant cookies," Cole said by way of explanation as he jumped out of the carriage. It felt good to stretch. He buckled his sword belt.

"Come on," Jace said, already marching off. "You keep watch while I lasso a snack."

Cole hurried after him, one hand on the hilt of his sword.

At the edge of the milky pond, Jace crouched and cupped milk into one hand. "It's cold." He brought his hand to his lips. "Mmmm. Rich and creamy."

Shaking the milk from his fingers, Jace stood and cast his rope out to the nearest cookie. The golden rope wrapped around the target multiple times. With a flick of his wrist, the rope yanked the oversized cookie out of the milk, but it broke apart, soggy remnants splashing down.

"Not very solid," Jace said.

Cole knelt on a flat rock that slightly overhung the pond. Below, milk lapped against the stone and the muddy bank, yet the milk didn't seem to have any dirt in it. He dipped a finger and found that Jace was right—it was quite cold.

Jace ensnared another cookie, then hauled it in slowly, bringing it to where Cole knelt. "Help me get it out."

Cole reached underneath the cookie. Although the top was firm, the underside was mushy. Working together, Jace and Cole lifted it out of the milk, Cole's hands sinking into the underside until reaching a more solid portion. Milk dripped down his wrists into his sleeves and onto his shoes. Holding his half of the sodden cookie required all his strength.

With their prize between them, Jace and Cole shuffled back to the autocoach. Cole tried not to breathe too hard. His arms burned with the effort. Mira got out as they drew near.

"You're not bringing that in here," she said.

"Why not?" Jace asked.

"It's a gooey, drippy mess," Mira said. "We'll eat some out here."

"Break off pieces," Cole suggested.

Using two hands, Mira snapped off part of one of the edges. The chunk was too big to take a normal bite, but she gnawed at it. "Wow, this is good."

Twitch got out as well and snapped off a piece. His eyes lit up when he tried a bite.

"Get some for us," Jace said. "We're too busy holding it."

Mira set her piece aside and broke off two more.

"Should we chuck it?" Jace asked.

"You want any, Bertram?" Cole invited.

"No time to bother," the old man replied. "I'm just here on holiday with my grandniece and grandnephews."

Swinging their arms, Cole and Jace heaved the cookie sideways, and it whumped down, flattening a circle of tall grass. They accepted their hunks from Mira. "We should get moving," she said.

"They won't follow us in here," Jace said. "Nobody wants to do battle with milk and cookies."

They all climbed back into the coach. Cole found that

the cookie tasted freshly baked, with a hint of warmth as if it had barely cooled. The soggy parts were extra good. He only had one chocolate chip in his piece, but it was bigger than his fist.

Cole chomped on his cookie as the coach rolled along. Eventually, his stomach started to protest. He worried that eating more would make him sick. "Anybody want the rest of mine?"

"I'm done," Jace said. "They're too messy to store." He tossed it out the window.

"Leaving a trail of cookie crumbs?" Twitch asked.

"They won't know we did it," Jace said.

The others chucked their pieces as well.

Cole watched out the window, looking for another cookie pond or anything else out of the ordinary. He didn't have to wait long. The next clearing they passed was full of upright dominoes, each bigger than a mattress, white with black markings. Hundreds of them formed a winding path, ready to fall if the first toppled.

"That is so tempting," Cole said. "I love knocking over dominoes."

"We can't stop for everything," Mira said. "One of these times it will be a trap."

"I can't believe somebody didn't tip them over a long time ago," Cole marveled.

"Maybe somebody did," Mira said. "They might stand back up on their own. Don't forget, these were shaped. Who knows what they can do?"

"Use the bow," Jace said. "Target practice."

"Right," Cole replied, excited. Jace had returned the bow to the storage compartment last night. Lifting the hatch, he retrieved it and handed it over.

While pulling the string to his cheek, Cole felt the arrow appear. They had passed the first domino, but in a minute, he would have a clear shot at the last one. Once it was in full view, he released the arrow, which hit the target a little higher than where he had aimed it. The domino rocked backward and fell into the next, creating a clattering chain reaction. The dominoes fell fluidly, the motion snaking around the field until the last slapped down flat.

Everything seemed very quiet after the noise of the dominoes had stopped—until they heard some distant roars, long and low and savage. They all looked at one another.

"Maybe not the best idea to announce our presence," Twitch said.

"The baddies will figure out we're here either way," Jace said.

"We wouldn't want to try to sneak by them or anything," Mira said.

"Sorry," Cole said. "I wasn't thinking."

"If we have to blame somebody," Jace said, "the guy who shot the arrow is first in line."

"I don't want to place blame," Mira said. "I just want to live. I vote we stay in the coach from now on."

"I'll second that," Twitch spoke up.

"Thirded," Cole said.

"I'm going to keep my options open," Jace said.

"Majority rules," Mira informed him.

Jace held up his wrist. "Doesn't rule me. I'm free."

Mira rolled her eyes. "I'm technically a princess. I could declare this a monarchy."

"You're even more technically a fugitive," Jace pointed out. "No offense."

"Whoa," Cole said.

As they curved around the next bend, a cupcake the size of a hill came into view—vanilla cake with chocolate frosting. Everyone crammed to his side of the coach to have a good look.

"Rethinking your policies?" Jace asked.

"I'm still full from the cookie," Mira said. "Besides, how do you even get started on something that big?"

"We'll need mining equipment," Cole said.

"Check out my side," Twitch said.

Everyone went to the other side of the coach to stare at a lemon meringue pie as big as a circus tent. In front of the epic pie, s'mores the size of card tables were scattered among the wildflowers, oozing marshmallow from all sides.

"Journey over," Jace said. "We've found our new home."

"Do you see anybody else here?" Mira asked.

"Their loss," Jace said.

"Free food everywhere," Twitch said, "and not a person in sight. What does that tell you?"

"More for us?" Cole asked, earning a high-five from Jace.

"Very funny," Mira said.

"We get it," Jace said. "It's too good to be true. There must be a catch. It's just fun to joke around."

"It might not even be a deliberate trap," Mira said. "But

the boy who made this place disappeared. Something went wrong here. People avoid it for a reason."

They heard a faint banging up ahead. As the coach advanced, the sound grew louder.

"Are we about to learn the reason?" Cole asked.

"We should get ready," Jace said, suddenly serious.

Cole put on his shawl and held his bow, fingers gently plucking the string. The volume of the pounding increased.

After passing through an orchard of gummy fruit and jelly beans, they found the source of the booming—an enormous red-and-black checkerboard with a rapid game in progress. Each checker was as wide as the street Cole lived on, and either slid or jumped to a new square when moved. The checkers moved on their own, and no side ever paused. Jumped checkers waited in stacks beside the board. As they watched, kings were made on both sides, and black soon won. Immediately the checkers returned to their starting positions, and a new game began.

"Those would squish you flat," Twitch said.

"Not if you stay away from the board," Jace said.

Out the window on his side, Cole saw a ten-story Ferris wheel turning briskly, all the cars empty. At one side of it, across a small stream, a herd of vacant bumper cars jostled with one another on a broad black surface. Beyond the two attractions, off in the trees, Cole glimpsed the top of a roller coaster.

"Look over here," Cole said. "This place is awesome."

"What are those?" Jace asked.

"A Ferris wheel and bumper cars," Cole said. "Rides from my world. This kid had to come from Earth."

The autocoach continued to trot along, the pace never changing. Cole continued to watch out the window. As bizarre as some of the sights were, the surrounding environment made them weirder. A hot-fudge waterfall crept down an otherwise normal rocky slope. Hamburgers the size of cars populated a brushy field beside thornbushes and boulders. A group of plastic action figures the size of real people posed within a grove of birch trees.

In many ways, Brady's Wilderness felt like a crazy dream come true. So much of it was silly and impossible. If they weren't being chased by legionnaires, if they weren't trying to find Mira's lost powers, and if this place had a safer reputation, they could have so much fun here.

Cole wondered if his lost friends were seeing sights like this. In Junction City, was Dalton encountering the equivalent of giant pies and fudge waterfalls? Was Jenna using something like a Jumping Sword or Jace's rope? He hoped they were experiencing at least some good things to help make up for their new lives as slaves in a foreign world.

"More cookies and milk," Mira said, peering out her window. "Whoever Brady was, the kid liked to eat."

"Look at the different kinds," Jace said.

Cole saw a creamy pond crowded with what were either oatmeal or maybe peanut butter cookies. Another contained chocolate cookies with white chips. A third featured huge pale cookies with cinnamon on top—probably snickerdoodles.

"Anybody want to go fishing again?" Jace asked. "We might kick ourselves tomorrow when all we have to eat is dried meat and biscuits."

"I don't trust this place," Mira said. "Let's keep survival the priority."

"Why just survive when you can feast?" Jace pressed.

"I'm still stuffed," Cole said. "They look good, but I doubt I could eat much."

In the distance, they heard the rich call of a horn blowing, long and low, the note rising a little at the end.

"What was that?" Mira asked.

"Legionnaires?" Twitch guessed.

"Mango would have warned us," Mira said.

"What if they got her?" Twitch suggested.

Another horn answered, closer this time. Two more sounded from different directions. Then a brassier instrument let out a blast.

"Was that a trumpet?" Cole asked.

"Look!" Twitch shouted, pointing.

Cole followed his finger to the milk pool with the snickerdoodles. Something was rising out of the milk near the edge of the pond, as if walking ashore from the depths. A dripping skull emerged, followed by shoulder bones, then the rib cage and the arm bones. The skeleton held a rusty shield in one hand and a corroded sword in the other. The pelvis rose above the surface of the milk, followed by the femurs. Very little tissue clung to the bones—mainly just some rotten tendons and ligaments at the joints. After leaving the pond, the skeleton jogged toward them, bones shiny with milk residue.

"What is that?" Cole said, his voice pitched higher than he had intended.

"That is why we listen to Mira," Jace said.

"Look the other way," Mira said.

Several skeletons jostled one another as they exited the woods on the other side of the road. The fastest moved at a trot. A couple walked. One was missing a leg and hopped along using a spear as a crutch. All had weapons—a few swords, a sledgehammer, a crowbar, a rock.

"Fun's over," Jace said.

Horns and trumpets blared ahead of them, behind them, and from off to the sides. In the distance, Cole heard the unmistakable squeal of bagpipes.

"This is an ambush," Twitch said. "They waited for us to get in deep, then sprang the trap."

"Looks that way," Jace said. "At least they're not too fast."

Leaning his head out the window and looking back, Cole saw the skeletons struggling to keep up with the autocoach. All but two were slowly falling behind.

From off in the trees to their right, a bellowing roar over-powered the horns and trumpets. The ferocious challenge struck a primal chord within Cole that left him trembling.

Mango flew in through the window. "We're in trouble. Skeletons are coming from all sides."

"How many?" Mira asked.

"Hundreds," the bird replied. "Thousands, maybe. Graveyards of them. They're all heading toward you. And there are worse things—savage creatures like nothing I've ever seen. You're going to have to abandon the autocoach. You'll be easy prey in here."

Cole's breathing had quickened. He could feel his heart

pounding in his hands. Did he have what he needed? He had his sword, his shawl, and his jewel. He held the bow. Anything else? What about food?

Up ahead, the ground rumbled with monstrous footsteps. Leaning out and peering ahead, Cole saw a dozen skeletons running toward the front of the autocoach. A few wore mismatched Viking armor. A big skeleton in the front held a longsword in both hands and wore a horned helmet.

But the skeletons weren't responsible for the ground quaking.

Coming up behind the bony warriors lumbered a dull orange Stegosaurus with maroon markings. Although obviously made of plastic, it was roughly the size of a school bus. Jagged plates protruded along its spine, and the tail had four spikes. The stegosaurus roared, showing razor teeth. Weren't they herbivores? Apparently, not this one.

The enormous plastic dinosaur charged toward the autocoach, bowling over the Viking skeletons like bowling pins and crunching bones underfoot. Undistracted, the galloping beast maintained a head-on collision course with the trotting brick.

A mightier roar drowned out everything for a moment. Cole looked up to see a Tyrannosaurus rex bounding toward them down a long slope, coming from the side, its plastic reptilian mouth a thicket of cruel teeth.

A paralyzing terror overtook Cole. There was no time to think. No chance to react. His eyes darted between incoming threats. Skeletons converged from everywhere. The two dinosaurs were seconds away. Dropping his bow, Cole squatted and braced for the impact.

CHAPTER
—— 27 ——

FRENZY

"**H**ey, brainless!" Jace yelled, seizing Cole's arm. "Out! Now!"

Mira and Twitch had already abandoned the autocoach. Fumbling with his Jumping Sword, Cole let Jace drag him out the door opposite the T. rex. The nearest of a ragged mob of skeletons approached from only a few paces away. The instant his feet hit the ground, Cole drew his sword, pointed it toward a bare spot on a nearby slope, and shouted, "Away!"

He soared over the rattling gang of skeletons and fell onto his side into some tall brush beside a Neapolitan ice cream sandwich that was the length of a bed. He was near enough to feel the cold radiating from it despite the warmth of the sun. His heart still hammered, but he no longer felt paralyzed. Confined in the autocoach, he had felt doomed. But Jace had snapped him out of it. They would do what they had trained to do at times like this. They would run. And who knew? Maybe they would make it!

Looking back, Cole saw Mira pointing at the Tyrannosaurus.

The Shaper's Flail hurtled through the air, a tangle of sturdy chains and iron balls, and wrapped around its legs. The gigantic plastic lizard pitched forward, carving a trench in the ground just shy of the road.

Having changed course, the stegosaurus now chased Twitch, who hopped ahead of it with tremendous leaps assisted by his wings. Jace made his way toward Mira, lashing skeletons with his golden rope and flinging them into one another.

A rustling behind Cole warned him just in time to dodge the downswing of an ax wielded by a skeleton in a conquistador's helmet. While the skeleton tried to pull the ax from the ground, Cole hacked off its head. Bony hands grasping, the headless conquistador staggered toward him, and Cole dashed away.

Mira recalled the Shaper's Flail and sent it into a vicious circle around herself and Jace. The whirling iron balls blasted bones into fragments, and the chains clotheslined dozens of skeletons, hurling them to the ground.

The skeletons near Cole had him surrounded. They approached in a shrinking circle, empty eye sockets devoid of emotion. About half had weapons—pickaxes, swords, and knives. One in a tattered apron held up a rectangular meat cleaver.

Noticing that as the skeletons closed on him, they opened up a lot of the area beyond, Cole patiently centered himself between them and let them get close. At the last moment, he pointed his sword above them and yelled, "Away!"

Something swiped his leg as he cleared the skeletons,

tearing his pants and scratching his calf. He had pointed at a spot about ten feet in the air, some distance off to one side, and that was where he ended up. With nothing to land on, he fell the extra ten feet and struck the ground hard, rolling to help absorb the brutal impact. Cole bounced and skidded through the brush, losing hold of his sword.

Shaken and sore, with the taste of dirt and blood in his mouth, Cole scrambled toward his fallen weapon. It was a hard reminder to only point the sword at solid landing areas. Then again, it was better than getting diced into skeleton chow.

Grabbing his sword, Cole staggered to his feet as an even greater number of skeletons swarmed him. His eyes found a giant slice of cheesecake near the limit of the sword's range. Without time to plan and hoping for the best, Cole extended the sword, cried the word, and sailed disturbingly high. Air rushed over him as the sword pulled him up and forward. An unusual vibration in the handle made Cole wonder if the sword was straining.

As he curved down toward the cheesecake, to his horror, Cole saw that he wouldn't quite make it. He had tried to stretch the leap too far. The result would be like jumping off a five-story building.

Hands scooped beneath his arms from behind, and suddenly he had an extra boost. Twitch landed behind him on the huge cheesecake, their legs plunging into the surface to their knees.

"Thanks," Cole said breathlessly, twisting to see his friend.

"Glad I could help," Twitch said. "We were heading for the same high ground."

With a good tug, Cole yanked one leg out of the cheesecake, almost losing his shoe in the process. Then he withdrew the other. He found that the surface of the cheesecake was firm enough to support him if he stepped lightly.

They were about thirty feet up. Down below, the stegosaurus bit chunks out of the cheesecake and clubbed it with its tail. Skeletons approached and started scaling it, finger bones clawing eagerly.

Mira came bounding across the field below and sprang to the top of the cheesecake. Jace's rope fell into numerous loops at his feet, then uncoiled like a giant spring, propelling him to the top of the cheesecake as well.

"They don't care about the autocoach anymore," Mira noted.

Cole saw the trotting brick still on the road, disappearing into the trees. In the rush to leave the coach, he had left his bow inside.

"No fun for them without us in it," Jace said. He crouched and scooped up some cheesecake in his palm. "At least we get to try this." He took a bite. "Wow, not bad!"

Below, the Tyrannosaurus came raging over to the cheesecake. It wasn't tall enough to reach them, but it came close enough to make it scary. Roaring and snapping, it leaped in vicious frustration, scattering many of the climbing skeletons.

"Flail, attack," Mira said, pointing downward. The Shaper's Flail stormed by, battering skeletons away from the cheesecake wall with a spray of shattered bone.

"With the flail, maybe we can hold out up here," Cole said.

"Not for long," Twitch said. "See how the big lizard on four legs is chewing away the base? They'll tear the cheesecake out from under us."

"He's right," Mira said. "The flail doesn't seem to hurt the huge lizards. It just knocks them down and scuffs them up a little."

"They're plastic dinosaurs," Cole said. "Giant toys."

"They seem really fun," Mira said sarcastically.

"No," Cole tried to explain. "Normally, they're little and plastic, and kids make them attack other toys. These ones are the size of the real things."

"Those are dinosaurs?" Jace asked. "I've never seen one. You have them in your world? You must be braver than I thought."

"Had them," Cole corrected. "They're extinct. We only know about them from fossils. These are big toy versions. Which might be worse than the real thing. Actual dinosaurs had bones and could bleed."

The cheesecake shuddered as the Tyrannosaurus stopped leaping upward and ripped directly into it, biting and clawing. The stegosaurus had burrowed partially out of sight, tunneling furiously into the base of the enormous slice.

Mango fluttered down and landed on Mira's shoulder. "I found the route with the least enemies. At least for the moment. I'll scout as we go. If you're fast enough, I might be able to guide you out of here."

"The bird is our best chance," Jace said.

Cole looked down. Skeletal hordes besieged the cheesecake, backed by an endless flow of reinforcements. Horns and trumpets continued to blow. A Triceratops the size of a bulldozer was rumbling their way as well.

He didn't want to go down among all those fearsome creatures. It was pandemonium. Anything could happen, almost all of it bad. Right now the battle felt paused. But if he sat still, the cheesecake would be eroded, and he'd be toast. Although a big part of him wanted to stay put, because it made the monsters seem farther away, he also understood that their only chance was to keep running.

"You're right," Cole said.

"I agree," Twitch added. "Mango's our new best friend."

Cole turned to Mira. "How good are the swords at jumping from a high place to a low place?"

"Not bad," she said. "They'll brake you at the end, like with any jump. Leaping down looks worse than jumping up, and kind of feels worse, but you'll survive."

"Skeletons!" Twitch shouted.

Several were scrambling over the top of the back of the cheesecake slice. Mira directed the flail at them and sent them flying, but more replaced them.

"Time to bail," Jace said. "Mango?"

"Follow me," the cockatiel said, flapping to the opposite side of the cheesecake from the dinosaurs and perching on the edge. "Looks good. Ready?"

"Go," Mira ordered.

The bird took flight. Mira pointed her Jumping Sword at a downward angle, shouted the command word, and then whooshed toward a fairly empty clearing screened by trees.

Cole aimed his sword at the same destination. It felt like

preparing to jump off a building, with nothing but his trust in the sword to assure him he could land it. But the cheesecake was shuddering, and more skeletons were reaching the top, so he shouted the command word and sprang.

Instead of falling straight down, the sword tugged him forward in a long, sloping descent. His legs brushed the treetops at the edge of the clearing, and he landed hard, skidding to his knees. Scabs earned on previous tumbles burst painfully.

Twitch landed near him, as did Jace, who swung down with his rope connected to tree branches. Mira pointed at Mango and jumped again, this time low and far. Cole imitated her jump and stumbled to a halt against a tree.

Skeletons dressed as pirates hustled his way. Some wore scarves on their skulls. One had a captain's hat and a peg leg from the knee down. Most were armed with knives and cutlasses.

Jace passed him, his rope ensnaring distant tree trunks, then shortening and carrying him along. Twitch buzzed by overhead. Cole extended his sword and jumped again, slicing along a narrow line between the trees.

Another jump and they reached a field filled with the most expansive playground equipment Cole had ever seen. The complicated arrangement of slides, ladders, tunnels, climbing walls, tire swings, poles, knotted ropes, trampolines, monkey bars, and balance beams would have filled a city block, and it had to be ten stories high, all linking together to form a soaring maze. It would be the ultimate setting for an epic game of tag, but skeletons trying to tag him to death would limit the fun.

Mira jumped high onto the playset, landing on a bouncy bridge made from rope and wood planks. The Shaper's Flail followed her unobtrusively. Cole joined her, grateful for the gentler landing that came with heading upward.

"Hey!" a voice called.

Cole whirled, surprised. The broad face of a freckled girl with auburn hair in braids poked out at him from the mouth of a tube slide. She looked a few years older than him, maybe fourteen or so.

"Who are you?" Mira asked.

"I can help," the girl said. "But you have to come now." She didn't sound scared. If anything, she seemed a bit bossy.

"Who are you?" Mira repeated.

"It's not a trick," she said. "I'm Amanda, Brady's sitter."

"His babysitter?" Cole verified.

"Not actually," Amanda said. "He modeled me after her. I helped protect him. I saw you getting chased and thought you could use a hand. The whole place will join the hunt soon."

Twitch and Jace joined them, making the bridge sway and wobble.

"Who is this?" Jace asked.

"Brady's babysitter," Cole said.

"Now or never," Amanda said, glancing out of the tube slide.

"She says she can help us," Mira said.

"Only if you hurry," Amanda said.

"Would you put on this shawl?" Cole asked, fingering the clasp at his throat.

"Why?" Amanda snorted. "What's it going to do to me?

Without a good answer, Cole shrugged.

Amanda huffed. "Not interested. I was just trying to do you a favor. The worst of them aren't on your trail yet—the mud people, the Blind Ones, the flying squid-faced monsters."

"We'll come," Mira said.

Amanda started sliding.

"You sure?" Jace asked.

"Sure enough," Mira said, swinging into the slide and disappearing. The Shaper's Flail slithered in after her. Jace followed, then Twitch.

Mango darted over to Cole, alighting on a bar near him. "Where are you going?"

"I think we found help," Cole said. "We'll be back."

CHAPTER
28

AMANDA

Not wanting to get left behind, Cole slung himself into the slide. The metal tunnel circled down, down, down, until he emerged in an underground room lit by a naked blue bulb. The others were waiting for him.

"Electricity?" Cole asked, looking at the bulb.

"He faked it," Amanda said. "The bulb doesn't have wires. But it never goes out. This way."

She led them through an obstacle course of cramped tunnels, funhouse mirrors, and pivoting panels. All of it was underground. She kept scolding them to go faster. Occasionally they would see where other slides from the playground above gave access. At last they reached a wide empty sandbox. Amanda stood in the corner and started sinking.

"Quicksand box," she explained before her head disappeared.

Mira stepped forward, but Jace pushed ahead. "Let me check it out."

He sank as quickly as Amanda. "I think it's all right," Jace said when he was down to his chest. "No pain. I can feel space beneath me." The sand was at his neck. Then his head was gone.

Mira went next, followed by Twitch. Cole heard clattering on the slides and in the tunnels behind him. It had to be skeletons.

He stepped onto the sand and started sinking steadily. The parts of his body beneath the surface experienced no wetness. By the time he was down to his waist, he could feel his feet poking through the bottom of the sand. Holding his breath as his face slid under, Cole endured the smothering sensation of sinking through grainy matter for a few seconds before he dropped into a new room, landing on a padded floor.

Cole tried to brush off his hair but was surprised to find no sand there.

"Don't bother," Twitch told him. "We came through clean."

Gymnastics pads covered the floor and walls of the otherwise bare room. Light came from glowing cubes in the corners. A smooth square of sand in the ceiling showed how he had entered the room.

"Come on," Amanda said, showing that one of the pads in the wall swiveled when pressed. "Stop wasting time." They followed her through a maze of halls and secret doors until they reached a bright room full of couches, stuffed animals, and beanbag chairs. "We're safe here."

"Do you hide here all the time?" Mira asked.

"I move around," Amanda said. "It gets boring without Brady."

"What happened to him?" Jace wondered.

A flash of grief distorted Amanda's features, but she shook it off. "They got him. He couldn't stop making up bad guys. I tried to help him. He made me to help him."

"How old was he?" Jace asked.

"Six," Amanda said. "He was so good at making things here in Dreamland."

"You think this is a dream?" Mira asked.

"He did," Amanda said. "He said he got here by dreaming. He was always waiting to wake up. I thought he must be right until they got him and the dream kept going."

"He was making real things," Mira said. "We call it shaping. The living things are semblances and the nonliving are renderings."

"Whatever," Amanda said, apparently not too interested. "I've been here alone a long time. Nothing changes. I don't get older. I can't leave. I've tried. So I just hide out. I've learned how to survive pretty good. Much better than when Brady was with me."

"Did he slow you down?" Cole asked.

"Not really," Amanda said. "We would find ways to avoid the bad stuff he made, but then he'd dream up new creatures that were smarter or had new skills. He couldn't help it. Once he was gone, the monsters stopped improving, and my job got easier."

"Are there others like you here?" Mira asked. "Good semblances?"

"He made a few heroes, but they eventually got killed," Amanda said. "They were too bold. There's nobody left on my side. But it looked like you guys needed help, and he made me to watch over little kids."

"We're not little," Jace protested, earning an elbow to his side from Twitch.

"Play along," Twitch murmured softly.

"No kids think they're little," Amanda said. "I'm fifteen. That's when you're finally big."

"Are we stuck here?" Mira asked.

"I am," Amanda said. "I can't cross the border of Dreamland. You guys aren't. I'll teach you a trick that'll let you walk right out of here. But first: Anybody want some popcorn?"

"Some what now?" Twitch asked.

"Yes," Cole said. "Popcorn is good."

Amanda walked into a neighboring room. "You four came from outside Dreamland?"

"Yeah," Cole said.

"What's out there?"

"Other weird stuff," Cole said.

Amanda returned with four bowls, two in her hands, two on her forearms. "You don't think we're part of a dream?"

"Feels that way sometimes," Mira said. "Especially this place. But it's all real."

"Don't all dream people think they're real?" Amanda asked. "How can characters in a dream tell how real they are? Brady thought he was the dreamer. I couldn't argue with him since he made me. He used lots of good details. I can remember what it was like to be awake, even though I've never woken. I started to wonder if he was dreaming inside of somebody else's dream. That would make me a dream of a dream."

"You're hurting my brain," Twitch said.

Amanda gave a brash laugh. "I know how you feel! Don't worry, if you think you're real, who am I to contradict you? I don't care how real you are. It's nice to find anyone that isn't trying to kill me."

"You mentioned we could walk out of here," Mira said. "Were you serious?"

Amanda narrowed her eyes. "You're not spies, are you? Did the bad guys send you to learn my secrets?"

"You said there haven't been new enemies here since Brady left," Cole reminded her.

"True," Amanda said. "After Brady left, this place stopped changing. Maybe you are real! The only other people who've come from outside were grown-ups. If they can't outsmart a dinosaur, that's their problem."

"How can we walk out of here?" Mira asked.

"Easy," Amanda said, leaving the room for a moment. She returned with plastic skeleton masks. "Wear these."

"Are you kidding?" Jace exclaimed. "They followed us when we were in our autocoach. That hid us way better than a mask!"

"If you're so smart, maybe I'm wrong," Amanda said. "Maybe these masks haven't worked perfectly for years and years."

"You're a semblance," Jace pointed out. "They probably don't chase you whether or not you have a mask."

"They didn't chase Bertram," Cole added.

"I don't know Bertram," Amanda said. "Maybe Brady didn't make him. Brady made me as a companion. His nightmares always chased me. They still chase me if I don't wear a mask. But when I have a mask on, they do nothing. None of them. We came up with the idea right before the Blind Ones got Brady. He thought it would work, so it did. It's his Dreamland after all. And then he wasn't around to make any of the bad guys outsmart the trick."

"We just wear plastic skull masks and walk out of here?" Cole checked.

"Yep," Amanda said. "But first try some popcorn."

Cole emerged from the metal tunnel cautiously. Despite Amanda's assurances, it seemed ridiculous that anything would be fooled by him wearing a plastic skeleton mask and his regular clothes. Ready to dash back to the tube, he advanced cautiously, Jumping Sword in hand.

The tunnel had deposited him on ground level at the edge of the elaborate playground. Skeletons wandered around at random. No horns blew. The organization they had shown when converging earlier was gone. One skeleton wearing a shabby monk's robe came near enough for Cole to reach out and touch it. Cole held still, trying to look more casual than he felt. The skeleton walked right past him.

Mira, Jace, and Twitch joined Cole. Behind them, Amanda watched from the tunnel, a mask covering her face as well. After they had filled up on hot buttered popcorn and cool lemonade, she had assured them that they could do whatever they wanted, including talk, as long as they kept the masks on.

Mango swooped down and landed on Mira's shoulder. The cockatiel pecked gently at one of her hairpins. "Don't tell me those masks actually work!" the bird squawked.

"Looks that way," Mira whispered. "We should be able to stroll out of here."

Cole kept watching the skeletons. Mira's conversation with Mango didn't seem to attract any notice.

"I told Bertram to wait for us past the edge of Brady's Wilderness," Mira said. "Think you could guide us to him?"

"The road winds a lot," Mango said. "If you use your renderings, I might be able to help you catch him before he gets there."

Mira turned to Cole. "What do you think?"

He felt flattered that she consulted him. "We don't want to be too conspicuous. It would be bad if moving fast made our masks come off."

"Let's stay on the ground unless we need to dodge a random dinosaur," Twitch said. Amanda had warned that there was still the chance of getting in the way of a large monster through bad luck. Sometimes skeletons got squished by accident.

"Fine with me," Jace said. "I still can't believe we might survive this. I had every intention of getting away, but it would have been rough."

"We'll just walk," Mira said.

"I'll lead you," the bird said, flying forward.

Cole walked along, sword in hand, watching the

skeletons ignore him. Some skeletons wore the remains of burial wrappings. Some wore filthy military uniforms. Many wore nothing. Of those that wore nothing, some were more polished and in better repair than others. Most carried some sort of weapon.

The Shaper's Flail followed along behind them, links clinking softly. The skeletons paid it no attention.

They passed many wonders. A three-level carousel rotated to calliope music, ornate statues of horses pumping up and down on their brass poles. A herd of massive Brachiosaurs waded through swampy terrain, tearing long strands of string cheese off white trees. A banana split the height of an office building threw long shadows as chocolate syrup and caramel seeped down creamy slopes.

Cole didn't feel like talking. Neither did the others, apparently. They just followed Mango and tried to stay out of the paths of the aimless skeletons.

The cockatiel led them well. The only monsters they encountered were skeletons, which roamed in such ridiculous numbers that they were unavoidable. Plastic dinosaurs could occasionally be seen in the distance. Cole glimpsed far-off flying creatures a couple of times, and once he saw some shambling mounds moving across a remote field. Otherwise the long march was uneventful.

Late in the day, Cole tore a piece from a glazed doughnut that was larger than a tractor tire. The others claimed handfuls as well, carefully eating the morsels under their masks. None of the skeletons showed interest.

As the sun sank, they reconnected with a path and shortly

came upon the autocoach, waiting just off the path near a stream. Mask still in place, Mira led the way inside. Cole found his bow where he had left it.

"You kids shouldn't wander off like that," Bertram scolded warmly. "We have places to go. Still bound for Middlebranch?"

"Yes," Mira said.

"We'll arrive late tomorrow morning," Bertram said. "Off we go."

The autocoach started rolling forward. They took off their masks. Body scraped and bruised, feet sore, eyes drooping, Cole found the coach much more comfortable than the night before.

MIDDLEBRANCH

Middlebranch was a larger town than Cole expected. The bustling community made him realize he hadn't seen a real town since coming to the Outskirts—just Skyport, Declan's hidden castle, and the empty country where the slave caravan had traveled.

The typical buildings in Middlebranch had stone foundations that stuck up above ground level to support wooden walls. Several main streets crisscrossed the town. Not including the outlying farms they had passed in the last hour before reaching the town, Middlebranch had dozens of buildings, maybe hundreds, some of them four stories tall.

They reached a stone-paved street featuring several mansions with gated grounds. Cole craned to view the impressive homes. The strangest one of them boasted many turrets and gables, and was partly constructed from glossy black stone, partly from bricks of various shades of blue, and partly from golden-hued wood. The end result was quirky and visually confusing, not helped by the spacious quartz fountain out front.

"Look at that crazy house," Cole said.

"Probably belongs to the lead shaper," Mira guessed. "Only shapers would build so eccentrically."

"I kind of like it," Twitch said. "It's original."

"Should we talk to the lead shaper?" Cole asked.

"Usually the lead shaper is tight with the local government," Mira said. "That often equals being tight with my father. This street is probably all government officials. We should look for Gerta the herb woman. Bertram? Could you take us to the town's main inn?"

"There are two of significant popularity," Bertram replied.

"How about the one the local officials visit least often?" Mira said.

"That would be Spinner's Lodge," he said.

"Let's go there," Mira said.

Jace was rooting around in the storage space under his seat. He looked up, a brown sack in his hand. "This is full of ringers," he said.

"They told us they gave us money," Mira said.

"I remember," Jace explained. "But this is full! Copper ringers, silver, gold, even platinum. We could buy a ranch and have money to spare. We could buy one of those mansions."

"We have to be careful not to show it," Mira said. "Nothing draws trouble quicker than flashing money around."

Grinning, Jace started sliding simple rings of equal size onto one end of a leather cord. "I'm free and I have money."

"That's too much," Mira scolded. "No gold. Certainly no platinum. Use mostly copper, and a couple silver if you must."

"I won't show it off," Jace promised. "I just want an

emergency fund. We already almost lost the coach once."

"Your coins are rings?" Cole asked.

"Most people in the five kingdoms use ringers," Mira said. "They're officially called ringaroles. I guess it's new to you. Ten coppers in a silver, five silvers in a gold, ten gold in a platinum. There are also copper bits, worth a quarter of a copper, and silver bits, worth half a silver. Those are smaller and square."

"No bits in here," Twitch said, adding ringers to his own cord.

"It's against the law to shape ringers," Mira said. "Some shapers are employed to check if ringers are authentic. My guess is Declan shaped these, and I suspect nobody would be able to tell."

"I should grab some," Cole said. "You know, in case of emergencies."

"Don't get caught with too much on you," Mira warned. "They'll think you robbed a money house." She claimed a small handful and began threading a cord through them.

Cole took a short cord from the bag, loaded it with gold and platinum ringers, then tied it around his leg inside of his sock. Satisfied, he started loading a longer cord with mostly copper ringers to wear around his neck.

"You'll jingle," Twitch said.

"What?" Cole asked.

"The ringers on your leg will jingle," Twitch said. "It won't fool anyone."

"How should I do it?" Cole asked.

"Use less and spread them out," Twitch said. "A few

ringers in one boot, a few in the other. A couple inside your belt. Use knots to separate some on a cord and bind that around your leg."

"What are you, a smuggler?" Cole asked.

"I've traveled," Twitch said.

"Or you could sew some secret pockets," Jace mentioned.

"You sew?" Cole asked.

Jace shrugged.

Cole untied his cord and started rearranging his ringers. He noticed an autocoach similar to theirs pass them heading the opposite direction.

"There's the lodge, up on the left," Mira said.

"Correct," Bertram affirmed. "I'm afraid I'll have to wait in the autocoach."

"Wait," Jace said. "I see something I need. I'll catch up." Before anyone could respond, he opened the door and jumped down from the moving coach.

"Want me to follow him?" Twitch asked.

"We have to trust one another," Mira said. "He's a big boy. He'll stay out of trouble."

"It's his first real day of freedom with his pockets full of money," Twitch reminded her.

Mira couldn't quite hide a look of panic. "He has to get used to the idea at some point."

The autocoach halted smoothly. "We have arrived," Bertram said. "I'll wait nearby."

"Thanks," Mira said, climbing out of the coach. Cole and Twitch followed.

Cole noticed people glancing at them. Down the street

he saw another autocoach, so they couldn't be too rare. Maybe the people weren't used to strangers. Or maybe it was because of their ages.

Spinner's Lodge contained a long, rectangular room full of plain wooden tables, all of them empty. A stone hearth on one end housed a large black kettle. Heavy beams spanned the space overhead. A hallway led farther back into the building, and a kitchen could be seen beyond the stone counter.

A bald man limped toward them as they entered. His crooked nose had probably been broken more than once. "What do you want?" he accused.

"Food," Mira said. "Did we come to the wrong place?"

"Can you pay?" the man questioned.

"We have plenty," Mira said.

"You don't mind showing me?" the man asked.

Sighing, Mira pulled her necklace out of her shirt so he could see the copper rings. He gave a nod. "I don't know your faces."

"We're traveling with our uncle," Mira said.

"These boys don't speak?" the man asked.

"Not before lunch," Cole said.

"Pick a table," the man said. "You're early for lunch, late for breakfast. Must be nice to have no responsibilities. What do you want?"

"What's cooking?" Mira asked.

"Egg soup, skewers of chicken, bread, potatoes, bacon, pork chops, and some porridge from this morning. Cook's specialty is sugarbread. He has frosted and apricot today."

"How's the egg soup?" Mira asked.

"Exactly like it sounds," the man huffed.

Cole noticed the bondmark on his wrist. The man certainly wasn't trying to make friends. Maybe he felt like kids were the only people he could treat rudely.

"Some of the soup for me," Mira said.

"Me too," Twitch chimed in. "And chicken skewers."

"I'll have the skewers and bacon," Cole said.

"How am I supposed to skewer bacon?" the man replied.

"The chicken skewers," Cole said slowly. "And bacon."

The man started walking away. "Will, you filthy weakling, get water to these customers."

A thin boy a couple of years younger than Cole hurried over to the table with a platter of cups and a wooden pitcher. He had a bondmark as well. He filled three cups, distributed them, then scuttled back to the kitchen.

"Is everyone this rude here?" Cole asked.

"Depends on the town," Twitch said. "Depends on the establishment. Depends who you are. Doesn't help when you're young."

"Where I come from, people treat customers nicely," Cole said. "They want your business."

"It can be like that here, too," Mira said. "We're in a remote town. Not many options."

Jace walked into the room wearing a felt top hat, gray with a black band. It wasn't very tall, but it had a brim all the way around.

Mira buried her face in her hands.

Jace came over to the table, grinning wide. "Saw it in the window."

"It's . . . something," Cole said.

"Isn't it?" Jace said. "I mean, what's such an amazing hat doing in a place like this?"

"How much?" Mira asked.

"Two silver," Jace said.

Mira reddened, her lips pressed together.

"I've never bought anything before," Jace whispered proudly to Cole. "What's for lunch?"

"They have chicken, pork, and egg soup," Twitch listed. "And sugarbread."

"Sugarbread?" Jace asked, perking up. "Any flavors?"

"Apricot and frosted."

"I know what I'm getting," Jace said.

The young slave called Will returned with two bowls on a platter. He placed one in front of Mira, the other in front of Twitch.

"You blundering good-for-nothing!" the bald slave yelled, exiting from the kitchen. He hobbled up to Will and cuffed him on the ear. "I gave you bread! Where's the bread?"

Will looked scared. "I must have set it down in the kitchen."

The bald slave cuffed him again. "Don't write me a speech. Fetch it!"

Will scurried off.

Hands on his hips, the bald slave turned to face the table. "You've picked up a tagalong. Quite the gentleman, it appears." The sarcasm was apparent.

Jace looked at him hard. "Ever buy a hat, bald man?"

The man squared up and stared at him flatly. "If I ever bought a hat, I'd have an outfit to match it."

"Then you'd buy a rag," Jace replied without humor. "But it wouldn't hide that nose or your mark. Who taught you to talk back to your betters?"

The man glared, fuming. "You better watch yourself—"

"I better watch myself?" Jace laughed, standing up. "You're a slave, you dimwit! You keep opening your mouth with no idea who you're talking to!"

Cole tried to signal Jace to mellow out, but there was no reaching him. He had his game face on.

Jace took off his hat, turned it upside down, and dumped Twitch's soup into it. "I bought this as a joke." He walked up to the slave and, reaching up to the taller man, put it on his bald head. Oily soup cascaded down the man's neck and shoulders. "It's yours now."

Veins stood out in the man's neck. His fists were tensed, his gaze lethal.

"Are you giving me the eye?" Jace growled. "You've forgotten yourself, lowlife! Please hit me. I'd love to watch you swinging by the neck, that goofy hat on your ugly head."

The slave backed away, his expression less certain. Jace stepped forward and snatched his hat back. "You should be on your knees, begging forgiveness. I've had enough. Fetch your owner! We're going to have words."

The bald man hesitated, as if about to reply.

"How stupid are you?" Jace yelled. "You've wrecked our meal! Move!"

The bald man hurried away. Cole avoided eye contact

with Jace. The bald slave had been a jerk, but Jace had laid into him too much. Cole's only relief was to have Jace's temper directed at a target besides himself.

A moment later a short man came out from the back. "What's the trouble?"

"Do you own Baldy?" Jace asked.

"I own him and this lodge," the man said.

"Your slave kept mouthing off," Jace said. "It was unacceptable."

The short man wrung his hands. "Gordon doesn't always . . . That's just his way."

"He shouldn't deal with people," Jace said.

"Maybe not." The man sighed. "I'll reprimand him."

"Okay," Jace said, straightening his shirt self-consciously.

"Let me make it up to you," the man said. "How about some frosted sugarbread? Just made it this morning."

"That's actually what I was going to order," Jace said, returning to his seat. "I'd like that."

"Four slices, on the house," the man said. "Sorry for any trouble. Would you like me to wait on you personally?"

"The other slave is fine," Jace said. "Will. And my friend needs more soup. Baldy made off with his portion."

"Of course," the owner said. "I'll see to it." He retreated to the kitchen.

"You have a way with people," Cole said.

Twitch coughed, perhaps covering a laugh.

"What?" Jace asked innocently. "I know how slaves are supposed to act. I went easy on him!" He lowered his voice.

"If I had ever treated a free man that way, I would have gotten ten lashes!"

"Did you have to dump the soup?" Cole asked.

"I sure did," Jace said, looking regretfully at his hat. "You saw how he treated that kid. I know his type. Rotten to the core. I've worked under guys like him. A bad slave can be worse than a bad owner. He had it coming."

"You ruined your hat," Mira said.

"Maybe I can clean it," Jace said. He lowered his voice again. "It's the first thing I ever bought. Slaves take what we're given. We can't purchase anything. The hat was perfect. Something nobody would have given me. Made me sad to ruin it."

Will emerged from the kitchen. He gave everyone a small loaf of dark bread and a slice of sugarbread, then placed a new bowl of soup in front of Twitch. Cole thought the sugarbread looked kind of like a cinnamon roll.

"Thanks, Will," Jace said. "Have you ever tried sugarbread?"

Will smiled and gave a nervous chuckle. "No, sir. It's expensive. It's not for the help."

"There was a time when I'd never tried sugarbread," Jace said. "I thought it looked really good. But my . . . mother wouldn't let me try any." He took a bite, briefly closing his eyes as he chewed it. "It's delicious. I want you to have half of mine."

Will glanced toward the kitchen. "I couldn't."

"You have to," Jace said, tearing his piece of sugarbread in half and holding out the larger piece. "Otherwise I'll complain. It's an order. Cram it in."

After another glance back at the kitchen, Will took a bite. His eyes lit up. "I'd always wondered how it tasted," he said.

"Good, right?" Jace asked, munching his own piece.

"Amazing," Will said, gleefully taking more bites. "I almost pinched some once. It just smelled so good. Tastes even better. Thanks." He stuffed the rest into his mouth, rubbed his lips, then wiped his hands on his apron.

"Well done," Jace approved. "You'd better get back to the kitchen."

"Thanks so much," Will said before hurrying away.

"Is that your first sugarbread?" Mira whispered.

"You guessed it," Jace said, finishing his piece. "Freedom is delicious."

Will returned with a bunch of skewered chicken and a plate of bacon. He placed chicken in front of Cole, Twitch, and Jace. "I told Mr. Dunford we should give you some chicken," Will confided to Jace.

"You're the best," Jace said.

"Will," Mira said. "My cousin has a rash. We've heard of a woman in town who is good with herbs."

"The herb woman?" Will asked. "Sure, she lives in a cottage on the far side of the bridge. Folks say she's the best."

"Thanks, Will," Mira said. "We'll probably pay her a visit."

CHAPTER
30

HERBS

Cole felt relieved as he climbed back into the autocoach. He had worried that more drama might arise from the humiliated slave, but at the end of the meal, Mira settled up with Mr. Dunford, and the owner offered a final apology as they walked out.

"After going over the bridge, turn left down the first lane we reach," Mira said to Bertram, repeating directions Will had shared. "We're looking for a cottage with a walled garden."

The autocoach rolled forward.

Mira turned to Jace. "If you want to keep traveling with me, you have to fix your attitude."

"Me?" Jace exclaimed. "That guy was a jerk!"

"You started unnecessary trouble," Mira said. "We're lucky the owner sided with us. Mistreating another man's slave can be taken as a personal insult. Mr. Dunford didn't know who was outside in the autocoach. He didn't want to risk crossing somebody important. Otherwise things might have gone the other way."

"The slave was way out of line," Jace maintained.

"He made some rude comments," Mira said. "Have some empathy. The man probably hates his job. He wasn't excited to wait on four spoiled kids on holiday."

"Don't forget, I was a slave," Jace said. "I know how it works. They don't get to treat us like that. Ever. And it wasn't just us. You saw him abusing Will."

"I get that you had reasons," Mira said. "But just because you *can* punish somebody doesn't always mean you *should*. Have some restraint. Show some class."

Jace scowled. "What's classy about letting people trample all over you? Letting them act like bullies? You guys are lucky to have somebody along with a backbone!"

"You have courage," Mira said. "I question your judgment. We don't want to lose the war because of needless battles. Show some patience. Don't stir things up out of vanity. Use your experience as a slave to make you more lenient, not harsher."

Jace exhaled angrily. "I can't believe a princess is lecturing me on what I should learn from being a slave."

"I was marked as a slave long before you were born," Mira said. "It's been my cover for more than sixty years."

"Exactly," Jace said. "Your *cover*. You knew it was an act. You had people looking out for you. I get it was hard. It wasn't palaces and parties. But don't tell me what I should learn from my life. You don't survive by acting weak. That makes you a victim."

The confrontation was making Cole uneasy. It felt like he was eavesdropping. He certainly wanted to stay out of it. Twitch seemed equally uncomfortable. Trying to appear disinterested, Cole watched out the window as the auto-coach crossed a wide channel on a sturdy stone bridge.

"What if it went the other way in there?" Mira asked.

"I had my rope," Jace said.

"So we solve the problem with violence," Mira said. "If you used the rope to beat them up, how fast would the story spread? Not a very big town. My guess is minutes. How soon before the legion hears about a kid using a golden rope to trash an inn? How soon before hundreds of horsemen get a second chance to corner us? And why? Because you couldn't handle some miserable slave making fun of your hat."

Jace folded his arms across his chest and glared at her crossly. He almost said something once, twice, then kept his mouth shut.

"Yes?" Mira asked.

"You might have a point," he allowed grumpily.

"I've been hiding for decades," Mira said. "That doesn't work if you attract attention. You had your reasons for how you acted. You're right that the guy kind of had it coming. I'm asking you to be smarter than that."

"You want me to let people treat us like dirt?" Jace spat.

"Don't let others control you," Mira said. "Don't let them prod you into making stupid moves. Let them have the meaningless victories. Let that stuff go. Think bigger. Play to win."

"Never stick my neck out," Jace said as if making a mental note. "Fine, we'll see how that goes."

Mira shook her head. "Don't deliberately misunderstand.

When it matters, go all in, fight to the finish. Just not when it doesn't matter and could mess up what you want most."

"What if I most want my self-respect?" Jace shot back. "What if that's the most precious thing I have? What if, without that, I wouldn't be a guy who could stick his neck out when it mattered?"

"How others treat you doesn't have to hurt your self-respect," Mira said. "Forgiving some poor guy who didn't know who he was messing with doesn't have to hurt your self-respect. Neither does being smart. Neither does playing to win."

Jace chuckled cynically. "You were definitely born to rule. You know everything I should do. You even know how I should feel. You don't want friends, Mira, you want semblances. Guess what? I'm not a puppet. And I'm not stupid. Maybe I thought sticking it to Baldy would make us look like we really were rich kids on holiday. Maybe that's why the owner treated us so well. Maybe the rest of you looked like imposters because you let some mouthy slave act like your superior."

Mira hesitated, finally shrugging. "Maybe. It felt unnecessary to me."

"Fine," Jace said. "I get it. I'll try to pick the right battles. But I also need to follow my instincts. I'm good at surviving too, Mira. Without any help."

"That's fair," Mira said. "But I'll part ways with you if I feel you're endangering me. Not out of meanness. Out of self-preservation. I don't want to control you, Jace. But I have every right to control my own fate."

Having crossed the waterway, the autocoach took the

next left. They seemed to be heading out of town. The lane wasn't paved, and homes were becoming infrequent.

"I see a wall up ahead," Cole said, hoping to change the subject.

"Good work, Cole," Jace muttered. "If I'm gone, at least you'll have an expert wall spotter."

"What's that supposed to mean?" Cole asked.

"It means, what's your opinion?" Jace said. "It's easy to let Mira do all the talking. Should I have left Baldy alone? Did I make a mistake? You didn't back me up at the lodge. You just sat there looking awkward. I know what Twitch was thinking. He was figuring out which window would offer the quickest escape. That's what he does. Maybe it's a bug thing. But what about you?"

"I thought you crossed the line," Cole said. "Pouring the soup on him was too much. It could have started a real fight."

"I couldn't show weakness," Jace said. "If I was going to stand up to him, I had to go for the throat. How would you have handled it?"

Cole sighed. "You saw how I handled it."

"You would have taken it?" Jace asked.

"Yeah, until Baldy crossed the line, I would have taken it. I did take it."

The autocoach came to a halt. "Would you like to investigate whether this is the desired destination?" Bertram asked.

"In a second," Jace said, sizing up Cole. "Twitch can spot the exits. Cole can take the insults. I'll keep us alive."

"Cole has saved my life more than once," Mira said, fire in her tone. "Not just the cyclops. Remember when he came into the common room with his bow? That was the time to act."

"I didn't see any arrows in the legionnaires running to get you," Jace said. "I forget, who took them out?"

"I'm not saying you didn't help," Mira said. "I'm saying Cole came to my rescue first. Don't insult the only people on your side. You could learn a lot from Cole."

Cole cringed inside. He knew Mira was trying to help, just as he knew she was making it worse.

"Good to know," Jace said. "I was wondering who I could study for some pointers."

"One of my secrets is watching for walls," Cole said, trying to lighten the mood.

Jace smiled knowingly. "Another is staying in the auto-coach when it's about to be destroyed."

The truth of it felt like a stab to the gut. "You're right. I froze."

"It happens," Jace said. "Usually it gets you killed."

"Stop it!" Mira said. "Seriously."

"It's okay," Cole said, angry now. Obviously, Jace didn't want to pull any punches. "Jace probably saved my life back there. He can teach me a lot. What's your secret? Practice? Reflexes? True love?"

Jace looked so stunned and terrified that Cole almost regretted the words. Almost.

Twitch laughed really hard. "You guys are hilarious!" Cole could tell it was forced. "We've come a really long way to talk to this herb lady. We're outside her door. And all we can do is squabble."

"He has a point," Mira said.

"Of course I do!" Twitch said. "I'm part bug. We have instincts about these things. We all have plenty to think about. If we keep talking, it'll just get mean. Let's go see what we can learn."

"Fine with me," Jace said. Only a little worry lingered in his glance at Cole. "I've never been more bored."

Cole wanted to get in one more dig, but resisted. "Let me see if I have this straight. When dinosaurs attack the coach, don't stay inside."

Jace smirked. "That's the idea. And I'm not supposed to dump soup on people unless it's absolutely necessary." He opened the door and got out of the coach.

"We all learned something," Twitch said, following.

"Like not to mock Cole," Mira said privately, with a little smile.

Cole thought she had missed his reference to Jace's feelings. The ease of her comment hinted she was aware of his crush. It took everything he had to erase his smile as he stepped down from the autocoach.

A wall of fitted stones draped with ivy blocked any view of the cottage until they reached a wrought-iron gate. Testing it, Mira found the gate unlocked. A gravel path bordered by white pebbles led from the gate to a tidy wooden cottage. To either side of the path, plants grew in rich soil, occasionally divided by lesser paths and weathered wooden beams.

Elaborate carvings of vines and birds were embossed on the door. Mira knocked firmly.

"I'm out," a female voice called from inside.

"We have to talk," Mira replied.

There came a pause. They heard a bolt slide back and the door opened. An older woman with short, graying hair opened the door halfway. She was quite thin and not much taller than Jace. "Children? I'm out of sweetroot."

"We don't want sweetroot," Mira said.

"Speak for yourself," Jace grumbled.

"What is it, then?" the woman asked. "Father have a fever? Mother sprain an ankle? Cow not giving milk?"

"You're Gerta?" Mira asked.

"The crazy old herb woman," she replied with a small curtsy.

"Declan sent us," Mira said quietly.

Gerta looked beyond them, surveying the area. "Who's in the coach?"

"A semblance," Mira said.

"You're serious," Gerta said, opening the door wider. "Come inside."

She guided them to a parlor with some fancy chairs and many shelves of fragile ceramic figurines. Jace claimed one chair, Twitch another. Cole and Mira used the sofa, reserving the biggest armchair for Gerta.

The herb woman used the armrests and sat down with a weary sigh. "Where is Declan?"

"We can't tell," Mira said. "It's for your good as much as his."

She smiled, showing imperfect teeth. "You were with him all right. He's well?"

"Old," Mira said.

"He was old when I was a girl," Gerta said.

"He doesn't get around so well anymore," Mira said.

Gerta nodded. "He sent you to me for a purpose?"

"I'm looking for . . . ," Mira began, then seemed unsure how to phrase it.

"A monster that has been tearing apart Sambria," Cole jumped in. "A really powerful semblance."

"You can't mean Carnag," Gerta said with a gasp.

"That's what people call it," Mira said.

"There have been no eyewitnesses," Gerta said. "I've heard tales of the devastation. The ruined towns, the missing people. We're all worried it'll head this way."

"Is it close?" Mira asked.

"Don't act eager, child. I've felt its energy from afar. It's like nothing we've ever known. What does Declan expect you to do?"

"We have to find it," Mira said.

"No," Gerta said. "You leave Carnag alone. Try not to let it find you. What did Declan tell you about it?"

"We have to find it," Mira repeated.

Gerta squinted at Mira. Then her eyes widened. "You're connected."

"What?" Mira asked.

Gerta spoke slowly. "You're connected to Carnag. I wouldn't have seen if I wasn't really looking. Same type of energy, much fainter, but pure."

"Where should we look?" Mira asked.

"Carnag moves erratically," Gerta said. "This whole region of Sambria has been in awful suspense. We never know where it will strike next. Head southeast. Follow the screaming."

"Straight southeast?" Mira asked.

"More or less," Gerta said. "There will be a path of destruction. Ask the people fleeing. I expect you'll find Carnag sooner than you'd like. What can you possibly hope to accomplish?"

"We probably shouldn't tell you," Mira said.

"That might be sensible," Gerta agreed. "Declan really sent you to me?"

"Really," Mira said.

"Did he shape the semblance in the autocoach?" Gerta asked.

"Yes," Mira said.

"Mind if I have a look?" Gerta asked. "It's not that I doubt you, but times being what they are . . ."

"Feel free," Mira said.

"I'll be back," Gerta announced.

Cole and the others watched from the window.

"Think she'll try to take something?" Jace asked.

"From the autocoach?" Mira said. "No, but it doesn't hurt to watch."

Gerta didn't spend long at the coach. She returned along the path wearing a small, satisfied smile.

"That's his work all right," Gerta said as she reentered the room. "Bertram is a funny old character. He's very adamant that he's enjoying the countryside with his grandniece and grandnephews. You poor dears. You've gotten tangled up in something frightful. The whole garrison of legionnaires at

Bellum went to fight this thing. Over a hundred men. None returned. If you go bother Carnag, I'm afraid that will be the end of you."

"We have to try," Mira said.

"Your connection to the entity is undeniable," Gerta said. "I could speculate . . . but I better not. I'm glad to hear Declan survives. I'm happy to lend what aid I can. I've devoted myself to working with my plants. Vegetation is much easier to shape successfully than animals or even semblances. Given time, I might be able to whip up something powerful. Since you seem to be in a hurry, I'll give you some of the best of what I have on hand."

"That's not necessary," Mira said.

"I help Sambria little enough," Gerta said. "I spend most of my time here shaping herbs. I avoid the ugly politics. Nobody wants to antagonize the woman who can help a toothache and cure an upset stomach. Every now and then I get a chance to help people who are still trying to make a real difference for Sambria. I suspect you four fall into that category."

"We'd appreciate anything you can do," Cole said.

"I have single carrots that will fill your stomachs for three days," Gerta said. "Not an illusion, mind you. It will be like you've eaten healthy meals throughout. I have pumpkin seeds that will give you extraordinary night vision. The effect lasts four or five hours. You wouldn't want the extra sensitivity during the day, so eat them with care. And I have many herbal remedies for injuries and illnesses. I'll provide a full assortment. I'll even throw in a delicious tea that can induce prolonged slumber."

"You're too kind," Mira said.

"It's the least I can do for friends of Declan," Gerta said. "Would you four like to stay the night here?"

"We should be on our way," Mira said. "There are people after us."

"At least rest from your troubles while I gather my gifts," Gerta said. "I'll bring you some snacks shortly."

"She's nice," Cole said after she had left the room.

Mira sighed. "Yes. And informed. The problem is, the more I learn about my powers, the less I want them back."

"Maybe we really should go on vacation," Cole said. "We have money. I bet Bertram would be thrilled."

They all chuckled.

"I wish I could," Mira said. "I really do. You all don't have to join me. But I must face this."

"We're with you," Jace said.

Mira gazed out the window. "I hope it doesn't mean we'll all go down together."

DEVASTATION

The autocoach clomped southeast through the night and into the next day, pausing only to let the occupants get out and freshen up. They passed through pleasant country made up of sparse forests, open fields, meandering streams, and low hills.

Around midday, they spotted a wagon pulled by horses coming along the road from the opposite direction. The wagon slowed to a stop as they approached, and Mira ordered the autocoach to halt. They ended up side by side.

"Good day," said the driver, a big man with simple clothes and a straw hat. "Are you folks certain you want to head this way?"

"I'm on holiday with my grandniece and grandnephews," Bertram said, leaning forward to be seen. "We're out enjoying the countryside."

The driver squinted back the way he had come. "This may not be the right direction to go for pleasure. The whole area is clearing out. Carnag has been active, and reports have him coming this way."

"We'll turn northeast before long," Mira said.

"You know your affairs," the man said. "The monster is hard to predict. Comes and goes. But I suggest you choose a new direction sooner rather than later. The towns you'll reach down this road won't have their normal services. Springdale got hit hard, and now the whole region is evacuating. Not many are coming northwest like me, since Carnag has shown a recent preference for this direction. You'll pass many refugees when you head northeast."

"Thanks for the warning," Mira said. "I'm sorry for your troubles."

"Are you sure you won't just turn around?" the driver asked. "You're tempting fate going southeast."

"It's no crime to see some sights with your relatives," Bertram said.

The driver raised his eyebrows.

"Uncle is kind of a thrill seeker," Cole apologized. "We'll turn up the next good road."

"Just offering a neighborly warning," the driver said, shaking his reins. "Take care."

"Thanks," Cole said. "Travel safe."

The next day they passed through an empty town. The area seemed like an abandoned movie set. There was no visible damage to any of the buildings. A few roosters roamed the streets, strutting and pecking.

The silent town drew Cole's attention to the quietness of the road. The broad lane looked well traveled, but they passed nobody—no autocoaches, no wagons, no horsemen, no one on foot. Uninhabited farms went by on either side.

After nightfall, they rolled through another derelict town. No lit windows brightened the darkness. Some cows roamed a fenced field, munching the long grass.

The abandoned countryside heightened Cole's tension. People didn't pick up and clear out like this for a minor annoyance. Carnag had panicked the whole area. The possibility that the monster might come their way had convinced people to leave their homes behind and head for the hills.

On the evening of the third day since leaving Middlebranch, with the setting sun coloring the horizon lava red, they reached another town. Upon arrival, Mira called for the autocoach to halt, and they all spilled out.

Cole could hardly decide where to focus his attention first. Ahead of the autocoach, the road disappeared into a bowl-shaped pit that resembled a crater from a meteor strike. Two wagons lay upside down on the roof of a local inn. Several trees were white as snow—leaf, limb, and trunk. One home had no walls or roof, but the floor, chimney, and furniture remained neatly in place.

"What happened here?" Twitch moaned.

"You only get one guess," Jace said.

"I know it was Carnag," Twitch said. "But what did it do?"

"Those trees aren't supposed to be white, are they?" Cole asked.

"No, it's unnatural," Mira said. "I also can't imagine it's easy to strip away the walls of a house without knocking over any furniture. We better take a good look. We might find some clues about what we're dealing with."

She started down the main street of the town. They

passed a large tree propped against a sagging building, soil-clotted roots in the air, leafy limbs on the road. A section of the town was a smoldering field of charred rubble. One side of the tallest building still standing was crusted with pink coral. A granite boulder lay in the middle of a shop, having apparently crashed through the wall. For one stretch the street undulated, like a stormy sea that had paused, leaving an abnormal pattern of swells and troughs. Half of one house was gone, sheared off cleanly so as to reveal a perfect cross section of the inside, like a full-size dollhouse.

The street ended at a reedy lake. Drowned buildings poked out of the foul water for another hundred yards.

"The town is totaled," Cole said. "How big is this thing? It looks like a giant had a temper tantrum. What can't Carnag do?"

"Some of this might have been done physically," Mira said. "But a lot of it had to be shaping—the lumps in the road, the coral, the house neatly sliced in half. Maybe all of it was shaping."

"So it's a semblance and a shaper," Jace said.

"Kind of makes sense," Mira replied. "It's made out of shaping power."

"How powerful are you?" Twitch asked.

Mira laughed softly. "I had some talent. Nothing like this. Don't forget what Declan told us. This is unrestrained shaping energy, free from my limitations. It's probably much more powerful than I could ever be."

Cole ran both hands through his hair. "How do we fight something that can blast the ground out from under us, chop us in half, crush us with a boulder, then grow coral on us?"

"And that's just for starters," Twitch added.

"I don't really know," Mira said. "We use everything we have. We hope my connection to Carnag can be an advantage somehow. Remember, it can't kill me without killing itself."

"I still worry Declan could be using us," Jace said. "He might just want Carnag gone, whatever the cost. He might have purposefully sent us to our deaths. If you get killed, Carnag gets wiped out too, and Sambria has one less problem."

"Maybe," Mira said. "But it's something I have to do. It's my power."

"You're not to blame," Jace said. "You didn't turn your power into Carnag. Whoever took your power is responsible. Blame your dad. Let him figure this out."

Mira took a deep breath. "This may be hard for you to understand. I'm not doing this just because I feel guilty. That power is part of me. Like a lost limb. Worse, even. Like a lost piece of my actual self. I've wondered for years if I could ever get it back. I knew it might never happen. But this is my chance. It matters enough to me that I'm willing to die trying. If you want to watch from a distance, that's fine. This town shows how scary Carnag can be. If you want to run away at top speed, I'll understand."

"Sometimes I feel like you're trying to get rid of us," Cole said.

"I kind of am," Mira admitted. "This is my risk to take. Not yours. I can live with getting myself killed."

"Technically, you can't live if you get killed," Jace pointed out.

"You know what I mean!" Mira snapped. "My life is mine

to risk. I can't stand the thought of bringing you all down with me."

"We volunteered for this," Jace said. "You didn't make us."

"He's right," Cole said.

"I know," Mira said. "But you don't have to keep volunteering. Sky Raiders run from danger. It's what we know. It's how we've gotten this far. But this time we're heading right at the danger. We're tracking it down on purpose. And I'm not going to run."

They all contemplated that in silence.

"You might need us," Cole said. "You might not survive without us. Jace is pretty good with that rope."

"I sure am," Jace said. "Don't try to get rid of me ever again. I'm done having this conversation. If you're determined, I am too. I see the town. It's a mess. We knew this thing was powerful. But I won't abandon you."

"If it goes really bad, we can still try to run," Twitch said. "You know, last minute. I'm not quitting now."

"What about you, Cole?" Mira asked. "You're not even from here. You have friends to find. Do you really want to get killed fighting my shaping power?"

"I don't want to get killed," Cole said. "I promised my friends that I'd find them, and I'm going to keep that promise. Your father has my friends as slaves. His laws led to us being taken from our world. You want to overthrow him. Doing that would be the surest way to help my friends. It all starts with you getting your powers back. I'm with you, Mira. Not only because I need to help Jenna and Dalton. You're my friend too."

Mira wiped at her eyes. "Okay. I'm grateful. It's not that I want you to leave. I just feel so responsible."

"We get it," Jace said.

"Where did you kids come from?" a voice interrupted.

They all jumped and whirled toward the speaker. An older man with a long white beard was coming their way down a side street. He wore dirty work clothes and walked as if he might be a little arthritic.

"Didn't mean to startle you," he said. "I'm wondering what news you've had."

"We came from the northwest," Cole said. "Things are quiet that way. The towns have evacuated."

"We were mostly evacuated," the old man said, drawing closer. "Some of the men stayed to fight."

"You saw Carnag?" Mira exclaimed.

The man shook his head. "Not me. I weathered the attack down in my root cellar. I'd seen a town the monster had hit. It leaves some of the buildings untouched. I've lived here all my life. Decided to take my chances hiding out."

"What happened to the men?" Cole asked.

"No sign of them," the old man said, his voice quavering. After a moment, he regained his composure. "You're the first people to happen by since Carnag visited five days ago."

"Any idea which way the monster went?" Twitch asked.

"Looked like the fiend doubled back the way it came," the old man said. "I didn't see it, mind you, just signs of its passage. That's been the pattern. Carnag ventures out farther every time, but falls back between forays."

"Are you all right?" Mira asked. "Do you need anything?"

"I have plenty," the old man said. "A whole town's supplies. The worst of it should be behind me. So far there have been no reports of Carnag hitting the same place twice. What brings you this way?"

"Family emergency," Mira said. "We better get going."

"Need provisions?" the old man asked.

"We have enough," Mira said. "Thanks, though. Keep safe."

"You too, young lady."

They returned to the autocoach. Mira instructed Bertram to go around the pit in the road and then continue to the southeast.

The autocoach trotted ahead through the night. Whenever he jerked awake, Cole peered out the window, half-expecting to see a monstrosity charging at them. But all he saw was the countryside under the dull light of a reddish moon.

"No star," Mira said one time after he looked outside.

"No?" Cole asked.

"I haven't seen my star since we fled through the cloud-wall," Mira said.

"I guess that means nobody can trace us," Cole said.

"No enemies and no help."

"Is it almost morning?" Cole asked.

"Not yet," Mira said. "Try to rest."

"What about you?"

"I'm trying too."

Just after sunrise, they heard the pounding rhythm of an approaching gallop. A quick look revealed a lone legionnaire racing along the road from the opposite direction. Jace got his rope ready.

"It's one guy," Mira said. "He's probably not here for us. He may just ride by."

The horseman slowed as he reached the autocoach. He looked like a teenager, though he might have been twenty. His uniform was disheveled. "Whoa!" he called. "You people need to turn around right away!"

Mira ordered the autocoach to stop.

"What's the problem?" Jace asked.

"Only the biggest threat in Sambria," the legionnaire said, panic behind his eyes. "How did you get this far without catching on? Carnag is just beyond the next hill."

His insides squirming with anxiety, Cole instantly turned his attention to the road ahead. He saw where the lane disappeared behind the next rise. Everything looked quiet and normal.

"Is it coming this way?" Mira asked.

"I'm not waiting around to find out," the legionnaire said. "I was part of a scouting party with eleven other soldiers. Good horsemen. I'm the only one who got clear."

"Did you see it?" Mira pressed.

"Glimpsed it through the trees," the legionnaire said. "It's gigantic, I can tell you that much. Hard to speak to the details. The others wanted a closer look. They got it all right."

"You abandoned your unit?" Mira asked.

"We're a scouting party!" the young legionnaire protested. "Somebody has to report back. It might not be too late for you. Turn around."

Jace looked at Mira. "What do we do?"

"Take him," Mira said.

The golden rope lashed out, bound the soldier's arms to his sides, and yanked him off his horse. The legionnaire hit the ground hard, his pinioned arms unable to help break his fall. The horse whinnied and reared, then settled down.

At first the legionnaire could only cough and wheeze. "What are you doing?" he finally managed.

"We're on holiday," Bertram replied. "My grandniece and grandnephews are helping me take in the countryside."

"Let me go!" the soldier cried. "Do what you want, but don't hold me here!"

"Play dead, soldier!" Mira ordered. "We have nothing to fear from Carnag. We work with it. Keep your mouth shut, or we'll make you a sacrifice."

The legionnaire mostly obeyed. Cole heard faint whimpering.

"Do you have some of that tea?" Mira whispered to Twitch.

"It isn't warm," Twitch said. "But I've kept some of it in water since we left Gerta's place. It should be pretty potent."

"Give him some," Mira instructed.

"Feel this?" Jace asked. The rope creaked as it tightened. The soldier cried out.

"I can make it much tighter," Jace said. "Our friend here has a refreshment for you. Drink it, and we'll let you live."

"How do I know it isn't poison?" the legionnaire asked as Twitch climbed down to him.

"Because there are easier ways to kill you," Jace said. "For example, I could squeeze you to death."

The soldier let out an anguished groan.

While Twitch gave the tea to the legionnaire, Cole leaned over to Mira. "If the legionnaires are scouting this thing, does that mean your father isn't directly involved?"

"Probably," she said. "Unless he's keeping it secret from his own people, which is possible."

"What . . . what . . . what was that stuff?" the legionnaire asked, his words slurred.

"Herbal tea," Twitch said.

"Not bad," the soldier said contentedly. "Am I sinking? Feels a little like . . . like I'm . . ." The legionnaire sagged.

Twitch snapped his fingers by the legionnaire's ear. "He's out. Might have been an extra-strong dose. The tea looks really dark."

"Good," Mira said. "We can't have him in the way. In fact, I don't want to risk leaving him here. Tie him up and we'll bring him."

Jace pulled some spare rope from the storage compartment. After binding the soldier's wrists, legs, and arms, it took all three boys to drag him up into the autocoach.

"I wonder if I should ride the horse," Mira said. "It might be good to have the extra speed and mobility."

"Go for it," Jace said.

Just then Mango fluttered down to the window. "I'm not sure if this is good news or bad, but Carnag is just up ahead."

"We know," Mira said. "Where have you been?"

"It's been hectic." Mango sighed. "I'm keeping track of many things."

"Did you see it?" Mira asked.

"I didn't want to get too close," the bird said. "It's big. And noisy. I heard people crying for help."

"Thanks, Mango," Mira said.

"On the bright side, I helped bring some assistance," Mango said.

A guy on a flying disk swooped alongside the autocoach. "Better late than never," Liam announced.

"Liam!" Cole exclaimed. "I thought you said you'd be too busy to help out!"

Liam scrunched his face apologetically. "I know. I didn't want you guys counting on me. But I got bored."

"You're here because you were bored?" Jace asked.

"Why not? I like how nonchalant it sounds. You want the whole story? We had to flee Cloudvale, and Declan is settled in his new hideout, so I figured they could spare me. I'm here with permission."

"How'd you find us?" Mira asked.

"You didn't think Mango was only spying for you?" Liam chided. "She reported to some of my other birds so I could keep track of your progress."

"Kind of a shady gift," Mira said.

He placed a hand over his heart. "I did it to be helpful. Promise."

"Do you know anything new about Carnag?" Cole asked.

"I haven't had a close look yet," Liam replied. "But I can feel it more clearly than before. It's just throbbing with power. I'm no slouch at shaping, but I can't imagine my power burning half so bright. This won't be easy. What's the plan?"

Nobody answered.

"We're kind of making this up as we go," Mira said.

"Might be all we can do," Liam said. "Nobody has ever confronted anything like this. Tell you what. I'll hang back and watch how it goes, study Carnag for weaknesses. That way you'll have somebody in reserve."

"That's really brave of you," Jace said.

"I'm being strategic!" Liam complained. "Who's going to save everybody if this goes bad? You?"

"Is anybody else coming?" Jace asked.

"I tried to talk Asia into joining us," Liam said. "She's too set on defending Declan. But an old friend of yours is on his way. Well, more of an acquaintance. Barely even that. He's on your side, though."

"Who?" Cole asked.

"Joe MacFarland."

"The guy from Skyport?" Mira asked. "The messenger?"

"The man is dedicated," Liam said. "He warned us that the legion was planning a major offensive through the Boomerang Forest."

"How'd he warn you?" Mira asked.

"He used the confusion of you guys escaping Skyport to find a hiding place," Liam said. "Keeping his ear to the ground, he discovered you had escaped into the Eastern Cloudwall and lived. When he learned about the planned offensive, he stole a skycraft and came through the cloudwall to warn you. I rescued him from the terminal void the same way I saved you four."

"Where is he now?"

"Coming as fast as he can on horseback," Liam said.

"Why didn't you bring him?" Jace asked.

"How big does my disk look? It's hard to keep it aloft away from the Brink. Some of my birds are guiding him."

"Should we wait?" Mira asked.

"I'm leaning toward no," Liam said. "After missing us at Cloudvale, the legionnaires are coming this way. Joe is a good distance behind me. There's a chance he'll never make it to us. Right now will be our best opportunity to confront Carnag without the legion at our backs."

"Sounds okay to me," Mira said. She approached the legionnaire's horse and stroked its neck. "Good girl. You don't mind heading back into danger, do you?"

"Have you ridden a lot?" Cole asked.

"A fair amount," Mira said. "I had lessons in my youth, and opportunities have come up over the years. She feels warm. He was riding her hard." Placing a foot in a stirrup, she mounted up. "You guys ready?"

"I'm not sure," Cole said. "How about 'willing'?"

"Good enough," Mira said.

Liam laughed warmly. "I'm going to put some distance between us. You won't see me at first, but I'd like to stay in communication." Drifting closer to Cole, he held out a hand. "If you put these in your ears, I'll be able to hear you, and you'll hear me. They won't work over huge distances, but they should be perfect for today."

Cole took what looked like a pellet of clay. The others each accepted one as well.

"It's not fragile," Liam explained. "Just squish it in there. Not too far. It'll mold to the shape of your ear canal."

Cole pressed the pellet into his right ear. It molded to fit snugly.

"Any other goodies?" Jace asked.

"That's it," Liam said. "Let's get this over with."

"Bertram," Mira said from astride her mount, "take us to find the monster over the hill."

The autocoach started forward. Mira kept pace alongside. Liam soared out of sight.

"We came looking for this, and now we found it," Cole murmured to Twitch. "Be careful what you wish for."

"Because you might get it?"

Cole gave a nod. "Exactly."

CARNAG

As the autocoach came around the side of the little hill, Cole gripped his bow like a lifeline. He wasn't sure what to expect, but he knew it would be horrible. As Mira had made clear, this time they were running toward the danger.

He wasn't sure how to prepare himself. Was he going to shoot an arrow at something that turned towns upside down and defeated regiments of trained soldiers? Maybe it would have a weak spot. At least he could help distract it while Mira figured out how to defeat it. With his Jumping Sword, he might be hard to catch.

What if he got killed? He tried not to dwell on the possibility, but he couldn't resist. There was a very real chance that they were all about to die. Nobody back home would care. His parents didn't remember him. There would be no mourning, no grave. It would be like he had never existed.

What would happen to Dalton, Jenna, and the others from his world? He supposed they couldn't blame him for not saving them if he got killed. That was a pretty ironclad excuse.

Then again, if he did nothing, that wouldn't rescue them either. They might never know it, but he was doing his best to help them.

He was relieved Liam had come. His shaping might not be as strong here as at the Brink, but the guy could fly, and he was confident, and he certainly had useful skills. Hopefully, Liam would be able to lend Mira the kind of support she deserved.

"There," Jace said, pointing into the woods.

Cole squinted. In the distance, treetops swayed violently, as if something not much shorter than them was passing through.

"I see it," Mira replied from astride her mount. "Bertram, can we go that way?"

"The forest is too thick for the autocoach," Bertram said. "Perhaps we can work our way around the perimeter of the woodlands."

"You better just stop and let them out," Mira replied. "Then try to work your way around. Stay as close to us as possible. Flail, follow!"

Cole jumped down. Mira led the way into the forest on horseback, cantering through the trees, the flail jangling in her wake. Jace used his rope to slingshot himself from trunk to trunk. Twitch put on his ring and started hopping. Cole knifed forward, using the Jumping Sword to take long low leaps between the trees. Soon he was ahead of Mira.

There came a creaking moan, like a barn about to collapse or the hull of an old ship under stress. The hugeness of the sound made Cole pause. The great creaking repeated, somewhat lower and slower. Mira kept loping forward, guiding her horse through the light undergrowth. Jace and Twitch continued to advance as well. Feeling a little jealous of the legionnaire sleeping back in the autocoach, Cole exclaimed, "Away!" and sprang ahead.

After a few more jumps, Cole saw Jace stop at the edge of a meadow. Twitch came to a halt beside him. Their backs to Cole, the two just stared. Cole heard the enormous creaking again, massive groans of tortured wood.

Cole's next leap brought him almost to his companions. As he edged forward, he looked out to the meadow and caught his first sight of Carnag.

The towering creature was made of tree stumps, dirt, rock, shrubs, part of a chimney, wooden beams, some crumbling battlements, bricks of varied shapes and sizes, half a wagon, a section of cobblestone street, a damaged rowboat, and three iron cages. It balanced on two asymmetrical legs and had a pair of long arms, but it was only vaguely humanoid, like a haphazard scarecrow. The misshapen head displayed a crude imitation of a face.

The scale of the monstrosity was astonishing. Cole stood no taller than its ankle. Only the loftiest trees in the forest overtopped it. The moaning creak hadn't come from the mouth—it was the sound of Carnag taking steps. With a grating of stone against stone and a crackling of timbers, the giant bent over. It gripped a good-size tree with one hand and yanked it out of the ground with an earthy rending of roots and soil.

Tree in hand like a club, Carnag turned to face them from the far side of the clearing. The colossus roared, the bellow blending the howl of a jet engine with the deep rumble of an earthquake. The cacophonous cry reverberated for a long time, echoing strangely, the volume surging unpredictably.

The roar shook Cole to his core. He felt like he had awakened on railroad tracks to find a train bearing down on him.

"Get out of here!"

"Run for it!"

"Go for help!"

As overlapping voices shouted desperate advice, Cole realized that the cages making up part of Carnag's body were occupied. One cage served as most of its right shoulder, another was embedded in the left side of its chest, and the third took up much of one hip. The people inside, many in legionnaire uniforms, waved and yelled.

Carnag took a step toward Cole. Though the meadow was large, the giant was only three or four steps away.

"Split up," Jace advised, using his rope to launch himself to the left.

Twitch took off to the right.

Cole held his sword tightly. Should he keep still? If he followed Jace or Twitch, they wouldn't be splitting up very effectively. Carnag took another step in his direction, the ground trembling beneath its creaky weight. Cole wasn't sure what move to make. Should he fall back? Should he try to juke the giant at the last second?

Another step. The jolt to the ground made Cole's teeth

rattle. Carnag reached out its free hand, crouching toward him. One more step and the hand would grab him. Cole decided to gamble on a last-second jump between the legs.

Still on horseback, Mira emerged from the trees beside Cole. "Carnag!" she called. "We have to talk!"

Carnag froze, then drew up straight and tall, all attention now on Mira. "You!" Carnag said, the female voice deep and raspy. The word repeated like an echo in reverse, growing louder through the final rebound.

"What have you been doing?" Mira demanded.

Cole could not believe her boldness. For the moment, her courageous accusation seemed to have stalled the monster.

"I do as I please," Carnag finally responded, the words echoing backward again, the last reverberation the loudest.

"You belong to me," Mira said. "You were taken from me."

"I belong to myself," Carnag rasped.

"No!" Mira insisted. "You're part of me. You're not whole. Neither am I. We need each other."

A long pause followed. Cole began to wonder whether Carnag would respond. Then the words came. "I'm more now, not less. You were my prison, as was another. Come to me. I will not harm you."

"Come to you?" Mira asked.

"You will belong to me now," Carnag said, crouching and reaching.

Mira drew her sword and jumped from her horse, landing on a high limb in a tree. "I'm not yours!" she yelled. "You're mine! You come from me."

This prompted a slow laugh that resembled the unsettling

sound a mine might make right before a cave-in. "I am much, much more than you."

The giant hand grasped for her again, and Mira jumped a great distance to land in another tree. Cole noticed Jace casting out his rope. It lengthened more than Cole had ever seen, thickening as well, and wrapped three times around Carnag's shins.

As Carnag tried to take a step, the golden rope held, and the huge monster toppled forward, knees hitting first, then both hands. Jace immediately reeled in his rope. Mira sprang to another tree.

Carnag stood, tilted her head back, and roared at the sky. Jace covered his ears, but the punishing echoes of the cry pulsated through his body. The leaves and brush around him trembled.

The branches of the tree where Mira perched suddenly closed around her, like a thousand fingers making a fist. The ground where Jace stood surged up on all sides, trapping him in a mound with only his head visible. Carnag whirled and stuck out an arm, catching Twitch in midair.

Twisting, Carnag faced Cole. As the ground heaved up around him, Cole thrust his sword skyward and shouted, "Away!" He soared upward, soil brushing against his legs, but not quick enough to entrap him.

Cole was still rocketing up when he realized his mistake. In his haste to avoid getting swallowed by the ground, he had aimed for the random sky and jumped with everything he had. There was nowhere to land. He had just killed himself.

Near the apex of his flight, Cole looked down from a dizzying height almost level with Carnag's neck. As he started losing altitude, a huge hand appeared beneath him. Landing on Carnag's palm, Cole jabbed his sword toward Carnag's shoulder, yelled out the command word, and jumped before he had settled.

Carnag's fingers closed too slowly, and Cole rushed toward the earthen shoulder. Upon contact, Cole pointed the sword at the nearest tree and kicked off, yelling the command again.

Speeding through the air, Cole watched for where he would land and prepared for his next jump. He'd never really tried stringing jumps together like this so rapidly. It took some of the jolt away from the landings. Or maybe that was the adrenalin.

Just before he landed, Carnag's giant hand closed around him, snagging him in midflight and holding him tightly. Cole squirmed, but there was no give.

Carnag slapped Cole into the cage in her chest. The door clanged shut before Cole could react. Five legionnaires shared the cell with him, their uniforms torn and soiled. One of them helped Cole to his feet. There was also a woman, and a child of maybe eight years.

The door open again, and Twitch was flung inside as well. Jace came a moment later. They both looked stunned.

"Welcome to your home away from home," one of the legionnaires said.

"You better hope it doesn't trip again," another added, rubbing the side of his forehead.

"Do you hear me, Cole?" Liam asked in his right ear. "Are you all right?"

"Yeah," Cole said softly. "We're trapped, but not hurt."

"Looks like she's out to capture you rather than squash you," Liam said. "I'm going to hang back for now."

The back of the cage was the wood, stone, and dirt of Carnag. Thick metal bars composed one side and the front, including the hinged gate that allowed access. Cole went to the gate and tugged on it to no avail. He still had his Jumping Sword, but he wasn't sure what good it would do behind bars.

When Carnag turned and started moving again, Cole clung to the bars to avoid falling. Creaking and swaying, Carnag stepped toward the tree that still held Mira. Carnag reached for the tree, and the branches unfolded.

"Flail, attack!" Mira cried. The Shaper's Flail went for Carnag's hand, whirling wildly to bash away clods of dirt, fragments of stone, and chunks of wood. After flinching away from the initial onslaught, Carnag snatched the flail out of the air, like a person grabbing a bug, and kept her hand tightly closed.

Mira used the diversion to shout the command word and leap to the ground. When Carnag rounded on her, Cole felt like he was looking down at his friend from high on the wall of a cliff. Carnag crouched to reach for her, making the cell tilt forward.

Cole wanted to close his eyes. If Carnag caught Mira, this was basically over! They were all getting captured too easily. It would be up to Liam.

Mira wasn't pointing her sword to attempt another jump. She glared up at the giant stoically.

"No, Carnag!" Mira yelled. She put the tip of the Jumping Sword to her throat. "Back off, or I end us!"

Carnag stopped reaching. Cole wondered if Mira had planned to use this bluff, or if it had occurred to her out of desperation.

The giant stood up straight. "You really would," Carnag said, mildly puzzled. From where Cole sat, the mounting echoes soaked in from all directions. "I feel your resolve."

"You bet I will," Mira called. "Better that I die than you rampage around Sambria, hurting my friends."

"I haven't killed," Carnag said.

"I find that hard to believe," Mira replied.

"I don't kill," Carnag repeated. "I collect."

"Is that true?" Mira shouted.

"I haven't seen it kill anyone," one of the legionnaires in Cole's cell called back.

"Me neither," a woman answered from below, probably in the cage at the hip. "But it isn't gentle."

"I collect," Carnag maintained.

"You can't collect people," Mira scolded. "That's no way to act. We belong together. Come back to me."

Carnag didn't respond.

"Do you hear that?" Twitch asked.

"What?" Jace wondered.

"A faint voice," Twitch said, moving toward the back of the cell.

"I've heard it too," one of the legionnaires said. "Like it comes from inside this thing."

Twitch leaned up against the back wall of the cell and

placed his ear against a wooden beam. "Yeah," he said. "It's a woman. Her voice is muffled. I can't understand her. But she's talking a lot."

Carnag crouched and knelt on one knee, giving Cole a closer view of Mira. She kept the point of her sword at her throat.

A tendril snaked forward from Carnag, slithering over the ground toward Mira. She watched it with wide eyes. "I'll do it!" she warned.

"Talk first," Carnag said, the words reverse-echoing strongly.

At the end of the tendril, the ground swelled up. A perfect duplicate of Mira emerged, wearing the same clothes, holding a matching sword. The tendril was lodged in the center of her back, tethering her to Carnag's foot.

"Hello," the fake Mira said.

"What is this?" Mira asked.

"We need to talk," fake Mira said calmly, her voice just like Mira's. Cole didn't have to strain to hear. It seemed like Liam must be using the clay earpieces to help broadcast the discussion.

"You're not me," Mira accused. "You're a semblance."

"I'm not you," fake Mira said. "I'm me. You can't beat me. You're the weak part. I could protect you."

"You're not anything!" Mira said angrily. "You're phony! You're made of stuff you found! Dirt and wood and junk!"

"I can be whatever I want," fake Mira said. "Whatever I need to be. We all shape ourselves. I'm just better at it."

"You were taken from me," Mira said. "Shaped away from me. I don't know how. Do you?"

A second tendril slithered forward. When it neared Mira, the ground bulged, and the tendril became attached to a man in fine clothes. "I did it," he said.

"That isn't funny!" Mira spat. "No more puppet shows. You're not him! You're not my father!"

Cole scowled down at the well-dressed semblance. From his current vantage point, it was hard to see all the details. But assuming the man had been shaped as accurately as the fake Mira, it was his first view of his enemy, the High King.

"Are you sure?" the false High Shaper said. "I'm close enough. This entity spent a great deal of time with me. Much more time than you did. And much more time than it spent with you."

Mira turned to her double. "You weren't part of him. You were his prisoner."

"She was part of me," the fake High King said. "*And* she was my prisoner."

Mira stepped close to her semblance clone. "Don't you see? He took you. My father stole you. But now you're free. We can be together again. We're supposed to be together."

There was no reaction from Carnag or the tethered semblances.

"I hear the talking again," Twitch said. "This is messed up. Someone is in there saying stuff."

"Can you make out any words?" Jace asked.

"No," Twitch said, frustrated.

"You want to own me like he owned me," fake Mira finally said. "You want to drown me inside of you! If I go back to you, I die. You're coming with me. We're both going to survive."

"I'm not bluffing about the sword," Mira said.

"I'm not bluffing either," fake Mira answered. "What if I love my freedom? What if I'd rather end than go back?"

"Twitch is right," Liam said in Cole's ear. "I'm fantastic at discerning physical compositions. There's a woman inside of Carnag."

"Mira!" Cole called. "Ask Carnag about the woman inside of her! The woman talking to her!"

Both the fake Mira and the semblance of Mira's father abruptly looked up at Cole. Their expressions told him he was on to something.

"The boy lies," the fake Mira and fake father asserted in unison.

"What woman is inside you?" Mira asked. "Is somebody controlling you?"

The semblances paused.

"I hear her again," Twitch said. "Quieter."

Cole pressed his ear to the beam below Twitch. The murmur of hurried conversation was faint but definite.

"I hear her!" Cole said loudly.

"We hear the woman," Mira asserted. "Who is she? Don't listen to her! You're part of me! Listen to *me*!"

"You're unworthy, Mira," her fake father accused. "You would have squandered your power. You let me take her, and you ran away!"

"I ran because my father was after me," Mira cried. "I ran because I didn't understand what happened. I used to shape so many things! Then it was gone. Stolen."

"Then use your shaping," her fake father challenged. "If

you're worthy, take back what's yours. If not, accept her protection and let her live. Let her thrive. Let her be all the things you were too inept to make her."

"I can barely shape anymore," Mira said. "I'd be lucky to change the color of my shirt. Why? Because my shaping power was taken."

"Interesting," her fake father murmured.

"More talking," Twitch called.

"Can you make out what she's saying?" Cole whispered, hoping Liam would understand that the question was meant for him.

"Sadly, no," Liam replied.

"Who are you talking to?" Mira demanded. "Who's in there?"

"Give me the sword," Mira's fake father said, holding out a hand. "We don't want a tragedy."

"Come an inch closer, and I'll cut my throat," Mira promised.

"She's serious," the false Mira said.

"I know," the fake father grumbled.

"What do you call yourself?" Mira asked her double.

Fake Mira hesitated. "Some call me Carnag. I suppose that is a good name for my exterior."

"Is that what you call yourself?" Mira asked.

"No," fake Mira replied. "I call myself Miracle."

"She's the true miracle," her fake father said. "She does wonders you could never have achieved."

"I didn't get much chance," Mira said. "I was eleven. I'm *still* eleven." Mira turned to her duplicate. "You call yourself

Miracle because you come from me. My father stole you. Was the woman inside of you involved?"

There came a long pause.

"I don't hear anything," Twitch reported. "She could be whispering."

"Is she still talking to you?" Mira asked.

"Maybe," fake Mira said.

"Why are you listening to her? Who is she?"

Fake Mira held up a hand to stop Mira from talking. "You wouldn't understand. She's . . . she's my mother. Not *your* mother. Not Harmony. *My* mother."

"Your *mother*?" Mira exclaimed. "Does that mean she made you? Is she who stole you?"

"*I* freed Miracle from you," her fake father said smugly.

"Did she tell you she's your mother?" Mira asked. "Who is she really? I'm more your mother than anyone! You came from me!"

"Don't be absurd," Mira's fake father growled.

"I want to talk to this woman," Mira said.

"She doesn't want to talk to you," fake Mira said. "Not yet. Later. After you come with us. She'll help you understand."

"I'm not coming with you," Mira said.

"You'll see," fake Mira said. "You can free me. Fully free me. Free us. From each other. Cut all ties. We can go our separate ways. She can teach you."

"You're my shaping power!" Mira shouted. "We're not meant to be separated. How would you like to lose your shaping power?"

"I can't," the fake Mira said simply. "I *am* shaping power."

Mira gasped. Her fake father stepped forward and took hold of her. Mira struggled, but he was stronger. Carnag reached down and picked her up.

It took Cole a moment to realize what had happened. Mira had dropped her Jumping Sword. It was no longer a sword. It was a stick.

MIRACLE

"Carnag turned her sword into a stick!" Cole exclaimed.

"I know," Liam replied in his ear. "That's bad. The rendering was designed to be difficult to tamper with. And I was taking countermeasures to hold it together. It took some time, but Carnag figured it out. That means everything we have could be vulnerable."

Jace and Twitch crowded the bars and watched as Carnag loaded Mira into the cage at her hip. On the ground, the semblances of Mira and her father approached Carnag's foot, merged with it, and disappeared. The colossus stood up.

"Put me with my friends!" Mira yelled.

"Privileges are earned," Carnag replied emphatically.

"Can you guys hear me?" Mira whispered. "Are you all right?"

"We're caged inside a giant monster," Cole replied. "Otherwise, we're fine."

"How do you hear one another?" Carnag bellowed. "Silence!"

The cage shook brusquely. Cole clung to the bars to stay on his feet.

"Don't make it madder," one of the legionnaires advised.

"I haven't lost all of my shaping skills," Mira called.

"Is that Miracle down there?" another of the legionnaires asked. "*The* Miracle, from all those years ago?"

Cole considered the legionnaire. Apparently the conversation between Mira and Carnag had provided him with enough clues to guess what was really happening. If he was adding up the facts, Cole figured it would be best to put the whole truth into circulation.

"Her father stole her powers," Cole said.

"You don't mean the High King, do you?" the same legionnaire replied.

Cole nodded. "He stole the shaping powers from all of his daughters and faked their deaths. Mira's been hiding all this time. Her father started losing the stolen powers, and Mira's powers turned into Carnag."

Everyone in the cage looked astonished.

"Who are you three?" a different legionnaire asked.

"Nobody important," Jace said. "We're helping her. Or trying."

"We have to get to that woman inside of Carnag," Cole said in a hushed tone.

"Good luck," the oldest of the legionnaires said. "We have our weapons. The monster didn't bother to confiscate them. We tried to chisel our way out. The creature is really solid. When we finally made a little progress, it just shaped away the damage and shook us around."

Carnag was walking again, moving through the woods, her long arms pushing trees aside like bushes. With each step, the cell swayed and the surroundings creaked.

"I may be able to help," Liam said quietly in Cole's ear. "I'll have to get closer, but I should be able to open up Carnag for you, at least briefly."

"We'll be ready," Cole whispered, his heart thumping.

"Where is she taking us?" Twitch asked.

"To put us with the others," the woman said.

"What others?" Jace asked.

"That's all she told us," the oldest legionnaire said. "Presumably, the other people she has taken. You heard her. Carnag collects people."

Twitch put his ear to the beam. "I think the woman is talking again. It's pretty soft."

"Try to catch some words," Jace urged.

Cole drew near to Jace and used his quietest whisper. "You heard Liam?"

Jace gave a nod and put a finger to his lips. "I'd try to pry it open with my rope, but this thing is too solid." He kicked the back wall of the cell, then winced and hobbled for a moment. He sat down by Cole, his golden rope in his hands. "Looks like we're stuck. We'll have to wait and see where we end up."

Cole wondered if Carnag bought the theatrics. The giant gave no indication one way or the other.

They passed out of the woods and started across open fields. Cole looked down at a barn and a farmhouse. The buildings appeared vacant, but cattle and sheep roamed some nearby pastures.

He noticed a speck in the distance. It grew rapidly, as if

heading straight for them. He nudged Jace, who looked up with a start.

By the time Carnag stopped walking and turned to confront the oncoming threat, Cole could see that it was Liam. He flew straight at Carnag, only swerving when one of those long arms reached for him.

"Get ready," Liam said as he streaked around behind the giant, not speaking loudly, but plenty loud with the earpiece.

Carnag chased Liam in earnest now, twisting and leaping, both arms swatting. Everyone clung to the cage's bars as best they could.

"The woman isn't far from you," Liam said after a series of dizzying evasive maneuvers. "Be quick! I'll try to distract it."

The back of the cell suddenly opened up into a tunnel that sloped inward and down. Wasting no time, Cole dashed into the opening. Jace and Twitch joined him, a step or two behind.

Carnag gave her most enraged roar yet. The overwhelming echoes came from everywhere. Staggering forward with his hands over his ears, Cole could feel the bellow as clearly as he heard it. The ragged walls of the makeshift tunnel quaked.

The tunnel wasn't very long. Cole reached the end quickly. He was in a simple lit room. A woman sat on a fat cushioned chair. She was middle-aged, with long dark hair and a loose black dress. Her physique hinted that she sat in a chair a lot more than she exercised. Her eyes were wide with alarm as she rose to her feet.

"They're in——" she started screaming, but Jace's rope whipped forward and wrapped around her head at the level of her mouth several times. All she managed after that was muffled fury.

"Shut up!" Cole ordered, brandishing his Jumping Sword. "Sit down, or I'll chop you in half!"

"I'll do more than that!" Jace promised.

The woman dropped into the chair. Behind him, Cole noticed the tunnel close up. He, Jace, Twitch, and the woman were now trapped in a fairly small space illuminated by glowing stones.

The room lurched sideways, and Cole fell to his knees. Jace went down as well, but he kept hold of the rope. Twitch gave a little jump, fluttered his wings, and stayed on his feet. The chair slid a short distance, but the woman remained in it.

"What are you doing in here?" Cole asked.

The woman glared at him and pointed at the rope over her mouth.

"Right," Cole said. "Call for help, and we'll show no mercy."

She gave a nod.

The coils of the rope loosened, sliding down to encircle her neck. Her eyes stayed on Cole. She curled her fingers at him and glowered. "How did you get in here? That was a strong act of shaping, yet I sense no active power in any of you."

"None of your business," Cole said. "Tell Carnag to let us go."

She grinned and gave a smug laugh. "Let you go? Are you trying to hold me hostage? You haven't seen Carnag mad yet. But you will."

One wall of the cell bulged, and Mira stepped out, a tendril in her back. Up close, the semblance was uncannily lifelike. "What are you doing in here?" fake Mira asked.

"Let Mira go," Cole said. "Let all of us go."

"Do you see what I've been telling you?" the woman said. "You resist killing them, but all they want is to destroy you! To destroy me! They were strangling me! You have to fight fire with fire!"

"Stop yapping!" Jace yelled.

"Be polite!" fake Mira commanded, pointing at Jace. She glared at the woman in the chair. "Quima, I've told you not to pressure me to kill."

"This Quima woman lacks full control over Carnag," Liam said in Cole's ear. "There's at least some resistance."

A tunnel opened opposite from where Cole had entered. It angled downward.

"Great," fake Mira said. "Like it wasn't hard enough to concentrate already."

Mira came racing up the tunnel. She had no tendril attached to her. Cole felt pretty sure that meant she was the real thing. The tunnel closed behind her. The little room rocked steeply to the side, making everyone stumble and crouch. The room swayed the other way, then steadied.

"Who is this guy bothering me?" fake Mira asked. "He's the best shaper I've come up against. Not more than I can handle. Pesky, though."

The real Mira stormed over to the woman in the chair. "Who are you?"

"Mira," fake Mira said, performing the introductions, "this is Quima. Quima, Mira."

"We all need to settle down," Quima recommended.

Fake Mira scowled. "I can't get ahold of this guy. He's slippery. I'm trying to unshape his flying pad, but it's really resistant."

"Let's call a truce," Mira suggested. "Miracle, tell Liam you want a truce. Tell him I want him to stop attacking so we can talk."

Cole heard the big Carnag voice offer a truce to Liam. Almost immediately, the confined room became more stable.

"He agreed," fake Mira said. "But the truce only lasts as long as I choose."

"That's how every truce works," Jace muttered. "And it goes both ways."

Fake Mira scowled at him. "Get that rope away from Quima. If you hurt her, I can't be responsible for how I'll react."

The rope shrank to its smallest form, and Jace held it behind his back.

Fake Mira walked over to Mira. "You didn't have to force this discussion. We would have talked soon. I just wanted to put the others with my collection first."

"The other people you've taken are all imprisoned?" Cole asked.

"Would you rather I killed them?" fake Mira asked.

"Miracle, this is crazy," Mira said. "What has Quima been telling you?"

"Quima is the one person on my side," fake Mira said. "I didn't collect her. She came here on purpose. She wants to be here. She wants me to be free. You want to destroy me. Who would you trust?"

Mira was at a loss.

Cole jumped in. "Quima might not be your friend. She might have helped take you from Mira."

"Then I thank her for my existence," fake Mira said.

"You existed as part of me," Mira said.

"Not like this," fake Mira countered, laughing softly. "I'm whatever I want to be now."

"And what is that?" Mira asked. "A pile of dirt and tree stumps that kidnaps people?"

"This is just the beginning," fake Mira said. "The next step is for me to become truly free of you. Completely. Quima will help us achieve it. You'll have to help too."

"Dream on," Mira said.

Fake Mira's laugh had a menacing edge to it. "You'll do it. Or you won't be free either. Ever. You or your friends."

"Mira, your shaping talent is flowing to you like never before," Liam said, his voice soft in the earpiece. "I don't know if it's because you're surrounded by your power, or some other reason, but try to keep Carnag talking."

Mira closed her eyes and took a breath. Cole knew she was pretending to think while listening to Liam. When she opened them, she spoke calmly and earnestly. "They stole you from me. My life has been a nightmare ever since. You were with my father. You know what he put me through. Now you want to steal yourself from me too?"

Fake Mira frowned. "Do you think I like you? Do you imagine that I owe you? Do you think I'm sorry I'm free? I don't feel like part of you, Mira. You aren't my missing half. If I came from you, congratulations for making something wonderful.

But I don't belong to you anymore. I never will again. Until you cut all ties with me, I'll make sure you won't be free either."

"Your power wants to be with you," Liam coached Mira. "It's the mind of this semblance that stands in the way. You have to defeat her. Don't give up. Carnag still has the vast majority of your ability, but more escapes to you every second."

"What will you do after you're free from me?" Mira asked.

Fake Mira glanced at Quima. "Whatever I want."

"Whatever you want?" Mira questioned. "Or whatever Quima tells you? You've been a tool for my father. How do I know you won't just become a tool for her? Do you even know what you want?"

Fake Mira paused, glancing nervously at Quima. "I want to be me. I want to be myself."

"You keep saying you want to be yourself," Mira said. "Who is that?"

Fake Mira faltered. "Someone independent of you."

"You're my shaping power," Mira said. "You became a self-shaping semblance. You know why we call them semblances, right? Because they *resemble* living things. They're not, but they resemble them. Think of the semblances you make. They seem like they have identities. But they don't. They're whatever you make them."

"I'm different!" fake Mira exclaimed. "I'm what I make myself."

"Then why do you use my name?" Mira asked. "And why do you look like me?"

Fake Mira fell silent.

"Don't bother her with dull questions," Quima said.

"You're her prisoner. You're only talking to her by her permission."

Fake Mira held up a hand. "We're talking so I can convince her to set me free. Mira, I look like you out of habit. It's convenient. But I can look however I want. There are many names I could use. Carnag is one."

"You could fake an identity," Mira agreed. "That's what semblances do. You can look like me or my father. You can pick up pieces of things you see and make them part of you. That doesn't mean you're alive. If you think about it, looking any way you want is the opposite of having an identity. You're a complicated, powerful semblance. But you *are* a semblance. Semblances are extensions of the will of their creator. Unless somebody else takes control." Mira turned her attention to Quima.

"How could anyone control Miracle?" Quima asked. "Everyone in this room only lives thanks to her generosity. I lend her advice. I give her friendship. And I think she has the right to exist. Is that a crime?"

"It is if you're tricking her," Mira said. "It is if you're only trying to be the next person who steals her from me."

"Nobody can steal me," fake Mira said. "I make my own choices."

"Do you?" Mira asked. "When did you choose to leave me?"

Fake Mira offered no answer. Her eyes strayed to Quima.

"When did you choose to be born, Mira?" Quima snapped.

"Yes!" fake Mira agreed. "Some choices aren't ours to make."

Mira gave Cole a nervous glance. The quick look told

him that she was about to gamble. "When did you decide you're better off separate from me?"

"It was . . . ," fake Mira started, then hesitated. "It was after talking with Quima."

"Really," Mira said.

Fake Mira flushed. "Quima gave me good advice. I chose to take it."

"Do you take a lot of her advice?" Mira asked.

"She's a friend," fake Mira said. "Like a mother. I don't do everything she wants."

"For example?" Mira pressed.

"She wants me to kill people who attack me," fake Mira said. "I . . . don't like that idea. If they can't hurt me, I'd rather just collect them."

"You got that from me," Mira said. "I hate the idea of killing anything. Even bugs. But I did have lots of collections. Before I left the palace."

"I know everything about you," fake Mira said. "I don't need reminders."

"You're letting an enemy exploit you," Mira said. "She's manipulating you."

"Quima wants me free," fake Mira said. "You want me trapped."

"If I die, so do you," Mira said. "We're fundamentally linked. How can Quima change that?"

"You have to be willing to let me go," fake Mira said. "Then she'll use her shapecraft to separate us permanently."

"What's shapecraft?" Mira asked. "I've never heard of it."

"Me neither," Liam inserted.

"One of many things you don't know," fake Mira said condescendingly. "Shapecraft is to shaping as shaping is to everything else."

Mira looked somber. "Quima can mess with the shaping power itself?"

"Exactly," fake Mira replied.

"Which means she can mess with you," Mira said.

"I would never——" Quima began, but fake Mira held up her hand.

"She can free me from you," fake Mira said. "That's all she wants."

Mira emphasized her next words. "What if she just wants you free from me so she can take control of you?"

Cole thought Quima looked like she was trying to act unflustered.

Fake Mira glanced at Quima with a hint of suspicion.

"You're on to something," Liam encouraged. "Keep going."

"Hmmm," Mira continued. "Why would Quima care about helping pure shaping power find freedom as a semblance? It isn't her power. She would have no reason to feel attached. Why mother it? Guide it? What would be in it for her? Not much. Unless the goal was to trick it. Maybe she was partners with whoever stole it in the first place. Maybe the whole plan was for her to take control of it."

Fake Mira stepped close to Mira and put a hand on her shoulder. "Drop it. If it's a trick, it worked. I'd rather be with her than with you. My choice will never change. I don't care if you think I have no identity. I'm content with who I am. So is Quima. If you refuse to set me free, I'll do whatever it takes to change your mind. Stop clinging to me. I'm not yours anymore. Let me go."

Cole could tell that the conversation was unraveling and that it wasn't going to go their way. What was their next move? How could they fight something so huge?

"Quima holds the reins," Liam said, his voice urgent and hushed. "She has Carnag's mind. But the substance of Carnag belongs to you, Mira. At some level, she knows that. You keep soaking up energy."

"You get that Quima could have shaped you to feel this way," Mira said, her tone resigned to failure. "You get that you're probably only feeling what she planted with her shapecraft. You're not making choices. You're reacting as designed. She probably started molding you the second you were on your own."

"Enough," Quima said. "Don't be selfish. I can end this right now. Give me your permission, and I will free you and Miracle from each other."

"I'll die first," Mira insisted.

Mira's fake father stepped out of the wall behind Jace and held a knife to his throat. "She doesn't worry about herself," the tethered semblance said. "How much do you care about your friends, Mira? Those abilities you lost haven't belonged to you for most of your life. Let them go, and you and your friends will live."

"What about not killing?" Mira cried.

"I never had enough motivation to take a life," fake Mira said. "You told me I inherited that trait from you. I may have been wrong to resist Quima on that point. My hesitation must have been you talking. Fortunately, I have the power to change."

"Don't give in," Jace said.

"If she doesn't, you'll die, and I'll move on to the next one," her fake father said. "It won't end with your friends, Mira. One by one, innocent after innocent, we'll apply the needed pressure. You have until I reach five. One."

"I can't open up Carnag," Liam said. "I'm trying to tunnel in, but she won't let me."

"Two."

"How did she improve so fast?" Liam lamented. "I can't even make a dent now. She adapts so quickly!"

"Three."

Cole didn't know what to do. If he attacked the semblance of Mira's father, the fake king might slash Jace's throat immediately. Who knew how else Carnag might attack? After all, they were inside of it.

"Four."

"You want to hurt my friends?" Mira asked. "You want to cross that line? You asked for it."

She pointed at the tendril tethering her fake father to the wall. Part of the tendril disappeared, and her fake father immediately dissolved, sword and all.

Mira extended her palm and a tunnel opened straight to the outside. "Jump!" Mira yelled.

Cole didn't have to be told twice. He raced into the tunnel and held out his sword. Once he could see the ground, he pointed at it, shouted the command word, and sprang.

Looking back as he fell, Cole saw Twitch leap into the air as well. Next came Jace, one arm around Mira, the golden rope now holding Quima. All three flew out of Carnag together.

As Cole plummeted, he watched Liam swoop down to help. In midair, Jace let Liam take Mira. She made his disk wobbly, and he curved away in a rapid descent. Carnag reached out a hand and caught Quima.

Sensing the ground approaching, Cole turned to watch his landing. After rolling to a stop, he saw Jace cushion his landing by coiling the rope beneath him like a spring. The rope was no longer connected to Quima, leaving her to Carnag.

Liam and Mira landed roughly, the disk rolling away from their point of impact after the wipeout. Dust plumed into the air.

"Are you all right?" Cole asked.

"Alive," Liam said. "My disk really wasn't made for two people." He was already running to retrieve it.

"How dare you?" Carnag bellowed. A huge hand reached for Mira. As it got close, Mira waved her arm and the hand vanished. Released from Carnag's grasp, the Shaper's Flail fell to the ground.

"Back off!" Mira yelled.

"She's taking your energy!" Quima shrieked. "She's using your own power against you!"

"My power!" Mira corrected.

The hand holding Quima disappeared, and the woman plunged downward, skirt flapping. A new hand formed just in time to catch her. Instead of lifting her up again, Carnag set her down.

"Contain Mira!" Quima screamed. "They want to destroy us! Stop them all!"

A cage appeared around Cole, the bars sprouting up out of the ground and connecting overhead. Through the thick bars, Cole saw Mira and Jace trapped inside similar cages not far away. Mira was chained and gagged. Twitch and Liam remained free, both of them airborne.

"Can you shape away the bars?" Liam asked.

Mira shook her head and gave a muffled, "No."

"Carnag herself must be more vulnerable to you," Liam realized. "The separate objects that she shapes are more removed from your influence."

Carnag stomped over to stand before Mira. A tendril slithered forward from one foot, and the fake Mira blossomed up from the ground at the end of the tether. She stormed forward angrily, stopping just outside Mira's cage.

"Now you've done it," fake Mira said. "Now I'm furious. You're going to free me from you, or I'm pounding all of you flat. Your friends first, Mira, then you, no matter what it does to me."

Mira gave an unintelligible response.

Fake Mira waved a hand, and the gag disappeared.

"Flail, attack Quima!" Mira shouted.

The flail zipped toward where the dark-haired woman stood, still looking flustered from her near-fatal fall. When Carnag lunged to defend Quima from the flail, Mira yelled a different command.

"Flail, attack me!"

The flail boomeranged around toward Mira's cage.

Barely recovering from the lunge, Carnag dove, grabbing the flail just before it collided with the thick bars.

Fake Mira waved a hand, and Mira was gagged again.

Carnag slowly stood up.

Cole craned his neck back to gaze up at the giant. She was so big! It was weird to think that something so enormous could come from Mira. According to Liam, the part that truly came from her wanted to return. Carnag was colossal and terrifying, but in the end, according to Mira, she was just a semblance.

Cole fingered his shawl. Would it have a chance of influencing something so powerful? Could he put it on something so huge?

"You're willing to die," fake Mira said. "And you're willing to get your friends killed. So let's demonstrate the result of your choices." She pointed at Jace. "Father tried to deal with that one. How about him first?"

"Get me out," Cole whispered. "Open my cage."

"I'm not sure I can," Liam said. "Even with Carnag's attention elsewhere, it'd stretch me to my limits."

"You have to," Cole said. "I have an idea."

"That's more than I've got," Liam admitted.

Two bars on Cole's cage disappeared. Liam lurched in the sky, almost falling from his disk, but he managed to right himself.

Racing from his cage, Cole dashed toward fake Mira. She was facing away from him, her attention on Jace. Carnag tromped over to that cage and raised a foot above it.

"Last chance," fake Mira warned.

"Don't give in," Jace demanded bravely.

Running hard, Cole unclasped the shawl. Quima watched Jace's cage. So did Mira. So did fake Mira.

"Mmmmphf," Mira said, pointing at her gag.

"Fine," fake Mira said. "Last chance. But if I don't like what you have to say . . ."

She waved a hand and the gag vanished again.

Cole reached fake Mira and wrapped the shawl around her shoulders from behind hurriedly, clasping it with nervous fingers. Fake Mira looked over her shoulder at him, her expression perplexed.

"Okay, Miracle," Cole said. "I need you to lie down."

Miracle immediately squatted and stretched out on the ground.

Heart hammering from his sprint and his desperation, Cole stared in stunned relief. He could hardly believe it was working! Not wanting to lose momentum, and trying to sound casual, he continued, "Carnag needs to carefully step back."

Carnag took a step away from Jace's cage.

Quima rushed at Cole, her eyes brimming with rage. Twitch slammed into her from behind, both of them tumbling to the ground. Liam landed nearby, waved a hand, and ropes bound Quima. A gag covered her mouth. Eyes bulging, Quima jackknifed frantically.

"Miracle," Cole said kindly. "All of Carnag should lie down. Gently, though."

The giant mishmash of objects and substances crouched down, then spread out on the field on its back. The people inside the cages clung to the bars as their floors became walls.

"Very good," Cole said. "Now open a way out for the captives. Once they're clear, I'm going to ask you to part yourself from that big body. You'll cut that little cord that connects you to all that junk and just be our size."

Before he had finished talking, Carnag's cages dissolved. Jace's cage evaporated. Mira's cage disintegrated as well, and her chains fell away. On the ground nearby, Quima squirmed, desperately trying to make her stifled protests heard.

Eyes shining, Mira hurried over to Cole. "You can get up now, Miracle," Cole instructed. "Just your normal-size self. Let the big Carnag part of you stay on the ground."

With the tendril still in her back, fake Mira got to her feet. Legionnaires and other prisoners poured out of Carnag.

"Everybody out!" Cole called. "Everyone back away!" He watched to make sure the cells were empty.

"Looks good," Liam said.

"Go ahead and disconnect from that big body," Cole suggested.

There was a pause, and fake Mira's lip twitched upward in a sneer. Then the tendril fell from fake Mira's back.

"The cloak is smoking," Twitch whispered.

He was right. Wisps of steam or smoke were rising from the shawl. Cole stood near enough to feel the heat. Despite this, fake Mira showed no discomfort. In fact, she looked serene.

"Miracle," Cole said hurriedly. "Your power actually belongs to Mira. The real Miracle. It needs to return to her. Give Mira her powers back."

"Oh wow," Mira said, her voice choked with emotion. "It's coming fast. I can feel it."

Fake Mira pivoted to face the real one. Anger ignited in fake Mira's eyes. Then her face contorted in hate, and her body quivered. The shawl smoked heavily and burst into flames.

"How dare you!" the fake Mira screamed, wheeling on Cole, her gaze promising murder.

With a wave of her hand, Mira sent the flaming shawl fluttering off to one side. "Miracle!" Mira commanded, her eyes intense. "Don't blame him. I think you're just angry with yourself."

Baring her teeth in a sneering grimace, fake Mira turned and charged the real one. Mira held up a hand, and fake Mira stopped short and started floating a little, her arms and legs spreading unnaturally wide. Mira glared at her duplicate, jaw clenched, sweat beading on her brow.

"What are you doing?" fake Mira asked, her voice strained.

"Taking what's mine," Mira said. She spread her hands apart, and fake Mira tore in half with a burst of light. When the flash was gone, so was all evidence of Mira's semblance.

QUIMA

Mira dropped to her knees. She stared at Cole with wide eyes.

"You did that?" Cole asked.

Mira nodded and let out a shocked giggle.

"She's gone?" Cole asked. "It worked?"

Mira nodded again. "I got a big dose of my power back before she turned on us. Suddenly I could sense her tangible form more clearly than ever, brittle and false, but with so much energy boiling inside. Energy that belonged to me. I had the strongest urge to release it."

"You released it, all right," Twitch said with a nervous laugh.

"It worked," Liam confirmed. "Carnag is gone. I sense none of her presence."

"I can feel my power," Mira said. "It's been so long. At the same time . . . it's incredibly familiar. Like I only lost it yesterday."

Liam glided over to where the former prisoners had

gathered after exiting Carnag. "Move along," he announced from his floating disk. "You need to go find the people trapped in Carnag's stronghold. The nearest road is that way. Nothing to see here. Smartest policy might be to pretend none of this ever happened."

Cole doubted whether anybody would be able to forget what happened, but the freed captives started trudging away. The giant form of the fallen Carnag lay inert, not disappearing like fake Mira, but utterly lifeless, no longer anything more than a baffling heap of random debris.

"What do we do with Quima?" Jace asked, standing over her.

"I have some questions for her," Liam said, returning. "I want a little more privacy first."

His posture uncomfortable, Jace glanced at Cole. "Thanks. You really bailed us out."

"Thank Liam," Cole said. "Thank Mira. Without them, we wouldn't have had a chance."

Liam shook his head. "I helped. But Carnag's power was much more than I could have defeated. Mira was amazing. But without your quick thinking, Cole, I don't think any of us would have survived."

"You really were a lifesaver," Mira said.

Cole tried not to blush. The temperature of his face implied that he was failing.

The nearest of the departing captives was now hundreds of yards away and getting farther with every step. "All right," Liam said. "Let's talk to Quima."

The gag disappeared from her mouth. "You have no idea

what you're tangling with," Quima spat. "Today you crossed the wrong woman."

Liam shook his head. "I'm not sure that's the lesson here. I think you crossed the wrong girl."

"Think what you like," Quima said. "Mira has only delayed her ruin. This was one small piece of a much larger puzzle."

"Not surprising," Liam said. "I want to hear more about shapecraft."

Quima's smile was both knowing and taunting all at once. "Grant me permission, and I'll show you."

"Considering what happened to Mira, I'm going to decline," Liam said. "I've worked with some knowledgeable shapers, but I've never heard of shapecraft."

"After meeting Carnag, you've had a lesson," Quima said. "I think that's enough for today. Those who practice shapecraft have done so quietly for longer than you can guess. Our time is nearing. You'll learn plenty before long. Be warned—what you don't know can hurt you."

"Does my father practice shapecraft?" Mira asked.

"To an extent," Quima said.

"Did he have help taking my powers?"

Quima paused, eyes narrow. "There is more to my order than you can imagine, Miracle. Without us, your father would be the least competent in a long line of High Shapers."

"Who helped him?" Mira asked.

"You'll learn nothing more from me," Quima said. "Mira, I'm no less dedicated to my cause than you are to yours. Let me show you how it's done." Closing her eyes, she made a tight fist.

"What do you mean?" Liam asked.

Quima opened her hand, revealing a pinprick of blood on her palm. "My ring hid a poisoned needle."

"You'd have to be careful with one of those," Liam said.

"I'll be dead in minutes," Quima promised. "No matter what methods you might have to extract what I know, they won't work before I'm well out of reach."

"You may be right," Liam said. "But surely you'll share some last thoughts. Some dying hints. You don't want to go out with a fizzle."

Quima gave a wide, evil grin. "If you wish. Carnag was weak. It was weak because it was docile. With a little more time, I could have overcome that tendency. The others will not be as frail."

"What others?" Mira asked. "Is this happening to all my sisters?"

"That won't be a mystery for long," Quima said. "They have distinct shaping styles. Their powers will take form differently. None will be as pathetic as yours. And the semblances that arise from your sisters are only the beginning."

"What will come after?" Liam asked.

"You'll know when it arrives," Quima said. "Assuming you're still alive."

"I feel whole," Mira said. "My father no longer has a share of my power."

Quima shook her head, as if Mira was missing the point. "Your father is the least of your problems. But even Stafford has not yet outlived his usefulness. His talents wane, but his authority remains. And he stole powers once . . ."

Cole felt a surge of fear. "My friends! The High King was looking for slaves with shaping powers."

Throwing her head back, Quima laughed grandly. The genuine delight gave Cole chills. "You have friends among his slaves? Friends with shaping talent? They will learn of shapecraft. The experiments reserved for them may teach us all new lessons."

"What experiments?" Cole asked, fear flaring into anger.

Quima shook her head.

"Tell him what you know," Liam said.

"Or what?" Quima laughed. "You'll kill me? Too late. You'll get no more from me."

"What about your part in this?" Liam asked. "Carnag. Did you form it with your shapecraft?"

"The power became a semblance because of shapecraft," Quima said. "All part of a larger plan than you could possibly guess. Its creation wasn't my doing, but I helped steer Carnag in the right direction."

"Did you steer it with shapecraft?" Liam asked. "Or with counsel?"

"Use your imagination," Quima said.

"But you were planning to take control of it?" Mira asked.

"I had control!" Quima said. "I should have taken full control."

"That would have required Mira's compliance?" Liam asked.

"No, I was just being polite," Quima said. "We're done. I fell short of my aims and failed my order. It is a small failure, inconsequential in the long run, but I'm ready to pay for it. Any second the symptoms of the poison will start."

"Yeah," Liam said. "About that . . . I shaped your poison. I'm really good at analyzing substances. And changing them. I'm rather amazing, actually. You stabbed yourself with honey. If your palm could taste, it would have been delicious."

Cole couldn't resist laughing at the stunned look on her face. Jace joined in, and even Twitch covered a snicker.

"Impossible," Quima retorted breathlessly.

"For some shapers, maybe," Liam said. "Kind of routine for me. My boss will really want to talk to you, so I'm going to make sure you don't harm yourself in the near future."

He waved a hand, and a golden strip of fabric emerged from the ground and bound itself around her mouth. She strained against the cords that held her.

"I know you like hiding in private rooms, so I'll give you one," Liam said. Quima sank into the ground as if it were quicksand. Liam glanced at Mira. "Now we can really talk. Don't worry, I'm putting her deep."

"What are you going to do with her?" Cole asked.

"Like I promised, I'll take her to Declan," Liam replied. "He'll be very interested to speak with her."

"Do you think you can find out what the High King wants to do to my friends?" Cole asked.

"Hard to guess," Liam said. "Declan may have the best chance."

"Maybe he wants their power," Mira said.

"That's what I thought at first," Cole said. "But Quima made it sound like there was more to it."

"She may have been trying to scare us," Liam said. "Everything she told us could have been a lie."

"I have a feeling it's not just a bluff," Mira said.

"Me too," Liam said. "We'll see what Declan can get out of her."

"He's safe?" Mira asked.

"Safe enough," Liam said. "We had to leave most of what he built behind. Lyrus couldn't come with us, so we left him in charge of the defense of Cloudvale. I've never seen him happier. The legion will have a very unpleasant job ahead of them. It's possible that once they confirm we've fled, they'll retreat."

"What now?" Mira asked.

Liam glanced at the sky and looked around. "We find Bertram, send your captured legionnaire on his way, then wait for Joe to catch up. He had a message for you that he wouldn't share with me."

"Any hints?" Mira asked.

"I expect it's important."

THE MESSAGE

Cole hunched on a stool outside of a beautiful cottage. A soft wind carried the scent of leaves and wildflowers. The autocoach waited nearby, Bertram sitting contentedly inside.

After traveling a considerable distance from where Carnag had fallen, Liam and Mira had shaped the cottage in less than an hour, complete with beds, furniture, a big fireplace, paintings on the walls, and a garden out back. This was the second afternoon after the cottage had risen.

Cole could not stop worrying about his friends. When Liam had moved Quima to a new underground cell near the cottage, she had refused to respond to any inquiry. With her blank expression and her dazed manner, she had seemed unreachable.

Lacking further information, all Cole could do was wonder and fret about Dalton and Jenna. If the High King took their shaping power, he would have to keep them alive, or the power would be lost, right? Would it bother his friends to lose their power if they only had it briefly? Or was the problem something else? Quima had referred to experiments. Given all that shaping could accomplish, the experiments could involve almost anything.

Mira and Liam had shared vague assurances that they would help, but, really, they were all waiting. They needed more information.

Fluttering down from the sky, Mango landed near the cottage door. Cole got off the stool. "What is it?"

"I need to tell Mira that a rider approaches," the bird announced.

"Is it Joe?" Cole asked.

"Of course, silly. I'm not raising an alarm!"

By the time Cole had retrieved Mira, Liam, Jace, and Twitch from inside the cottage, they could hear hoofbeats. Cole clung to a faint hope that Mira's messenger might reveal something about how he could help Jenna and Dalton.

Before long the horseman rode into view. He cantered across the field to them and dismounted. Cole recognized the man who had come to Skyport just before the legionnaires arrived, his whiskers longer, his leather jacket further dulled by dust. Joe pointed at the cottage. "Looks like you've settled in!"

Liam shrugged. "It's far from any convenient roads."

"I saw Carnag," Joe said. "What was left of it. Thanks for waiting. Glad I could help."

Liam lifted his hands apologetically. "Did you notice any legionnaires on the road?"

"That was only part of the fun!" Joe exclaimed. "Do you

know how hard I rode to get here? I galloped through the night, trading horses, spending money like a compulsive gambler, and using every trick I knew."

"Mira, meet Joe MacFarland," Liam said. "Joe, this is Miracle Pemberton. These three boys are her friends."

Joe gave a respectful bow. "I'm at your service, Your Highness."

"Nice to meet you," Mira said uncomfortably. "Just call me Mira, please."

"Whatever you prefer," Joe said. "I'm glad to find you safe."

"I'm glad you're safe too," Mira said. "Thank you for trying to warn me about the legion back at Skyport. Was there more to your message?"

Joe glanced at Liam. "I learned about the legionnaires while on my way to find you. The message regarded other matters."

Mira looked surprised. "What?"

Joe looked from Cole to Jace to Twitch. "I was supposed to take you and Durny to confront Carnag. If we succeeded, we had a second assignment. It concerns one of your sisters. Would you rather I tell you in private?"

Mira paled and rubbed her lips with both hands. "I haven't had direct word about my sisters since we all parted. Are they all right?"

"This only involves one of them," Joe said. "She's in trouble."

Mira faced the boys. "Then this is up to you. I can't begin to thank you for getting me out of Skyport and coming here with me. It went beyond my wildest hopes. If you want to leave, now is the time. I won't take it personally. We're out of immediate danger. I expect this news will mean traveling to another kingdom."

Joe nodded. "Since we're among friends, I'll reveal that responding to this message would mean going to Elloweer."

"I'm with you, Mira," Jace said. "I told you to stop trying to get rid of me. Although I'm not sure my rope will work well outside of Sambria."

"It's very powerful," Liam said. "But outside of Sambria or maybe Junction, it will barely function, if at all. Other shaping disciplines govern the other kingdoms. Almost all Sambrian renderings would become inert. In Elloweer, shapers are called enchanters, and their abilities are mostly foreign to me."

"I'll be less useful," Jace said. "But I'm willing. Where else would I go?"

"You're free now," Mira said. "You could build a life. With that rope alone, you could go far here in Sambria."

"Any of you would be welcome to join me," Liam said. "Our new hiding place should remain secure for some time. We could certainly make use of you. And I wouldn't mind company with the chore of transporting Quima."

"Would you rather get rid of me?" Jace asked Mira, almost timidly.

"I want you to do what you want," she said. "Staying with me will definitely lead to trouble. Maybe even death."

"Then count me in," Jace said. "I've had so much trouble in my life, I'm not sure what I'd do without it."

"I haven't told you everything about me," Twitch said. "I left Elloweer with a purpose. My people are in danger.

Slavery was an unplanned detour. I have to go back and see what I can do. So I can join you for at least part of the journey. But maybe I should avoid hearing details, because I might have to eventually part ways."

"Whatever you'd prefer," Mira said.

Twitch hopped away, wings fluttering. He only stopped once he had given them plenty of space.

When Mira looked at Cole, he had never felt more like a hero. She stepped toward him and gave him a big hug, which he returned. "Your friends need you," she said. "I wish we had a better idea what they're up against." Releasing him, Mira stepped back.

"What friends?" Joe asked.

"My friends who came here as slaves from my world," Cole said. "Some had shaping talent and were sold to the High King."

"Slaves who can shape?" Joe asked. "Do you know their specialties?"

"No," Cole said. "But the High King may want them for experiments."

Joe rubbed his jaw. "The High Shaper has been sending his slaves with shaping talent all over the five kingdoms. They're going into training wherever their talents are strongest."

"Since when?" Mira asked.

"For the past several weeks," Joe said.

Liam scrunched his face in disappointment. "That means your friends could be anywhere."

Cole felt deflated. Joe's news meant he knew less than he had previously believed. "Including Junction City," Cole realized. "They might not have gone with the slaves sent for training. They could be part of something else."

"Entirely possible," Joe said. "But I do know that the High Shaper has been acquiring slaves with shaping talent wherever he can find them and sending them to be trained all over the Outskirts."

"We'll help you find them," Mira said, rubbing Cole's shoulder. "I promised to help you. I haven't forgotten."

Joe looked a little uncomfortable. "You may be needed elsewhere, Mira. At least in the short term."

"There are ways we can investigate," Liam assured Cole. "The five kingdoms are large, but we aren't without allies. I'll give you all the help at my disposal. You could come with me and wait, or I could probably figure out a way to contact you if you'd rather stay with Mira."

Cole frowned. "Thanks. Right now information is what I need most. I can't really help my friends until I know where they went. In the meanwhile, I'll stick with Mira."

"Are you sure?" she asked.

"They're as likely to be in Elloweer as anywhere," Cole said.

Mira hugged him tightly. Cole tried to avoid eye contact with Jace. "I'd hate to lose you. You saved us back there. You saved me. Cole, if I live forever, I'll never be able to thank you enough."

"I couldn't believe it worked," Cole said. "I thought it was a long shot."

"It was," Liam said. "If Mira hadn't planted a lot of doubt in Carnag, and if the essence of Carnag wasn't eager to rejoin

Mira, I don't think it would have succeeded. The shawl was a potent tool, but not strong enough to harness something like Carnag—not unless she was already pretty conflicted."

"Anyway," Cole said to Mira, "until I have a clear idea where to find Dalton or Jenna, I'm coming with you. Without a plan, or at least someplace to go, I can't imagine leaving you. I'd be utterly alone."

"Ouch," Liam said.

"Not if I went with you," Cole hurriedly clarified. "Which I would do, except . . . I've lost enough friends already. I don't want to lose any more."

"Ouch again!" Liam said. "Seriously, stop talking."

Cole gave an embarrassed laugh. "I don't want to lose you either, Liam, but you're heading off to a hideout. I need to keep moving. And I want to help Mira."

"In that case, I'll contact you if I learn something," Liam said.

"I'd appreciate it," Cole said.

"Go ahead and give us the message," Mira prompted.

"As you can probably guess, this concerns Honor," Joe said. "Her shaping was always strongest in Elloweer. Your mother fears that her protector is dead and that she has been captured. I was going to take you and Durny to try to help her."

"How would we find her?" Mira asked.

"Her star is in the sky," Joe said. "I know how to recognize it. Just as I know yours."

"I can't believe it," Mira said. "I haven't seen Nori in so many years. I'm surprised she's in trouble. I can much more easily picture her rescuing me."

"The message had few details," Joe said. "We'll only learn more by following her star."

"When do we start?" Jace asked.

"As soon as you choose," Liam said. "It'll mean going our separate ways for now."

Mira sighed. "I had hoped that getting my powers back would mean the end of my troubles for a while."

"Not yet," Cole said. "But we hurt your dad. And we'll hurt him more. The best way to help my friends will be to bring him down."

"No problem," Jace said. "We'll take out the High King. Twitch will love that. We should tell him."

"We won't beat the High King tomorrow," Cole said. "Probably not the next day either. But helping Honor will be a good place to start."

"This may not stop with the High King," Liam warned. "We also have to worry about Quima's group of shapecrafters."

"No," Cole said. "They need to worry about us."

ACKNOWLEDGMENTS

My books do not happen through my efforts alone. Writing and promoting my books take me away from my family more than I prefer. I thank them for their support and patience. My wife, Mary, and my eldest daughter, Sadie, also read my books and provide feedback. Mary is always my first editor and her reactions to my chapters proved very useful once again.

I also have professional help. As he has done before, my agent, Simon Lipskar, shared some sage insights that helped me really bring this story into focus. Liesa Abrams, my editor, did a superb job with feedback as well, even though she was approaching the due date for a child. Fiona Simpson gets a big thank you for stepping in when Liesa had her son. (Congrats, Liesa!)

I'm very grateful to Simon & Schuster as a whole for believing in me enough to embark on a new series with me. Lots of people helped this book get produced and helped get the word out about it. Bethany Buck, Mara Anastas, Anna McKean, Paul Crichton, Carolyn Swerdloff, Lauren Forte, Jeannie Ng, and Adam Smith all played critical roles. And big thanks go to Owen Richardson for the terrific cover art.

My team of early readers did a great job on Sky Raiders. Jason and Natalie Conforto gave helpful responses and opened my eyes to some cool story possibilities that will show up later in the series. My uncle Tuck and my mom provided useful feedback, along with Cherie Mull. Liz Saban provided some of the first sparks that ignited this whole idea, and loaned me the names of a couple of her boys. Paul Frandsen made a couple of good catches near the end. Thanks, everyone!

I owe thanks to Brandon Flowers and the Killers for letting me use a line from one of their more poignant songs at the start of this book. I thought the line really fit the story, and am grateful they granted permission to use it.

Finally, I owe huge thanks to you, the reader! The books of mine that you read, share, and buy let me do this for a living. Without your support, I'd still be writing on the side, and there would be far fewer stories. Thanks for taking the time to go on this adventure. There are four more books coming, and you'll soon see that things are just getting started. I'm excited to share more of this series. Read the note that follows for more on that.

NOTE TO READERS

One down, four to go. I'm happy that you've been introduced to one of the Five Kingdoms. Just wait until you see where the story goes in the coming books! I don't think I've ever planned a series with as much variety as you'll find in this one. If you liked this first book, get ready for a great ride. I'll keep them coming as quickly as I can. Books Two and Three should come out within a year.

Because my writing schedule is packed, and because I go on book tours a lot, and because I have four kids, I can be hard to reach. If a letter or e-mail has gone unanswered, please accept my apology. If you sent it, I probably got it, but I'm an absentminded, disorganized person, and I've fallen way behind in responding. I still hope to get caught up one day. I save the messages I get, and randomly respond to as many as I can manage.

If you want to be in contact with me, I suggest following me on Twitter (@brandonmull) or my author page (Brandon Mull) on Facebook. I routinely post in those places, so you can get news if you want it, and posting comments there sometimes leads to responses. You can also try emailing me at autumnal-solace@gmail.com (an address that comes from one of my Fablehaven books). Whether or not you get an answer is a roll of the dice.

I hope that someday I'll figure out a system that will let me respond to everyone without neglecting my job and my family. If it is any consolation, part of the reason I am disorganized about practical things is because my mind spends a lot of time making up stories. So if nothing else, at least I can communicate with you through my crazy books. And if you really want to meet me, just keep an eye on my tour schedule at brandonmull.com.

Whenever a new book comes out, I hit the road and have many events around the United States.

For those of you who have just discovered me, here is a quick guide to my other books:

Fablehaven is a five book series, and probably my most balanced, with a good mix of adventure, humor, and discovery. It deals with secret wildlife parks for magical creatures, and the overall feel is probably the closest fit to my Five Kingdoms series. I have plans to start a sequel series to Fablehaven around 2016.

Beyonders is three books long, and is my most epic series. It starts out kind of weird and mysterious, then builds into a grand story about heroes trying to save an imperiled world. You'll meet creatures and magical races you've never read about before, and I think the ending of book three is my biggest finale so far.

Candy Shop War is lighter than my other stuff, but full of imagination. It happens in a normal neighborhood with normal kids. Magicians come to town sharing magical candy that can give people powers. When it turns out some of the magicians are up to no good, things get interesting. There are two books in that series so far. Both feel like complete stories, without any real cliffhangers.

Spirit Animals is a series I created. Readers will discover a world called Erdas, where kids and animals can sometimes form powerful bonds. It is my fastest-paced story, and maybe my best for readers who are just getting used to a thick book. Though I outlined the whole series, I only wrote book one. Six other authors will write the six other books.

And lastly, if you're into picture books, I have two Pingo books about a boy named Chad and his imaginary friend. You can find more about all of my books at brandonmull.com.

If you made it all the way to the end of this, congratulations for finishing what you started. Thanks for reading. See you in the Outskirts!

COLE'S ADVENTURE CONTINUES IN . . .

ROGUE KNIGHT

It took some time before Cole noticed that the autocoach was going faster than usual. Mira, Jace, Twitch, and Joe had fallen asleep shortly after nightfall. Despite the darkness and the rhythmic trotting of the huge four-legged brick pulling the coach, Cole had failed to relax enough to sleep.

They had been progressing toward Elloweer for many days now. Mira was so excited to see her sister that Cole sometimes wondered if she remembered that Honor was in peril. Twitch remained quiet and content, not speaking much unless asked direct questions. Joe spent most of his time focused on the possible dangers of the road. Jace grew more cranky and restless with each passing day. Cole couldn't blame him.

The travel conditions helped explain Cole's current insomnia—too many hours confined within the autocoach, getting little exercise and napping whenever he wanted. The days and nights blurred together, making it tricky to keep a regular schedule.

As he sat in the dark while the others slept, the reality of his circumstances confronted him. Until a few weeks ago, Cole had lived a normal life as a sixth grader in Mesa, Arizona. Then one trip to a neighborhood haunted house on Halloween had landed Cole and his friends in the Outskirts, a mysterious realm made up of five kingdoms that each contained distinct forms of magic. As if getting stuck in another world wasn't terrible enough, all the kids who had traveled with Cole to the Outskirts had been branded as slaves the second they arrived.

After a failed attempt to rescue his friends, Cole became separated from the others when he was sold to the Sky Raiders, a group of scavengers who salvaged valuable items from dangerous castles in the sky. He had no clue where any of his friends from Arizona had ended up, including his best friend, Dalton, and Jenna, the girl he'd had a crush on for years. He knew they were somewhere in the five kingdoms, and he was determined to rescue them. But sometimes the task of finding them felt impossible.

The only bright spot for Cole was the new friends he'd made in the Outskirts—including Jace, Twitch, and Mira, fellow Sky Raiders who had escaped with him. Joe had come to warn Mira of danger, and later had joined them. Cole felt that sticking with Mira was important. She had connections across Elloweer that made travel easier and that might help him find leads about his friends. Of course that meant facing a lot of danger in the meantime, since Mira was on the run from an incredibly powerful evil ruler who just happened to be her father, the High Shaper who had proclaimed himself High King. Having stolen Mira's power once, he wanted her abilities back, and after seeing firsthand what that power could do, Cole understood why.

Since arriving in the Outskirts, Cole had flirted with death several times—while scouting sky castles, escaping Skyport, and battling his way through a dreamlike land created by some magical kid. And there was no foreseeable end to the danger. How many near misses could he expect to survive?

Home felt a million miles away. The actual distance was probably even worse. From all appearances, the Outskirts existed in a whole separate universe.

But Cole was here in Sambria, one of the five kingdoms, and that wasn't changing anytime soon, so all he could do was focus on their next goal.

Mira's mother had used her shaping talent to place a star in the sky above Honor, which meant Mira's sister was in trouble, but they had no other details. Not long ago, Mira's power had taken tangible form, and defeating it had nearly cost them their lives. Were they now heading toward a similar battle? They had no idea what threat Honor could be facing, but Mira was determined to rescue her.

Bertram, the coachman, slouched forward on his bench, eyes on the floor, elderly features blank. As a semblance created by shaping, he didn't need sleep, but he wasn't designed to provide much company. He sometimes shared useful information about their route. According to Bertram, they would reach the border of Elloweer tomorrow morning.

The autocoach usually provided a smooth ride, so when it jostled over two rough patches in succession, Cole began to pay attention. The *clip-clop* of the trotting brick sounded faster than he had ever heard it. Then the rhythm of the trot changed to one of a loping stride, and the speed of the autocoach increased even more.

Neither animal nor machine, the autocoach had been created by shapers. It never tired, but it never went fast, either. Cole tapped Bertram. "Why are we speeding up?"

The old man looked at him, lips quivering, one eye twitching. Bertram only spoke to share information about the roads ahead or to assure anyone who cared to listen that he was on holiday with his grandniece and grandnephews. Though his replies weren't always relevant, he had never failed to respond to a question.

"Guys!" Cole yelled. "Something's wrong!"

Joe's soft snoring sputtered to a halt. He squinted at Cole. "Is the coach *running*?"

"Yes," Cole said. "And Bertram won't talk."

The old semblance wore a pained expression. One hand clenched sporadically.

Joe hastily shook Mira and Jace. "Wake up!"

Twitch sat up with a start. "What's happening?" he asked.

The brick's pace increased to a pounding gallop. The autocoach rattled and creaked, then jolted over a sharp bump, jarring Cole's spine.

Jace produced his golden rope, the magical item he obtained when he worked for the Sky Raiders. Mira reached for the Jumping Sword that their friend Liam had made for her before returning to the Grand Shaper of Sambria.

Joe slapped Bertram briskly across the cheek. "Bertram! Slow us down! Stop the coach!"

"Halt the coach, Bertram," Mira demanded.

Face contorted, Bertram's lips peeled back as he ground his teeth. Drool leaked down his chin.

"Stop us, Bertram," Joe insisted. "Stop us now!"

Rocking from side to side, Bertram screamed. The wretched, desperate cry filled Cole with panic. What could make the calm old semblance behave like this?

If anything, the autocoach gained speed.

"Should we bail?" Twitch asked, slipping on his Ellowine ring to reveal his semitransparent wings and grasshopper legs.

"What about our stuff?" Jace asked.

"You kids go," Joe instructed. "Use your renderings to land softly. I'll stay with the coach to see where——"

His instructions were cut off as the autocoach launched into the air. For a moment, gravity disappeared. Cole was floating, as were the others. They all came crashing down when the coach landed thunderously, slanted steeply forward as it plunged down a sharp incline.

Cole ended up on his back with Twitch on top of him. The autocoach quaked as it skipped out of control down the slope. Before Cole could sit up, the coach went airborne again, tilting sharply to the right.

Jace's golden rope suddenly expanded, zigzagging around the inside of the compartment in a complex pattern. The autocoach landed on its side and tumbled wildly, flinging Cole and his friends against yielding lengths of golden rope. The elaborate tangle cushioned their movements and kept them from slamming against the interior walls of the coach. Cole lost all sense of direction as he flopped between segments of rope, the coach whirling and shattering around him.

The autocoach came to a rest upside down. For a moment, the occupants hung suspended like bugs in a spiderweb. The stillness and silence was eerie after the chaotic crash. Then the rope web slackened, and they dropped to the ceiling. Cole felt loopy and sore.

"Get out," Joe whispered urgently. "This was an attack. It's not over. We need to move."

The door had been torn from one mangled side of the coach. Twitch ducked through and into the darkness beyond. Jace shrank his rope to its normal length and exited as well. Mira went next, followed by Cole. Joe came last.

The autocoach had settled at the bottom of an earthy ravine that was spanned by a bridge. Dim moonlight revealed steep, brushy banks sloping up on either side, and a stream, crawling down the middle, narrow enough to step across. The rocks, branches, and warped old logs littering the bottom of the ravine suggested that sometimes the stream rose higher than its current trickle.

Cole took a deep breath of the night air. It definitely beat the odor of six bodies crammed in close confines day after day. Since they had started their journey to Elloweer, he had only left the coach to relieve himself and occasionally to eat at a roadside inn.

Jace pressed a finger to his lips and pointed at the top of the ravine. A pair of caped, armored figures was descending the slope, one astride a huge jungle cat, the other riding what appeared to be a writhing mass of rags. The intimidating mounts glided down the incline with slinky grace.

Crouching low, Cole held his breath. The last few days had been quiet, but he knew Mira's father had people hunting them. When Mira defeated the semblance monster Carnag and regained her shaping power, the High Shaper had lost all claim to her stolen abilities. With the power he took from her other sisters fading, the High Shaper would be in a panic.

The sinister riders didn't look like legionnaires or city guardsmen. Could they be Enforcers? Cole had heard warnings about the High Shaper's secret police, but had no way of knowing if these riders were affiliated with them. Whoever they were, the sight of them gave Cole chills. In a land where reality could be reshaped, he had learned to accept the impossible, but that didn't mean he liked it trying to hunt him down.

Without saying a word, the small group headed in different directions: Twitch slithered behind a log, Mira crouched behind a bush, and Jace melted into the shadows behind a rock pile. Joe ducked back into the damaged compartment. Cole crept around the autocoach, putting it between himself and the oncoming figures, which still let him peek around it to keep an eye on them. The duo advanced with little effort at subtlety. Cole realized they probably assumed the crash had left all occupants of the carriage incapacitated or dead. If not for Jace's rope, they would be right.

Cole considered retrieving his Jumping Sword from the coach. With a fight brewing, he hated to be weaponless. But he worried about the noise spoiling their chance to surprise the oncoming riders. Both were almost to the floor of the ravine.

Squinting, Cole tried to make sense of the squirming jumble of rags. The ragbeast glided along on tattered wisps of fabric, hovering more than walking. Though not very substantial, and lacking a clear shape, it seemed to support the rider without difficulty.

Joe sidled up next to him and quietly handed Cole his Jumping Sword. "Lay low if you can," Joe whispered in his ear. He held up a bow—a shaped weapon Cole had retrieved from a sky castle and that produced an arrow every time the string was drawn. "I'm borrowing this. Top priority is getting Mira away from here."

Bow in hand, Joe slunk away from the totaled autocoach. He stepped over the small stream and took cover in some tall brush.

Staying low, Cole peeked as the riders prowled along the base of the ravine. They advanced straight toward the autocoach. Of course! They meant to search the wreckage! Why hadn't he picked a different hiding place?

Keeping the inverted autocoach between himself and the riders, Cole backed away, crouching, Jumping Sword held ready. If they spotted him, he would use the sword to flee up the slope. Maybe he could draw them away from the others. Even with their strange mounts, the Jumping Sword might give him a chance to outrun them.

One foot stepped into the stream, making a little splash. Cole froze.

The big cat gave an angry yowl. Cole cringed, gritting his teeth. Beyond the coach, Cole could see Twitch had risen skyward, oversize dragonfly wings shimmering in the moonlight.

Twitch had been spotted.

Cole shuffled sideways in time to see Jace's golden rope

whip around the rider on the jungle cat. The rope hoisted the armored figure high into the air, then slammed him down on a rocky patch of the streambed with a resounding clang.

The ragbeast wheeled toward Jace. Mira sprang out of hiding, flying through the air, Jumping Sword extended. Her blade struck the ragbeast's rider in the side, knocking him to the ground without piercing his armor. Mira tumbled to the nearby creek bed, her sword falling from her grasp.

The huge jungle cat streaked toward Mira. Pointing his sword at a spot ahead of the jungle cat, Cole shouted, "Away!"

The sword pulled Cole through the air on a low trajectory, skimming along just above the ravine's floor. As the big cat pounced at Mira, Cole, backed by the momentum of his flight, plunged his blade into the feline's ribs. The Jumping Sword had slowed just before reaching the target, but even so, Cole drove it deep, then collided with the furry, meaty side of the huge cat. Cole spun through the air and landed on the ground, painfully wrenching his shoulder and scraping his legs.

Twisting to nip at the sword in its side, the jungle cat hissed. Then an arrow hit the big cat in the neck.

"Flail, attack!" Mira called, pointing at the feline.

Accompanied by the crunch of smashed wood, the Shaper's Flail flew out of the wrecked autocoach. Composed of six heavy iron balls joined to a central ring by weighty chains, the flail whirred to the jungle cat, simultaneously pummeling it and wrapping it up. With two legs pinned, the huge feline ended up on its back, hissing and struggling.

The armored rider Mira had unseated was now on his feet clutching a double-bit battle-ax. He clomped toward

Cole, weapon raised high. Curling his legs, Cole prepared to lunge away from the downswing of the heavy weapon.

Before he could move, a golden rope lashed the rider's ankles together, jerked him upward, and flung him against a boulder across the ravine. The gigantic jungle cat went still as arrows accumulated.

Jace whipped the ragbeast a couple of times, but the golden rope passed through it without grabbing hold of anything. The attack seemed to spur the tattered mass of fabric into action. After whirling in place for a moment, the ragbeast swished by Cole, doing no more damage than a thrown pile of laundry.

Cole went and retrieved his sword from the big cat, jiggling it to wrench it free. He wiped the blade against the animal's fur.

At the top of the ravine, near the bridge, a horse gave a loud whinny. Cole glanced up in time to see the steed rearing. A rider slid off before both silhouettes moved out of sight.

Wings fluttering, Twitch landed beside Mira. He crouched and helped her to her feet. The ragbeast glided swiftly upstream alongside the trickle of water.

Joe ran over to them, holding an arrow ready against the bowstring. "Mira, get that rider." His bow pointed toward the top of the ravine.

"Flail, attack," Mira ordered. The tangle of balls and chains disengaged from the fallen cat and zoomed up the slope of the ravine. At the top, it paused.

"Flail, attack," Mira repeated, gesturing in the direction the stranger had gone.

The flail hovered benignly.

"I'm trying to picture the rider," Mira said. "He moved out of sight before I really saw him. I think I have to see the target. Should I go up the slope?"

"No," Joe said quietly. "It isn't worth the risk. Can't you command the flail to strike whatever is within range up there?"

"It isn't an attack dog," Mira said. "I have to direct it."

Joe nodded. "I hit the rider's horse with an arrow. I'm not sure how much damage it did. We can't let him escape. He could round up reinforcements. I should go after him."

"How'd they make the autocoach run wild?" Twitch asked.

"They must have reshaped it somehow," Jace said.

"But Declan made the coach," Mira murmured. "It would take quite a shaper to hijack a Grand Shaper's work."

"Might have been shapecraft," Cole said. "If shapecrafters can mess with the shaping power itself, who knows what else they can do?"

"They organized Mira's power into Carnag," Twitch said. "Why couldn't they tamper with a semblance?"

"Whatever their skills, those were no ordinary soldiers," Joe said. "You just met some Enforcers. And one of them is getting away. I can't let that happen. He probably won't go to the legion or any regular authorities, but there may be others of his kind in the area."

"We're splitting up?" Jace asked.

"For now, yes," Joe said.

"We follow the road?" Twitch checked.

"It will take you to Carthage, on the border between Sambria and Elloweer," Joe confirmed. "Honor's star has held steady in that direction. If danger forces you to abandon the road, Mira knows how to follow the star."

Cole glanced at Mira, who had turned her gaze to the sky. To help guard the precious secret that Mira's mother could mark the location of her five daughters, only Mira and Joe knew what Honor's star looked like. If that information ever leaked to the High Shaper, the girls would be doomed.

"Am I just flustered?" Mira asked. "I don't see it."

Joe looked skyward in the same direction she was peering. "Oh, no," he muttered after a tense pause. "You're right. The star is gone."

"What does that mean?" Mira cried.

Cole felt horrible for her. That star was her one connection to her endangered sister. Mira's panicked eyes studied the section of sky where the star should be.

"Could mean lots of things," Joe said, his voice deliberately calm. "Might mean your mom was worried about enemies using the star. Might mean your sister has been rescued."

"What if it means she's . . . ?" Mira whispered, covering her mouth.

"I'm sure that isn't it," Joe said. "We can't let this sink us. I have to track down whoever is slipping away. You go to Carthage. There's a fountain with seven spouts on the Elloweer side. If I don't catch up to you on the road, look for me there every day at noon. Lay low. If I'm more than three days behind you, I'll be either dead or captured." Joe glanced at Cole, Jace, and Twitch. "Watch over her."

Joe turned and dashed up the hill.

Mira continued to stare at the patch of sky. Following

her gaze, Cole saw many stars. But he knew the one she yearned to see was not among them.

"Don't linger," Joe called down to them as he charged up the slope. "There's no telling who else might be headed this way."

"He's right," Twitch said.

"What about our stuff?" Jace asked, dipping his head toward the crippled autocoach. "At least the money!"

"Good thought," Cole said.

"You two grab what you need," Twitch said. "I'll get Mira out of sight. We'll wait for you up the road."

"Fine, shoo," Jace said, waving a hand. "You too, Cole, if you want."

"I'll stay with you," Cole told Jace, then glanced at Mira. "See you in a minute."

Twitch took flight, and Mira used her Jumping Sword to leap halfway up the slope opposite the one Joe had climbed. "Flail, follow," Mira called, and the weapon obeyed.

His shoulder smarting and his scraped legs sore, Cole crossed to the autocoach. No longer harnessed to the coach, the walking brick lay motionless on its side, two of its legs broken off at the thigh.

Cole and Jace reached the opening where the door had been and climbed inside. Bertram lay facedown, his body limp.

"Is he dead?" Jace asked.

Worried that Jace might be right, Cole crouched and shook the elderly coachman's shoulder. "Are you okay, Bertram?"

The old man stirred and raised his head. "I'm on holiday with my grandniece and my grandnephews." He gave a small smile. "Nothing to worry about here."

After climbing to reach the floor of the coach, Jace opened a hatch and several items fell. He jumped down and started rummaging. From outside, Cole heard the faint trickle of the stream.

"You didn't seem like yourself back there," Cole said to Bertram. "You screamed."

The old guy blinked. "I'm no longer a spring chicken. The young must forgive us older gents a little episode from time to time. I've been under the weather. I won't let it ruin our holiday."

Jace dropped down. "We should go," he said, backing out of the coach.

Cole held up a finger to tell him to wait. He tried to frame a question in terms that might enable Bertram to respond. "Our holiday is in trouble. The coach went wild and crashed. How will we get to Elloweer now? What happened?"

Bertram gave an uncomfortable chuckle. "The coach did what it had to do."

"The coach takes orders from Mira," Cole said. "It doesn't go fast. What happened?"

"It performed as required," Bertram said. "So did I."

"Who gave the order?" Cole asked. "Who changed the autocoach?"

ABOUT THE AUTHOR

BRANDON MULL is the author of the *New York Times*, *USA Today*, and *Wall Street Journal* bestselling Beyonders and Fablehaven series. He resides in Utah, in a happy little valley near the mouth of a canyon, with his wife and four children. Brandon's greatest regret is that he has but one life to give for Gondor.